THE
WORDSMITH'S
TALE

THE
WORDSMITH'S
TALE

STEPHEN EDDEN

Beautiful
Books

First published 2011.

Beautiful Books Limited
36-38 Glasshouse Street
London W1B 5DL

www.beautiful-books.co.uk

ISBN 9781907616969

9 8 7 6 5 4 3 2 1

A catalogue reference for this book is available
from the British Library.

Cover design by Christina Griffiths.
Typesetting by Misa Watanabe.
Printed in and bound in the UK by CPI Mackays, Chatham ME5 8TD.

For

M.B.E & S.J.H

AUTHOR'S NOTE

Throughout *The Wordsmith's Tale* I've attempted, wherever I can, to use phraseology rooted in Old English.

Very occasionally, where the appropriate word has eluded me (for example, if it sounds too Latinate for comfort), and something jars, I've added an Old English word in italic. Hence, *ofergeatu* for 'oblivion'. Each time, I've tried to make the meaning obvious, so as not to slow the reader down.

Although I've presented these words in modern script, I wanted to remain as true as possible to what the narrator, Thomas the Piper, would have said. I've therefore used the different endings, as appropriate. (Mercifully, barring a few exceptions, we're spared these in modern English.) So, to use the above example, *ofergeatu* might appear as *ofergeate* in a different context.

I hope that these choices are the right ones. I'll let you be the judge of that.

Part One

OLD MOTHER HAGGARD

I

Some call me Thomas the Piper. Great-grandson of the far-famed Tom Thumb. At night, I pick up a whistle and place it to my lips. I play softly, so as not to awaken Tolland and the others. My piping coaxes memories – one hundred years of memories – from their hiding places. I line them up and dust them down, ready to call my young scribe into the room at first light, so that he can pin them, wriggling, to the vellum. Stories of how we danced, my forebears and I, to the tune of history, felt its pulse, played our part, wove tales of our own, and how each of our wishes, even in the face of hopelessness, was fulfilled.

Last night I summoned a faint song, wrapped it in a minor key and I played it so quietly that only the dead could hear me, only distant memories were stirred.

Wintercearu, the whistle piped gently.

Wintercearu: the sorrows of winter. A sadness that shrouds you. When the days are short and the nights long. When the cold bites your bones and hunger eats into you.

The winter of Nine Hundred and Eighty-Seven, though they were all one and the same. Great-Grandmother Fleda hadn't stirred since daybreak. She was faint through not having eaten. For a week or more only rank water had touched her lips. On her lap, she cradled her last ten acorns. Her only food since the glut of autumn, lifetimes ago. Little more than ballast and likely to leave a nagging, persistent pain, deep in your guts. Beside her lay her half-tamed half-wolf half-dog. She knew she must summon the strength to slaughter him for his meat. For all his wilfulness, Wolf-Dog deserved better than that. Perhaps his flesh might taste less bitter if she undertook one last act of kindness. Fed him those acorns before his gruesome end. Assuming he didn't turn his nose up at them.

She wavered for hours before holding them to him.

He scoffed them. More like a wolf than a dog. Then looked trustingly, longingly into her eyes. Her resolve took flight. How could she kill him now?

Great-Grandfather Tom – far-famed, fairy-tale weaving Great-Grandfather Tom – knew all about longing. He'd spent more than twelve years searching for Fleda and the pain had never subsided. Tom was a dwarf. And his dwarf's bones ached from the fruitless hours and days and weeks and years he'd been trudging around these hills – retracing his steps more times than he could recall – looking for the woman who, in her youth, had been so lovely to behold that she'd had him trembling. Tom had never doubted he'd find her one day, that his faith would be rewarded, though it often seemed like searching for a speck of silver in some murky, sun-starved pit.

He reckoned he'd have missed her, yet again, had it not been for Wolf-Dog.

Wolf-Dog had growled. Tom had turned and noticed something or someone in the gloom. He wasn't yet aware it was Fleda, propped against an oak tree. Somewhere between life and death.

'I'd have done the same for any old hag,' he'd claim. 'I'm just brimming with thanks it was *her*.'

Wolf-Dog eyed Tom. Dribbling as he smelled the mouth-watering stench of rotting meat wafting from the grubby old sack slung over Tom's shoulder. Without a word, the dwarf laid down the cloth, drew his blunt old knife from his belt and tore off a piece of the brown flesh. He lobbed it a little way from Wolf-Dog, who stirred himself. A new best-friendship secured. Dogs always liked their lives to be straightforward. You were a friend or a foe. Never any middle ground.

Tom kicked at the remnants of a fire. No life there.

It was an ordeal, lighting a fire. A craft he'd never mastered in his fifty-two years. Setting a room ablaze with many-hued stories was one thing. Mastering your tinder was another.

He cleared a patch of earth and arranged a bed of the partly burnt remnants lying there. Then he reached into the tree. Fleda hadn't moved, seemed not to know he was there. Tom grasped some dried, beetle-burrowed wood. Crumbled it over the coals. Then some crusts of dead fungus, as dry as his old bones.

Wolf-Dog had scoffed his meat and was asking for more. Tom glowered at him and shook his head.

'No,' he barked. Wolf-Dog looked at him forlornly, but sat down. The happiest friendships with wolf-dogs are the ones where they know you're the lord-and-master.

Fleda had stirred as the dwarf had raised his voice, but still she didn't look up.

Tom struck his flints again and again over the tinder but the sparks wouldn't bite.

He cursed.

But then one spark landed on the wood and clung to life. Blowing hard, Tom began to cough. Wolf-Dog sidled around, sensing his luck was in, while his new best-friend was rasping away. He grabbed the rest of that brown flesh, but Tom turned and grappled with him.

Scolded, downcast, Wolf-Dog slunk off. He'd only secured a scrap of the meat.

Tom noted that the beast would need a little more taming before they were done.

The fire was set, now. He placed kindling carefully on to it and waited patiently for it to catch. Then he cut strips of the rotting goat-meat and laid them over the flames.

Hearing the sizzle, smelling the lovely stench of burning flesh, Fleda began to stir again. For the first time, she was aware of Tom's presence. The sound of his tread, his mutterings, the spit of the fire. They washed over her like dull pain. Then she felt the food he'd thrust into her hand. Warm and tempting. She ached from hunger but hadn't the strength to lift the meat to her lips.

Tom pulled a morsel and held it against her mouth.

Fleda wanted the food so much she'd have sold her soul just for the joy of swallowing it, feeling it slide down her throat, but instead she retched.

Tom withdrew the meat and started to stroke the hag's hair, unconcerned that his hand still dripped with fat. His touch was tender. His heart welled with warmth. She managed to tilt her head and lift her gaze. She stared at him. Old Mother Haggard. Broken by her forty winters. Worn by the cares of this world. But in her eyes there was a flicker to match the fire now glowing beside them.

'Fleda? Is it you?'

She didn't reply, but his heart leaped. Nothing could have shaken him from the belief that it was the girl he'd searched so long for. His Elfleda.

'Fleda . . . My love, my life, my sun, my moon, my day, my night, my north, my south, my breath, my . . .'

Her head had lolled again, but he carried on stroking her hair. Touched her sunken cheeks.

'Hear me, Fleda. I'll never forsake you. I'll make you whole again.'

He tossed the piece of meat towards Wolf-Dog.

'Good dog,' he whispered. 'Between you and me, Best-Friend, I've been working on that little speech for the best part of twelve years and I don't think she took in a word of it.'

Wolf-Dog cocked his head. The dwarf was clearly asking for something or other. Perhaps it was to do with that meat. What does a wolf-dog do to help on such occasions? Perhaps show Top-Dog you're happy. He wagged his tail and approached Tom with his head low, his ears back and nuzzled into those delicious goat-fat-tasting hands.

'Good dog, Best-Friend. Thank you for looking after my

Fleda. Now we must give her back her life. Slowly. Bit by bit. You give her your warmth while I make her a thin gruel of water and goat-flesh. We all have to start somewhere.'

He ordered the dog to lie across Fleda's lap, then took out a bowl, poured water from his hide-flask and shredded some scraps of goat-meat into the brew.

He wrapped up the rest and hung it out of Wolf-Dog's reach.

Wolf-Dog whined but stuck to his task. There are times when you must curb your wolfish urges. If you do as Top-Dog says then he'll give you more meat later. And Top-Dog says you must lie across Old Mother Haggard. Besides, she may make for a bony dog-bed but she has a good bad-smell to her: ripe and rotten like that lovely burnt flesh that filled your belly.

Wolf-Dog settled down to sleep. Warmed by his body heat, Fleda was already dreaming about the sun dimming as her breathing became shallow and sparse. In her dream the shadow of a dwarf came and placed some gruel on her lips and when she sipped it, she felt its warmth inside her. The glow of the sun was no longer waning; it began to brighten again.

Wolf-Dog and Fleda were both fast asleep as Tom began to drive stakes into the ground in a wide ring, grumbling all the while about his stiff old bones. Then he threaded twigs between the stakes. It would be little more than a crude shelter from the cold, the wind and rain. Enough to barter time, though, before he built a more robust dwelling.

Wolf-Dog awoke to see the shelter that had unaccountably appeared. Rising up, he stretched, yawned and slunk sleepily over to inspect this new thing that either a man-spirit or perhaps the dwarf top-dog had put there. A good thing to mark these things before some other wolf-dog lays claim. Men and women aren't very good at marking things, so he must help. He cocked a rear leg to do the deed but was met with a blow to his haunches that sent him reeling.

Why was Top-Dog angry? This was hard to understand. Life is confusing for a wolf-dog. You do your best to work things out but life out-thinks you. Hovels appear from nowhere and Top-Dog beats you for pissing.

Now the dwarf-man is rubbing your fur as if to say you are a good wolf-dog, that only the pissing on the hovel bit of being a wolf-dog is bad. The rest is good.

'Good boy,' Tom muttered. Wolf-Dog pricked up his ears, pretending to listen, just in case he was supposed to be taking it all in. Best not to earn another rap on his haunches.

'Hard to believe I was once King Edgar's very own tale-weaver, eh, Wolf-Dog? The King of all England, no less. My star's long since shot across the sky and trailed off to *ofergeate*. To oblivion. But I never stopped believing I'd find Fleda one day.'

Tom lifted Fleda and carried her over to the newly wrought shelter. She was as light as a moonbeam. As he laid her carefully, tenderly, on a bed of leaf-mulch, she opened those once lovely, daylight-dancing-in-them eyes, aware of the presence of a man. Not yet aware it was *him*.

'A little more gruel?' he asked her.

She nodded.

As he held it to her mouth, she gulped at it. It tasted like her wolf-dog's piss might well taste, but it was as soothing as a dock-leaf balm on nettled skin.

Fleda was guzzling her gruel greedily, now. At one point, she stopped and struggled to summon words. Not easy when you've not spoken to a soul for – how long? – maybe years.

'Shush,' he whispered, placing one of his tiny goat-fat-dripping fingers on her lips. It tasted good, did that finger.

'Just drink, Fleda, my bread of life. I'll be your shelter from the storm, your fleece in the frosty cold, your shade in the summer, your fire-blaze in the icy winter, your moonlight on the darkest nights . . .'

Wolf-Dog had had enough. He got to his feet again and shaped to leave the hovel, farting loudly before he departed. Fleda still hadn't the strength to raise herself. No escape from the dwarf and all his prattling. Words enough for the three of them.

II

'Can you hear me, Fleda?' he asked.

She nodded.

'I'm going out, but I'm not leaving you. I need to find more food and fresh water. Materials to make a proper home, too. One that won't keel over when the next storm brews. Daub, wattle and enough legroom for the three of us. You'll want for nothing.'

He took her silence as assent.

Fleda and Wolf-Dog watched in wonderment as Tom unearthed morsels of this and that, sometimes a true feast. She began to fill out, the soft blush returning slowly to her cheeks.

Every now and then her dwarf came back with goods that must surely have been stolen. That chicken looked too plump to have been eking a living in the wild. Loaves of bread – still warm – were hardly likely to have been left by one of the spirits of the woods.

She'd give him a wary look and he'd appear suitably chastised.

When he came home one day, tugging a reluctant a pig by its nostrils, she broke into her first, toothless smile. He could see her delight from the way her eyes leaped with laughter. If it had been down to Tom, he'd have slaughtered the animal there and then, but it was clear Fleda planned to keep the thing for the time being.

Fatten it up for a rainy day, perhaps. Either that or she'd taken a liking to the beast.

Wolf-Dog was less welcoming, snarling at the newcomer wolfishly, though the pig ignored him. Wolf-dogs were sly. They had this way of cosying up to top-pig-men and becoming their best-friends. A true pig knows that you should mistrust all men and all wolf-dogs.

Tom gazed at Fleda and felt a warm glow at having unearthed the joys of a shared life. Fancied he could see, with every passing day, a little more of her former beauty.

Just fleetingly, once in a while, she was that lovely servant girl again. The one who'd had to suffer the late, lustful King Edgar's hungry gaze and who'd perhaps been unaware that the dwarf had looked at her longingly, besotted, from the shadows. Edgar, King of all England. Anointed by the sainted Archbishop Dunstan at Bath Abbey in Nine Hundred and Seventy-Three. Declared God's mouthpiece on this earth, though far from otherworldly in his appetites. A man famed, just as Tom was, for his lack of inches, though not a lack of ruthlessness. Tom – wondrous wordsmithing Great-Grandfather Tom – will have stories enough to spill about his sometime master and king. Some of those can wait. Best not to spoil their nights by the fire. He'll unfurl only gentler tales for now.

III

Once in a while, Fleda assented silently to Tom's manly fumbling. Lay back and allowed him his piece of heaven-on-earth. A fair reward for all he'd done. And he was always so kindly. Not the sort of man who overwhelms you with his brute male strength.

> *I fall into my Fleda's*
> *grey-green, sea-green,*
> *daylight-dancing eyes.*
> *I see their strength and calm,*
> *from the soft, salt-balm tingle and tide*
> *to the high, storm-brewed heft and heave.*
> *When we make longing love, I'm*
> *lulled by her lovely gaze,*
> *bewitched by her grey-green,*
> *sea-green pull. I long to plunge,*
> *to throw myself into her darkest depths.*

One night, emboldened by lust, Tom thought the time was ripe for him to climb on top of his beloved again. But she slapped his face. Stopped him in his tracks. Wolf-Dog watched her warily. The pig dozed.

Tom spluttered his apologies, but she'd turned away from him. Later, troubled that she'd been too harsh on him, she softened, took his hand and placed it on her belly. Not much other than a mound of skin, tauter than the last time he'd stroked it, but evidence enough that he was to be a father.

> *From one mere dry and paltry pip, the*
> *bountiful, appleful bough is begotten*
> *(though it is graft that grows us together,*

love that binds us tight, when blossom-bursting,
leaves-unfurling, spring-like, sunlit days are done).

She'd feared he might turn on his heels and hobble over the horizon. In truth, she'd grown used to him. She'd have felt his leaving keenly. Patterns, once woven into your life, are hard to change without risk of unthreading the whole.

She needn't have worried. He wasn't going anywhere.

IV

When the day of the birth arrived, Tom was ushered out of their one-roomed hovel on the end of Fleda's roughly hewn besom. She'd no intention of letting him anywhere near her as she underwent the trials of childbirth, whether she needed him or not. The goddess Frig took a dim view of the presence of any man when she was overseeing such things. The gaze of a man would be a bane on the newborn.

So Tom sat outside, prodding the earth nervously with a stick. Wolf-Dog snuggled up to him. You knew where you stood with Top-Dog. Old Mother Haggard and the hog were harder to please.

'What do you think, Best-Friend? Boy or girl?'

Wolf-Dog cocked his head, unable to resolve dwarf top-dog's concerns.

Neither Wolf-Dog nor Tom noticed that the pig, tethered a distance away and burrowing its snout in the earth, was about to be mounted by a wild-boar of eye-watering girth. A not unwelcome surprise for the old girl, though her back fairly buckled under the weight of the brute. Mind you, it was over in a flash, a quick snuffle of thanks and then the boar was off again. That was boars for you.

Blood-curdling shrieks emanated from their dwelling as Fleda forced the newborn from her slight body. The gut-wrenching agony bit into her, but then came the joy-falling, silence-descending, relief-bringing moment when he emerged at last.

The child cut the air with its first cry and Tom ventured to the doorway. Stole a glimpse of his newborn son. He could have sworn that was almost a smile lighting Fleda's gnarled, lovely old face.

She didn't shoo him away as he handed her water in a

new bowl he'd crafted on one of those happy, storytelling nights beside the fire.

'Hold him,' she whispered. 'Our boy.'

She watched as tears streamed down his wizened cheeks.

As he cradled the child . . . his child . . . their child in his arms, he was a giant. He kissed the newborn's crumpled skin and felt a tide of some sort of longing overwhelming him.

'I've warmed a little water. Shall I bathe him?'

She nodded. Then she watched as he set about his task. So softly, as if afraid that harm could come to this gift the spirits had granted him.

The strange thing about love is that it's like us. It can beget more of its own kind. Love can give birth to more love and then watch it grow. It knows no bounds.

He bathed the boy and then wrapped him in a woollen fleece he'd stolen not many days earlier.

The child was born late in the year Nine Hundred and Eighty-Eight. Old Mother Haggard's bastard boy.

Delighted that there were new ears to hear his tales, Great-Grandfather Tom didn't wait long to start telling his son a story or two. They were all beside the fire. Tom, Fleda (tired and not listening to a word), the wolf-dog (loyally pretending he could understand), the pig (now several hours pregnant and feigning indifference to Wolf-Dog's best-friend-dwarf) and newborn-son, who seemed to gurgle with pleasure at the sound of dwarf-giant's babblings.

Once upon a time . . .

The dwarf looked lovingly into his son's eyes. Uttered the four words some might reckon to be the most spellbinding, the most songful and most taken-for-granted in the mother tongue. Words which, if Great-Grandfather Tom's claims were true, he'd been the first to summon.

Tom began to unfurl his story of a dwarf no bigger than a thumb . . . named *Tom Thumb*. A tale in which ill-luck and soaring triumph come in wave after wave. Old Mother

Haggard looked up, swept back to that time when as a young woman she'd heard him in full flow. She smiled, just fleetingly, but he caught it and turned his gaze on her. Before he could meet her eyes, she was looking down at the fire and had started to prod it. He saw it though. The embers of her fair, carefree youth were still burning. He sighed and then ploughed on.

'Where was I, my beloved boy? Ah, yes. A dwarf, no bigger than a thumb.'

Wolf-Dog looked out through the doorway, growling. Fleda pointed a finger. Tom turned around. They looked on in horror as the sky began to bleed. A great open wound appearing above the port of Watchet.

'The Vikings are back,' Tom muttered, holding the child tightly.

Fleda took in the bright red sky and the pillars of smoke. Her face hardened as she turned to their own fire and prodded it again. What was it with men? Why did so many of them lust after what wasn't theirs? Lands, wealth, maidens. Why couldn't they just live in peace? It seemed that men had blighted most of her life, one way or another.

The port of Watchet burned. The red sky was lovely to behold in its way. Sat here, you couldn't hear the screams or feel the anguish. A thousand tragedies as lives were trampled underfoot, hopes were snuffed in the choking smoke. And flames and bloodlust consumed all in their wake.

The boy, barely out of her womb, was witnessing his first piece of history. What sort of world had she brought him into?

Tom placed his son carefully down beside Wolf-Dog and hobbled over to Fleda. Put an arm around her shoulder.

'You'll be safe with me,' he told her.

Who was he fooling? But at least he had the heart of an aurochs.

'I know what you're thinking,' he joked. 'The roar of

the eagle and the wings of a bruin, the fleetness of an ox, the strength of a hare. I reckon the Almighty was on the right lines, though he muddled things a tiny bit.'

A shame the gift of the gab wasn't the best of shields against a wielded sword.

Would that the spirit of Alfred could be summoned from the cold earth. Alfred the Great, who'd rallied the English when all hope had seemed lost.

'We've been here before,' Tom mused. 'The pulse of the English nation little stronger than a corpse's. Though things were even bleaker then than they are now. Our island enshrouded in darkness.'

Then he stirred himself, pushed out his Anglo-Saxon chest and began to chant.

He came brandishing, bold-shouldering hope,
his head held high-and-mightily,
slashing his sword, so lord-and-masterfully.
Our foes faltered at the right-handed wrath
of our table-turning saviour, our tide-turning,
our walking-on-water king; and even the grass
beneath his tread bristled with green English pride.
Thus, doubt and disbelief were driven clean away.

'We shan't see another Saxon like Alfred in my lifetime,' old Tom Thumb sighed wistfully.

Nor – sadly – in anyone else's lifetime.

'Don't fret, Fleda, my love. We'll keep our heads down and all will be well enough. I know the way these Vikings are. Wait for the harvest to be gathered in before they swoop. Then they're off. Why do all that back-breaking work? Better to get some dim-witted Saxon to do it all for you. They'll not come hunting in the woods, what with winter setting in.'

V

Tom Thumb was right. No Vikings came. Nobody came. Why would they venture into such a godforsaken place? And what a winter, too. The frost gnawed at your very bones. Huddled in their one-roomed home, they wallowed in each other's warmth.

Their boy was thriving. Forever hungry and guzzling his mother's milk. Growing faster than ivy twining its way up bark.

'That'll be because he came so late,' Tom reckoned. 'You wait fifty-odd years for your firstborn and he makes up for lost time.'

Fleda reckoned she'd never heard such hare-brained nonsense.

They'd named their boy Bas. Tom would later claim this was because it was less of a mouthful than *bastard boy*, but can you ever believe a word a story-weaver tells you?

Four months after Bas's birth, the pig was lying on the floor of their dwelling, grunting as her litter of offspring began to make their way into the world. Bas sat, transfixed, as they appeared, one by one, bloodied and squealing. He watched as they sought their mother's teats and suckled.

Tom was there, too. And a thought struck his bright, story-crafter's mind.

There was more than one teat too many for the sow's litter, so he placed young Bas among the piglets and watched while he drank greedily.

Pig seemed happy enough. Probably too tired to care who was having their fill. Fleda sighed with relief. Help at last in the struggle to slake her son's thirst.

There were seven piglets. Mouth-watering, they'd be: roasted, one by one, in the fullness of time, on a roaring, fat-spitting fire. In the meantime, while his teeth formed, Bas would have to make do with a regular dose of sow's milk and a feast of stories.

VI

Yes, the old dwarf had always been able to summon a story. Even the late King Edgar had spotted that.

'You look like a lad who might spin a good yarn,' the king had said.

'You saying you think I'm a lying little know-it-all, my lord?'

'Think of yourself as a *diminutive, fairy-tale-weaving omniscient*,' the king had suggested. 'It has a much better ring to it.'

Good advice. The right sort of title can open doors.

Great-Grandfather Tom tossed a silver penny. Bas watched as it caught the firelight. Fleda remembered the last time she'd seen it arc through the air, lobbed towards her dwarf.

'Is that *the* penny?'

'The very same one.'

Later, Fleda allowed the dwarf to curl his little body beside her as they settled down for the night.

There's an art to telling a story. If you're asked to entertain the king, you start by finding out what *spices his gruel*, to conjure a phrase.

King Edgar: a black-and-white king who ruled with an unerringly ruthless streak. A king with twin obsessions: the deflowering of nuns and a determination to render wolves extinct.

'The nuns bit I can understand. But wolves? Extinct?' Tom had enquired of one of the king's courtiers.

'Trust me, urchin. It's true. He's even granted Ludwall overlordship of the Welsh on condition he presents him with the carcasses of three hundred wolves each year – though, to be fair, he was probably drunk at the time. As for nuns . . .'

A very disturbing habit that began when he raped a nun whom at least he had the decency to make his first queen. In return she presented him with a son (who would, in time, become a king and a martyr).

Her place was soon taken, though. By the ill-famed Queen Elfrith, who'd in time become the subject of many a story from the lips of Tom Thumb and who'd soon learn she'd have to sit – mute and uncomplaining – while her king turned his lusty attention elsewhere . . .

Fleda shuddered at the distant memory.

'I want you to know I loathed every moment of being groped by him.'

'I know, my beloved,' Tom reassured her. 'I knew how alone and frightened you were. I hated what he did, too. Which was why I . . .'

His voice tailed off.

'But you must have known I was in love with you. I was prepared to do anything for you, that I'd never stop trying to find you.'

'I didn't know it, but I hoped it.'

'You'll go down in history, my beloved. His other women are all forgotten, tossed on the scrapheap of the past, but I'll tell folk about my Fleda as long as there's breath in my lungs.'

Fleda, the lovely serving-maid, who'd become the reluctant solution to a thorny royal problem.

It had been a year of aching famine, though, to judge from the ample spread laid out, the king and his followers had been spared the bite of hardship.

Standing up suddenly at the end of a feast, roaring drunk, King Edgar had pointed towards a thane's daughter.

His meaning had been clear.

As the king had stumbled off to his bed and fallen through the damask draping, the chosen girl had pleaded with her mother to save her.

'I think I may have a solution,' the mother had announced. 'My servant girl Elfleda will have to do instead.'

'Very wise,' Ludwall, Overlord of the Welsh, had said, drinking in the comely vision of loveliness standing her distance: slim and dark and adorable.

Fleda was led, trembling with terror, to where the king waited in his bed. Drunk and impatient.

The next day, as the sun rose, it dawned on King Edgar that things had taken an unexpected turn for the better. He woke up and saw – in the sober, hungover light of morning – what he'd not noticed in the drunken, candled half-light the night before. Given the choice between this servant girl and the thane's daughter, no sane man would have settled on the second.

She must have moved him uncommonly, because he'd instructed her she was to spend the rest of her life within his grasp. She'd said nothing as he'd informed her of her fate. She'd cast her eyes downwards. Choked back the treasonable tears that welled up, aborting them before they were born.

VII

Eternities later, Fleda feels the warmth of Tom's embrace as he snuggles up to her. She's unable to sleep, what with all those memories stirred up by the sight of that silver penny spinning through the air, glinting in the firelight.

Tom can't sleep, either. His head's swarming with tales.

New to the royal court, a wordsmith who – if you can believe his tales – had blagged his way to the top from the meanest of beginnings and shown uncommon skill as a story-weaver from time he could draw breath. And now he'd been instructed by the king to stand on the mead table and conjure a story. A straightforward request. So why had it carried such a weight of menace? Why had it had him quaking in his shoes, overcome by gut-wrenching terror?

Nuns and wolves. A simple enough task to weave a fairy tale about them . . . but the words had all fled from his mouth. Tom groped forlornly for the story he'd spent days honing. He heard the sound of knives and cups being beaten impatiently on the table.

'Speak, speak, speak,' they were chanting.

There was one person making no noise but staring earnestly at him. Her lips broke into a nervous smile of encouragement. Her grey-green eyes held his gaze as he took a deep breath. Calmness fell on him, like snow, blanketing the furrowed ground. He took three more breaths and then raised his right hand. Slowly, with an authority beyond his years. He waited for silence to fall.

'Once upon a time, a novice nun named Black-and-White Wimple Head lived in a wolf-infested forest—'

'Excellent,' the king purred.

And suddenly Tom Thumb was into his stride. Cantering, as he unfurled his spellbinding new tale.

He held them in the palm of his hand. Teased them as he growled the wolf's words or fluttered his eyes, mimicking the novice nun's innocence. Leaped like a wolf at one of the serving-girls, baring his teeth. Bounded on to the table again and continued with the story. This was story-weaving such as none of them had ever heard or seen.

They were on the edge of their mead benches as the dwarf told them how the king, hearing the novice nun's screams, came rushing to the girl's rescue. Wrestled the wolf to the ground.

'"My, what a big sword your mightiness holds in his hand," the novice nun gasped as she fell into the king's arms.'

'Very good!' King Edgar roared and he nodded to a courtier to toss a silver penny into the dwarf's hands. Newly minted and gleaming brightly, it span through the air.

A coin bearing Edgar's own noble profile.

'Ludwall,' the king suddenly barked at the Overlord of the Welsh.

'Yes, sire.'

'Have you reached your allotted three hundred wolf carcasses yet?'

'I fear that, such is your mightiness's foresight, the stay of wolves on our blessed island is nearing its end. They are becoming much harder to find.'

'Bring me three hundred wolf carcasses or you're dead.'

Then his tongue was searching inside Fleda's mouth. Thomas turned away, unable to face his own impotence in the face of such abuse.

King Edgar lived in a world clothed only in black and white. Perhaps this helped to explain his obsession with nuns.

VIII

Once Bas's teeth had pushed through, he moved on from drinking the sow's milk to devouring her offspring.

Fleda always winced when she heard the blunt axe come crashing down on a piglet's neck. One by one, the young swine were dragged outside, squealing, and Fleda would turn away. Watching them taken from their mother, Fleda recalled those times when her own newborn had been taken from her. How she'd wept as they'd snatched away her first child. Was it a boy? Was it a girl? Her pleas had been ignored. It was better not to know these things. She'd wailed loudly and one of the midwives had slapped her face. What was she doing, brewing such a storm of noise? The king might be in earshot. Under no circumstances was he to be reminded of the results of his lust and his slut's compliance. So she fell to sobbing, holding out her arms in supplication. To no avail. They'd carried the newborn out of the room and out of her life.

Then they'd washed Fleda. Told her to get some sleep. Ready herself in case the king was overcome with the need to take her that night.

That was why she looked away whenever one of the litter was led from the hovel. But at least the pig had felt her young press against her teats. Felt their flesh against hers. Heard their contented gurglings and snufflings. And Pig seemed happy enough to have another try at piglet-making when the old boar came sniffing around some months later.

IX

By the age of four, fed on a diet of stories and suckling pig, Bas was already a strapping lad, taller than his father and ready to take the axe from old Tom and wield it with a cleaner blow than the dwarf had ever mustered.

'Look into the beast's eyes and thank him when you bring down the axe,' Fleda had told her son. 'A happy, carefree life and a clean blow to the neck, a sweeter one for being struck with reverence. Every beast deserves such a fate.'

It was Bas who was called on to put Wolf-Dog out of his misery.

Best-Friend was old now, barely able to drag his hind legs around. The boy knelt down, took Wolf-Dog's head in his arms and wished him well in the afterlife. Then he brought the animal's suffering to a swift end, tossing his head and torso into a clearing. An offering of carrion. Rich pickings for the crows, to give Best-Friend wings and hasten him to a new life.

'A cleanly wielded sword and a strong unwavering arm. Loyalty to your friends and a steely indifference to death. These are the materials from which a fine warrior is honed,' Tom observed admiringly.

He was fiddling with that silver penny again. He always did when he was launching into one of his homilies.

'The right ingredients and a big dollop of luck – which is where this little silver penny may come to your aid. I doubt that I'll ever have need of its wondrous powers . . .'

And he was off again. He couldn't help himself, could he? Whenever words began brewing in his head he couldn't contain them. They had to come bubbling out. He was drunk on words, besotted with stories, was Great-Grandfather Tom. Whether walking alone in those hills for twelve long years or commanding a roomful of ears, it was one and the same. Tall stories or short ones. It was the unbridled joy, the unfettered love of the spoken word. As precious to Tom as the very air he breathed.

'This silver penny, graced with the head of King Edgar, was tossed into my hands by the king's very own sorcerer.'

Fleda looks at old Tom and rolls her eyes. The story changes as regularly as the tides. They have a life of their own, stories do. It's as if you're sitting astride a wild horse. You may be tugging on the reins, imagining you're in control, when suddenly they go galloping off to places of their own choosing.

The important thing with stories is for the facts to fit. Facts are like clothes. They should be changed to suit the occasion. Wear your best, most sober facts for a formal do. Wear bright, colourful facts at a drunken feast. Particularly if you want to grab some attention. Perhaps, however, you should be more guarded in a court of law, and stick to witnessed truths. Even Great-Grandfather Tom would have accepted that.

It was a bright, sunlit, yarn-spinning sort of day. A day when tales are like the clear light coursing through the running stream. Distorted and refracted in the telling.

A day when the coin positively sparkled as Tom Thumb flicked it up and it span.

'Have I ever told you about this penny, my strapping young lad?'

'Not in a while, Father.'

'Well, then. It was Merlin himself who kissed this penny with his old, pale lips. Blessed it before he slipped it into my hands. Yes, blessed by the sage himself, it was. Enough to grant the holder any three wishes of his choosing.

'"Take your time," Merlin advised. "I was too hasty with my choices when I was granted the same . . . The Gift of Sorcery, very useful when you want to shape history; the Gift of Omniscience, which is to say knowing everything that's going on around you; and the Gift of Foresightedness – the chance to know what's coming round the corner . . . And by the way, things are about to take a turn for the worse. You'll not be entirely without blame for that, though I suppose I'll pardon you now, given that it's your capacity for love that will be our undoing."

'"You're talking in riddles, your blessedness," I said.

'"Indeed I am. Not a gift I can attribute to any wishes. Just a propensity we Saxons all have, in varying degrees," he joked.

'Anyway, Merlin blessed the coin with the touch of his sorcerer's lips and with it comes the power to summon three wishes of your choosing. And here's the best part, son. Many's the time I've been tempted – especially while I spent all those years looking for your mother – but I've not used up even one of the wishes. So with any luck, I'll be passing them on to you when I'm dead and gone. All three of them.'

Fleda takes Bas to one side later and quietly tells him:

'Don't raise your hopes too high, lovely. If there ever was a Merlin, then I don't recall seeing him. I reckon age is catching up on the old dwarf. Your father's started imagining things. If you ask me, most of his stories have about as much weight as a sparrow's fart.'

X

While Tom was off, more and more, somewhere in story land, Bas continued to take on a giant's share of the workload.

Fleda walked with him through the woods, secure with her strapping son at her side. She showed him the tracks of various animals. Which berries could be picked, which to avoid at all costs and which – like rowan or haw berries, bitter to taste – were the food of last resort. The various types of mushroom, too.

'Believe me, my darling boy, in this uncertain world, it's useful to know which ones you can fill your belly with and which will teach your foes a short sharp lesson . . . Now, let's garner a meal for that daft old father of yours, though if his stories get any more rambling we might have to put him out of his misery with some of those poisonous berries I've been telling you about.'

Bas loved these moments. He was taller than his mother now and a good head and shoulders higher than his father. He'd need that sturdy frame, too, the way the Vikings were now running amok over much of the West Country. The exploits of King Alfred – about which Tom often waxed so lyrical – were a mere memory, though still cherished by most Saxons. King Edgar might have briefly offered up the hope of peace but such dreams would prove short-lived. The country had lurched once more into a state of unruliness. The wooded hills now seemed the only safe place to be.

XI

Tom's up and about, defying his creaking bones, stirred by having his audience of wife, son and pig, though, of the three, Bas is the only one showing much interest.

He's weaving a tale about a giant who lives at the top of an ivy twine that's grown all the way up to the heavens.

He puffs out his chest, lumbers around and from his lungs there comes a deep, sonorous, unearthly roar.

'"*Fifel, fah, feond* . . . Giant, foe, fiend . . . I smell the blood of an Englishman."'

Then he's overcome by a fit of coughing that shakes him to the core.

'I'm not long for this world, my young warrior. You must promise me you'll keep your head down and keep weaving stories: the secret to a happy life. And take this penny. Remember what I told you. It comes with three wishes, though if you find a young woman and love her only half as much as I love your mother, then I doubt you'll even need any other wishes to come true. Maybe you'll pass the penny on to a child of your own. Along with all those stories.'

XII

Bas held the frail old dwarf as he rasped, unable to fetch up the tales that were still bubbling inside him. Holding his father in this way called to mind the dying wolf-dog whom he'd always seen as a dog-brother as well as a best-friend. The boy who could have wrestled bruins suddenly understood why he'd been brought into this world by the union of Tom Thumb and Old Mother Haggard.

Bas reckoned the spirits had breathed air into his lungs and strength into his body for a reason.

The strong needed to protect the frail. It was the strong who nursed the dying. The strong who stayed the fist of a brute who'd strike a woman as soon as reason with her. The strong who crushed the thug who'd torment the helpless, from a shy beast to the smallest of insects. The strong who thrust his spear calmly, firmly into the heart of a hunted stag, hastening its path to the afterlife, delivering it from pain – while the weak gleaned sport from the chase, the terror of a fleeing animal.

Strength coupled with compassion, or *soft-heartedness*, wasn't to be confused with sentimentality, or *soft-headedness*. Compassion was the steady gaze into the eye of the suckling hog you slaughtered, grateful for its life and its death. Sentimentality was the squeal of a young child as they saw blood gush from the beast's neck.

A soft heart and a hard head were the preserve of the strong.

Fleda put her head to Tom's chest. Listened until she was sure he was no longer breathing. Then she motioned to her strapping ten-year-old son to dig a grave in the clearing. He set about his task without complaint. As she watched him, she wondered if she'd been wrong to deny him his childhood. The chance to mingle with others of his age. But other children were as likely to be venomous as serpents as they were to offer best-friendship. His time would come.

Bas dug deep, with his crudely fashioned shovel. He cut through the soft, mulchy ground as if it were the tender flesh of cooked lamb, though even the hardest-baked clay would have been no match for his strength.

Fleda stanched her tears as she scattered the rich earth over Tom's body. Then, when Bas had shovelled the rest of the soil, she knelt down and pressed into the ground not a wooden or a stone marker but an acorn. An acorn, like the ones she'd held in her hand when nearly all hope was gone. Like the ones Wolf-Dog had bolted down before the dwarf had struggled into their lives on those rickety old legs and granted them the gift of happiness. An acorn to remember him by. One that would grow into an oak tree from which his spirit could watch over them and guard them.

Slow-row me to a safe shore.
Cradle me to my heaven-haven home.

'We'll need to fence it,' she said. 'Otherwise the deer or brocks will snuff its life before it's rooted.'

She stirred the mess of vegetables, threw in a handful of snails.

'This is a day for celebration, not grief. And a day for wall-fish soup,' she informed Bas. 'Your favourite, my darling. We've not had wall-fish soup for I can't remember how long. Your father never was keen on snails. So not everything will change for the worse.'

She looked up from her cooking and watched her well-built son as he drove posts in a circle around the grave. Protection for the oak sapling when it emerged in its own time. Alone, Fleda let her guard slip. Tears welled in her eyes.

When Bas returned to his mother's side, she was muttering.

'Why did I never tell him I loved him? Was it really so hard? Did that brutish king and the rest harden me so much?'

When the skin's grazed it dries itself and heals into a hard clot. When your heart's repeatedly wounded, it hardens and you form a protecting barrier around you. When love comes so late – and after so much hurt – it can seem too much of a miracle for you to believe in it.

'Why did I never tell him?'

'You did, Mother. Not with words but in other ways.'

Bas was wise as well as strong beyond his years.

XIII

Fleda hauled herself from her bed. It was time to move on. A fresh start. It was a birdsongful morning. Bas was still dozing after all that digging and grief. She hadn't the heart to wake him. It was sometimes easy to forget that he was still a child. But suddenly, seeing him asleep, fatherless, she was struck – for all his strength and stamina – by his vulnerability. She let him rest a while.

Where had his stature come from? Was it down to all that suckling at Pig's teat and all that pork? Or was it gifted to him by the gods who'd granted her a son? Or was he doing all the growing his father never had?

For all Fleda knew, he'd inherited her own father's build. There was no telling because Fleda's father had fled long before she'd opened her eyes to the world. Her mother had been tight-lipped. Never said a word. Not about Fleda's father. Not about anything.

There had been all sorts of stories to explain this. There was one tale where Fleda's mother was supposed to have upset the woodland spirits in some way; she'd wandered off into the woods and emerged a day or so later looking dishevelled, lost and robbed of the power of speech. Another said that she'd been on the receiving end of a marauding Viking's attention. The man had been built like a stag and rutted like one. She'd been struck dumb with awe. This story might have perhaps explained why Fleda herself (presumably the result of such a union) might have herself borne a giant, but, when push came to shove, no one seemed to have seen this seven-foot Norseman. Another tale was that, as a young girl, Fleda's mother, being a fiery wench, had cursed her thane when he'd made an improper advance. The thane, fearing the truth would out, had ordered that her tongue be removed and then tossed it to a hungry cat. Truly a case of the cat getting her tongue.

All probably a load of nonsense, but presented with a problem that's out of the ordinary, people will launch on a tireless search for understanding.

Fleda never heard her mother speak a single word. By the age of ten she was in service, cursed by the absence of any past but blessed with the striking loveliness that set her apart.

She'd been whisked off from a childhood coloured by no words and no past to the nightmare of her time as the king's whore. For three short years in between she'd been treated well enough by the mistress, who'd then offered her up to the king.

Her looks might have melted the most powerful man in the country, but when King Edgar died, she'd been discarded as soiled goods. That was the spark that had fired her resolve to fly from his court, hiding herself away in the hills those twelve lonely, fearful, looking-over-your-shoulder years. Hoping no one would ever track her down . . .

No. Hoping against hope that Tom Thumb would. That he loved her like no other, loved her enough to track her down where nobody but the most dogged of men could have found her. Far enough from the reach of the king's power-hungry queen, who was about to pour wrath and venom on all around her. Queen Elfrith had been waiting to wreak her terrible revenge. But that was a different story: a toxic brew that can ferment a while yet.

In Fleda's own fairy tale, Tom Thumb had spent twelve years scouring the countryside after she'd fled. Searching everywhere for the woman he loved. Finally he'd tracked her down in the Quantock Hills: shrunken almost beyond recognition, aching with hunger and awaiting death. To old, arthritic Tom Thumb, though, she was still the comely servant girl he'd always worshipped and always longed for.

She sat silently beside the newly dug grave, staring into the beyond. She heard Bas stirring now. Heard Tom Thumb's life stories drifting on the air in the tree-sighing breeze and the birdsong. Her dwarf. Not much to him in a physical sense, but she'd felt safe in his arms, at peace when he'd shared her bed and curled himself against her. Not consumed by lust but simply yearning for her touch. And how it warmed the soul to be so needed.

I fell this sun-blessed morning beneath the spell
of a linnet so bright-blood-red and brilliant
there welled in me a warmth
one human only could ever induce.
I heard song-singing from a high
tree-top, a throstle so tuneful, so
unaware that it lit in me a glow
one lover only could ever ignite.
I saw two buzzards together sweep the sky,
so clean, so cloud-high up they
summoned a sense of awe that
only you could ever command.
I sat beside your silent grave and felt
the chill-cold wind of my utter loss,
an emptiness that nothing on this earth
could ever hope to fathom or fill.

XIV

Bas was ten years old but the only two people he'd ever known were his mother and father. Fleda knew it was time to seek work for her boy. Perhaps a quick dip in the river would be in order, to take the edge off ten years of accumulated stench. And work some charcoal into his teeth. Not that she could really see the point of all that palaver. You waste an hour scraping all the filth off and scrubbing the stench away and within a week you're back to where you started. Back in those black, wish-you-could-forget days in the court of King Edgar, she'd heard of some folks who were reckoned to bathe as often as once a month. The churchmen were supposed to be the worst. Did they think their God was interested in outward appearance? If you were really set on masking all those odours, what was wrong with something like crushed lavender? Did the Romans teach us nothing? They'd spent too much time bathing and look what had happened to their empire while they sat there, preening themselves. It had crumbled. And who'd made it crumble? Hordes of unwashed barbarians, more interested in fighting than sitting in a warm bath. That was who.

There were times, though, when you had to do your best and this was one such. You didn't want to offer yourself up for service and find the thane turning his nose up at you in more ways than one.

There wasn't going to be a better time to act. Tom Thumb was off to his afterlife. Pig – now well past the age for bearing young – was dying and ready for the pot, though she'd need a few hours on a spit to soften up that tough old meat. A nice send-off, that would be. Fleda sensed that Fate was telling her now was the time to go, though she prayed that Bas would fare better than she had when she'd embarked on her journey into the big wide, swallow-you-up-and-spit-you-out world.

XV

They'd feasted well and Bas was sucking the last shreds of meat from one of old Pig's trotters when Fleda broke the news to her son.

He didn't question her, trusting that she knew best. After all, the words of parents carry more weight of wisdom than the wishes of their young.

'You know every tree in this wood. Remember it well in case you ever need a place of refuge, somewhere to hide. Though, by the look of you, I don't imagine you'll ever have to run from any man . . . Most of all, remember the place where we've laid your father to rest. And if ever you need some wise counsel and I'm no longer there to give it, then come and seek his advice.'

Bas gripped the silver penny, nestled in the hem of his left sleeve. As long as he had his penny, he'd not forget his wonderful story-conjuring father or the stories he'd told in their hovel. As long as the acorn they'd planted continued to grow, his father would be there for him.

Love knows no limits. Plant its seedlings and it will blossom again if properly nurtured.

XVI

They were half a day's walk from the nearest settlement. They'd followed the stream, then the river. Walk far enough down a watercourse and you find a settlement of sorts. The first one would do. Find a place where there wasn't much in the way of rich pickings for all those marauding Vikings. A small community, getting by. That would suit the two of them. Fleda heard the yelps of children, the banter of adults. Tom Thumb had come back with stories of a place like this one. Hard by the woods, a cluster of dwellings around the thane's home. Perhaps this was where he'd found Pig.

Fleda knew they would be tempted to turn and flee. For Bas's sake, she must greet this challenge with the strength she herself had shown as a child. Set a hardened face against the wind that whispers misgivings into your head, take whatever Fate blows your way. Bas's first shock would be the sight of other children. Sure enough, he clung to the shade, looking on warily at the buzz of people.

'Come.'

The thane was summoned. Everyone was watching the strangers. Some looked on brazenly, though most snatched only glances.

Their new lord-and-master waddled out to meet them. First he looked the hag up and down. Not much use, he reckoned, and not very pleasing on the eye.

'What can you do?' he asked Fleda.

'Sew as well as any other, tell a story, cook pleasingly well and carry more than you might think on this old back of mine.'

Then he eyed the boy. A good build.

'How old is he?'

'Ten years. Not a day more.'

'Why would you lie to me, woman? You can certainly spin a tale, right enough.'

'It's the truth. As honest as these old hands that would work themselves to the bone for you. You'll watch him grow another few years yet. If I'm lying you can have me flogged and marched back to the woods we've come from.'

'He's a fine enough young man already. I'll offer you shelter and land and, in return, you'll give me no trouble and enough hard graft to keep me happy, though I've no doubt the boy will be doing your share of the work as well as his . . . I see you have an axe, boy. Before I get someone to show you your bed, you can hew down that birch tree there and your mother can carry the logs over to the store. What are your names?'

'The Widow Haggard,' Fleda replied, still keen to cover the tracks that led back to her brush with royalty, however old and overgrown those tracks might be, because you never knew who was still watching and waiting to pounce, to finish the story that Tom Thumb was always loth to tell.

'And the boy?'

'This is my ten-year-old son. Bas.'

'Ten years old. Yes, I heard you the first time.' And he still didn't believe her, though he didn't feel inclined to flog her for her lies. Winfrith the Thane didn't have much stomach for floggings. Not like some overlords who took relish in meting out punishment. Floggings quelled unrest, but the unrest would erupt again in another place, like a plague. Besides, a full-blooded flogging was too tiring.

Winfrith looked on in awe as the mother and son made light work of their task. They were going to give good service, these two. As night fell, they were led to their quarters. Bas clung on to his mother, tears welling in his eyes as he was told he must leave her. Those without a home of their own – a flimsy, dark, one-roomed *sundorwic*, but nonetheless a home – slept in two outhouses. One for women, girls and babies. One for men and older boys. That was Winfrith's way of stifling the curse of *jiggery-pokery*. The more jiggery-pokery there was, the more the women were hampered either by carrying a child in their bellies or suckling them when they could be working. Fewer women to tend to tasks and more mouths to feed. Winfrith the Thane had nothing against children, was in fact quite fond of some of them, but it was at least eight years before a child could start doing any proper work. Of course you could never stop the men and women getting up to their high jinks. But if there was to be any lusty jiggery-pokery, then the time and place for that was at dusk, in the woods.

Snivelling and clinging on to his mother, Bas suddenly seemed like a ten-year-old and not a strapping young man.

'It's all right,' Fleda whispered. 'I'll see you in the morning.'

Had he not been so tired, Bas might have struggled to sleep in a new place, without the sound of his mother's breathing or that comforting smell she gave off. No stories to lull him and, of course, the irretrievable absence of other reassuring noises, like his father's best tale-weaving voice, pig's snufflings and – in the not-too-distance – Best-Friend's growlings as he dreamed wolf-dog dreams of chased hares.

But Bas sank into a deep, dreamless sleep such as he'd never known.

Awakened by two crowing cockerels, each staking their claim to the settlement, Bas took a moment to gather himself and recall that he was no longer safe in his hovel. A frail boy – who looked, perhaps, as if he needed a friend – came up and shyly suggested that Bas tag along with him and his sister.

When they took their place behind the men and women, Bas couldn't help but notice that whereas the men tore into their bread and milk, the women held back.

'They save it for us,' the new friend explained. 'Old Winfrith never gives us enough. Always saves it for his own belly.'

At this point another boy, one with a slight frame and the quick, darting movements of a rat, came up, pulling at the pony-tail of New-Friend's sister. Bas was unaware that his peers, unable to find words to give wings to the feelings welling inside, often fell back on such actions to glean some attention, even if only a mild scolding. Nor could he see that the girl was probably as flattered by the rat's attentions as she was annoyed by them.

Bas grabbed the boy's wrist and squeezed it, so that he had to release his grip on the pony-tail. Then he lifted him up and placed him down away from the girl, as gently as he would have laid a fledgling bird back on a branch. Without a shred of ire.

'Please don't pull my friend's sister's hair,' Bas said quietly.

The rat and the sister were shocked in equal measure. New-Friend looked pleased that he'd summoned the courage to offer Bas his friendship. He also looked secretly pleased that the rat had been put in his place.

Bas would be slow to understand that the power of unspoken words can be greater than those we utter. The unseen gale can buffet a man more forcefully than the loudest roar.

But the other children would learn, swiftly enough, that Bas wasn't to be crossed. Built like a shire horse and with the strength of one, too.

Having bolted down his breakfast, found his mother and eaten the extra bread she'd saved for him, Bas was reluctant to leave her side. Fleda watched with pride as her son bent his broad back into serfdom, furrowing the field like a grown man. She looked into her giant of a son's eyes and knew that she would be safe in her old age, with or without the dwarf who'd offered her love and companionship when she'd assumed she'd never be granted such blessings.

The blade bursts boldly through the burnt-brown soil,
but from the weeping wound, life springs afresh.
The earth is chilled and cold but offers flowers,
sun-sweetened and soft-scented in your gathering arms.

XVII

Rat was sitting in the corner, rearranging a pile of straw. Most of the children preferred lying in their serried ranks, but not Rat. He'd made his bed in a corner of the dormitory and wasn't happy until he'd placed it snugly around himself. He sat there, picking at the fleas that seemed to favour his bed over the others. He also had the rodent's habit of licking his hands and slicking down his hair.

'He's not like the rest of us,' Bas's shy new friend Elric explained. 'He doesn't have a mother or father like us.'

How was this possible? Bas had been led to believe you couldn't be ushered into this life unless you started out with a mother and father. Perhaps the boy in the corner – curled in his straw now and twitching his nostrils – belonged to a rat family but had been magicked into a boy by a sorcerer.

'I think his mother did some jiggery-pokery before she was wed and she died when she was giving him birth but no one was his father, so he had to be looked after by everyone. He's always been a bit different.'

Rat was peering at Bas. Mystified by the boy who had twice his girth and twice his strength, but the mind of a ten-year-old. Rat was probably about fourteen, though no one could remember for sure.

The next morning, there was no pulling of pony-tails.

'I didn't mean nothing by pulling her hair, Bas,' Rat squeaked in his thin voice. 'I wouldn't mind being your friend, too. You and Elric and me can all be mates. You're allowed two best mates each, I reckon.'

Bas agreed. His second day and he'd already garnered two friends and a friend's sister. Rat was holding a stick in his thin hands and gnawing on it.

'What are you doing with that stick?' Bas asked.

'It's me kissing stick,' Rat explained.

Bas looked at him in puzzlement.

'Don't you use lips for kissing?' he asked.

'Well. Yes and no. I've heard only sissies use just their lips. For proper kisses you need tongues.'

'Tongues? Aren't they for story-weaving?'

'Yeah, but they're for proper kisses, too.'

'What's that like then?'

'You just get a girl and you stick your tongue in her mouth, I reckon.'

Rat licked his right hand and slicked his hair.

'You've stuck your tongue in a girl?' Bas asked, in disgust as much as awe.

'Not yet. That's why I've got me kissing stick. It's like this. You chew on the stick and spit out all the bad stink and then a girl lets you stick your tongue in her mouth. If your breath stinks too bad, she'll just let you do a sissy kiss on her lips, 'cause they don't taste as strong.'

Rat had obviously given the matter a lot of thought.

'Well, he could spend a year chewing on that stick, but his tongue's not going anywhere near my mouth,' Pony-Tail announced.

Rat scratched at a flea that seemed to be drawn to his armpit.

'There's plenty other carp in the pond,' he informed her. 'Anyway, it's like tickling trout. You gotta take your time and do it right. Then you can flick 'em out of the water and they're flapping around and you're in control.'

Then he was grabbing at his breakfast rations and scurrying off to a quiet spot to sit down and nibble away.

'What's he mean about carp and trout?' Bas asked Pony-Tail.

'Don't know and don't care,' she answered, though it sounded to Bas that she did.

Fleda was pleased that Bas seemed to be spending more time with his new friends. It was what she'd both dreaded and hoped for. Her boy finding his feet, beginning to go his own way.

'I got sommat to show you,' Rat informed Bas one evening. 'But it's gotta be a secret.'

XVIII

'You ever seen a girl's tuffet?' Rat asked.

No, Bas hadn't.

'I got this special place,' Rat said. 'You can see the privy and watch them lifting their skirts.'

'Doesn't sound right,' Bas said.

'Things is only wrong if you get caught,' Rat explained. 'I been burrowing in this old brocks' sett. Smelly sods. That's where I got me fleas, I reckon. Mind you, it's worth it.'

'Follow me, Bas.'

Rat slipped into the sett. It was clear to Bas that his ten-year-old giant's shoulders were never going to fit.

'Can't get in,' he whispered.

'Boy, you're gonna miss out, Bas.'

There was a sound of further scratching and scurrying and then Rat's whisper echoing strangely in the tunnels, seeming to come from at least two directions.

'I can see four of them raising their skirts,' Rat gasped, breathlessly. 'I don't suppose you know how to make curds and whey with your winkle, Bas.'

'Why d'you have to go sneaking around?' Bas asked Rat when he emerged from the sett.

You couldn't go looking inside women's skirts in broad daylight, Rat explained. If you did that, you got something called *short shrift*. And kissing sticks aren't much use when you were getting what's called a *tongue-lashing*, which was not to be confused with *tongue-grappling*, which was much more fun, by all accounts.

Rat looked up suddenly and darted for cover.

Bas turned around as a twig snapped.

'Caught you red-handed,' announced a wiry crone who'd

stolen up on them. 'Young boys shouldn't go looking under women's skirts.'

'Why not?' Bas asked. 'Rat said it was all right.'

'Did he? And would you believe Rat if he said he'd seen a cockerel laying an egg?'

'That's plain daft,' Bas pointed out. He was rewarded with a cuff around the ears before being taken to his mother.

Fleda slapped Bas's face.

So this was what was meant by short shrift. Short shrift stung your cheeks and brought tears to your eyes.

Bas felt crushed. He'd lost three portions of love already. His father's tell-you-a-story-to-cheer-you-up, arm-around-your-shoulder sort of love, his wolf-dog best-friend's looking-loyally-into-your-eyes, follow-you-to-the-ends-of-the-earth love and Pig's suckling-and-warming love. He feared that as the palm of his mother's hand smacked against his cheek that he might have lost her soft, yielding always-there-for-you love.

'I'm sorry,' he said quietly, shocked by Fleda's actions. 'I didn't know I'd been bad.'

Fleda immediately regretted what she'd done. Striking Bas was akin to crushing a pearl under a hammer blow. The trouble with violence was that it created ripples that would create others in turn. She'd seen the way children who'd suffered beatings themselves went on to be bullies. Bas, gentle giant that he was, might be stung by her blows to violence of his own. Her sins would have returned to haunt her.

'You stupid, stupid boy . . . I'm sorry, Bas. I shouldn't have hit you. Please promise me you'll never hit anyone.'

'Why would I hit anyone?' he asked.

'I'll never forgive myself for what I've just done, Bas, unless you promise me that – because of this – you'll always come and talk to me if you want to know anything. Don't listen to the likes of Rat. Boys like that'll lead you into more trouble. You swear to me?'

'I swear.'

Fleda kissed him on the cheek, on the spot where she'd slapped him.

'You run off to bed, now.'

'Don't listen to Rat,' Elric's sister Catte told Bas. 'You only needed to ask. I'd have shown you my tuffet if you'd shown me your winkle. I could do tongues, too, if you wanted. It's just Rat I don't want to do it with. Nobody likes Rat much, apart from the fleas. Fleas like Rat a lot, I reckon. '

'Thanks, Catte, but I think we'd best leave it. I don't want any more trouble.'

XIX

'Sorry I ran off and landed you in it,' Rat muttered, grooming his hair nervously as he seated himself beside Bas and Catte, listening to a man who seemed to be the settlement's chief storyteller.

'Can you pipe down and let me listen?' Catte hissed.

It was a long, rambling sort of story, delivered by an old codger who'd not grasped the fundamentals of his craft.

Bas sat watching the interesting lumps and bumps on the man's skull, left exposed by his thinning grey hair. The codger's eyes seemed to have disappeared somewhere deep into their sockets. He looked more dead than alive.

It was one thing having all that knowledge stored away in the lumps and bumps on your head. Quite another to bundle them into a story that had your listeners on the edge of their seats. There was no point in possessing a chest of the finest of gold and silver if you didn't have the old iron key to the lock. Bas became aware he'd not been listening for some while.

The lumpy old codger was looking up to the heavens. Probably seeking inspiration. Droning on about Hengest and Horsa, the fearsome founding fathers of Anglo-Saxon England.

'I don't want to worry you,' Rat whispered, 'but he's still got about another couple of hundred years to get through.'

Bas watched an intrepid flea leap boldly from Rat's soiled tunic and on to Catte's pony-tail. A desperate bid for freedom, perhaps. Though Catte wouldn't be best pleased once the flea had worked its way up the pony-tail and nuzzled into her skin. Bas imagined the flea would find the taste of Catte's flesh and blood more wholesome that Rat's. Quite a journey it must have been on. From some mangy old brock, via Rat, to Catte. That flea would have a story to tell.

By the time Bas had stirred himself and was listening to the old codger again, Hengest and Horsa were long since gone and the last of the twelve great battles between the Saxons and the Ancient Britons – the Battle of Badon Hill – had reached a bloody (though surprisingly tedious) end.

Bas stifled a yawn.

But wait. What was this? Excitement at last. Something was stirring. This must be what they call a *heckler*. The best sort of storyteller gives the heckler short shrift, dances mockingly on his words, maybe draws him into the tale.

A drunkard stands up, sways unsteadily and yells at the codger to bring his ramblings to a close. 'I've had more fun watching the moon wane,' he says.

The old man continues to plough on, undaunted. Perhaps he's so wrapped up in his words he's no longer aware he has an audience.

Where heckling fails, fruit may succeed.

Something brown and rotten narrowly misses the codger and hits the wall. Bas watches as it slides slowly towards the ground. It's an apple or a pear, Bas isn't sure which. It's certainly interesting the way it clings to the wall to slow its fall, as if hanging by the fingertips on to the last shreds of its dignity. Not unlike the codger.

Still he drones on.

Bas wonders if those lumps and bumps on the man's head might, after all, be the swellings where he's been struck in the past by fruit of a firmer sort, rather than a storage place for all that knowledge.

The unrest is growing. Insults are being exchanged. Unaccountably, some of the listeners want the drunkard and his friends to remain quiet, let them hear the tale.

'I can tell you the ending,' the heckler says. 'A lot quicker than Old Lumpy, too.'

'I'm fetching Winfrith,' says one of the listeners and he stands up.

Lumpy's not stopped to draw breath.

The drunkard stops heckling as he weighs up the facts. The thane will be displeased to be fetched from his fireside to resolve a dispute. These meek fools will all side with Lumpy. Besides, there's that rotten fruit still sliding down the wall of Winfrith's barn. They call that *evidence*. The drunkard has a sudden change of heart and opts to sit down, though his attempt is ungamely and he lands heavily on his arse.

A brawl averted by the calm voice of reason and the threat of a good flogging. *The carrot and the stick*, they call it.

Calm descends again and, to his credit, the codger skips the odd war, a Viking raid or two, fairly canters past the finishing post.

There is polite applause for Old Lumpy when eventually he stands down. Flat on his back, not even roused by the odd half-hearted kick, the drunkard snores.

'You should tell some of your stories, or Father's stories,' Bas suggested to Fleda.

'I'll not waste them on this lot,' Fleda responded.

But what tales she could have told.

Fleda looked at her giant of a son, at his trusting gaze and his open face.

'Dearest boy,' she sighed. 'You're a gift.'

> *He fell like a feather to our newborn world,*
> *bringing to mind the settle of snow –*
> *gleaming, untarnished on mud-tainted ground.*
> *I cradled, caressed him and curdled his cries;*
> *and then when he stared at my joy-smitten eyes,*
> *and mapped all the lines of my lived-in old face,*
> *I knew it was Love that had landed so soft,*
> *Uplifting, redeeming my now-sunlit life.*

A giant of the gentlest sort and still an innocent child. And yet, in a couple of years or so, in a few giant strides, he'd be a man.

Part Two

YNGA

I

I, Thomas the Piper, sit back and stretch my arms.

'Are we done, Eam?' my scribe asks me, hopefully. A polite boy. He addresses me as *Uncle*.

'I fear we've only just begun, Pup,' I reply.

I hear him groan. I can hardly blame him. He's a good boy, is Aart. He knows nothing other than the cloistered life of devotion and service. Perhaps he wishes that – like Bas – he could stumble belatedly on the joys of childhood, though I fear it's too late for that. His voice has broken. Already I hear that slight tremble whenever the name of one of the novice nuns passes his lips.

'All this scribing will hone your skills, but I'll grant you a day's grace while I gather my memories,' I tell him.

'Thank you, Eam.'

He came to our cathedral at Exeter when no more than a babe in arms. It had been his father's dearest wish that Aart should learn to read and write. I might flatter myself that I'm a wordsmith but I'm master only of the spoken word. I leave the reading and writing to my friend Tolland. He's taught Aart well. The father would have been proud of the way the son took to his lessons so well. Perhaps not so pleased with the use he soon put his learning to. This place is divided between the former minster, where the monks are housed, and – mere cloisters apart – the building where the nuns live, watched over by a forbidding abbess. Aart, who, with his shock of curly wheaten locks, looks like one of the cherubs painted on the plaster walls, has always roamed freely between the twin houses of God. Aart's regularly called upon to deliver love letters for the more ardent of the brothers and sisters. Yielding to his curiosity and reading those letters has opened the boy's eyes. They might lead a life of quiet devotion, the brothers and sisters, but they're still slaves to the lustiest of thoughts.

'You have your freedom. But for one day only, Pup,' I remind Aart.

He catches his breath as if he wants to say something.

'Speak up, Pup.'

'I know they had a rough time of it, these forebears,' he said, 'but I envy them their freedom.'

'Two things, Pup. First, this. Pain and joy are never quite so unfettered in a told story as they are in life. When you pen hardship and glee on to the vellum with that feather, you only scratch the surface. Second, I know freedom and I know imprisonment. I was bound for many years to a rogue named Isaias. He grew fat on my story-weaving and all the time he had me fettered by fear. I knew that if ever I crossed him my life would be over. But I've known freedom too. And though at best freedom is a blessing, at times it has you howling for the torment to end. This God of Israel the brothers have bound you to may be a vengeful, wrathful oaf with his constant threats and his endless demands for prayers and penance, but believe me, there are worse places, far, far worse places to be than here, where we're safe from our barbarous conquerors – about whom we'll have time enough to tell when you and I are good and ready. Go now, Pup.'

Alone again, I tease more memories from their hiding places. I can summon all manner of stories on my worn old wooden whistle. Notes to conjure Fleda the comely servant girl: sweet and soft and firm as fruit. They have a soulful strain to them. And then Great-Grandfather Tom makes his presence known. Sometimes his spirit – for all his old joints are stiffened – skips lightly up and down the scales as easy as a smile. Then, just when my fingers are dancing a jig, he slows me down and we conjure a melody full of longing. Twelve years' worth of longing.

The giant Bas is bringing me a thoughtful, steady tune. But then other, shrill notes make themselves heard. My story in song is marred by the spiteful sprites that (when they lived) were Rat and Catte. My mouthpiece suddenly tastes as sharp as an unripened apple.

II

Rats are inquisitive creatures. Eager to explore the new. Rats don't give up easily, either. Scratching at his flea-ridden body, this particular Rat was itching for some action. A chance to become a hero. An opportunity to impress Catte.

However many times she curls up her lip in disgust and tells you she'd rather kiss a sheep's arse than allow you anywhere near her lips, you don't give up. Not if you're a rat, you don't. You keep on gnawing at your kissing stick and hoping for better times to come. You keep looking for that little chink, that moment of weakness when she softens. The secret is to keep nibbling away. Wear her down. Just as you wear down all those kissing sticks. You chew at the rough bark and then you grind away at the fibre with your teeth. Working, working at the same spot until their resistance goes. Then that delicious moment when the soft, moist pulp in the middle yields.

'I think it's called *boring the skirts off a girl*,' Elric suggests.

Rat and Elric are eighteen years old now. Both of them men, but both of them still boys. Elric's not obsessed with girls in the way Rat is. Having a sister, he's always seen them as part of the fabric of his life. He's at ease with them. Doesn't need to take out his frustrations on a stick the way Rat does.

Elric quite likes the idea of being a warrior. Anything has to be more fun than hanging around this place all day, every day. Toiling on the land. It's all right when the sun's on your back, but most of the time, it's as miserable as hell. At least if you're a warrior, something out-of-the-ordinary's likely to happen. Being cursed and blessed alike by the gift of youth, Elric has no sense of his own mortality. The fear of death, pain or defeat of any sort just doesn't enter his head.

Elric's bosom-buddy Bas is only fourteen, though it's hard to credit. He's already taller than any man any of them has seen. Catte knows she likes Bas a lot more than she likes Rat, but she's unsure what feelings he stirs in her. Some soft flutter of her femininity, but is it *lover-love* or is it *sister-love*? Probably more sister-love than lover-love because, for all his strength, Bas is still the first to suggest they all play *Serfdom-and-Freedom*. Poor Bas. Too trusting by half. He's caught and rounded up all the prisoners one by one and there's only one person to find. It's always Rat. Rat invariably comes up with the best hiding place ever and Bas is on edge, wondering what surprise will be sprung on him. He fears Rat's rodent cunning. He knows Rat will give him the slip, scurry silently up to touch them all and thus free them, so that they'll scatter from Bas's grasp and Bas's heart will sink. Again.

Catte will spot Rat. From a distance he's wiry and sleek, not mangy. She'll feel the flush of excitement at her impending freedom, but she'll feel a sister-sadness for Bas, who's fallen for Rat's wiles again. Here comes Rat, padding quietly. He puts a thin finger to his lips, warning her to be silent. Catte loves Rat . . . because he's going to give her her freedom and every peasant girl's best but scariest dream is the dream of freedom. She hates him . . . because Rat's going to enjoy his power over her. She loves him . . . because he's going to touch her and she's away. She hates him . . . because he's going to touch all the others first and he's going to taunt her, pointing to his kissing stick, trying – but failing – to exact a promise. She loves him . . . because Rat can't stand not to win, and so just at the final moment, he's going to grant her her freedom and with Bas bearing down on the two of them, they'll escape those giant's hands in the nick of time. She hates him . . . because although she's escaped, Bas is gaining on her and she'll be the first to be caught, entrapped in Bas's holding pen, again.

Most of all Catte hates the fact she loves to play these

children's games. She wishes she hated them and looked down on them. Maybe she will, one day soon. Maybe things will never be the same again, now that Rat, Elric and Bas are being asked to join the menfolk and become warriors.

III

It's a hare-brained plan, if you can flatter it by calling it a plan at all. The blame lies with Ethelred the *Unræd,* the Ill-Advised. Did he really believe he could eradicate the Danish threat by launching a raid on every Danish settlement on one fateful night? Did he and his ill-advisers really not understand? If you wound a beast while its back is turned it's likely to turn round and savage you.

Queen Elfrith had secured the throne for Ethelred. Elfrith: the woman from whom Fleda and Tom Thumb had taken flight. Just in time.

And this is how Fleda tells the story.

She speaks quietly.

'Walls have ears,' she tells Bas and he looks at her questioningly because he doesn't recall ever having met a wall with lugholes. Perhaps he wasn't looking hard enough.

'What I'm trying to say, my love, is that Elfrith is the scariest, most hateful stepmother who ever lived. And the most vengeful spurned wife who ever pursued a king's reluctant whore. If she'd found me, she'd have strung me up. Believe me. She'd have stood there, laughing, as they pulled out my entrails.'

Bas gave her another of those questioning looks. She could spin a yard of yarn from an inch of truth, could Fleda.

'It's not a lie, Bas. She wrested the throne from her stepson and handed it to that wastrel son of hers. King Ethelred.'

Ethelred's half-brother, Edward – a king for only three years, but a martyr for much longer – had seen no reason to flee the grasp of the late King Edgar's second queen. He was, after all, the rightful and undisputed King of all England. But, back in Nine Hundred and Seventy-Eight– while Fleda was hidden in the Quantock Hills and looking over her shoulder, while Great-Grandfather Tom was only three years into his long, wearisome search for his beloved – Edward had arrived at Corfe Castle. On a hunting trip. Ready to offer the hand of friendship to stepmother and half-brother. He left the place with a dagger thrust into his side by one of her henchmen. Falling from his horse, clutching his open wound, he was dragged along by a stirrup for some distance while his lifeblood drained from him. A sudden and unexpected and bloody ending to a pitifully short reign. The coast was clear for Ethelred to be crowned king. The scheming Elfrith's wishes had all come true. She was, of course, duly contrite. Prayed to this new-fangled Redeemer whom kings and queens seemed to put their faith in. But no amount of monastery-building by way of atonement could save her from being branded the original wicked stepmother.

Ethelred – now more than twenty years into his seemingly endless, hopeless, woeful reign, beset on all sides by foes and famine in equal measure – had listened to his counsellors: a group of men who couldn't have found their way out of a six-foot tunnel with a shaft of sunlight beaming into the end. This was the same bunch who'd advised paying off the Danes in silver as a way of staving off attacks. Have you ever emptied your pockets for a bully? Did he wave you past and thank you for your generosity next time you were cornered? Or had he concluded that extorting money from you was quite rewarding and demanded more?

The plan was to attack every Danish encampment and cleanse the country of its unwelcome guests.

Bas's and Fleda's lord-and-master, Winfrith the Thane, was under strict orders to supply every fit and able-bodied man. Young and old. None of his usual tricks.

Winfrith's belly was so swollen he looked ready to topple over. Fleda put it down to more than mere greed.

'Nobody could get a belly that big just through eating. It

must be worms.'

He was a decent enough thane. Ruthless in his extraction of his tithes and other rightful dues, though. Perhaps he needed to be. His land wasn't up to much. The crops it yielded were never going to be bountiful. Maybe he resented this and so felt no particular obligation to respond with alacrity to any call to arms. He'd usually muster a group of old codgers and warn them to arrive after the heat of battle had begun to cool.

No point in sacrificing the fit young lads, he reckoned.

'Tilling this blasted soil's backbreaking work. I need lads who can put a bit of spirit into it.'

What Winfrith was good at (apart from shirking and eating) was raising taxes for his shire reeve. And therein lay the secret of his success. He overlorded a happy-go-lucky community, sufficiently off the beaten track to avoid most of the marauding armies. Prepared sometimes to go short themselves in order to feed their thane's astonishing belly or add to the royal coffers and keep the peace.

This time it was different. Winfrith sighed and, with a heavy heart, imparted the news that all the men and boys – all bar the children – would be taking part in the raid. But the odds were so stacked in favour of his lads and men that, in truth, he felt a twinge of guilt about it all.

Was there something about the way he'd delivered the tidings that betrayed his misgivings? Fleda was on her stiff old knees, begging Winfrith:

'He may be built like an ox, but he has the heart of a lamb, my lord. He's still a boy.'

Winfrith hated himself for being so soft. Would that he were one of those stone-hearted types who'd have given the whingeing crone a good thrashing for haranguing him and then walked off with no shadow of guilt clouding him.

'My hands are tied. The plan's foolproof, anyway.'

Fleda shook her head in despair.

'The plan's doomed to failure.'

'Go back to your work,' Winfrith commanded her. He was a patient man, but he'd heard enough. A plate of cold meats awaited and he'd rather be grappling with that than with his conscience or with the old crone tugging at his boots. An unedifying sight.

The old hag was no doubt right. The whole thing would be botched and in no time the Danes would be back. Baying for blood. How do you go about stopping the violence that keeps on repeating itself as surely as a horse-drawn millstone continues to turn and crush the wheat beneath it?

Crestfallen and sullen, Fleda sloped off and began attempting to whet Tom Thumb's old knife – his *seax* – though she wasn't entirely sure whether she was blunting it or sharpening it as she swept it across a piece of gritstone. At least she was bringing a gleam to it as she worked off the rust.

'Men!' she muttered. Just as she'd done as she'd looked on from the hills as Watchet was torched.

'You'll need this,' she said, handing her son the weapon. She didn't dare look into his eyes. 'I don't suppose I have to tell you to look after yourself. Be staunch, watchful and unshrinking in your defence and merciful to your foes.'

'I don't understand why we need to do this, Mother.'

'Because we must trust our leaders,' she said, without conviction.

Had she been younger, she might have summoned the will to up and run. Take Bas away from this poison. An atmosphere dripping with male vigour and hatred was not one she wanted her boy to be part of. But what could she do, apart from worry? She was powerless. So was Winfrith. She could hardly blame her thane, though she found herself despising him. Hobbling around their settlement with that enormous great belly of his. Clearly a man who'd never had his body honed by the cut and thrust of battle.

IV

'This is a night for bloodshed but not for heroes,' Winfrith addressed the lads.

It's hard to be a hero when you steal up on a foe who's sleeping soundly in his bed, though that didn't stop Rat from darting about the place excitedly, a sharpened stake in his hand in place of that soggy kissing stick.

Elric looked at the weapon with contempt.

'My gutting stick,' Rat told him proudly. 'Took me an age to whittle this little wonder with flints, but it'll slice into some Viking innards like a knife through warm butter.'

'Remember the date well. The thirteenth of November, in the year of our Lord One Thousand and Two . . . Remember the night when many of you became men,' Winfrith intoned.

'Once a rat, always a rat,' Catte taunted her would-be lover.

'How many dead Danes will it take for me to get my tongue into that insolent mouth?' Rat enquired.

'I reckon I'd rather kiss one of the dead Danes,' Catte scoffed, though secretly she felt a shimmer of excitement about it all. The idea of Rat returning from the fray and taking her in his arms, planting a manly kiss, seemed mildly intoxicating. So long as she closed her eyes when he tried it. There was something about being in the arms of a blood-splattered, sweat-soaked warrior that both disgusted and aroused her.

Winfrith was nearing the end of his rallying call.

'No risks to your persons. Listen and look out for one another. God grant you good speed and I hope to see you all safe home.'

Fleda was glowering at her thane. There was something powerful about the old hag that Winfrith couldn't put his finger on. Had he but known it, it was the complete absence of any deference. Old Mother Haggard – she who'd sometimes had the late King Edgar aching with longing, she who'd outsmarted King Ethelred's mother – didn't suffer fools gladly. Even well-meaning fools like Winfrith.

Unable to withstand Fleda's gaze, Winfrith looked in the direction of his own ample belly. Deep inside his voluminous guts, he knew Old Mother Haggard was right to be angry. He wanted to tell her that the wellbeing of all his subjects mattered to him. Yes: in part because they were a valuable commodity. But young Bas was the one he cared about most. There was something special about the boy. The heart of a warrior, but a soul as soft as fallen fruit.

V

The talking was done and the moon was up. Rat and Elric were having second thoughts. They were strangely subdued. Fleda was staring into the fire as Bas departed from her. Seemingly speaking to the spirits that danced in the blaze, she said:

'The world's gone mad. If any harm comes to my son, my life is over.'

Bas backed out, awkwardly.

The plan was for them to surround a Danish settlement and torch it. Spare not a single soul. Now it began to spit rain.

'That'll dampen the fires,' Elric suggested forlornly.

Rat trod on an old twig. Leaped in terror as it snapped.

'Frig. I'm feeling jittery, Bas.'

Rat was unnerved by the moonlit wood with all its secret sights and sounds. Not Bas. The shadows, the hoot of an owl, the scratchings of mice: these were his friends. He recalled his and Best-Friend Wolf-Dog's delight as they'd both explored the night-time woodscape. Loved the certain knowledge that the spirits were watching out for them.

Bas looked at Rat. Saw fear in his eyes. Something else, too, that he didn't quite understand: a look of murderous hatred. For no one in particular. For the foe in general. Murderous hatred borne of fear.

Where did violence stem from? Fear or self-loathing, Fleda always said. Sometimes from an inability to put a point of view. The man whose lips are muted by powerlessness will sometimes speak with his fist or sword. For all his soft-heartedness, Bas knew no fear. He recalled a moment when an enormous maybug had landed on Catte's clothing and how, stricken by terror, she'd screamed. Rat had urged her to brush it to the ground and tread on it, but Bas had gathered it in his right hand and freed it. Wished it well as he'd sent it on its way with a gentle breath.

'That's what sissies do,' Rat had mocked him as he'd blown the maybug away. Catte knew Bas was no such thing.

'Thanks,' she'd said. 'That was very brave, Bas.'

She'd curled her lip in contempt at Rat.

Assailed by no fear, only misgivings, Bas led Elric and Rat through the woods with their moonlight and shadow, haunted by the owl cries and the soft tread of deer and foxes.

Rat's nostrils started twitching. He was the first to sniff the wood smoke drifting from a Danish settlement. The fine rain was not persistent enough to snuff out the fires but it brought the smoke lightly back down to earth. Rat tasted it on his tongue and licked his lips, excitedly. Laughed nervously as he thought about what he might do to one of those Danish girls, once he'd wrestled her to the ground. All the things he'd wanted to do to Catte, but she'd rebuffed him.

'I reckon I could get used to this,' he whispered. 'I reckon I could be good at rape and pillage.'

'Shush, Rat,' the leader urged him. 'Form a circle, everyone, and then, when you hear me hoot like an owl, we'll move in.'

Rat gripped his gutting stick tightly as he moved into position.

An owl hooted and Rat was off, creeping forward.

'Not yet,' the leader urged. 'That wasn't—'

Too late. Chaos ensued. One of the Danes had raised the alarm and there were people bumbling in all directions. Screams. Flames. Some people grabbing clothes and running from their homes.

Rat saw his quarry. She was limping: one of her bare feet had been pierced by a thorn. She cried out as he caught up with her. Her scream cut the air as sharply as any thorn into skin. Rat felt another surge of excitement as he grappled with her and felt her firm-soft flesh. She screamed again as Rat pinioned her . . . and then he felt a blow to the back of his head. Like a thunderclap. He was vaguely aware that the girl had been picked up and was being carried off. Rat pulled himself into the shadows, holding his crown. By the time the sun rose, Rat's head would be as sore as a swarm's worth of bee stings. The Danish girl would be reunited with her family. And Rat would have had enough time to concoct some tale of his derring-do. Meantime he'd lie low.

'You search that place, Bas.' Elric motioned towards a boarded opening. 'Call if you need me. Torch the place when you've taken anything you want.'

Then Bas was gone. None of them saw him again. And when they gathered together, some of them still trembling with horror or elation or both, and when they called the names out, one by one, there was no Bas.

Who would impart the news to Fleda? She'd be beside herself with grief. What was that saying about the way folk box the ears of the bearer of bad tidings?

'I reckon you should be the one to tell Old Mother Haggard,' Rat mumbled to Elric. 'You're good at that sort of thing.'

'I'm sorry, missus,' Elric was confessing to Fleda. 'Last I saw of Bas he was going into this place to torch it.'

'My Bas? Torching someone's home? You're lying.'

She slapped Elric across the face.

'Sorry, missus,' Elric added, as if he deserved the punishment Fleda had meted out.

'And, you. When did you last see Bas?' she shouted at Rat.

'Rat didn't see nothing, missus,' Elric offered. 'He was being a hero. He had them coming at him from all sides, did Rat. Cornered by four of them. As big as Bas, one of them was, but Rat got the better of them.'

Fleda rolled her eyes.

'Him? A hero? Is that what he told you?'

'It's true, missus,' Rat scowled. 'For once in his life, Rat was the hero. No stupid old hag's gonna say otherwise.'

Fleda slapped Rat's face.

'That's your hero's welcome.'

Winfrith waddled over.

'What's going on?'

'If any harm has come to my Bas, I hold *you* responsible,' she cursed him.

Fleda had turned and gone before Winfrith could reply.

'Someone should teach that old hag a lesson,' Rat chuntered.

'What lesson?' Winfrith asked. 'That all war is bad? That nothing good will come of violence? That the worse fate to befall a woman is to lose her only child? I think she knows these lessons well. Go about your work, you two. I'll send some men to retrace our steps and account for the missing. You boys stay out of trouble. We've had a bellyful of that already.'

Winfrith hobbled off, his stomach clamouring loudly

for more food.

Fleda went and sat down at the edge of the woods.

If he's been slain, she muttered to herself, *then my life is over.*

VII

Bas had lifted the wooden boarding that blocked the entrance to the hovel. For a moment he'd been lost in the lightless black. His flaming torch was adequate for setting hovels ablaze but useless at shedding light on a darkened room. The first things he saw were the glowing coals: the embers of a fire, hastily snuffed out. He was aware of a presence before he saw anyone. A true warrior would have known that now was the time to strike. Not Bas, though. Were there children hiding there, scared out of their wits? Or a wife, perhaps, widowed only moments ago? Trembling for fear of the hordes of raping-and-pillaging men?

If I were still a child, thought Bas, *I'd be shaking like an autumn leaf.*

His eyes were adjusting to the light. The first time he saw her, she was a shadow.

'Your son, this giant of a Saxon, fell in love with my shadow,' Ynga would tell Fleda.

'All men fall in love with shadows,' Fleda would respond. 'They fall in love with what they imagine us to be. Poor foolish things.'

Bas fumbled in his pocket and drew out a crust of bread. He offered it to the shadow but she stayed cowering in the corner. So he held his knife by its blade, presented the handle to her. Still no response, so he laid it on the ground and took two steps back.

'Stay hidden.' He spoke slowly, lest she should struggle to understand him. 'I must wreck your home. Otherwise someone else will. Sorry. This way you may be spared.'

Bas held the torch up to illuminate his features.

'Look at my face. You'll be safe if you trust me. Shout if

you need help. I'm Bas.'

Then he piled up a small amount of cloth and wood and threw his torch on it to set it ablaze. No one would enter the hovel now. He bowed and backed off. Outside, he caught sight of a knife being wielded as the moonlight glinted on it. It could have been a Saxon or Viking knife. Another pointless death. Bas beat a hasty retreat into the woods: the safest place, he figured, for an unarmed warrior. The rain was still falling, though fine and more mist than rainfall. As Bas sank to the ground, he caught his breath, thinking he'd heard someone's soft tread, not many yards away. He sat stock still, wondering what the dawn light might reveal. Fearing he might not live to see the new day. Perhaps he'd been foolish to hand his knife to a shadow. He closed his eyes in a silent prayer for deliverance.

Bas was so tired and on edge he was half-awake and half-asleep. His head was spinning. Had he heard her voice, breathing from the darkness? As gentle as dewfall. He'd no right to be falling in love with the shadow of a Danish girl with a voice like dewfall . . . He was just a miserable serf. An old hag's bastard child. They made a chap feel unworthy, those Danes. Even their dwellings smelled different. Not the same stench as a Saxon hovel. Though – just maybe – when you were grateful to a strapping Saxon lad for saving your life, it might take the edge off the stench.

VIII

Bas woke with a start. He could hear voices. The rain had ceased, but his clothing clung to him. Still sodden.

He crept forward to gain a better view. These were men he knew, though he stayed put. Perhaps he feared being branded a coward for having left the fray and hidden himself away. The men spat on the few dead Viking bodies they saw. Bas couldn't understand how something like the body of a dead child could conjure such raw hatred.

'Self-loathing,' Fleda would remind him. 'It's hard to despise your fellow men if you're happy in your own shoes.'

The men kicked at the smouldering embers of the homesteads. Then Bas heard one of them pointing out the one intact dwelling with the charred doorway.

Her place, Bas thought. What would he do if they dragged her out? He knew the answer to this. He'd come charging down the steep mossy bank and utter a blood-curdling giant's yell for them to stop right there. Because she was his girl.

Bas waited, his senses heightened.

One of the men entered the dwelling. Bas heard dull thuds as the man kicked out, overturning stools and venting the vestiges of his hatred.

'Nothing left,' he muttered.

The shadow had spirited herself away.

Some impulse drove Bas to stay rooted to his mossy bank while the Saxon men lashed out at whatever remained of the buildings.

Perhaps they were angry with themselves because they knew that by botching the whole attack they'd have sparked fresh reprisals. It would be a matter of waiting. Remaining on their guard. It might be days or it might be years. But as sure as the green shoots pushed through the earth each spring, the Danes would be back.

When they'd spent the last of their anger and turned to go, Bas dithered. Should he follow them or should he stay and wait for the Viking girl's shadow to return? He might have had courage enough for five men, but courtship remained a source of dread.

Tortured by misgivings, Bas opted for the certainty of home. Before he went, he righted the stools, cobbled together some partially burnt slats to form a makeshift barrier to wind and rain. Then he gathered together whatever food he could: the bitter berries that the wildlife had left alone. He lit a fire from the smouldering remains of another hovel. A welcome-of-sorts. Supposing, of course, that she'd summon the courage to return.

'I shall be back,' he roared from the charred clearing and his giant's bellow rippled out in all directions. Rooks leaped from their winter quarters, wheeled above the ash trees, cawing in alarm. Foxes, slumbering in their dens, woke with a start and sat bolt upright. The Saxon men, having spent all their anger and frustration, were suddenly assailed by knee-trembling fear and scrambled away from the voice they imagined to be the spirits of the Viking dead, announcing their vengeance. Rumour had it that one of them shat himself, though no one was sure because he stank to high heaven at the best of times.

Not far away, a fifteen-year-old Danish girl looked up and wondered if it was a sign that she should return or run. Return to what? Run to where? A fifteen-year-old girl as slim as a shadow and with the most astonishing pale-blue eyes.

Bas walked up to his mother. She greeted him, just as she'd greeted Rat and Elric, by shaping to slap his face. But then she checked herself as she remembered her promise never to strike him.

'What've I done wrong?' Bas asked, startled.

'You died and I died with you. And all the time you were alive.'

Bas looked confused.

'They're saying your friends are heroes but you ran from the fray. Even that nasty little Rat's walking around like he's conquered the world.'

'Rat did nothing. He tried to do bad stuff to one of the Danish girls, so I rapped him over the head and knocked him out cold.'

'Good boy, then. But keep that to yourself. Don't make an enemy of that Rat. He's the sort to turn round and bite you when your back's turned.'

'I saved another girl, too, and gave her my knife.'

Fleda broke into a toothless smile.

'Well, in that case, I forgive you for dying and coming back to life. Here. I saved some crust.'

'Thanks . . . Leastwise I think it was a girl and not a shadow and I reckon she must have been Danish, too.'

Fleda shook her head in disbelief.

'Mad as a hare. Just like your father,' she muttered. 'Promise me you'll never change,' she added, looking into her son's eyes.

Fleda stirred the fire with a twig.

'Oh, and another thing. Always listen to what that soft heart of yours is telling you. Perhaps Fate meant you to be there to save those young girls.'

She wondered how they would be feeling. That girl Rat had tried to deflower and the other one, whose shadow Bas had handed his knife to. They'd be terrified out of their wits. Cold and hungry. She knew how it felt to be at the mercy of others, prey to the violent attentions of men.

'By the way, if you want to go and find that shadow, I'll not stand in your way.'

'I might do that, so long as it doesn't land me a cuffing from you.'

Fleda was still studying the fire, still stirring it.

'I'll not box *your* ears. I need to save my strength to give that Rat another good hiding for all his lies.'

'You'd have been proud of me, Catte,' Rat said, gnawing on his kissing stick. 'I was sorting out those Danes until I got knocked on the head. Reckon it might have knocked some sense into me. Reckon you should be my girl, now I'm a warrior.'

Catte was warming to the idea. Rat didn't look the part, but a warrior was still a warrior, when all was said and done.

'I dunno,' she responded. 'Maybe. But I still ain't gonna let you use that lying tongue of yours for no funny business.'

'Well, we warriors can't wait for ever. I'll maybe have to find another tasty nibble instead.'

Rat was sulking now.

'Maybe,' said Catte, turning away haughtily.

Rat eyed her lovely little rump as she walked away.

'Don't know what you see in her,' Elric said.

'There's no one as blind to a girl's virtues as her brother,' Rat advised him.

'And no one as blind to her faults as a horny little bastard on a promise,' Elric replied.

'I got something to show you,' Rat shouted after Catte.

'I bet it's nothing to get a girl excited,' Catte responded, dismissively.

'You'll be glad I showed you if the Danes come back wanting their revenge.'

'That's the limpest excuse I've heard yet.'

'No. I've got this secret place. Only Bas knows about it and he won't fit in it. You would, though,' he said, observing her slender hips.

'I dunno,' Catte said and skipped off.

'Gotcha,' Rat crowed as he trapped a flea between his thumb and forefinger before thrusting it into his mouth. 'You gotta know the right time to pounce, Elric.'

IX

Ethelred's ill-advised plan to eradicate the Danes had failed spectacularly, sparking a flurry of violent skirmishes. Catte and Rat would need their hiding place in the deserted, flea-ridden badger sett overlooking the privy. It would be one of the few places the Danes were unlikely to go.

Their ruthless and infamous leader Swein Forkbeard waded in, sweeping the Saxon mongrels aside in his marauding wake. It would be another winter scarred by mindless brutality, with stores of corn up in smoke and livestock driven off into the woods. Another winter to get by on acorns, once everything else was gone, summoning bitter memories of winters past for Fleda.

Rat was generous in offering his sett as a hiding place for anyone with a narrow enough torso to wriggle in. That included Catte and a reluctant Fleda – whose distaste for Rat was only trumped by her fear of an untimely, violent death – but not Bas or Elric.

'I need to go off to the woods,' Bas announced. 'I've got unfinished stuff.'

'Follow that soft heart,' Fleda advised him. 'And don't go dying again this time. I couldn't bear the grief.'

'What you babbling about, missus?' Rat asked.

'None of your business,' Fleda snapped, but Rat's face had disappeared back into the sett before she could slap it.

'Don't you need a knife or something?' Elric asked.

'Nah,' Bas shrugged. 'I got these.'

He held up his two enormous hands.

His huge hands, hardened to leather. And one big, soft heart.

X

The deserted Viking encampment was barely changed.

The shadow's home still stood but its fire had died. The wooden stools were still in place but the pile of bitter berries he'd left had been eaten. Bas sat down in the corner to rest and wait. He tried to resist sleep, but it nagged at him insistently until he succumbed. His nap was fitful and troubled. Bas dreamed of his father, Tom Thumb. Was the same impulse that had driven old Tom to pursue Fleda now visited on the son? Bas sighed in his half-sleep at the thought of chasing a shadow for twelve years. He woke up muttering.

When he'd come to his senses, he became aware of the sad offering on a platter of leaves. Bas realised there were only two likely explanations for this. A gift from some friendly woodland spirit or a welcoming present from the shadow of the Danish girl. He found it disconcerting that she must have been watching him, perhaps studying him while he slept. Troubling, but also comforting that she should still have left a peace offering.

Although he searched tirelessly all day, he found no trace of her. Perhaps she still feared this Saxon giant was trying to ensnare her. But Bas wasn't one to give up easily. His patience was rewarded the following morning with another miserable but well-intentioned platter of wizened crab apples and, beside them, his father's old knife.

So. It was the girl, then, and not a woodland spirit.

Bas sat down and set to work. First he gathered dried wood and spent fungus, just as his father had taught him. Then he began striking two pieces of flint together, inhaling the lovely burnt smell of the struck flint until a spark flew in the right place and took root. Then he breathed life into the fire: gently at first until it was set. Warmed, he began to fashion a crude ring from birch wood. Worked at it all day, though with his blunted knife it was never likely to be as perfect and smooth as the finger he imagined it encircling.

Finally, he placed it on the stool and busied himself until nightfall. He lay beside his fire, awaiting her arrival. Instead, sleep caught up with him again. It was a night of blustery winds. Threatening to tear the roof off.

When he managed to drag himself awake, he became aware that pressed against him and still fast asleep was the Danish girl. On her finger was his ring. It looked better on her than it had done resting on the stool. His leg was deadened but, for a while, he decided to bear the suffering. Revelled in the warm glow of the girl's proximity. Gritted his teeth until he had to turn, to ease his discomfort. She stirred.

Easing himself up, he walked off his dead leg. She lay there, one shoulder exposed. Those lovely shoulders of hers.

Once the feeling had returned to his right leg, he nestled down beside her to doze. After a while they found themselves making half-sleeping, half-waking love. Bas didn't know a lot about love, but he sensed in his very bones that nothing would ever be the same again. What was it Fleda had said? The sky will be a brighter blue, even on the dullest day. The birds will sing more sweetly. The flowers glow like suns . . . He sighed heavily and slumped back. Then for the first time he looked into her lovely eyes and stared at her, longingly and silently. Unable to find words to match the occasion.

'Thank you,' she said.

Unsure how to respond, he began to laugh. A great snorting giant's guffaw. She joined in, holding her delicate but grubby hands over her mouth to cover her teeth, which she reckoned to be her worst feature since one had been chipped when she'd fallen a few years back . . . though Bas found her laughter and her teeth bewitching.

'No, I mean it.'

And they were both gripped by uncontainable laughter again. Perhaps giving voice to their undiluted joy.

She tried again.

'Thank you for waiting to make love to me when you could have raped me.'

'I've found you,' Bas sighed. 'Remind me never to lose you.'

Now she was weeping.

Probably relief, she told Bas. Relief that – miraculously – she'd made the right choice.

She gazed at him again. Her startlingly pale-blue eyes seemed to reach into his very soul. And even though her hair was matted after days and nights spent in the wind and rain, her plaits beginning to unravel, and her face and her hands grubby with ash and soil, she was beautiful. The loveliest girl he'd ever beheld. She tried to stop herself from smiling but was unsuccessful. She covered her mouth again to hide her broken tooth.

'I don't think I'll love you any less for the loss of a piece of tooth,' he informed her. 'I love my mother and she has no teeth. I think you should meet her.'

She felt an undertow of terror at the prospect of being plunged into a settlement peopled by a bunch of warmongering Saxons.

'Just in case you decide to introduce me to your mother, I'm Ynga,' she whispered.

'Bas,' Bas responded, embarrassed at his oversight.

'I know,' she said. 'You told me, that night you saved me. You said I should look into your eyes and that I'd be safe if I trusted you and then you said you were Bas.'

'Good . . . Do you want to do anything before we go? Say your farewells to any of your kith and kin who died?'

'My family were already dead long before you all came.'

'Sorry.'

'Perhaps we could do one thing before we leave.'

She looked up at his face again and he felt that chipped tooth of hers on his tongue as he explored her mouth.

XI

My scribe coughs. It's his polite way of slowing me whenever I race ahead of him. His feather fairly flies across the page now that he's grown accustomed to etching my words on to the vellum. Nevertheless, we story-weavers sometimes find that words come tumbling, all in a rush, from our lips.

'Like horse shit being tipped from a cart,' my dear friend Tolland sometimes remarks.

'Like purest gold pouring from a furnace,' I correct him.

'I hate to slow you, Eam,' Aart apologises.

'Then let's talk a while, Pup, and rest that overworked right hand of yours. Is all this talk of lovers troubling your young mind?'

'I confess I've often wondered what it must be like to kiss a maiden, Eam. I fear the Lord might strike me down if I do.'

'Were you to kiss one of the novice nuns, I imagine the abbess is more likely to box your ears than the Almighty is, Pup. I also imagine the wrath of the abbess is more fearsome to behold than the wrath of the Almighty.'

'You still haven't told me what a maiden's kiss feels like, Eam.'

I tell him what I can, though I'm hardly well schooled in such matters. I tell him that the lips of a gnarled old wordsmith such as I may be able to conjure feelings of joy. That these are as nothing compared to the joyous touch of a young maiden's lips. That a lover's lips can conjure feelings of more longing than the heart can bear.

'Thank you, Eam.'

He's still troubled. I can read his voice the way he can read the written word.

'What troubles you, Pup?'

'I fear I might have sinned and seen things I ought not to

have seen, Eam.'

'A brother misbehaving?'

'In a manner of speaking. I read a letter and one of the brothers plans to eat a nun.'

'Eat a nun?'

'Those were his words to one of the sisters, Eam. He said he could eat the sister alive. If I tell the abbess, I'll be damned for having read the letter entrusted to me . . . Why are you laughing at me, Eam?'

'Dear, dear Aart. Though it shames me to say it, I've been driven to eat the flesh of a fellow man. Driven by hunger such as you could never know. Believe me. Such flesh is flavoursome enough, but it leaves a guilty taste in the mouth. That story must wait, Pup. For now, rest assured this brother speaks in the words of a lover. He talks only of the lust that devours him.'

Aart sighs with relief.

'Run along now, Pup. You've earned some respite. And try not to get up to any mischief, though I'm not averse to hearing what the brothers say in their letters today.'

XII

Catte took one look at Ynga and felt her hackles rising.

Rat watched her. Twitching. Scratching at his fleas.

The flooded river overspills where the bank lies lowest. You make your strike for your girl when she needs you the most.

So he sidled up to her as she bent down plucking weedlings from between the crops.

'Seems to me you don't want to be my girl, so I guess I'd better give up trying and find some nice little Danish girl who likes the taste of my tongue.'

'I didn't say you couldn't ever. I just said not yet.'

'Well, my patience just set off walking over the hills.'

'All right. Maybe tonight when no one's looking. And if you go telling, I'll bite that tongue of yours off.'

'See ya later,' Rat squeaked happily as he danced off, giving his kissing stick a vigorous gnawing.

'Don't you worry about what people say, you two,' Fleda advised Bas and Ynga. 'A sharp tongue's blunted by the spilling of too many insults. It's the silences and things not said you should guard against. Those that store up their bile are the dangerous ones. They'll poison things . . . But Winfrith'll have no complaints. Looking at the shoulders on the pair of you, you'll do the work of five men and two women.'

Bas looked adoringly at Ynga's lovely square shoulders. He couldn't stop thinking about them. He loved them. And her blue eyes and her long, fair hair, now shining and neatly plaited. Fleda saw the way her son looked at the girl and was pleased he'd found the right one. She and Tom Thumb had wasted half a life before they'd struck lucky. It hadn't escaped her notice, either, the way Bas had started to wash himself with alarming regularity – sometimes more than once in a week – and even change his undergarments and comb his hair on occasions.

'A regular little Viking that girl's made you into,' Fleda teased him. 'There are things I need to tell you both about the *meeting of flesh*,' she added, clinging to the myth of her child's complete ignorance of such matters.

She sighed. It would be bittersweet, teaching her daughter-in-law all her stock of *womanly wiles*, the ways she'd found of pleasing the demanding, voracious King Edgar. Hastening the day when she'd cradle her first grandchild in her arms was a good reason to impart her hoard of wisdom. Stirring up all those painful memories wasn't so good.

Bas couldn't take his eyes off Ynga, couldn't wipe the smile off his face. Felt blessed by Fate. Not just because of the womanly wiles old Fleda had passed on to her daughter-in-law, but because of the mere fact that he should have stumbled upon her. Couldn't quite figure why a girl like Ynga should have given him a second look. But she loved him all right, as much as he did her. And nothing could beat the feel of her warmth as they pressed against each other at night or – fleetingly – during the day.

Ynga ignored the snide insults that flew her way, borne on the breeze. Shrugged her lovely square shoulders and got to work, clearing stones as Bas worked the soil. He bent down and kissed her lightly where her shoulder met her neck.

We all should have a strapping shoulder
to cry, to weep our wet tears on, or one
that leavens, that lightens a load and
I'll admit to longing to taste on my tongue
a tender, herb-smothered, slow-ovened,
melt-in-your mouth shoulder of lamb.
But Ynga's sun-gilded shoulders,
the ones I caress or I cling to in our bed are
beautiful, comely, beyond compare.

Bas sighed. Fleda smiled. Ynga continued to lift stones, her neck still tingling from Bas's touch.

XIII

Catte followed Rat over to the old badger sett. Standing at the entrance he took a good look at those slender, boyish hips of hers.

'Yup,' he said. 'A nice fit, I reckon. You follow me in and I'll show you my kissing room.'

She wriggled in and followed him to the brocks' main sleeping chamber.

'Afraid there's not much headroom, Catte, so we'll have to lie side by side and make the most of it.'

Rat tried to stay composed as he placed his mouth next to Catte's.

What did he taste as he searched her with his tongue? A rat relies on his senses of taste and smell more than his sight. In the dark badgers' sleeping chamber, Rat's senses were heightened. In her mouth, which resisted him at first but then slackened, he tasted not spittle but spite. On her breath he smelled not the bread she'd just eaten but the odour of bitterness.

Rat felt a growing confidence and his paws began to explore Catte's slender frame, but pretty soon she made it clear which parts of her body were out of bounds . . . in particular, her breasts and that tuffet he longed for.

Catte twitched uncomfortably as a flea pierced her skin. She scratched at it as she wriggled her way out of the sett.

'Not all it's cracked up to be,' she said dismissively and then skipped off.

But she'd been bitten by a bug: a desire to be kissed over and again, though she hoped she could do better than Rat.

Yes, Catte had been let out of the bag.

'Man mad,' Fleda would chunter. 'I've seen her sort before. Vixens. Wedlock-wreckers.'

XIV

Few folk approved of Bas's girl. Many of the wives felt threatened by her beauty.

'Madness,' Fleda muttered. 'She's clearly only got eyes for my Bas.'

Admittedly they were the loveliest, pale-bluest eyes any of them had ever seen. Even cast modestly downwards they could set a man's heart fluttering and a wife's pulse surging with jealous concern. When she looked up, they could turn a grown man's bones as soft as unbaked dough.

'Can't they see?' Fleda growled. 'That little Catte's much more of a threat, wiggling those slender hips of hers in front of them. She thinks she's so clever. She thinks she has the men in the palm of her hand and before long she'll find herself out of her depth. She'll be satisfying some man's needs but she's too full of herself to realise she might be quelling a fire, but her slender hips only ignite lust. Ynga's blue eyes light a far brighter fire of longing.'

Old Tom Thumb had talked about *longing* and *shorting*. When a woman inspired longing, you'd do whatever you had to in order to make her love you. Even trudge around the country for twelve years trying to find her. When a woman conjured not longing but shorting, if a quick rough-and-tumble in the bushes wasn't on the cards, you had to find another outlet for your lust. Then you'd take a deep breath and get on with your life.

No one was listening to Fleda as she muttered darkly about Catte and the shorting she conjured in men.

Winfrith waddled up to Fleda.

'I don't want any trouble with that Viking girl. I've a mind to banish her from this place, the stirrings she's caused.'

'She's not caused them,' Fleda snapped. 'Is she to be punished for being so comely? She doesn't ask to be ogled by any of them.'

Fleda still felt keenly the injustice of having been chosen as the late King Edgar's whore because she'd been gifted her dark, bewitching, elfin looks. Why was it never the fault of the men, whose brains were lodged well away from their heads?

'I'm not talking about anyone ogling her. I'm talking about her being an outsider.'

According to Winfrith the Thane, those barbarians in places like Mercia might accept inter-tribal marriages, but here in Wessex, the heart of Anglo-Saxonness, it wasn't the done thing. A Viking girl was bound to be an object of mistrust and endless gossip.

Fleda believed we're all outsiders, one way or another. She'd not put her trust in any of this lot.

And what about you, Winfrith? she thought. *Didn't your forebears, just like mine, come along and wrench the land from those tribes now skulking in the far-flung corners of this island? What makes you think it belongs to you any more than it belongs to the Danes or even to the few wolves we've left cowering in the deepest, unpeopled woods?*

'I could have her banished,' Winfrith threatened. He tried to puff out his chest, but succeeded only in raising his enormous belly slightly before it collapsed again.

'Could, but won't. Because she does the work of two of those gossiping, giggling little vixens. And my Bas does the work of five men. You're smart enough to know which side of the bread your dripping's larded on.'

Chuck in a little compliment along the way. In Fleda's experience, men always fell for that. It softened their heads while they mulled over their own importance.

'I could have you flogged for your insolence,' Winfrith said, without any conviction.

'Could, but won't,' Fleda said, turning her back on him. *Because you're a coward*, she might have added. But you had to allow your thane to walk around with some of his dignity intact. Without some nod to the rule of law, there'd be chaos.

'Just heed my words,' Winfrith said.

'And mark mine, too. It's not my Bas's Ynga likely to give you heartache. That'll come from other quarters.'

'Meaning what?'

'Meaning you need to keep your ears to the ground and your eyes on your serfs and snuff out any trouble before it brews.'

'I'll thank you for your advice. Perhaps I was mistaken but I thought that offering snippets of wisdom was the meat and drink of thanes, not serfs.'

It was always good to finish a bitter exchange with one of your serfs with a withering put-down. It helped to reassert the pecking order.

Winfrith even began to whistle as he waddled off. Catte looked up at him and smiled invitingly, pushing out those budding breasts of hers. Winfrith felt stirrings in his groin. Perhaps the old hag Fleda was right. He ought to watch his step and keep his eyes open for trouble from sources other than Bas's comely Danish wench.

XV

'Be careful, you two,' Fleda warned Bas and Ynga. 'I don't want you coming to any harm.'

Fleda nodded her head towards Ynga's belly, which was looking very slightly swollen. You could have missed it, if you didn't have an eye for these things.

'Anyone told you two about babies?'

'Rat did tell me some things,' Bas mumbled, blushing hotly.

Fleda turned her eyes towards the heavens.

'Well, that'll be a load of nonsense he's planted in that brain of yours . . . If you two are going to be presenting me with a grandchild, then there are things you need to know – especially you, my dear.'

She looked at Ynga. 'You need to know the pain you'll suffer. Try to imagine going for nine months without squatting over the privy and at the end of it, you pass a stool as hard as rock and a hundred times bigger than any stool you've ever passed in your life. Then you'll begin to understand what awaits you . . . And you, young man. Don't you ever forget what you inflict on your Ynga every time you start getting all excited of a moonful night.'

XVI

Once she'd spotted that Ynga was pregnant, Catte felt her
hackles rise again. A surge of spite and a determination not
to be outdone. And if someone was going to go planting his
seed in you, why not make it the top dog? That would get
one over on that outsider with her pale-blue eyes, her fair
hair and those plaits you just wanted to pull.

Catte knew, each time she pouted at Winfrith, it was she,
not Ynga, who had her thane practically salivating. It wasn't
going to take a lot of skill to entice her lord-and-master
beneath her skirts. She watched as a half-feral cat played
with a mouse it had cornered. Kept letting the animal free
before pouncing again. Eventually, perhaps after a dozen
attempts, the mouse gave up the ghost. As if finally accepting
it was in the cat's thrall. The cat ate the doomed mouse with
an expression not unlike boredom before sloping off. Not
a bad way to approach that lively mouse inside her thane's
pants that seemed to have a life of its own. Tease him and
torment him until he was in your thrall.

'Don't think I've not seen the way you look at old
Winfrith,' Rat hissed. 'You're my girl, so I don't want his
tongue in your mouth.'

'I'm not interested in tongues and mouths. That's for
boys,' Catte dismissed him. 'Besides, I'm not your girl. I'm
nobody's girl.'

'Or everybody's, the way some men talk of you,' Rat spat.

'That's a lie and you know it. I hate you.'

But Rat wasn't to be denied. He pinned Catte by her wrists
and forced his tongue into her mouth. Catte squirmed and
then she bit Rat's invading tongue. Rat screamed in pain.

Winfrith came waddling round the corner. As he scurried
off, Rat heard Winfrith's promise of a flogging drifting on
the wind. You can run, but the voice of your thane and the

whip-crack of his punishment run faster.

'Come here, child,' Winfrith comforted Catte. She rested her head against his chest as he stroked her hair.

Yes, thought Winfrith; *she's purring now*.

He felt those shortings again, surging through his veins.

'You know I care about all my little orphans. It's not easy watching some of my pretty little waifs grow up without their mother or father and then to feel tenderness welling up when you become young women.'

Catte allowed Winfrith to press against her.

'Do you understand that I could love you, my little waif? Not just as a father might love you.'

'I like to please you, my lord, but I don't wish to displease the mistress.'

'The mistress will mistake my attentions for fatherly concern . . . if we're careful.'

'I understand, my lord, but now wouldn't be the right time. Rat'll sneak up on us and spread his gossip.'

Catte drew away from her thane.

'Take care, my waif,' he warned her. 'This thane is a lusty, impatient fellow. And mark this. A thane expects to help himself first to the finest meats at a table. He has no taste for other men's cast-offs . . . Now go away and find Rat. Tell him to be at my door at first light tomorrow and ready for his flogging.'

'Thank you for your love and care, my lord,' Catte pouted.

Then she walked off, wiggling her slender hips and smiling.

'She will be mine,' Winfrith muttered to himself, 'and the Rat will feel the bite of my whip and the sting of my justice in the morning.'

Beatings at the hands of Winfrith were a rarity, and therefore well attended when they cropped up.

'She's trouble, that one,' Fleda whispered – not for the

first time – as she turned her head away while ten whip-cracks landed on Rat's back. 'Mind you, it's about time that little rodent was put in his place.'

Fleda shuddered as the tenth and final crack echoed in the morning air. She looked at Bas.

'Go to him. He may be a filthy rodent, but he's your friend. No one will stand in *your* way. Not if they've half a brain, they won't.'

Bas carried Rat over his shoulder so as not to inflame the disturbed flesh on his back and laid him down on his own bed – in their own dwelling now, their *sundorwic* – while Ynga bathed his wounds. She did this not to ingratiate herself, because she cared not a jot what any of them thought of her. She did it because she reckoned she might bring a little peace and calm to Rat's weeping wounds. Stem the tide of his suffering. Stifle thoughts of revenge seeping in through his broken skin.

Ynga knew that bad spirits could invade your body while you lay there with open wounds. Sometimes the bad spirits got into your head and whispered how you might avenge the injustice. Sometimes the spirits brought you low and cursed you with the fever or plague, or even death itself. As a little girl she'd seen her own father's flesh, breached by an enemy sword, grow green and swollen. She'd smelled the stench of death on him as the spirits dragged him from this life. She wouldn't have wished that on anyone. Not even Rat.

Catte heard Rat's groans – was that pain or pleasure? – and felt her back arching with hatred for the Danish outsider.

Ynga was swelling very visibly. Some of the older serfs on the settlement would sometimes venture to wish her well, even to touch her belly and feel for signs of movement.

There was nothing like a new life to draw people together and consign old hostilities to the dung heap. A new life and a fresh start.

But Catte still seethed with envy. Ynga's belly tautened and Catte's resolve hardened. She had Winfrith where she wanted him now. It was so easy, she smirked secretly. Men were putty in her hand.

Winfrith's breath quickened as she led him to the storeroom. It was cooler here. Quieter, too, with little chance of their being interrupted.

'Wicked temptress,' Winfrith rasped as his chubby hand grasped a buttock.

Catte felt a mixture of dread and elation. The loss of her virginity was moments away.

She winced as he entered her. Winfrith mistook her gasps for pleasure.

There was a cold look in his eyes.

Catte gritted her teeth. It wasn't meant to be like this. Her dreams had been of fine bed linen. A woollen mattress beneath her. Her thane looking needingly into her eyes, promising her the world.

He held her hips in his chubby hands. Gripped her too hard for comfort. Thrust into her with something more akin to violence than tenderness. How could this be? She'd given herself to her thane and he seemed to be cursing her, not thanking her, as he whispered his obscenities into her ear. Not a word about love.

Then he withdrew from her and allowed her skirts to fall.

'Go now,' he instructed her.

'Do you not love me, my lord?'

'No less than you have always loved me, child. Which is all a girl could hope for.'

'What if I bear your child, master?'

'Unlikely,' he replied, tersely. 'And if seed grows in you then I'll couple you with some man in my charge. Simon the Simpleton's without a wife.'

'Simon has no wife, nor any brain, either. I'll not be tied with him in wedlock.'

'As you wish. Just remember old Winfrith will keep his

eye out for his little vixen.'

He patted a buttock, as if to confirm – if there was any doubt – that he was her lord-and-master now in every way.

Winfrith waddled off, having passed on to the hapless Catte the gift of the clap. Walked away, too, aware of the infertility that had been a curse and a blessing of sorts in his childless life. The only seeds likely to be growing inside that elfin belly were the seeds of bitterness and resentment.

The waif was on her own now. She was sharp, that one. As sharp as unripe fruit. But she'd bewitch some serf or other with her charms, such as they were. They had to learn, these wenches. And better to learn from your thane than from some wastrel.

Alone, Catte sobbed.

Perhaps Rat loved her. Perhaps she should settle for him. Although she'd like to try her luck elsewhere first. What did she have to lose? The damage was already done. What was that saying? You may as well be flogged for stealing gold as for a farthing.

Ah, but poor Catte. She would have to learn that before you can truly be loved – loved with unquenchable longing – you, yourself, must learn to love.

XVII

Secrets will out.

'Poor foolish girl,' Fleda muttered, shaking her head. 'Another wench who'll be tossed from man to man. Fodder, to satisfy their shortings. Some girls seem able only to satisfy that sort of manly urge.'

She looked into Ynga's pale eyes.

'Consider yourself twice-blessed, my love. The spirits have granted you the looks to inspire longing and the good common sense to handle that. Maybe they gave you that strumpet Catte's share of looks and common sense.'

Fleda had also learned the hard way that there's an ocean of difference dividing the *meeting of flesh*, as she called it, and the *meeting of minds*.

The meeting of flesh was like the fall of snow. A girl might anticipate it with growing excitement, and, yes, it could sometimes blanket your sadness for a while. More often than not, it soon became as cold and disappointing as muddied slush, though that never stopped you eagerly anticipating the snow's next visit.

But love, the meeting of minds, was like the sun. Sometimes too hot for comfort. Sometimes dimmed and cooled by the clouds. But most of the time it was warm as a summery, bird-singing, bee-humming day.

Fleda sighed as she remembered how summer had come late into her life. When Tom Thumb had loved her so much he'd made her happy to be in her own crumpled skin.

Would Catte find happiness one day?

Probably not, Fleda thought. Rumours and gossip could poison people's minds against you. Where did they start? Rumours sprang up like toadstools on cow shit. Perhaps some sprite had danced from person to person, whispering the secrets in their sleeping ears. But Fleda doubted that.

That poor, stupid strumpet, Catte, had probably sought comfort and reassurance by sharing her secret with Rat in their flea-infested badger's sett and Rat, knowing that to be in possession of gossip can make a man feel inches taller, had scurried around twitching that mean, pinched face of his and squeaking his nasty little stories.

'Here. Take some of my bread,' Fleda muttered to Catte in the morning. 'And if you've a brain in your head, you'll also take my advice. Try to have as little as possible to do with men. There's good and bad in all of them, but more bad than good, by my reckoning.'

Catte was grateful for the bread, but opted not to heed the old hag's dire warnings.

She continued her search for love but found only brief, squirming-inside moments of heaven that somehow compounded her sadness. Rat refused to give up hope and his patience was finally rewarded. The fleas cavorted wildly in the badgers' sleeping quarter while Rat fumbled blindly and ineffectively before he had his moment of delight.

'You should be my girl, Catte.'

Her pride might have long since fledged and gone, but even Catte drew the line at that idea.

Fleda had dire warnings for Winfrith, too. She told him she sensed trouble ahead.

'Nothing new there, then, old girl,' Winfrith noted dryly.

'Big trouble. Believe me, I've known big trouble. I once had the whole kingdom in the palm of my hand. Then my dwarf and I . . .'

Her voice trailed off. Fleda spat absent-mindedly at his feet.

Winfrith let it pass. The old crone was becoming increasingly wayward. Wrapped up in her little world.

'. . . And another thing. I'm not long for this life. Any harm comes to my Bas or my Bas's Ynga and I'll be watching you from beyond the grave.'

Now that *did* worry Winfrith. The old crone looked old and careworn enough to have one foot in the afterlife already.

XVIII

Ahead of any of the troubles or any parting-this-life, Ynga's first child, Fleda's grandchild, announced her arrival. Screams of pain came from the same bed from which sighs and groans of ecstasy had emanated.

It was easy for the men, Fleda chuntered. They thrust in their sausage – their *gehæccan* – and weep a few cloud-white tears. Don't have to worry about the thing the size of a good haunch of ox that comes out crying clear-water tears at the end of it all . . . Not the end, in truth, but just the beginning.

Scolding Bas, encouraging Ynga, Fleda helped to bring her grandchild into this life. She was the first to hold the baby. Cut the cord with the same knife Bas had offered to Ynga's shadow. Wrapped the baby in clean cloth, rocking her cries away. Then placed her beside Ynga's swollen breast. Gazing all the while directly into the baby's eyes as if she were in love.

'A girl,' she told Ynga. 'A beautiful baby girl who'll break as many Saxon hearts as she breaks Danish ones. Thank you for the most wonderful gift I've had since old Tom Thumb gave me back the gift of my life . . . This little girl must never go to the dark places I've been.'

'Emma,' Ynga whispered.

Emma is swathed in freshly washed cloth.

'I've a few stories I'll tell you, little one, before I'm done,' Fleda says. 'A good thing, having a girl first. Softens up the birth canal for when the boys come along. Never start with a boy.'

As if we have any choice in the matter.

Old Mother Haggard's gabbling. Emma gurgles happily. Trying to focus her eyes on the world that has only just been born anew.

'You can come in now,' Fleda calls to Bas. 'Be careful with your bairn,' she chides him, before he's even seen the girl. Bas of course doesn't know how to be anything other than gentle. His giant's right hand supports the body and his giant's left hand is bigger than the baby's head.

Bas weeps buckets.

'You great soft-hearted lummox. There's a woman's heart inside that warrior's body,' Fleda says.

XIX

Fleda's so thrilled her tongue won't sit still now. Now that the dam has burst, a torrent of stories comes tumbling from that parched old mouth of hers. They'll struggle to shut Old Mother Haggard up.

'You've both chosen well,' she says. 'Beautiful Ynga, who'll break every man's heart but Bas's . . . and you, my very own Bas, strong as a stag but nesh as a lamb. And now we have another mouth to feed. We may have nothing, but we're blessed.'

Her former loveliness that so bewitched her king and her dwarf is dancing in her green eyes. Dancing by the light of the fire. All sorts of stories are about to start tripping over themselves to come out.

She starts with the story of three warriors who beat their path to the door of three sisters.

The first warrior offers the eldest sister a chest of gold in exchange for her hand in marriage. The chest measures two feet by one by one. As she empties the chest of its gold, she's allowed to fill it with secrets. A bountiful hoard of secrets. There's only one catch. He's allowed the same quantity of secrets. They wed.

The second warrior offers a chest measuring only half as big. Otherwise, the deal's the same. They marry.

The third warrior offers no gold or secrets. Only his undying love. They, too, become husband and wife.

A year later, the first sister's plagued by emptiness. She's spent her gold. What gnaws at her is not regret for the lost gold or her secrets, but worry about what her warrior's secrets might be. All two feet by one by one of them.

The second sister's eaten up by jealousy. She has only half as many secrets. She's missed out on all those guilty pleasures.

The third sister is happy with her lovely gold-free, secret-free life.

'So. No secrets.'

Fleda was looking at her son and daughter-in-law, no longer addressing her soundly sleeping granddaughter. She prodded Bas in the ribs.

'You listening to me, sunshine?'

Bas grunted.

'No secrets,' he agreed.

'Best not to hang around too long, you two,' Fleda ploughs on, in the spirit of openness and honesty. 'I reckon you should try for a boy next. Your babies'll need a grandmother and a grandmother needs babies.'

It makes some sort of sense but it begs a question. How on earth does she reckon on making certain it's a boy that'll result from their meeting of flesh? Besides, Ynga's exhausted. Bas will have to wait until she's good and ready.

Fleda carried on with her stories. And while Bas was out ploughing the fields, she picked up where she'd left off in imparting her extensive knowledge of womanly wiles in the matter of the meeting of flesh. Some of the suggestions were enough to make Ynga blush. But she'd overcome her shyness soon enough.

'When I said *no secrets*, this is an exception to the rules,' Fleda informed Ynga.

XX

Catte hissed and cursed in a jealous rage. Spat on Ynga's clothing as she passed her.

'Danish whore,' she growled, the irony of her calling Ynga such a name lost on her. Catte longed to be loved. But each time a man withdrew from her, rolled off her, she knew she'd only satisfied their shorting. Ynga was loved and now she had a child, too.

Bas's erstwhile bosom-buddy Elric tried to reason with his sister. His pleas fell on deaf ears.

'Can't do much about it, Bas. Like casting wheat on to bare rock, trying to reason with Catte. So much fire in her belly she'll be burned to a crisp by her own flames.'

'Tell her I'll always love her for the way she became my sister when I had no friends. Tell her she needn't go hating Ynga. I love Ynga in a different way but I love Catte as a sister, though I'd rather she didn't spit on my girl, 'cause every time she does that it makes loving her a little bit harder.'

'You're a good sort, Bas. I'll tell her.'

'Maybe one day she'll learn to love herself. My mother says you can only be properly loved when you learn to love others. Otherwise it all goes belly up.'

'She's a wise old crone is Old Mother Haggard. Wish I had a mother.'

'Maybe Fleda'll agree to be your mother, if I ask her. Makes sense if you're my brother and Catte's my sister.'

'As I see it, she's got her hands full being a grandmother. But thanks all the same, Bas. Besides, I don't see Catte staying in the same room as your Ynga for long without having one of her hissy fits.'

XXI

Old Mother Haggard had her hands more than full being a grandmother. As well as spending hours scraping weakly at Winfrith's meagre soil, she had her stock of stories to tell.

'What's the point of having a headful of stories and not passing them on to the next generation?' she muttered. 'It's a bit like . . .' She searched for the right words. '. . . like having a crop of apples and watching them rot when you could be eating them.'

Fleda peered at Ynga's belly.

'Do I see what I think I see?' she asked. 'Good breeding stock, is our Ynga.'

She glowed with pride that she should have been granted the gift of such a daughter-in-law.

'I reckon it's a son this time round,' she announced. 'Well done, the two of you.'

These were glad tidings.

'We're blessed,' Bas announced, feeling unworthy of such unremitting joy.

Blessed indeed. Putting up with the mean-spiritedness of your kith was a small price to pay for such happiness.

He fished out the silver penny his father had handed him. Perhaps him and not Fleda because Tom Thumb had wanted to spare his lover's blushes, given that it bore the image of King Edgar. Not that it looked much like the king. Nevertheless, you didn't want to risk rubbing salt in a woman's wounds.

Bas owned up that he'd nearly summoned the first of the silver penny's three wishes, hoping that he could track down Ynga and make her his wife.

'Sounds to me like you narrowly avoided wasting a good wish, my boy. It's pretty clear you'd have become man and wife whatever. You'd never have got by without each other, like a milkmaid's hand and a cow's udder.'

With his silver penny, its three wishes all intact, and with the sort of wife any man would have longed for, Bas felt nothing could defeat him or make him glum. Not even those who ribbed him for having stooped so low as to marry a Dane.

That's their problem, not mine, Bas mused. *They don't know what they're missing.*

Ah, but they did know something of what they were missing. The men who heard those sighs and gasps colouring the still night air: they knew all right. All those sweet sounds fuelled the fantasies of the hot-blooded Saxon lads. Why didn't their Saxon girlfriends make love like that? And when you came to think of it, it was usually the women who spat on Ynga as they passed her. Not the men. The men secretly burned inside not with hatred or resentment but longing. Besotten with the fair-haired, blue-eyed goddess who'd breezed with comely grace into their enclosed world. No wonder most of the women resented Ynga.

'You allow sunlight into a room and people see their own imperfections,' Fleda told them. 'They need someone other than themselves to blame, so they blame the sun.'

XXII

The baby was a boy this time round, just as Fleda had said it would be, though Bas could never figure how his mother had worked this out.

Fleda tapped the side of her nose, knowingly. She'd possibly convinced herself that it had been something other than guesswork.

'Thought we might call him Thomas,' Bas mumbled.

Fleda smiled.

'Let's hope he can conjure stories like his grandfather and that he's a hard-headed, soft-hearted warrior like his father . . . Shall we tell your brother a story, Emma? Which one shall we choose?'

'Silverlocks and the three bruins, Grandma,' Emma replied.

'Ah, Silverlocks, my little darling. Silvanlocks. The playful spirit of the woods; half-man, half-tree. Leaves sprout from his head and mouth . . . And why must we always be good?'

''Cause if we're good he'll look after us and if we're bad he'll play tricks on us.'

'Good girl. Let's tell Thomas the story about the tricks Silvanlocks played on the three bruins when they were out stealing honey.'

Once upon a time. Fleda always savoured the four words. They reminded her of her dwarf more than anything else could . . .

'Are you all right, Grandma?' Emma asked.

'I'm sorry, my dear. I was in another place. The world of memory and spirits and the departed. Your grandfather lives there now and it mightn't be long before I join him. So listen well. Just in case you need to summon my stories one day.'

Once upon a time there lived a father, a mother and a baby bruin . . .

It wasn't the best of times for a boy to enter this life. Ill-timed rains and faltering sunshine had led to the worst famine in years. Fleda might have been able to recall times as hard, but neither Bas nor Ynga had known anything quite like it.

Perhaps that was why Emma wanted her newborn brother, Thomas, to be told a story about a hungry and cold Silvanlocks tucking into someone else's porridge and sleeping on their bed.

Thomas rasped as Fleda wove the tale.

'Why's Thomas making a funny noise?' Emma asked.

'I reckon he's trying to growl like one of the three bruins,' Fleda replied, masking her alarm.

'No point in worrying our Bas,' Fleda suggested to Ynga, 'but I'd be surprised if that little tyke outlives me. Men are about as much use as a cart without wheels in these circumstances. Being a good warrior's one thing, even a soft-hearted, hard-headed warrior like Bas. But coping with a baby boy who's cursed with the death-rattle before he's learned to speak is a different thing altogether.'

'I thought you said *no secrets*,' Ynga replied.

'That was mainly for his benefit. I think we can make an exception when it comes to life-and-death matters.'

'And meeting-of-flesh secrets. You told me to keep those from Bas, too,' Ynga pointed out, wondering if there were any other exceptions to what seemed a very unwatertight – in truth a very leaky – rule.

'A stubborn little lad,' Fleda conceded a week or so later. 'Not letting go very easily. His grandfather was the same. It takes a particular sort of cussedness for someone to spend twelve years searching for a woman the way old Tom Thumb searched for me.'

Thomas's growling hadn't abated any. And when he wasn't growling he was seeking out Ynga's teat, trying to extract some sort of relief. Spluttering and weeping with frustration.

'Perhaps we all have the same degree of suffering and Thomas is getting all of his out of the way,' Fleda muttered, more in hope than out of unshaken belief.

Bas was working over the soil when he sensed, with a shocking suddenness, that something was very wrong. He set down his spade and ran for home.

'What is it?' he asked as he entered, though he knew the answer already.

'Too lovely for this world,' Fleda sighed. 'Silvanlocks wanted him for his own.'

It was Fleda who suggested that Thomas be buried beneath the shade of the departed Tom Thumb's tree. A burgeoning oak, now eight feet tall – at least twice as tall as the old dwarf had been – and grown strong on the dead man's remains.

'A long walk, but it'll be worth it. Let Thomas's grandfather look after the boy. He's more time on his hands than we have. Less to occupy him. About time he had someone to talk to as he whiles away the years.'

Thus it was that Tom Thumb and the infant Thomas came to meet one another.

Bas sobbed quietly. His late father would surely have been trying to tell him trouble was brewing, if only Bas had taken the time to listen to Tom Thumb's spirit voice borne on the wind. But we don't listen, do we? We go about our noisy lives, rarely stopping to hear the voices of the long-gone dead. If only. If only he'd made it home earlier, then perhaps young Thomas's life could have been spared. And then there was the penny, too. The one Tom Thumb claimed was a gift from Merlin. Now in Bas's safekeeping. What was the use of a three-wish penny if you weren't in the right place at the right time?

XXIII

'Will we ever get over this?' Bas asked Fleda.

'Oh, yes,' she replied. 'We get over everything . . . but we never forget. There isn't a day that passes when I don't wonder about your half-brothers and half-sisters.'

The news hit Bas like a bolt from the woad-blue yonder.

'Brothers and sisters? You never told me.'

Fleda shrugged.

'You never asked.'

For one so full-to-overflowing with her advice, Fleda could be very tight-lipped when it suited her.

'I thought you said *no secrets*.'

'That was between husband and wife. Not mother and son.'

Bas was itching for stories about these half-brothers and half-sisters of his.

'Nothing much to tell,' Fleda replied. 'They took them away. I never saw them and that was the end of it. But they never took the pain away. The pain in here . . .' She pointed to her chest. 'They let me hang on to that.'

'How many?'

'Does it matter?'

'It helps me understand the amount of pain you feel inside.'

Clever, thought Fleda. *Not just all brawn. He knows how to wheedle a number out of me. Knew how to choose a good wife, too.*

'There were four in all.'

Fleda sat silently for a moment.

'At least I have *you* and if I'd not had the others first – all that practice, softening my birth canal – then there's no way I'd have managed to push a hulking great lummox like you out into the sunlight.'

XXIV

Old Mother Haggard had been right about never forgetting. When Bas heard the sigh of the wind through the trees he heard his son's voice – clearest of all in Tom Thumb's oak tree whenever he made the trek. When he saw the trees weep in autumn, he knew they wept for Thomas. In winter, when the family all gathered around the fire, Bas would clutch his penny every time his daughter Emma so much as coughed or spluttered. Ready to make his first wish. But spring, the time of new shoots and birth, was when his son's absence cut him most keenly.

Bas was blessed in so many ways. But he felt cursed, having been unable to get to his boy before he died.

He'd prove twice cursed . . .

It was now the year One Thousand and Six. Winfrith was reluctant to risk the best of his workers in the endless battles, skirmishes and tit-for-tat raids that sprang up who knew when and where, like toadstools springing to life on the forest floor before they shrivel and die. He knew, though, that he'd been pushing his luck for too long. Pointed questions were arrowing his way.

Was it really the case that those old codgers he'd offered up were the best he could muster? What about that giant some had heard tales of? The one who could do the work of ten men?

'Ah, yes. Bas, the Haggard's son. I was forgetting . . . though I think the tales about him have been sumptuously embroidered, my lord reeve.'

Tales usually grow in the telling. Become taller each time they're recounted to the next man. It helps to satisfy the appetite, does a tastier story. There's a danger that history would be dry and bland without being spiced by untruths.

'Since I humbly offer my lord reeve the services of a fine warrior, a giant who's as likely to do the work of ten men, by your own account, then I beg my lord reeve to allow me to offer some wise old heads alongside the Haggard's son. Brawn enough for ten men and the wisdom of another ten.'

'See this most remarkable of thanes.' The reeve turned to the other members of his moot council. 'He offers me a strange band of men: ten warriors' hearts, a further ten wise heads and only twenty-two legs between them. I feel as fleeced as a shorn sheep. Go back to your meagre soil, Winfrith, and send me this weird and wonderful army of men.'

XXV

'Sorry, Bas. I tried to stand my ground,' Winfrith sighed.

'Can't we live in peace with the Danes, for Frig's sake?' Fleda scowled.

'A choice beyond my grasp,' Winfrith admitted. 'Frankly, I believe in live-and-let-live . . . As you know, I'd whet my appetite ahead of whetting my sword any day of the week.'

'Spineless,' Fleda cursed. Too publicly. Winfrith struck the old crone and she crumpled to the floor.

'Insult me again and I'll have the very life flogged out of you.'

'I'd have you flog me before you lay another finger on a helpless old woman,' Bas growled.

'Not so helpless,' Winfrith muttered. 'She has more acid in that tongue than a viper.'

But Winfrith felt shrunken by the experience. A lesser man. One who was losing control of events. Yet he'd return to his old self soon enough. He always did. A blow to his pride here, an obstacle to be overcome there, but a thane must not show his doubts. Allow your men and women to share your moments of weakness and all is lost. It hurt when the reeve humbled him, pained him when that troublesome crone defied him. But a deep breath, a hearty meal, a serf bowing low before him as he chastised them, and his pride would be restored.

Fleda turned to Bas.

'I'll be fine,' she said. 'Just you be careful. Don't go risking your life. Remember what awaits you when you return. A wife most men could only dream of and a daughter who'll break more hearts than you'll ever know.'

Fleda was wise enough to make her peace with Winfrith before her son left. She might hold him in contempt, but she knew that, with Bas gone, it wouldn't be sensible to go stirring things up. Like all cowards, Winfrith would feel the stronger for the absence of someone he feared.

So she cast her eyes to the ground and spoke quietly.

'I don't blame you for sending my son away, master. Nor do I blame you for striking me.'

Winfrith nodded.

'Enough said.'

'. . . But I reserve the right to blame you if my son is harmed.'

Defiant old crone, Winfrith thought. *Can't help herself. With any luck she'll not last another winter like the one just past. That'd be some sort of blessing.*

So Bas was thrust if not into the heat then maybe the warm, smouldering remains of battle. Bas and ten old men: Winfrith's reluctant twenty-strong, eleven-headed, twenty-two-footed army of men – though one of the old feet had a pronounced limp, two more were riddled with arthritis and two others were deformed by rickets.

As they reached new settlements, they gleaned tidings of where their enemies might be. Hard to track down, these Vikings. You followed them towards the west. Next thing you hear, they're back in the east, five miles behind you and terrorising the very people who gave you food and shelter the night just past. So you turn again, to face your foes. Bas and the others walked for five days, often in circles, none of the men with much of a stomach for fighting – and with Bas on occasions having to carry on his back either the man with aching bones or the one with rickets. (The one with the limp proved fiercely independent.) It was comical. It was miserable. Too much rain, so they shivered as their clothing clung to them. Not enough food, so their stomachs uttered war cries more fearsome than they themselves could muster. Bas wove stories as they sat around the camp fire with other dispirited groups of men, though his tales of warfare were too even-handed for most of their tastes. They wanted stories about out-and-outly bad Vikings and godlike Saxons. Where was King Alfred in all of this? The faultless paragon of Saxon virtues: wise king, lawmaker, a shiningly bright mind and the finest of all warriors? Where was the heartless, faultful, hateful Ivar Ragnarsson – a Viking with no bones, principles or a shred of mercy – and his band of marauding villains? What was the point of a tale of warfare and derring-do with shades of grey to it? It was hardly going to stiffen your resolve. Mind you, half of the audience was out of it anyway, some of them drinking, others of them falling asleep (among them the old one with the limp who collapsed with exhaustion each night and fell sound asleep within moments).

Once again, perhaps because his head was spinning with tales, Bas failed to listen to what the spirit of his father, Tom, was trying to tell him. The rain, which had been falling persistently for several days, had now ceased and Bas and his fellow reluctant warriors were warming themselves by a blazing fire as he recounted half-hearted, even-handed war stories for them. But back home, troubles were raining on Ynga. She lay there shivering, mouthing Bas's name.

Fleda found her. The old woman's heart sank as she saw her daughter-in-law's state of dishevelment. Ynga looked up.

'How can I tell him?' she sobbed.

'No secrets,' Old Mother Haggard said quietly. 'No secrets, remember. And no lies.'

'He'll never love me again.'

'If he's worthy of you, he'll stay beside you. I know my Bas. He'll be a tower of strength.'

As she spoke, Bas, many days away, finally heard that spirit voice whispering to him that not all was well.

'Got to go,' he said, in alarm. The codger with rickets stopped rubbing his aching legs and looked at Bas.

'You can't just disappear, Bas.'

'No one would notice, would they?'

Sure they wouldn't. He only stood a mere head and shoulders above anyone else.

'What I meant was: who the hell is going to carry me if you go, Bas?'

Bas shrugged his enormous shoulders.

'Got to go,' he said again. 'Can't see the point of all this, anyway.'

And he was off. Let the rest of them do what they had to do.

XXVI

Bas strode out. Unencumbered by his fellow warriors, he ate up the miles, and all the while the spirits – chief among them his father's – whispered their warnings. He walked a day and a night before he bowed to the need for sleep. Then he walked another day and night. No backtracking this time. No enemy to have him running around in circles, though he kept well clear of peopled places, aware that he'd be branded a deserter if word of his flight reached his reeve. At last he saw his home there in the distance . . . His tiredness took flight and he broke into a run. And coming to greet him with her arms held out was his three-year-old daughter, Emma. His darling child. He lifted her into the air. She was so beautiful, so perfect that he felt he could crush her with his love. Thank heaven she was alive and well.

Fleda appeared in the doorway, concern written on her lined old face. Bas stopped babbling with Emma. There were no words of welcome from Fleda. She just said, very quietly:

'Remember. You've a treasure worth more than all the riches in the world. Don't lose it.'

No lies and no secrets.

Ynga hasn't got up to greet her beloved Bas. She's sapped of all energy like a plant starved of rain and sun. She stays seated in a corner, huddled on the dirt floor. Her eyes are cast downwards. Now she's sobbing.

Fleda has walked across and begins to stroke Ynga's hair.

'Take your time, my dear.' Then she turns to Bas and motions that he should hand Emma over.

'Come with me, little one. We'll leave your father and mother to talk in peace.'

'Why hasn't Mummy stopped crying? I thought you said

Daddy would be able to make her stop weeping.'

'He will, my darling.'

The story was garbled in the telling. There were ten. Or was it more? They were hungry for her. They pinned her down and one by one they raped her. Some of them took their turn at the back and raped her once again.

'I tried to scream, but one of them forced some rag into my mouth . . . I gagged . . . I was struggling to breathe . . . I tried to fight, but I couldn't . . . So I had to lie there, let them help themselves to my body while my spirit took wing to another place . . . And all the while I thought I must survive for Emma.'

She'd tried to close her mind to the pain . . . She'd bled where they'd dug their nails or their teeth into her . . . In the end, she'd passed out.

Why were they filled with so much hatred and violence? Do men not long to lie with a woman? When does that longing become something so crippled and deformed?

'Why?' Ynga wept.

If they'd come to me for bread, I'd have given them all I could spare. Or water. Or friendship. I'd have been their friend. The one thing I wouldn't have given them was my dignity: my body. Why was this the one thing they demanded? And if they had to take it, why was it done with such violence?

Perhaps they were like the thief who steals from a poor man and then beats him. The thief does this because he blames the poor man for the fact that he (the thief) has been diminished by the crime. The poor man – who's had to part with his pence – is the richer of the two . . .

Bas's mind was racing, but words wouldn't come to his aid. Wrong time and the wrong place again. He should have pulled his penny out and wished for Ynga's deliverance.

Will he ever get to make his three wishes?

'Did you see who it was?'

Ynga shook her head.

Didn't know? Couldn't bear to say? Wiped it from her memory the way you'd scrape dog shit off your shoe?

Bas didn't press her. He could work out at least eight of the names without even trying. What's a man supposed to do?

Fleda was standing in the doorway. Emma was beside her, but absorbed in studying a puff of dandelion seeds.

'Think about it before you jump in, Bas,' Fleda said, calmly.

She turned to Ynga.

'Don't worry, my love . . . Bas'll need to go and have a word with his late father. The dwarf'll put him straight. He was a wise old fool.'

'Look after Ynga and Emma,' he said to Fleda. He was shaking: with rage or frustration and sleeplessness.

Sometimes it seems a curse to have the soft-heartedness of a lamb and the brute strength of an ox. How much easier to leap in without a thought and wield your knife in anger.

Bas knew he needed to take his time, talk to his late father, think through the problem. Not hastily in black-and-white. But with thoughtful, many-hued calm.

XXVII

He was still shaking as he knelt beneath Tom Thumb's oak. Slowly the tremor subsided. It was clear his late father wasn't going to talk to Bas until the boy was ready to listen. You could never hear the voices of the departed unless you were able to give them your rapt, undivided attention. You had to close yourself to the crashing sounds of the living: the fox's bark, the nightingale's song, the breeze's sigh, your own breath.

You had to wait until the spirits felt you were ready to hear what they had to say.

Where's the point in revenge? Bas found himself thinking. Revenge is a lusty, rapacious beast that breeds like wildfire. It should be snuffed at birth.

Tom Thumb's great hero King Alfred had understood that, hadn't he? The Dane, Guthrum – routed at Edington and lying face down in supplication – had already figured out that Alfred was the greatest warrior of his age and that his men would march to the ends of the earth for him. But, as Guthrum lay prostrate on the floor, humiliated, in front of what remained of his army, Alfred showed him mercy: he lifted Guthrum to his feet, looked into his eyes, spoke to him as an equal, made him feel tall; and Guthrum knew he owed Alfred not just his life and his unswerving loyalty, but his very soul. And what followed was a happy period free of bloodshed, where Saxon and Viking lived in peace.

No. Don't seek revenge. Strangle it. Snuff it out. Bury it. Shame your enemies with your mercy. Leave them awestruck by your self-control. Strike terror into them with your calm silence. Make them tremble before your strength of character . . .

He could still bang on, could Tom Thumb. Death hadn't stayed his tongue.

'Thank you, Father,' Bas whispered. 'Take care of my little boy, young Thomas, while I take care of Ynga.'

XXVIII

'Sorry to hear your bad tidings, Bas,' Winfrith said.

Bas grunted. He supposed he could hardly blame Winfrith. A thane can't be everywhere at once. Crimes will happen on any master's patch.

'And, by the way, Bas, I'll need you to hide yourself away if one of the reeve's men comes sniffing around and asking where you slipped off to. I'll deny you've shown your face. And if any of my lot murmurs so much as a word about desertion, I'll have them strung up by their balls. Enough said.'

Bas's resolve to resist revenge would be sorely tested. He set about trying to forget. Put his energy into tilling the stony soil for Winfrith. The sun broke out and warmed his bent back. Not one person so much as whispered about his flight from the warriors' encampment. But other stinging insults rained on his ears.

From the men's mouths there were bawdy mutterings. From the wives came the worst vitriol. Unable to swallow the hard truth of their husbands' savagery, they had no doubts about whom to blame.

Danish slag, he thought he heard a woman's voice spit, like a drop of water sizzling on a fire. *Lined them up*, someone was whispering. *About a dozen of them, while poor old Bas was doing his duty . . . Wore them all out she did . . . Couldn't get enough of it.*

When Ynga shuffles out beside Bas, they spit on her from behind with greater force. If Bas has to leave her alone with Fleda or Emma any longer than moments, they abuse her worse than ever.

Whore. Wedlock-wrecker. Bitch. Not satisfied with stealing just one good Saxon man, she has to help herself to as many as she can get her hands on.

Ynga shields her daughter Emma and hurries silently on her way. Her eyes fixed forever on her feet these days.

'This can't go on,' Bas sighed. Fleda agreed.

Maybe the old dwarf was only half right. Yes, revenge wasn't the answer. But what about good old Anglo-Saxon justice, so fair and so lauded? Where men and women are able to state their case, where their words are weighed in the balance and even the mighty can be brought low by a heavy enough weight of accusation? Then again, the quality of justice depends less on the letter of the law and more on the judge. Winfrith proved himself as inept as he would have been on the field of battle. He raised his hands in a gesture of helplessness.

'I know they should all have their *pride and joy* cut off, Bas,' he conceded. 'Every last one of them. But how can I prove their guilt? I have the word of one woman against the testimony of a dozen men . . . And all their wives will line up and swear blind their men were in their own arms at the time. If there's any punishment to be meted out, they'll be doing it themselves, behind closed doors.

'Here,' he said, handing Bas a basket of grain. 'For your wife and child . . . and tell the old crone that I'll turn a blind eye if she and your Danish woman don't pull their weight for a day or two.'

Winfrith was ever the peacemaker. Or always seeking the easy way out. It depended which way you looked at it.

'I wash my hands of the matter, Bas. You must forgive and forget.'

Winfrith had wisdom enough to know his words had a hollow ring to them.

Some women might – in their righteous wrath – have sent the basket of grain flying across their hovel floor, making for an unexpected and welcome gift for the rodents who also considered the place their home.

Not Ynga, though. Her fighting spirit had already flown. Silently, she took Winfrith's peace offering and then, in a whisper, she said to Bas:

'Of course, it's your baby I'm carrying.'

She held her hand against her belly. She'd started lurching unsteadily between the unspoken thought and the uttered word. Surprising Bas and Fleda by sometimes not answering their questions or by fielding ones they've not asked.

'Never . . .' Ynga mutters as she scrubs her washing.

Fleda is looking increasingly alarmed.

'Bad spirits sneaked in when those vermin did what they did to her,' she tells Bas. 'I know how this happens. Your spirit takes flight from your body. It's the only way you can cope with being raped like that. But while your own spirit is away, the bad demons steal in. There's only one cure. You need to give her so much love that the demons are driven back out, my son.'

Bas was going through torment. He wanted to believe Ynga was carrying his baby. More than anything. Because if it were true then maybe Ynga could be whole again. One voice in his head told him he should be jigging for joy that another child of his was growing in the womb of the girl he loved so much he'd die for her. But another voice was mocking him. Some bad spirit or other, too cowardly to reveal itself. That voice was telling Bas that the father could be just about any of the hot-blooded men in the village.

Ynga was sure.

'Your baby . . . I know it.'

She raised her head for the first time in weeks and her pale-blue eyes bored into his. Ynga at her most lucid. But when she sensed his doubt, her head dropped again.

It wasn't anything he'd said. It was what he'd not said. You can hide many things. You can smile sweetly at an enemy or you can cloak your scorn from someone you despise.

You can sometimes look unmoved when, in truth, you're quaking inside with fear. You can feign indifference when inside you're churning with emotion. But hiding your doubt from someone you love, someone who knows every twitch and tremor of your skin, every modulation of your breath and every flicker of your eye ... that's a near-impossibility.

Bas felt overcome with a wave of tenderness for his lovely, haunted wife. Nothing could have diminished that. Not even if she'd spawned the very Devil himself. All she had to do was gaze at him with those pale, troubled eyes and he would do anything she asked of him.

Those eyes that she kept fixed on her feet for much of the time now.

'They shan't destroy us. You'll have so much love we'll smother the demons who've invaded us.'

Fleda was watching them, listening to them.

Male bluster, she thought to herself. Though if Bas was right, they had a fight on their hands. Demons such as Doubt or Despair wouldn't let go of their hold without one hell of a fight. They were among the most tenacious of bad spirits.

'. . . in the supping,' Ynga mutters.

Bas looks at her quizzically.

'The proof of the ale,' Fleda explains, patiently. 'The proof of the ale's in the supping.'

Bas is still unsure.

'Have you none of your late father's wits, boy? She's trying to tell you you'll see right enough who the father is when the child's born. Am I so cursed that I have a son with no wits and a daughter-in-law who's had hers wrenched from her?'

So Ynga was haunted by Despair and Bas by Doubt. But he threw himself into his work. That way he was less likely, amid the bustle and thrust of daily life, to hear the voices in his head. He didn't want to think about it. Didn't want to know.

Elric, working beside his old buddy, shaped to say things at intervals but the words didn't want to come, so he swallowed them, though they tasted bilious.

If Bas asked him straight, how would he reply? What if Bas had asked him: *Was Rat one of them?* Would he have the courage to say: *Yes, Rat was one of them.* Or would he cloud the truth? Would he twist things and say: *How can I know that if I wasn't there, Bas?*

But what if Bas pressed him? What if Bas asked him: *What if you'd been there, Elric? What would you have done?* How could he answer that? Would he have the courage to admit that he fancied the skirts off Ynga and – in the heat of the moment – might have been swept up by everything . . . and, of course, if he had done what the other vermin had done, then he'd have been racked with guilt until his dying day . . . So, after a long, long pause, he might have said to Bas: *I pray that if I see a group of men setting on a girl I'd have the strength to defend her.*

But what if Bas wouldn't let go? What if Bas looked at him and asked again: *I ask you directly, Elric, as the dearest friend from my boyhood. Were you there in my home and did you, too, rape Ynga?* Elric would have looked his friend full in the face, held his gaze and told him: *No, Bas. I swear by all the saints I had no part in it.*

And Elric would have known that he was now damned twice over by his own lips to eternal fire and damnation. Not just for his actions but for lying under oath.

Each time Elric shaped to speak, his mouth was filled with the sour taste of his guilt for his part in destroying Ynga and betraying Bas. It was never going to go away.

Sometimes, as Ynga struggles with her demons, she thinks out loud. At other times, she forgets to open her mouth and utter the words she's saying. Fleda takes on the role of her interpreter. If Bas harbours any doubts about whose father the unborn child is, Fleda has none. Frail, bent and slowed by the blessing and curse of her old age, she remains a rock.

'They won't break you, child,' she says, grooming her daughter-in-law's lovely hair, unravelling and then reworking and binding her plaits. Pale as ripened wheat. 'When your Bas's babe comes into this world, we'll give him a welcome fit for a prince, shan't we? And his mother'll be looking like a queen. Now let me pick these wretched fleas off your skirts.'

But in her heart, Fleda's thinking other thoughts. Such as: *When I'm dead and gone (which can't be long, now), who's going to look after this poor, wretched, broken girl and my little grandchildren?*

'. . . hurt so much I just wanted to die,' Ynga mutters.

'I know, my dear. But Bas will love you more than ever when you pull through this. You and the child. He'll love you both.'

Fleda bit her lip. She'd allowed a slight shimmer of doubt to creep into her voice. She'd begun to wonder if Ynga ever truly would pull through. Being raped by the King of England night after night was one thing. But by ten men – or was it twelve? That was so much worse. And Ynga, cherished, adored wife, had fallen so far. When you're already at the bottom of the heap – a mere servant girl offered up to preserve a thane's daughter's chastity – there's not far to fall.

XXIX

Ynga was standing there. Sobbing and confused, because her waters had broken. She grasped her back as she felt the first spasms. Fleda led her to a bed of fresh straw.

Thank the saints it's her third time of asking, the old woman thought. There was no way Ynga would have survived the ordeal of ridding her body of a firstborn in her current state. It would have torn her apart.

The child seemed happy enough to slip quietly into the world. There had been only eight moons since the rape. Surely there was no doubt about who the father was now. Was there? Fleda was determined to whip up some sort of celebration. Whatever Ynga's been through, she's gifted Fleda another lovely grandchild. In those moments you just rejoice, even if your tired old body's too stiff to do much dancing these days.

'By the bones of St Swithun,' she announced. 'It's a beautiful boy. A perfect little boy. He's got his mother's lovely straw-white hair . . . And look at those heart-melting blue eyes.'

His mother's hair and his mother's eyes and . . . therein lies the problem. The boy is the spit and image of his mother. Which is all for the good because that little lad is going to get every woman clucking and cooing like a broody hen and he's going to get the hearts of all the girls pounding when he becomes a man. But it does nothing to drive out the demon of Doubt.

You silly, thoughtless old fool, Fleda thinks to her late husband. She hopes he can hear her reprimand, though he's resting a good few miles away under that oak of his and he always was a lazy old good-for-nothing, so he's probably asleep anyway . . . *Do you hear me, Tom Thumb? Why couldn't you have taken a moment to sort things out? A*

*word in the right places? The Creator could at least have
given him Bas's nose or put that funny kink in his left ear.
Anything that was unmistakably Bas ... But no. You couldn't
even manage that.*

*What's the point of your husband's being dead if he
doesn't look after his family?*

'. . . Harry as his own,' Ynga mutters, either finishing
an unspoken sentence or allowing her thoughts to spill out
loud. Who can say?

At least she has her wits about her enough to be grappling
with names. And it seems her mind's made up. The boy's
going to be . . . is it Harold or is it Harald? Harry's a good
name. Half-Dane and half-Saxon.

Bas is happy enough.

'Harry,' he says, picking the child up. 'My son.'

'There you go,' Fleda whispers. Bas already thinks of the
boy as his own, even if there's a smidgen of a chance that
Ynga's deluding herself and one of those vermin has sown
his seed in her.

'. . . they'll throw the baby in the fire,' Ynga mutters.

Bas is cradling the boy.

Fleda puts her arm around Ynga.

'Not Bas,' she whispers. 'It's all right, my dear. Bas is the
one who loves you. Remember? Bas is the one who'll stand
by you and protect you and the children.'

There's a dazed look about Ynga. The life has drained
from those pale eyes. Perhaps it's down to the birth and she
needs her rest.

Fleda strokes Ynga's hair again.

'Go fetch some fresh water from the well to refresh your
mother,' she says to Emma, who goes skipping off, unaware
that anything is wrong. Which is how it should be.

When Emma gets back, Ynga gulps the water down.

'Thank you, my love,' Fleda says. 'Mummy's very
grateful.'

Ynga's led to her bed. Confused about the tall man with

the big nose. She's so exhausted she feels she'll fall asleep in moments. But Emma's dancing around the stranger, shouting excitedly for the stranger to tell a story for the newborn boy.

Bas is worn to the marrow after toiling on the land for a day. His shoulders are burdened by all his troubles. But he looks into Emma's eyes, then at the baby he's cradling, and he launches into his performance, unaware that he's picked up his father Tom Thumb's movements and mannerisms.

XXX

Harry proved stronger than his brother Thomas, who'd been unable to cling to life. But Fleda hung on all the same, just to be on the safe side. For three years, she fussed over the child. Still the image of his mother. Not so much as a freckle to mark him out as Bas's (or anyone else's) son.

Fleda was muttering about what an idler her late husband had turned out to be. He might have been the best sort of story-weaver while he lived, but he'd been a waster since he'd died. Not done a thing to help.

Emma was seven by then and already the mother of the house.

They have the snows of the North Lands in their white hair and the blue of the North Sea in their eyes, Fleda mused.

She adored them. Would have happily stayed with them. But she knew she was breathing her last. That rattling noise sounded like someone from another world knocking on her door. Telling her her time was up. She looked over at Ynga. Poor, wretched Ynga, who heard and saw nothing these days, just sat there or ate her gruel whenever Emma fed her. Those once-lovely eyes, which could conjure longing in any man, were now dead, those once-perfect square shoulders hunched. Her lips, where words had danced with soft grace and that bewitching foreign accent, now dribbled gibberish. Her skirts, which had clung to her so exotically, were grubby and flea-ridden. And she smelled worse than a Saxon.

Fleda beckoned to Emma and whispered in her ear. Old Mother Haggard's voice and her fight were both fading.

'I want you to know, my dear, your mother was once the most beautiful woman I've ever seen in my long life. When your father walked in the door with her, it felt like another sun had come out. She radiated so much loveliness it was as if she was a spirit come down from another world. Which

I suppose she had, in a way. I looked into her eyes and I looked into Bas's and I knew he'd chosen well and they were in love.

'You'll be as lovely a woman as she was. You'll have every man promising you the world because he wants to share your bed. Good men, bad ones, middling ones. But wait until you're sure you've chosen the right one . . . I'm off to the afterlife, soon, to see your grandpa and your brother Thomas and I shan't be coming back. So you look after everyone. And if you need any help, call on Tilly. She's a good sort.

'Now fetch your father for me. I've something to tell him.'

XXXI

Once upon a dark, bleak time there lived an old crone who, in the final years of her life, was blessed with grandchildren: a girl and a boy. When she sat them on her knee and told them tales, her cares fell from her shoulders. The light danced in her eyes again. She chipped away at the tallest of her dwarf-lover's tales. Brought them down to size, missing out the more far-fetched ones. Added stories of her own that would wend their meandering way to posterity.

Emma, in particular, listened and tried to capture every tale. Taking note of its shape and substance. Ynga sat staring into space, sometimes stirring herself to go and fetch water.

Fleda heard Bas's voice and looked up.

'Emma said you wanted me, Mother.'

'She's a fine girl. Like her mother . . . like her mother was. Like she will be again.'

Then Fleda launched in.

'None of us is entirely without guilt. We carry our guilt around in our heads, like our stock of stories . . . only we tend to be less eager to tell everyone about our guilt. We bottle it up.'

'Unburden yourself, Mother. I'll carry it for you.'

'Thank you, my darling boy. I knew you'd understand. I'd a mind those broad shoulders of yours could carry the weight of my guilt easily enough.'

Then, in a quiet, faded voice, Old Mother Haggard spills her secret.

King Edgar, King of all England, died suddenly and unexpectedly, having not long since turned thirty years of age. About the same age as the Galilean when the Romans crucified him. The king's men, all with an eye to winning their master's favour, were forever comparing him to the

Galilean. He'd started to believe them.

'It was Tom's idea, but I take the blame,' Fleda whispered to Bas. 'I didn't know one herb from another, but I knew the king's ways inside out. The ale beside his bed. The way he gulped it down in the morning before he started groping me and I gritted my teeth again and began to sigh with feigned delight . . . as guilty of pandering to him as any of his spineless cronies. Tom knew about poisons. He'd learned a thing or two from someone. Merlin, he said, but he was a lying little know-it-all . . .'

Fleda offered her king the fatal brew. Watched as he began fighting to hang on to his life. Gasping for breath. Looking at her imploringly. Fleda, certain that the king knew she was to blame, had to look away. Knowing that if the dwarf had blundered and the king survived, she was as good as dead.

'Then I fled, with my dwarf hot on my heels, though I didn't know it . . . and it only took him twelve years to catch up with me. He was no ordinary man, though, Tom Thumb. Didn't give up easily . . . Anyway, that's not the point. The point is, Tom Thumb and I killed King Edgar and then we fled. Before the wicked stepmother, Queen Elfrith, could wreak her revenge on everyone . . . The point is we changed the course of history and I want you to bear the burden of my guilt, but not my regret, because I have none.'

Regret eats you up like a canker.

'I've no regrets, Bas, because if things had been any different then I wouldn't have fled, you wouldn't have been born and . . .'

Her voice trailed off.

'I understand, Mother. We change anything and it changes who we are.'

So. Tom Thumb and Old Mother Haggard altered the course of history. Snuffed out the life of the last Saxon king who'd been able to impose the rule of law enough to bring peace – however short-lived – to the land. Snuffed out King Edgar's life and plunged England into darkness. Had Edgar not died on the eighth of July, Nine Hundred and Seventy-Five, then perhaps . . . No, that would be engaging in fairy tales. History is littered with enough of those already.

'One last thing, Bas. Put me near your fool of a father when my time's up. If I'm to have any chance of tracking him down and giving his ears the boxing they deserve, then I'll need to be buried near his oak tree.'

Old Mother Haggard waved him away. She needed to sleep.

She never woke up.

XXXII

Fleda was gone.

The year was One Thousand and Ten. The old order was collapsing. The Danes were squeezing out the last of the famous Anglo-Saxon resolve. Even outposts like Winfrith's coombe had been ransacked by passing groups of marauders at some point. Places whose salvation lay in their impoverished soil, from which it took boundless energy to extract a decent crop.

Where Saxon hope was dying, Saxon hatred of anything Danish bloomed like some poisonous, deformed growth.

When Ynga walks uncertainly out to fetch water, mumbling to herself and with her eyes cast downwards, they spit on her with even more force than before. Ynga ignores them. Nowadays, when she gets home, she doesn't even bother to wash the gobs of spit off her clothes and hair.

They still call her *Danish slut* and *wedlock-wrecker*. They accuse her of madness and say she's possessed of an evil spirit. They say she's dirty and unwashed and you can see the lice crawling in her hair. Bas or Emma sometimes try to help her bathe, but what's the point?

The story of what happened next was garbled.

One of Ynga's tormentors raised the alarm: Lippy Maggy, a woman cursed with a mouth that didn't know how to stop talking and a simple-minded husband who barely ever said a word. She was running round like a headless chicken.

'It's the end of the world,' she shrieked hysterically. At first no one paid much heed to her warnings. They recalled that Maggie had led much of the end-of-the-world-is-nigh breast-beating ten years earlier, when someone clever had told her it was the thousandth year after Christ's birth and that this was likely to herald the Second Coming.

Someone slapped her face to bring her to her senses.

'The water,' Maggie sobbed. 'The well. It's turned to blood.'

She was right. The water had taken on a red hue. So someone fetched Winfrith, who waddled breathlessly to the scene. A chance to take command without risking life or limb.

Here were his orders. A boy – *You, lad. You'll do* – was placed in the bucket and lowered, a candle in his hand. After they'd winched him down, there came a muffled sound and to the mixture of blood and water was added a fair amount of vomit. It would be some weeks before anyone summoned the courage to drink water from the village well.

On being hauled back to the surface in his bucket, the boy imparted the information that – as he put it – *Bas's whore* was down there, with her head smashed open. The boy's mother boxed his ears.

'You don't speak ill of the dead in that way,' she scolded him. It struck the boy as mightily unfair: if you're going to speak well of someone, isn't it best to do it when they're around, rather than waiting 'til they're dead?

The tidings reached Bas. It was Tilly who sought him out.

His shoulders sagged visibly, those broad shoulders that could do the work of so many men.

'Perhaps you could mind his children, Tilly,' Winfrith whispered. 'They mustn't see their mother like this.'

Elric insisted on being lowered into the well so that he could tie a rope around Ynga's waist and haul her up. Bas stood there, refusing to budge. Determined to witness with his own eyes what they'd done to his beloved wife.

When the sacrifice was laid at his feet, dripping and crumpled, Bas began to sob. Great juddering giant's sobs. The stench of shame clamped the onlookers' mouths. Even Bas's lord-and-master Winfrith knew he'd wronged Bas and Ynga. He'd bought peace with a basket of grain when justice might have helped to drive the demons from the place.

Elric came up to Bas and put his arm around those sagging shoulders.

'Sorry, Bas.'

Elric was sorry because he'd been swept up in that tide of lust and he'd felt tortured by it ever since. He was one of the few who'd never had a bad word to say about Ynga. He knew the truth. And now he was being torn apart because it had come to this.

'I'm really sorry this has happened to you, Bas.'

A shy girl named Ellie has plucked up the courage to come forward. Courageous because she knows she'll be tongue-tied, but – slowly – she forms each word. It's like laying a nestful of eggs. She takes her time but she gets there in the end.

'I seed who done it, Bas. It were no fall. She were pushed right and proper, she were.'

'By whom?' It's Elric who asks.

Ellie's exhausted herself fetching up all those words. Eighteen of them. More than she normally manages in a week. She points her finger – but it's at a group of three women.

'Liar,' one of them hisses. 'Viking-lover. Whore.'

Which is tantamount to an admission of guilt.

'Catte?' Elric is shocked that his sister should have been named.

'Stop this!' Bas yells, his voice exploding like a crack of thunder.

For once in his life, Winfrith grasps the nettle, as any good thane should. The accuser and the accused – Ellie and Catte – are to come to Winfrith's hall and they'll resolve this in an orderly way, as the law demands. Each of them is allowed a supporter.

'I'll need you, Bas,' Ellie says. 'I got the truth in there' – she taps her head – 'but it just don't come out too easy.'

'I'll look after myself.' Catte stares defiantly at Winfrith.

'I reckon there are things I know that no one else does and they might have to be said.'

Winfrith stares her down. 'I'll not have any idle gossip in my hall. We'll stick to the facts of this case. You'll condemn yourself to be hanged if you start spreading malicious, rancorous bile.'

'I'll help Tilly take care of your children, Bas,' Elric says. 'And I pray my sister's innocent or the shame would kill *me*, too.'

'The only man in this godforsaken place I'd trust,' says Bas. Which is like a knife-thrust to Elric's heart.

The case for the prosecution crumbles when it becomes clear Ellie's view of events was impaired. She knows in her heart of hearts that Catte's the guilty one, but there's a smidgen of doubt because she was quite some distance away and her eyesight's not the best. So. The word of a *Viking-lover* – as Catte keeps calling Ellie – against a spiteful young woman who swears under oath that she never touched anyone.

'Which is more than can be said for some folks,' Catte says, staring directly at Winfrith, 'though such folks know what it takes to keep a person quiet.'

Catte swears Ynga must have jumped in of her own accord, because she'd lost her mind.

'What am I to do?' Winfrith shrugs.

Bas shakes his head, wearily.

'I'm off,' he says. 'I need to put my Ynga in the ground before the sun dims.'

First his mother, trampled on, though she found happiness in the end. Now Ynga, dead, through none of her own doing. He longed for her, as he'd always done, ever since he'd fallen in love with her shadow. What had she ever done to deserve her fate? What was that rubbish Bas had been told about the earth-inheriting meek? A tale as tall as any ever told. No. Here was the unburnished truth:

Blessed are the braggart, the bully, the brute
for it is thoughtless thug – the nithing – and not
the pitiful, picked-upon, penniless poor or the
cursed and curmudgeoned mean and meek
who shall surely stand to inherit the earth.

Bas buried his wife beside his mother, father and his own son, Thomas. When he arrived home, Emma and Harry were sound asleep. Elric had gone but Tilly was watching over them. Someone had left another basket of wheat on the doorstep. Probably Winfrith. A peace offering in place of justice, again. Bas kicked the basket over, scattering the grain.

Old Mother Haggard would have been watching and scolding him.

Stupid boy. Never had your wits about you . . . Old Tom Thumb managed to get a word in once I'd stopped boxing his ears. Told me to ask you why in Frig's name you didn't use your blasted three-wish penny to sort things out.

XXXIII

Secrets. Once you've spilled them, they've a habit of spreading. Like the fleas that leap, unseen, from one person to the next.

Catte was in the badgers' deserted bedchamber with Rat. Seeking comfort.

'Tell me you love me, Rat. I need someone to love me . . . Tell me you love me and I'll tell you the worst secret I know . . . and you must swear never to tell. Remember, I never told on you and that Danish whore.'

'She wasn't no whore.'

'It wasn't me who raped her.'

Ynga had gone to fetch water and, looking up, had been startled to see it was Catte spitting on her. In a sudden moment of lucidity, of *lihtnesse*, she'd recognised the woman not as Catte but as the one who could have helped her but spurned her instead . . .

She'd slipped from the grasp of the first man after poking him in his eye. In the confusion, she'd got to the door, overturning a stool behind her. She'd pulled the door and shaped to scream. She'd felt relief as she'd seen Catte outside the door.

'Thank you,' Ynga had gasped. 'Thank you for saving me.'

But that look on Catte's face . . . It was like hatred. And Catte had pushed her back into the doorway, back into the clutches of those men and the demons waiting to invade her.

At that moment, the hope – which had sprung so briefly to life – had been crushed. Ynga's head fell; her heart sank. All her fight left her. And Catte was smiling . . .

Standing by the well, it had all came back to Ynga.

'It was *you*,' she'd said. 'You.'

Catte had panicked. If Ynga were to tell Bas . . . Ynga had to be silenced. She bundled her over the edge of the well and ran.

She'd spend the rest of her life running from the uneasy truth, but it would keep pace with her, forever closing in on her. As if in a nightmare.

Catte had spilled her secret and Rat hadn't even told her he loved her.

Part Three

THE BABES IN THE WOOD

I

Evil feeds off goodness like a half-starved fox, tearing at its prey. Wherever there's light, darkness lurks, ready to pounce and smother it. How do I summon joy and sadness in one moment on my beloved ha'penny whistle? I try, but the trick eludes me, so I play as the mood takes me: happy then gloomy then gleeful again. I conjure not only the endless dance of light and shade but also the relentless march of birth and death and birth. As fixed as the rising and setting of the sun or the waxing and waning of the moon. And though the sun might hide itself, blushing hotly, behind a thundercloud, it hasn't deserted us. Nor the awful truth of death or the unfettered joy of birth. They'll never go away. And though I might be playing some well-known, well-honed melody on my pipe, a sad, sonorous, soulful note might impose itself or an unexpected tune might take hold and have me soaring with happiness.

Tolland wanders in, while Aart and I sit back and recover our breath after so much wordsmithing and scribing.

'Prayers and more prayers,' he sighs. 'Count yourself blessed, young Aart. Your labours are more fruitful than mine, however wearisome they may seem. Your written words are etched for ever on that vellum. My prayers are but a fart – albeit a holy fart – that wafts away in the breeze.'

'Not unlike your riddles, Tolland. None of which ever remains lodged in my failing memory,' I tell him.

'Talking of riddles, try this one, Aart. What stands erect in a bed and brings tears to a maiden's eyes?'

Aart mutters something apologetic.

'You embarrass the lad with your ungodly jests, brother,' I say. 'Besides, this talk of maidens and beds isn't good for him.'

'An onion,' Aart pipes up.

'Very good,' Tolland says. 'You have a mind as sharp as a shining new *seax*, lad. I'll have to try harder to outwit you.'

'Your prayers may be as insubstantial as a fart, Tolland,' I quip. 'But at least you could scribe those riddles.'

'I like that thought, Thomas. *The Exeter Book of Riddles*. It has a ring to it. Perhaps I might call on your young scribe.'

'I think Aart has enough to occupy him. Unlike some.'

'A gentle reprimand, Thomas. Wisely spoken. I'll leave you two workhorses to plough your wordy furrows.'

He leaves, humming some chant or other to himself.

'Is it sin to have thoughts about wishing to feel a novice nun's flesh, Eam?'

'Novice nuns in general or one novice nun in particular?' I press him. 'Has Tolland's talk heated your blood, Pup?'

'One in particular,' he admits, shyly.

'Good. To answer your question: that depends, Pup. In truth, I'd recommend a life of devotion to the woman you adore ahead of a pure, untainted life of devotion to the Almighty. But where a maiden's concerned, there are good and bad ways of thinking about her flesh. First you must know the difference between love and lust. The meeting of minds and the meeting of flesh. If you wish to hold her in order to possess her, this is bad. If you want to hold her because you cannot imagine living if she slipped from your grasp, this is good.'

'I think my thoughts are good then, Eam . . . though perhaps I should still confess them before the Almighty.'

'I imagine the Almighty has grown tired of such confessions. He'll have heard them from every devout man or woman who ever lived. Let's attend to our writing instead, shall we?'

Poor lad. My wordsmith's tongue is loosened now. Otherwise, I might have let him go. There'll be time enough to woo his beloved when our task is done.

II

Tilly had longed for children and *true love* but been denied them both. She'd had *false love* aplenty, where a man has his way and then doesn't want to know you. Tilly reckoned there were two ways most men found their way into a woman's bed. The first was true love, which spoke for itself. The other was false love. All those honeyed untruths that softened a woman's resolve and that some men excelled at. Tilly was past attracting the true-love sort of man. Only likely to meet them when she was dreaming.

She'd longed for true love and for children. She'd given up hope of finding either, so was more than happy to take care of Bas's kids while he was out toiling. Furthermore, she wasn't bothered that when they lay together, his soul was elsewhere. She was happy enough to offer her own sweet balm to the gentle giant who'd had the hope knocked out of him. She might not have been the lusty thing she once was, but she still loved the feel of a man beside her at night.

So. Bas was satisfied and Tilly hadn't felt needed like this for years. Where was the harm in it? It was what you'd call a *marriage-of-convenience*. In Tilly's opinion, if many marriages started out based on love, most of them became marriages-of-convenience in the fullness of time. In her case, she'd settled for being a *wife-of-convenience* from the off.

Bas's soul was elsewhere. The country was in ruins. The West Country had been the last bastion of Saxon England back in Alfred's day, when he'd held his country together by a thread. Where the strong – which is to say ruthless, black-and-white – rule of King Edgar had kept the invaders at bay, the reign of Ethelred – placed on his throne by Queen Elfrith – had heralded a descent into chaos. For thirty-five years, man and boy, Ethelred had hung on, like a leaf taking on a blizzard. Finally he'd fled to Normandy (only to return briefly before his death at the age of fifty, in One Thousand and Sixteen). Now the West was being ravaged as two leaders fought for the throne: the fearsome Swein Forkbeard's son Cnut (whose name, of course, was the butt of endless Saxon jokes) and Edmund Ironside, the son of Ethelred, hailed by some as the true King of England. No more stealthy raids or foxy cunning. This was full-frontal, gale-force brutality. One settlement after another forced into submission as the two sides advanced.

The worst of the action mercifully passed the village by. No one was bothered about such a godforsaken place.

But there comes a time when you can no longer hide. Winfrith was under orders to round up some men for battle. *And none of the usual old has-beens. I want some strapping young lads, Winfrith.* Which meant the likes of Bas, Elric and Rat.

None of them is absolutely sure whom they'll be fighting against. Or for. The trick – in these confused, uncertain times – is to guess the likely winner and take sides with them. Trust only your most steadfast friends and no one else, though some are inclined to keep a watchful eye on their friends, too.

Bas had long since stopped believing in any causes. Whoever's side he was on, he didn't care whether they lost or won. He was first in the queue to go to war. Winfrith could see in those dead eyes that Bas's zest for life was gone. In this frame of mind, the giant of a man would be a boon to any bunch of warriors.

Still haunted by his regret and his shame, the thane Winfrith handed the peasant Bas his finest sword – a sword as sharp as it had been on the day it was forged, never having left its sheath.

Bas eyed the weapon warily. Whoever heard of such a thing? Peasants were supposed to make do with whatever they could lay their hands on. Not wield swords such as this one.

'I know. I know,' Winfrith agreed. 'But I'd like to see the man who tries to wrest this one from you . . . Feel it, Bas. It's as light as a feather, but in your arms it will fall like an anvil from the sky on anyone who crosses your path.'

'I'm not supposed to carry a thane's sword, master. Besides, I won't know what to do with it.'

'Go on, Bas. Take it. I've no need for it. A man such as you needs little schooling in swordsmanship. Watch how I cut the air. Like this.'

Winfrith brought the sword down in an ungainly but effective enough swipe.

'Your brute strength, your giant's reach and your fearless heart will see you through. When you bring the sword back, you can tell me your stories of the mayhem it wrought.'

Before he left, Bas entrusted the now-tarnished silver penny to Emma's safekeeping.

'Still three wishes,' he said. 'Neither your grandfather nor I have used them.'

Perhaps neither Tom Thumb nor Bas had had sufficient faith. Half-hearted, weakly wished-for wishes are rarely fulfilled. The best wishes, the most life-changing, joy-bringing, fairy-tale-come-true wishes are the ones where you dream the highest and the hardest. That takes faith. And faith – along with hope – had all but deserted Bas.

'Look after the penny, Em . . . And look after your brother. I may be away a very long time.'

III

Bas strode out and, raising his sword in the air, his arms taut, his eyes glazed, his soul having taken flight, he set about butchering the enemy, whoever they might be. Always in the front line, Bas would throw himself into the fray like a raging bull, as if defiantly inviting Death to consume him. As if he wanted to hasten the day when he'd have a chance of catching up with Ynga again, in the afterlife.

No stories tumbled from Bas's lips these days. He might as well have been mute, for all the company he offered his fellow warriors. He sat there, staring into space, his mind in another place. Sometimes he took his eyes off the yonder and studied the sword Winfrith had handed him – now stained by the blood of so many warriors. As a young man, Bas might have shuddered to think of the lives he'd destroyed. Not so much the lives of the warriors he'd laid low – a single, well-struck blow and it was all over for them. No pain; release, even, from the terrors of war. Bas might have been more worried about the wives and children left behind, waiting in vain for the warrior to return, only to lose hope, which trickled from them until it was finally gone, like a dried-up spring. Left to face a life of hardship and want, without a man to provide for them. But Bas was beyond caring about such things, these days.

Only once was he roused to anger. That was the first time one of his fellow Saxons opted to involve himself not just in some pillage but in a dose of rape. The terrified woman watched, wide-eyed, as Bas lifted up the wretch, flung him against a wall and, in so doing, broke the man's neck. The woman curled up into a ball, sobbing and shuddering, perhaps expecting Bas to take the place of the warrior who was now slumped against the wall and stone dead.

Bas wrenched the dead warrior's tunic from him. He

placed it on the woman's shoulders and left. Perhaps, if he'd not been so hot with anger, he might have thought to drag the man's body from the room.

Nobody remonstrated with him. No one else tried anything similar in his presence.

IV

Bas met his own bloody end in the month of October in One Thousand and Sixteen. Far from home, at the Battle of Ashingdon, where Cnut triumphed. Bas's last words were his instructions to Elric to bear his sword back to the thane Winfrith.

'I promised to tell him my stories,' Bas gasped. 'Leave the cakes of blood on his sword. They'll tell the story clearly enough . . . Bear the tidings of my death to my children and tell Winfrith to warn every man that if any harm comes to them, they'll have the spirit of Bas the Giant to answer to.'

Bas had already become the stuff of Anglo-Saxon legend. Perhaps his death marked the end of Saxon hopes. Maybe that was the point where King Edmund knew he was fighting a lost cause.

Cnut was crowned King of all England (to add to the rest of his vast kingdom) early the following year. Saxon story-weavers everywhere – refuting the yarn spun by the Danes – would delight in telling the tale of how, egged on by his followers, Cnut tried – and humblingly, wave-drenchingly failed – to demonstrate his almightiness by turning back the tide, at Bosham.

Bas had been right about some wishes not having a rain cloud in hell's chance of being granted.

'Why are men so daft?' Emma would ask Tilly.

Tilly didn't know the answer.

'I'm not much good at answers,' she admitted modestly. 'I'm not much good at questions, either . . . I can make a nice gruel, though.'

Harry and Emma always listened delightedly to such stories. Emma wasn't sure how to take the anti-Viking tales. Maybe they were just a dig at warmongers and overlords everywhere, which was much more praiseworthy.

The best stories were the ones they gleaned from warriors returning from the wars – trying to eke a living, now that, having lost a limb or two, they were no longer fit for tilling the soil.

Some of them were jokers.

'Have I told you the tale of Rat the Fearless?' Elric asks, having hauled himself on to the dais. 'Have you heard how Rat boasted he'd removed the leg of a Viking warrior? "A leg?" says I. "Aye, a whole leg," says Rat. "Wouldn't it have been bolder and braver to remove the Viking's head?" says I. "Indeed it would," says Rat. "Except that the head had long since been severed from the warrior's body by Bas."'

The story-weavers who summoned the warmest glow were those with tales of Bas the Bold. The stories of his bravery spread and grew like a forest fire in a parched summer.

Bas was by now taking on whole armies single-handedly. Swatting the enemy as if they were flies. Crushing them underfoot as if they were weevils . . . and then, as people began to tire of stories about war and started yearning for peace to fall at last on the kingdom, new tales sprang up like fresh saplings. About Bas the Giant who pulled a plough it had taken six oxen to haul through the mire. Sometimes, Bas became a fearsome ogre living in a faraway land of magical castles and more gold than it was possible to wish for.

But Harry and Emma loved it most when the giant of legend was an affable great lump who only ever slew his enemies in his righteous wrath. According to Emma, that sounded more like their father. Tilly agreed.

V

Cnut had succeeded in doing what he'd failed to do at Bosham. He'd turned the tide. Peace really *was* falling on the land, like welcome, crop-swelling rains. Bas was lying in his warrior-in-action's shallow, unmarked grave when he might have wished to be beside his beloved Ynga. But at least he'd banished his demons. Released from the drudgery of mortality, he was now firmly set on looking after the welfare of his two children. Of course they had Tilly to look after them and – if the worse came to the worst – the silver penny and its three wishes to call on. You didn't want to go putting all your trust in the untried powers of a mere coin, though.

Bas wouldn't have blamed Tilly for what she did: spiriting the children away and selling them into slavery. Because they were born to serfdom anyway. A *Judas Iscariot*, she was called by all and sundry – and with special venom by Catte, who seemed to have forgotten that she'd caused the children the bulk of their pain: first when she'd colluded in Ynga's rape; then when she'd pushed her into the well. Whether you're King Cnut at Bosham or just plain Catte, it's easy enough to whitewash over past events, recraft them as any storyteller might.

'Thirty pieces of silver,' Catte hissed.

'You'll go without bread for a week,' Winfrith barked at Tilly. But he'd relented within a day. Tilly *had*, after all, ministered to his needs on many occasions. Perhaps the loss of two young pairs of hands was a price worth paying for such pleasures. Besides, once you'd heard the other side of the story, you could see why Tilly had done it.

'Too reasonable for my own good,' Winfrith muttered as he handed Tilly a crust. 'Too fair-minded to be a thane.'

Bas would have understood, too. Tilly said she'd done

it to protect the children. After Bas had died, she'd got in with a bad-un. She'd let him into all of their lives. He wasn't like Bas, this one. Bas might have charged around wielding his sword like a dervish, but he was a gentle soul. This new man scared Tilly witless. Frightened her so much she daren't risk trying to leave him. His need for alcohol was unslakable. If he wasn't as high as a buzzard on that mouldy rye bread that lifted your spirits, he was sinking ale as if the barrel was about to run dry. It made him tender at first: soothed his sore head; but he never knew when to stop. One moment he'd be pawing Tilly like a great bear and the next he'd be growling at her. And he had his eye on little Emma, too.

One day, Tilly saw him slipping his rough hand under her tunic and whispering to the girl.

'You'll be a fine wench one day soon, little lass.'

That was too much for Tilly. She could take the man's sudden turns of mood, but she wasn't going to stand by while he molested Bas's girl.

So she sold Emma and Harry into serfdom, a safe day's walk away from him. And – in doing so – gave them their freedom.

'Be brave, Emmy,' she'd said, as she'd handed over the children.

Emma had looked at her so forlornly that the tears had fairly choked Tilly. Her eyes said that Tilly had betrayed them. Harry had held Emma's hand; his gaze held only terror.

'I don't know much, Emmy. But I knows this is the best for you two mites. It's what Bas would have wanted me to do.'

Yes. Bas would have approved.

And if that spirit of his had had arms and legs, he'd have lifted that great drunken, child-molesting oaf off the floor and thrown him on to the dung heap.

The pennies she'd gleaned from the sale (many fewer

than the thirty pieces of silver Catte had claimed) were soon shed in meeting her oaf's thirst for strong ale. They did nothing to ease Tilly's lot in life. Not that she'd ever imagined they would. Or even dared to wish they would. Poor Tilly. A heart of glistering gold. For all too short a time a handful of tarnished silver. And a dull, unglinting, leaden life without the true love for which she'd craved.

VI

The children clung together. Tired to their bones and terrified. They made a striking pair: the two fair-haired, blue-eyed angels. Never apart: day or night. Their new thane's wife took one look at Emma and decided she'd have her as her personal maidservant (a task Fleda could have told her all about). But Emma, stubborn as a cornered badger, would have none of it. By the power of the mighty Bas (may the Creator rest his troubled soul) she'd not be parted from her brother Harry. The new thane struck her across the head and told her she'd do as she was told. Emma just clammed up and carried on hoeing the soil. Determined to show no reaction, however shocked she was. Shocked, because although her previous thane, Winfrith, had been a man of many faults, he'd never once struck a child.

Here, however, was a very different thane to Winfrith. This one had sought favour with his reeve by offering up many a strong young warrior. In return, he was allowed to take liberties when it came to hiring slaves on the cheap. Wretches, with no one to turn to, nothing that they could call their own. The reeve was hardly likely to grumble while these slaves, robbed of any rights, were being toughened up to become the next wave of battle-fodder.

Here was a thane who'd spent his life being obeyed. He raised a stick and struck the girl a further blow, this time across the back. Emma grimaced and staggered slightly, but continued to hoe the soil. The thane felt growing anger and – something worse – a sense that he was being humiliated. In full view of his other serfs, he was striking a slip of a girl, but there was no backing down. Next, perhaps balking at the idea of hitting a slight and powerless girl again, he struck her brother. Harry – taking his cue from Emma – gritted his teeth and refused to allow himself to cry.

A serf, standing only yards away, spoke up.

'You'll not be able to hurt them childs, sire. They be the childs of Bas the Giant. You could strike 'em 'til kingdom come with a red-hot iron and they'd not feel a thing.'

'Quiet, serf. Get on with your work or you'll have a lashing from more than my tongue, too.'

Then, determined to prove the serf wrong, to prove himself the equal of this legendary giant – a giant who was dead, for Frig's sake – the thane continued to rain blows on the two children until they lay on the soil.

The eerie silence was cut only by Harry's quiet whimpering. Emma was still silent. Therein lay victory.

By the time he'd reached his hall, the thane was ashamed of himself. Would he have done what he'd done had the mighty Bas been standing there? Of course he wouldn't have. He turned to his wife.

'Both Viking children shall work for you, but mind them well. They need the demons to be driven from them.'

VII

Harry was sobbing as he held Emma tightly in the dark. Where Emma was stoical, defiant and faced adversity with an unerring gaze, Harry was a quiet child, shyly avoiding the eyes of all these strangers, speaking to no one other than Emma. Where Emma could remember how Bas had danced around their *sunderwic* and how she'd felt safe and loved, Harry had little sense of how it felt to be in a father's embrace. Where Emma had loved Ynga as the bright, beautiful woman who'd lit up a room before the spirits stole her, Harry had only briefly known the Ynga who'd muttered at shadows. As they lay on their bracken beds, their life-tinder spent but in too much pain to sleep, Emma clutched the silver penny in the lining of her outer skirt.

'One day we'll be free,' she whispered. It was no mere wish. It was an unyielding vow.

Emma was a fighter. It would take more than the odd thrashing to break her spirits. Her dead father, wherever he was, must have been thinking that he wouldn't need to keep a watchful eye over this one for much longer. She was perfectly capable of looking after herself.

Harry cuddled up to his sister.

'I miss Tilly,' he said.

Tilly was flesh-and-blood, Ynga and Bas no more than a memory.

In her mistress's kitchen, Emma learned to prepare meat and vegetables. She was taught how to identify the various herbs: those that could make the dullest of fare sing on the palate and those that were grown for their healing properties. Or the ones that could drive out the demons that laughed in a man's head the morning after a night supping too much ale and the ones you wanted by your side when you waged war on sickness and disease. Harry was learning to slaughter and skin an animal or to chop wood for the fire.

Emma was fourteen years old now and Harry ten, though both so slight they looked much younger than that. At night, on their bracken bed, Emma comforted her brother, whispering the tales she was able to recall. Some had started life as her grandfather Tom Thumb's stories and some had been spawned by Fleda. There were stories of Ynga's making, with a Viking lilt – strangely bewitching as they fell on Saxon ears – and there were fairy tales by or about the legendary Bas the Bold. Finally she threw into the heady brew some fables of her own.

Emma didn't know it, but a number of the other serfs, feigning sleep, were listening in. She'd inherited her grandfather's silken story-weaving gift. More than one of them was besotted by the comely, silver-tongued maiden with the golden hair and the pale-blue eyes and wondered how they could part her from her brother for long enough to declare their undying love.

'Once upon a time . . .' Emma whispered. Calling to mind poor Tilly, still staggering, no doubt, under the blows of that oaf who'd marred all their lives, she span her yarn. About a grouch in search of a wife . . .

A tinker said to him: 'Sir, I've just the companion for you. She'll never leave you. She'll never answer you back. She'll never nag you and she'll never cook you a bad meal.'

And then he drew from his bag a cat.

The loathsome old grouch looked angrily at the cat and rained curses on the tinker.

'But, sir,' the tinker said. 'This is no ordinary cat. Be kind to her and, after a year, she'll turn into the most lovely, breath-taking wife a man could ever dream of.'

So the loathsome old grouch took the cat home and gave her fish and milk.

Very soon, though, he sank back into his miserable old

ways. Each night he would kick the cat and the cat would run howling and yowling from the room . . .

After one year, he came home one night and the cat was no longer there. Strangely, he began to miss it, even to feel remorse.

Then, as he was walking down the lane, he saw a woman whose beauty left him trembling. She was so lovely, his knees began to buckle under him . . .

Emma mimicked the man. Harry felt her knees shaking as she curled against him. He giggled.

. . . Clear as a lightning flash, the old grouch knew the woman was the one who'd been released from her year-long spell. He begged her forgiveness and promised he'd prove the most loyal husband a woman could wish for.

'Too late,' she said. 'It's easy to make such promises to a woman you long for. A man shows his true worth in the way he treats the sort of helpless creature I once was.'

She turned and walked away.

And the loathsome old grouch lived miserably and regretfully ever after, though he never again kicked a cat.

Harry was drifting off to sleep.

Alfie the Stammer, who knew what it felt like to tremble all over and have your knees buckle under you, was listening to the honeyed tones and thinking that he would never, ever treat Emma badly if she would be his girl. He watched as she scratched at one of the fleas troubling her and prayed that it might hop over to him, because he reckoned that was the nearest he'd ever get to touching her himself. Alfie felt he'd never be able to get down on his trembling knees and declare his undying love. It would take him from here to the blue beyond to spit it out. Meantime, if that flea would just take a little bite out of her lovely skin and jump over here, he could dream for another night.

VIII

Alfie the Stammer was a dreamer. When words fail you, dreams are the best refuge. *Alfred*, his mother and father had named him. In honour of the greatest of Saxons. In the hope that their son might grow to be blessed by the spirit of the long-departed king, perhaps graced with just a smidgen of his greatness. Yes, to be sure, King Alfred was fallible. We're all prone to weakness. Even the Galilean – for all his talk about love of your fellow men – lost his temper once in a while. But the spirit of Alfred surely had some spare gifts to bestow on young Alfie. He might have burned the widow's cakes at Athelney, but was he not a master of the written word? Was he not fluent in the *Englisc* and Latin tongues (though the latter wouldn't be much use to Alfie)? Was he not a renowned warrior? Was he not a man who could summon thoughts from the yonder, such as conjuring the notion of a candle clock? Yes, a smidgen of King Alfred's greatness would be a blessing indeed.

So the parents had high hopes for young Alfie, though those hopes were soon borne away like dandelion seeds on the wind. Words taunted Alfie; they lodged in his mouth and refused to come out however much he willed them to. Alfie tripped about the settlement, anything but a warrior. And his mother and father soon accepted that perhaps the only skill King Alfred's spirit had gifted their son was the ability to burn cakes as well as any fool. Alfie had grown to be an affable young man. Tall and handsome, too. But he was cursed by his stammer; at his happiest when dreaming. Since this lovely, stoical, story-telling girl, Emma – half-Saxon, half-Dane – had arrived, Alfie had lurched on different nights between bliss and cringing frustration. In his best dreams Alfie shed himself of the curse of his halting speech and words flowed from him. In his worst nightmares, Alfie gasped for air as he tried to express his emotions, but the power of speech had deserted him completely. Emma would breeze past him in these nightmares, unaware of his silent presence.

In the end, Alfie's moment came and he was wide-eyed awake and able to enjoy it, bittersweet though it was.

Alfie always looked out for Emma and Harry when it came to snatching their meals. To be standing behind her as they waited for their rye bread and milk was a heady delight. So he was alarmed when they didn't appear at midday. Bolting down his bread, he went off in search of Emma, fearing she might be in some sort of trouble. He found her with her brother behind the barn they all slept in. The place she graced each night with her story-weaving that charmed all the boys.

'Thank heaven it's only you,' Emma whispered.

Only you. Not someone of any note. That cut Alfie to the quick.

'You mustn't let on we're leaving, Alfie,' Emma urged him.

Alfie wanted to go down on one knee and tell her that without her, he'd be lost. If she stayed, she could become his girl and he would strive to make all her wishes come true.

But Emma had only one wish: to flee.

You can take a beating here and there, but what her thane now wanted was too much to bear. When a drunken oaf lifts your skirts, dear Tilly can lead you away to another place. When your thane starts whispering lusty thoughts in your ear each time his wife's back is turned, you have to take the law into your own hands. Sometimes he tells you he longs to caress you. Sometimes his mood darkens and he tells you you'll satisfy his needs or be damned. Whether this is longing or shorting he feels, you know it's wrong. You fear it will end the way it did for your mother.

So – unbeknown to Alfie the Stammer – Emma had plotted her escape.

No honeyed words of persuasion came to Alfie. He knew

the score, anyway. The thane's wife was probably the only person who hadn't noticed the way their lord-and-master looked at Emma that greedy way. So, instead of pleading, he made a promise.

'S-s-s-s-s-shan't s-s-s-s-s-say nothing, Em-Em.'

Alfie was close to tears that his parting words to the girl he adored should be so abject. Of course, it was precisely because he adored her so much that he couldn't spit out what he wanted to say.

'Thank you, Alfie. I knew you, alone, were the one I could trust.'

What happened next was little short of a miracle. In a moment of sudden tenderness, Emma kissed Alfie lightly on his cheek. That kiss, and her trust in him, were so remarkable that Alfie was to find himself blessed for the first time with the power of more or less untroubled speech.

Alfie opened his mouth and replied to her, slowly but clearly:

'Good luck and w-watch out for the w-wolves . . . I shall pray for you every d-day.'

Emboldened, Alfie then returned Emma's kiss and gripped Harry by the arm.

He covered for them long enough for them to spirit themselves away. Alfie's failure to report their escape until the following morning earned him a long and painful thrashing but he was so distracted – by the loss of the girl who'd left him the gift of unhalting speech – that the beating seemed somehow unreal.

Who's to know whether or not that version of events is true? The thing about history is if you're going to go swallowing it, make sure you take it with a healthy sprinkling of salt. Preferably a lot more than a pinch. Story-weavers don't like loose threads to be hanging from what they've woven. To have left Alfie stammering or speechless would have been cruelty beyond measure. So much neater if we all live happily ever after.

IX

Emma's and Harry's grounding as servants had been some sort of blessing. They'd been cocooned from the harshest the weather had to throw at the settlement and their chores, although dull, were at least varied. That meant they were more than able to cope with life in the depths of the forest. Their combined skills: killing and preparing meat, gathering herbs and fruits, building a rough wattle shelter and maintaining a fire allowed them to make the most of their newfound freedom. In the depths of the forest, inhabited only by beasts and the spirit world, they felt secure. Unfounded fear kept others away. Emma and Harry looked to the various elves and sprites – Silvanlocks chief among them – to protect them. It was known that they watched over children.

There were times, of course, when the rain refused to stop falling and the sun refused to come or the frost wouldn't let go of its grip. But they never regretted having fled.

Emma was as strikingly lovely as Ynga had been. Harry, too, had similarly been blessed. And yes, they were happy. Carefree. No mistress to bark orders at Emma; no lord-and-master to bow before. And Harry no longer had to squirm whenever someone looked in his direction or spoke to him. Here, watched only by Emma, he moved with feline grace. Never take your happiness for granted, though. Disaster can be a blinking-of-an-eye, unforeseen moment away.

Unbeknown to his sister, Harry watched, fascinated, as she rubbed the ash from a spent fire on to herself and washed her body. It was a trick their mother had taught her before . . . before she'd lost her mind: one of the ways to make sure you avoided smelling like a Saxon. Harry was distracted by this troubling vision of naked beauty, struggling to understand the strange feelings welling inside him. As Emma bathed herself, two young men stole through the bushes towards her. They, too, were transfixed by what they saw. Her loveliness was overwhelming. A sight to stir any hot-blooded male.

With the harvest safely gathered in, Alfie and one other young man had been sent to track Emma and Harry down. An example had to be made of the brother and sister. If their break for freedom weren't rewarded with violent suppression, who knew where it would end?

They all knew the thane was bent on having his evil way with Emma. And they all knew Alfie was in love with the girl, would have walked to the ends of the earth for her. Now he was having to reel in the girl he loved in. Humiliation for poor Alfie the Stammer. It's called having your nose rubbed in the shit.

During the search, his misgivings will grow like a canker. His longing, too. Each time he thinks about her – bewitching, story-weaving, knee-weakening, breath-stopping, tongue-tying Emma – he feels another surge of longing for her. And he feels, too, the threat of his stammer, all those words dammed in his mouth and refusing to flow.

By the time Alfie found Emma, he'd endured two weeks of misgivings. Fourteen days in which to craft the words he'd use to announce himself. A fortnight for the doubts to ferment about his ability to say what he must say.

He caught his breath when they heard the fugitives. Stole up on them as quietly as cats stalking their prey. Froze when they saw Emma in the clearing. As naked as a newborn. A breathtaking, speech-stumbling sight for a lovestruck lad. Alfie spoke first, controlling the slight tremor in his voice as he cast his eyes downwards, unable to allow himself to drink in such loveliness. Humbled by his unworthiness. Ashamed to have invaded Emma's privacy.

She was like a pale, unblemished bloom. Perfect. She clutched her tunic in front of her.

'I'm s-sorry, Em-Em. Been s-sent by the m-m-m-master

to bring you . . . bring you home. He s-says if you return w-w-with us, no harm will c-come to you.'

The stammer she'd so miraculously chased away with that parting kiss had come to visit him again under the force of her gaze.

'You believe him? Because if you do, you're stupider than I gave you credit for being.'

When she spoke, it was a heady, intoxicating brew of firm, fleshy Saxon laced with a spicing of Viking.

Alfie felt wounded. He couldn't bear to be thought of as stupid by Emma. He didn't give a damn if every other person on earth thought him a fool. But not Emma.

He wanted to lift her up, there and then. Take her in his arms. Tell the world in clear, ringing tones that if any man so much as laid a finger on his beloved, he'd crush the life from that man's body.

'I'm s-sorry, Em-Em,' he said. 'The m-master's orders is ord-ord-orders.'

This appeared to him to be the crassest thing he'd ever said.

Harry stepped forward. His cunning had been honed over his short, eventful life and he knew this was no time for threats. He and Emma would easily be overcome.

'Alfie,' he said. 'You saved us once . . .'

His companion – chosen by the thane more for his brawn than his brain – eyed Alfie warily. If Alfie were to have second thoughts, that would be three against one. Yes, he could look after himself in a brawl, but this was going some.

Harry cut in. Looking down at his feet as he spoke.

'Stay with us, Alfie. The thane'll beat us to a pulp if we return.'

Worse than that, thought Alfie. *The thane promised me, though. 'No harm will come to them,' he said. But can I trust the word of my lord-and-master?*

It wouldn't feel good, would it, Alfie? Listening in as the thane starts pawing at Emma and she's nowhere to run.

You might love her, whatever he does to her, but could she ever love you? Not if you pass sentence on her by taking her prisoner again. But, then again, could she love you anyway? Harry's leading you into a trap, isn't he? They'd only laugh at simple Alfie if you let them go.

Alfie looked up now at Emma and asked her a straight question.

'W-what d-do you s-s-say?'

She waited while he'd fetched each word. Then Alfie stood there patiently, his eyes averted, as she dressed herself. Emma caught Harry's eye and they both turned and ran. He might have been slow of speech, but he was a fleet runner, was Alfie. In moments, he'd caught up with Emma and, grappling with her, pinned her to the ground. Young Brawny came up behind Alfie, panting. Strong as an ox, he might have been, which was why the thane had chosen him to search with Alfie for the fugitives, but he was no runner. Alfie longed to stay there, holding her, feeling her warm proximity and her breath on him. He wanted to whisper to her that he had always loved her and always would. But she scowled at him for the indignity he'd visited on her.

'W-w-what do you s-say, Em-Em?'

'I say you're a simpleton if you take me back to the thane.'

'S-s-sorry,' he said, although he knew that a real man – the sort that Emma would find her insides dancing for – wouldn't allow such an insult from her.

Reluctant and ashamed, he rose to his feet.

Emma will repeat the story many times: Alfie stoically does his duty by his thane, taking Emma and Harry back to the settlement.

('And not a day too s-soon,' Alfie will interrupt her, 'because w-winter's about to s-set hard and the forest is no place to be at that time of year.')

The thane proves untrustworthy. Emma and Harry are led to him; he orders them to be tied up so that he might make an example of them. He calls the rest of the village to come and witness the spectacle. He begins by flogging young Harry so hard and so repeatedly that Harry sinks to his knees. The thane bellows at him:

'Stand up, boy. Off your knees.'

With a worthy effort of will, Harry rises again, but, after another onslaught, he sinks down for a second time. After a third and fourth thrashing, Harry collapses, fainting.

Then the thane turns to Emma.

'It's your turn now, wench,' he growls and then he whispers in her ear. 'You're a comely vixen. I've a mind to roast you on my turnspit.'

Emma grits her teeth.

'Alfie,' the thane yells. 'Thrash the wench until she passes out.'

Alfie steps forward reluctantly and takes the whip from his master. He knows why the thane's chosen him. To ridicule him and to add spice to the entertainment. Young Brawny looks a mite put out. Surely he would have been a better choice to mete out a good thrashing? Didn't he earn the right when he went off searching for the fugitives? Why choose Alfie when he's as slender as a sapling? Not enough strength in those arms to put bite into a lashing.

'Come on, simpleton. What are you waiting for?' the thane barks at Alfie.

'I c-c-can't d-do it, my lord.'

'Just do it, boy, or I'll thrash you instead.'

'S-s-shan't d-do it,' Alfie continues. At which point, his master grabs the whip and lays into him in a frenzied attack that only comes to a halt when the thane is unable to summon the energy for a further blow. The fact that he has spent so much of his life-tinder in breaking Harry's will moments earlier is possibly what saves Alfie's life.

Ah, but it was worth it, wasn't it, when Emma knelt down and bathed his back and placed a poultice of comfrey over his wounds? It was worth the pain he'd suffered for this.

He would have walked through the gauntlet of hot coals for this. To be tended by her, to feel her compassion. Not her contempt any longer, not even her pity: her compassion. And she was bathing not a simpleton but a man.

Alfie groaned. Pain had never felt this wonderful.

Alfie grew in stature after his ordeal. Even the thane seemed wary of him. Alfie was never the defiant sort and certainly not a shirker. He continued to throw himself into his work. But when the master circled around his beloved Emma, strutting and feasting his eyes on her, Alfie vowed he'd not have his girl defiled by the old goat. He narrowed his eyes as they followed the master and the master knew that he would have to choose his moment well. Bide his time.

For nearly a month the thane bore his shortings, with increasingly bad grace, until he could wait no more.

'Wench,' he barked. 'There are things to be done in the house. Follow me.'

Emma cast a worried look towards Alfie.

'If Em-Em c-c-comes, then I c-come, too.'

'What I have in mind for the wench, I don't require your help with, simpleton.'

'Stay w-where you are, Em-Em,' Alfie commanded, all lord-and-masterful, with only traces of his stammer. Emma did as she was bidden.

'How dare you cross me, simpleton,' the thane barked.

'You will have to k-kill me before you lay a finger on her, m-master.'

'Don't tempt me, serf. Who do you think you are, speaking to me in this way? This wench is no concern of yours.'

'Alfie's worth twenty of you. I'd sooner die than lie with you. And if you lay another finger on Alfie you'll have the rest of us to contend with.'

'Bluster,' the thane scoffed.

But there were murmurings and the low hum of discontent in the air. The thane felt exposed enough to back off.

'Mark my words,' he said to Alfie as his parting shot. 'You're finished, simpleton.'

'W-we must g-go. Harry, you and I. Now.'

Which was a proposal of wedlock of sorts. A vow-of-sorts that was as steadfast as any other. Alfie's love had been immediate and all-consuming, like fire. Emma's was slow and more considered, enveloping her like the warmth that comes from the sun on a bright spring morning. Dear Alfie. Slow to speak his mind and measured in the way he drew the facts together before he forged a point of view, but he had a good memory and was a skilled craftsman. As he bent over his work, whittling or chopping wood, she would watch his back and feast on the beautiful, ugly scars that marked him. The scars he'd borne for her.

Yes, it was warm love Alfie conjured. Not a hot, soon-fading fever of longing. Emma knew she'd chosen well.

He was a good husband, was Alfie, and fiercely protective of his wife, but not in a jealous or possessive way. He saw her as something rare and beautiful he hoped the world would never despoil. Each morning, as he awoke, Alfie would feel like singing out loud to the rising sun in thanksgiving. He couldn't believe his good fortune in having landed his catch. That feeling never lessened over the years. Not in those looking-over-your-shoulder early months that Fleda could have warned him about, when the thane's search party was hot on their tails. Not in those times – deep in Tom and Fleda's Quantock Hills and guarded by their forebears' spirits – when they felt, at last, that they were finally free of the thane's clutches. Not ever.

X

Harry knew well enough when to leave the two of them alone. Understandably for a boy who'd never been blessed with the unfettered joys or cursed with the hurtful barbs of childhood, he was quiet and withdrawn. Days would go by and he would say nothing. This wasn't because of any sullenness. Harry was easy in his own skin. But why talk? Don't actions speak louder than words?

'Look at me when you're mumbling,' Emma would sometimes coax him, when words emerged. Harry would look up briefly, and then go back to muttering something or other into the fire again.

Alfie would tell Emma to leave her brother alone. He'd point out that not everyone had her gift for words. Not everyone found it as easy to summon that withering gaze of hers.

Emma watched, amused and undetected, while Harry carefully tried to count the number of hairs that had now sprung into life around his . . . well, you couldn't quite call it his manhood, yet. Harry was beginning to think – for the first time in his life – that the number was beyond counting. This was a good thing. A good thing because, if what Alfie had said was true and not just another example of his trickery (and he sounded truthful enough), then you could work out how many times you were going to lie with a woman in your life by counting the number of those strange, curly hairs. At least it was more than a hundred . . . a lot more than a hundred, which offered some hope.

'Busy?' Emma coughed.

Harry scrambled off, leaving his knife and his dignity lying on the floor. The trouble with this great, unpeopled forest was there was no one to run to. But Emma would help him to laugh it off when he slunk back. He knew that. She always did.

You could do a lot worse for a sister.

Harry had noticed the changes happening to him when he was about thirteen. That was the time he'd asked Alfie, shyly. And Alfie had given him the benefit of his wisdom on the meeting of flesh. Harry was already aware of the way Emma and Alfie clung to one another doing their joined-together, lying-down love dance. Occasionally – unable to fight temptation – he'd watched invisibly from a distance while they made sometimes quiet and sometimes grunting-and-groaning love.

By the age of eighteen, he was becoming restless. It was as clear as a cloudless sky that what he really needed was a woman and he needed one badly. He had no one particularly in mind. Just a vague hope that once he'd secured himself a woman, then he might in time learn to fall in love with her, whatever that entailed. It was time for Harry to go on a journey.

'I'm off,' he announced to his sister and Alfie.

'To do what exactly?' Emma asked.

'Can't say.'

'*Can't* say or *won't* say?'

'Won't say.'

'You want a woman. Harry wants to run off to find a woman, Alfie.'

'Don't laugh at me, Emmem.'

Harry often addressed her fondly by that name; the one Alfie had come up with as he'd struggled to splutter out the word *Emma*.

'You can't just go and pick a woman and take her away, like gathering berries. You have to win her heart.'

'And how am I supposed to do that?'

Harry was still veering towards the rape-and-pillage school of courtship. At the very least, he'd assumed he might carry off his bride-to-be and ask questions later.

'Tell him, Alfie.'

'I don't know. I suppose you sh-show her you love her . . . But d-don't tell her, for Frig's sake. And then you wait until she sh-shows you she loves you, w-without telling you. And that's . . . that's when you're allowed to tell her w-what she knew anyway.'

Said with barely a stammer.

'So how will I know all those signs?'

'You just will. If you're not . . . not sure, then it's p-probably not love. But if you are sure, then it's love. You get my d-drift?'

'And what about giving the right signs?'

'Put your trust in the sp-spirits of the forest. Just as they put the right s-songs in the throats of birds, so . . . so they put the right looks and the . . . the s-sighs and w-words into the m-mouths of lovers. B-besides, if she *is* the right one, she'll love you even m-more if you make a right . . . right s-sow's ear of the whole th-thing.'

'How come?'

Two reasons, Alfie reckoned. First, if you make a hash of it, it shows you're besotted and she's turned you into a gibbering wreck; that'll make her feel wonderful about herself. Second, it's easy for a woman to *worship* someone who's perfect, but difficult to *love* them . . .

'Thanks, Alfie.' And then, before his brother-in-law launched into another wave of explanation, Harry added: 'Right, I'm off.'

Not such a simpleton after all, then, was Alfie. Though sometimes you wished the stammer would come back in all its former glory. He'd always said fewer words when he was struggling to gather them.

XI

Breezing into a settlement – one big enough to offer a fair choice of maidens ready to be swept off their feet by a stranger – was risky. So Harry sought out some of the homesteads within tramping distance of the isolated clearing in which the three of them had set up home.

When he'd found a likely place, he watched from a distance, waiting for the sort of signs that Alfie had warned him about. Perhaps a knotting of his stomach or a tightening in his throat. He wasn't having much luck, though.

The search continued until he found a little place that must have been a good three days' hike from his home: a small settlement nestling near the Quantock Hills. They were lost in May Day revelry. The dancers seemed to be in high spirits. Harry didn't feel he had it in him to dance around with such abandon. And then, some distance from the rest, he saw her. A shy girl, not joining in the frivolity. Probably about sixteen years old but very slight, which lent her an air of elfin charm. Her face was strong but pretty, although her upper lip was scarred. The spirits of the forest had chosen to mar her lips and – in a moment of purest and unexpected clarity – Harry knew why this should have been. He knew instinctively that the friendly spirits in the forest shadows had chosen this girl for him. He reckoned her harelip was the reason this pretty girl was standing apart, too ashamed to join in the dancing. And he knew, too, that the harelip was the reason why boys weren't panting around her, showing off and strutting like cockerels. Harry also knew something that not many other eighteen-year-old boys knew: that scars are only skin-thin but beauty shines from the inner sun of the soul. Harry knew this, of course, because of the deep scars that disfigured his back. Scars like those that his sister's husband Alfie wore proudly as the badge of his love. As he wallowed in his moment of epiphany, Harry understood the reasoning behind his savage beating all those years before. Any resentment he might have felt towards his erstwhile master evaporated. The hand of Fate – the Wyrd – and the invisible spirit world had landed his lashing. Not the thane.

Harry continued to feast his eyes eagerly on the pretty girl with the harelip. The longing that welled up inside was not of the lusty, rape-and-pillage sort. He wanted to wrap his arms around her and he wanted to kiss her, full on her marred and lovely lips.

So this was what Alfie had been babbling about. Love was about wanting to become two halves of a whole.

She must have become aware of his scrutiny, because suddenly she looked towards where he was hiding in the bushes. It was a fleeting look and, a moment later, her eyes were cast down again. But her expression had changed; a barely perceptible flush of excitement warmed her.

Harry stepped back a little further into the shadows and watched. Twice she looked up again in his direction and twice she looked downwards again, blushing.

His nerve failed him.

His sleep was shallow in the night. He turned and writhed. You sleep only when your heart is ready to let you. If it beats too wildly, it won't release you. Harry woke before the sun. He watched it rise. This was the loveliest time of day. Drenched with birdsong. Then he watched the unmistakable dipping flight of a green plover. Once seen, forever lodged in the memory. He knew that rising-and-falling feeling. The flight of the heart, like the flight of the many-coloured, many-named plover or lapwing or peewit.

I watched the plover's wheeling flight,
its high-heave and its dip and dive.
I felt the lover's painful plight,
the swell and swoon, the soar and swoop.

The lapwing looped; it rose and plunged.
My heartbeat leaped and – lovesick – lurched and lunged.
The peewit's high, fleet flight reflecting my own
land-locked, rise-and-falling, faltering pulse.

Returning to his vantage point, Harry found no sign of the girl. Only a bowl of milk and some scraps of bread. He devoured them. He waited.

In the evening, she came. A starlit and moonful sky. As she touched the bowl, she smiled. He could see her but she couldn't see him. Her lovely, scarred lip curled awkwardly, struggling to get to where it wished to be. Alfie's garbled advice was slowly beginning to make more sense. The language of love wasn't something that danced superficially on the lips, like flattery, lies or even everyday pleasantries. It sprang from somewhere deep inside. It needed no words. It didn't matter if you stumbled over what you wanted to say. If halting imperfection was a good thing, then Harry sensed he might just be in with a chance here.

The pretty girl with the harelip poured a supply of fresh milk into the now-empty bowl. Still Harry hesitated. Too shy to venture forward.

When she'd gone, he drank the milk. It tasted not just fresh and thirst-quenching. It tasted of her in some indefinable way. As if her fragrance had permeated it. As if it were some love potion that was weakening his knees and turning his head.

What was it Alfie had said (though not in as few words)? *Women are different to us. A man may spend all day chopping wood for his beloved, but she'd prefer a posy of flowers that took moments to gather.*

Harry opted to give it a go and washed out his bowl. Filled it with stream water and a display of flowers that he spent the best part of an hour trying to arrange.

When it came to it, the flowers did look more appealing than the pile of logs he might have placed there for his beloved.

The following day, there was a bowl of warm gruel waiting for him. Delicious it was too, if you're fond of gruel, as Harry was. He tried to recall how his father, Bas, had brought his fairy-tale courtship to a swift end and then, from somewhere deep inside him, he heard that rich, storyteller's voice and it came flooding back. He matched the gruel not with another show of flowers but with a ring hewn from ash wood and carved with a crude pattern of leaves. He sat still and brimful with worry. Hoping she'd be pleased with the offering.

He needn't have worried. She placed the ring on a finger, smiling serenely. Then she looked up.

Harry, his heart pounding, chose to make his move. It was as Alfie had advised him: your heart tells you what to do.

In the first telling of this tale, at this moment she looks up and sees that Harry is flesh and blood, not a sprite. Alarmed, she runs back to the safety of her homestead. Rocked by this setback, Harry takes several weeks before he plucks up the courage to make himself seen again. This time she doesn't run.

The girl is called Hazel, born when spring was trying to assert itself and the hazel catkins were in flower.

Emma will cling tenaciously to this telling of the tale. She'll cast gently mocking glances at Harry who, in truth, never overcomes his shyness.

When Harry tells the story, it's different. He walks forward. Lifts Hazel in his strong arms (well muscled after all those years chopping wood). Plants his eager mouth on her marred and beautiful lips. And when they come out of their heady trance, the two of them are surprised to find he's walked about five miles with Hazel in his arms.

Since they've walked this far, they think they might as well continue heading towards his home in the woods.

Two days later, they arrive back and the group has grown to four.

'I love this place,' Hazel sighs, dancing a May Day dance inside. Much better than those dances-for-real she'd had to endure back in the settlement.

Alfie splutters something about May being the best time of year. Emma adds that life in the woods is like a slice of heaven on earth for two-thirds of the year, the months when unbridled joy falls upon you, like the sunshine and birdsong that spice the air. It's hell in the winter months, though, she says.

'You've done well, Harry.' Emma smiles. 'Much better than you deserve. How in the name of every saint did he manage to persuade you to be his girl, Hazel?'

But she knows without being told. They're more alike than two fledglings in a nest, are Harry and Hazel.

Later, she speaks to Hazel alone.

'Be warned, my new friend. Men take some getting used to. Our task is to plane the roughness from them. I reckon you'll need to draw Harry out of himself. Stop him looking at his shoes all the while . . . and talking of bashfulness, I don't suppose he's summoned the courage to talk about the meeting of flesh?'

'Not talked, as such. More leaped in and helped himself. Not that I offered any resistance.'

'Good. At least we've sorted that one. Alfie didn't need much coaxing on that matter, either. I imagine all men are the same. Sometimes we women need time alone. I find it best to send Alfie and Harry off to the borough whenever I need peace and rest. Get them to barter some of our spare meat or the fruits of the forest for milk and tools and suchlike. Keeps them out of sight for a whole day by the time they've trudged there and back.'

Hazel smiles as Emma whispers stories about their men. She's found true friendship here, away from her crowded settlement.

'With Alfie, the problem is his rules. It's laws here, laws there. Has me tearing my hair out. He means well. I thought he was a simpleton when I first met him, but he's as bright as a beacon. Always coming up with these ideas, though, about what we must do for the best. Always changing our dwellings to bring in some betterment or other. He's always right, of course. Nothing worse than a man who's always right. Anyway, try not to snigger next time Alfie announces some new law. And have a quiet word in my ear if we need to send the boys off to the borough and have some time to ourselves. Meantime, if you need any tips on the meeting of flesh you only need ask, though it sounds as if you're both doing fine on that score.'

Indeed they were. Unbeknown to Hazel, a child was beginning to form inside her womb. All that hungry lovemaking would herald a new arrival. Sow your seed and you reap a harvest of sorts. A child to spark as much pleasure and pain as this unfettered, sun-blessed and cold-cursed life in the woods will bring you. And – once he's made his way into the daylight – a captivated listener who'll soak up all their stories. Tales that, in the fullness of time, he'll offer up to Posterity, for its safekeeping.

XII

My scribe has just coughed again, quietly and politely. To slow the flow of my outpourings. To catch his own breath and rest his aching wrist while I gather memories as a lover would flowers. And rightly so, for Thomas the Piper has finally found his way into the story. Yes, I must guard my words well now. One slip of my wordsmith's tongue and I might damn myself forever.

'Is all this talk of courtship troubling you, Pup? Or is it those infernal noises coming from the walls?'

Tolland has just belched alarmingly in the next room, interrupting our thoughts. Perhaps – given his musings on the matter of farts and prayer – I might take this to be one of his shorter exchanges with the Almighty. A prayer of rebuke, maybe.

'I think I may be in love, Eam,' Aart confesses, his earnest thoughts a stark contrast to Tolland's burblings.

'. . . If what Alfie says about the language of love is true,' he adds.

Ah, the heft and heave of the aching,
faltering, helplessly-in-love-falling heart . . .

So, he does take note of the thread of my story-weaving as he scribes it down, then. I'd hoped he might. Spare the lad's blushes as I tell him about Harry's blunt attempts at courtship.

'What's your beloved's name?'

'Edyth . . . Edie.'

'You must learn to woo Edie well,' I tell him. 'Have you given her flowers?'

'I was hoping she wants kisses, not flowers, Eam.'

'Take my advice, Aart. It must be flowers, because when

you give her flowers, it'll make your kisses taste like nectar to her. That way she'll want many more of them.'

'Thank you, Eam . . . Have you ever loved a maiden?'

'Once, Pup,' I confess. 'Love looked me in the eye but my courage fled through the open door. I may be able to summon a story as well as any, Aart, but I never found the words to tell her how she moved me. Her name was Ottillie. She was the sweetest girl. I should have thrown myself at her feet and asked her to be my wife. But here I am, married to the spoken word. Don't make the same mistakes as me, Pup. Don't listen to the brothers when they tell you to turn your back on earthly delights.'

'I'm sorry, Eam. I hope that doesn't make you sad.'

Such a thoughtful boy.

'Not sad, Pup. Nor regretful. We must learn from our mistakes, not wallow in them. Though if she walked through the door I'd take her in my arms and not let her from my embrace until she agreed to be my wife.'

I dismiss him. He's worked hard, has Aart.

'Flowers,' I remind him. 'The rest will follow as surely as day follows night. I'll see you tomorrow.'

Time enough to gather my thoughts. We're rowing through dangerous waters, now. I must tell him, soon enough, about his mother and father. I mustn't open wounds that have healed over. But it's the story of Thomas the Piper that worries me most. Me, myself, I. *Me, mec, ic.* A corrosive sort of truth, is the story we tell of our own lives. The most unreliable of all histories.

XIII

It was clear, from the moment the boy tumbled into the waking world, that he was small – very, very small – though he had a voice that more than made up for this. A storyteller's thunderclap of a voice, Emma reckoned. Just like his great-grandfather, Tom Thumb. They'd even called him Thomas and his arrival sparked a retelling of all the old dwarf's tall tales. They dusted them down and relished them once again.

Harry was sure, now. All those whispers about his own beginnings had been lies. If the child Thomas was the image of his great-grandfather, Tom Thumb, then it followed, didn't it? Harry was without even a shimmer of doubt the son of Bas the Bold. Not grown from the seed of one of the curs who'd raped his mother. No shred of doubt about it. Thomas was the living proof.

A gift from the spirits of a dwarf was more than Harry could ever have wished for.

Alfie stands up and raises a stuttering toast to the newborn, wincing as the vile-tasting elderberry wine touches his lips. At least the stuff makes you pleasantly drunk.

He was a tall man, over six feet and with a slight stoop. As if he felt ashamed to be higher up than his peers. As if he felt he didn't merit his elevated position.

'F-f-five of us, now. I think we'll n-need some ground rules, some n-new laws,' he continues.

Hazel doesn't dare to look up at Emma, for fear she'll splutter her broth over the fire. Alfie has a point, though. Emma's right. No simpleton, is Alfie. He's been mulling over his new set of laws the way his namesake King Alfred once had; though the late king was bringing order to a rather larger realm than Alfie the Stammer's. It's Harry who breaks ranks and starts chortling.

'Wh-what have . . . have I s-s-said?' Alfie asks. The words seem more knotted in his mouth than ever.

'The trouble with Alfie is his brain's always working too fast for his mouth,' Emma says to Hazel. 'There's so much going on in that head of his he just can't spit it out. What's more, he's so tall his head's up in the clouds.'

Then she turns to Alfie.

'Don't worry, though, my love.'

She knows Alfie loves the way she often gently mocks him. Yet sometimes he needs a little reassurance. Don't we all, when we're beset by self-doubt?

Alfie looks less troubled by Harry's chortling now.

'My Alfie's the apple of my eye,' Emma says, sighing heavily and exaggeratedly, 'but what's the point of an apple without pips?'

The point of an apple without pips, Alfie points out, is that it tastes better, right to the core.

'And that will explain all that grunting and groaning and squealing that you two get up to,' Hazel suggests. 'My apple Harry has too many pips for his own good.'

She adjusts her baby's bedding.

'These rules,' Alfie proclaims.

He's been giving it a lot of thought.

He's heard it said that the Galilean came up with a simple plan. Love one another and you didn't need those Ten Commandments. Simple truths are best, just as unblemished jewels shine the brightest. If they had only one rule, which would be that they always gave to someone else what they themselves wanted, then they wouldn't go far wrong.

'Isn't there a danger of our forever passing things in circles, Alfie?'

Alfie had thought about that. It was fine with some gifts, like love or comfort. If you ever felt the need for them, you didn't ask for them. You gave them instead. But with everyday things, once you'd given them, that was it: they belonged to the new owner. If they wished to give a gift in return, then it had to be something different.

'Let's give it a try,' Emma chimes in. 'See if there are any flaws in Alfie's laws.'

She winks at Hazel, who suppresses a giggle.

Alfie sits down. Harry hands him the flagon of that venomous elderberry wine. Alfie gulps at it, thirstily.

'Anyone want the gift of another swig from this flagon?' Harry asks.

XIV

The apple of Emma's eye he may have been, but Alfie's pips still refused to grow inside her. She watched, never once feeling even a shadow of envy or bitterness, as Hazel's belly began to swell again.

Late the following summer, Hazel ushered her second-born into the world. She looked at the screaming, screwed-up ball of flesh that gurgled in her arms. Her new daughter was the most perfect gift she could have hoped for. A girl, whom she loved as much as she loved her son, Thomas; a daughter she perhaps loved even more than she loved her soul-mate, Harry (because that was a different sort of love: one of equals).

There was a wistful longing in Emma's pale eyes as she watched the mother and child. Hazel knew exactly what Alfie's Law required of her. The law that had served them so surprisingly well this last year. She carried her daughter over to Emma and placed the child in her friend's lap.

'I'll carry on feeding her, as I must. But she's yours. Your daughter to name and to keep and to love as your own. I'll never stop loving her, of course. But she's yours.'

And though it hurt Hazel much more than she'd ever admit, it felt wonderful to see the joy she'd brought to Emma's eyes.

Later Emma came over to Hazel and said:

'I'm afraid all I have to give is a paltry offering. I'd like you to have this silver penny King Edgar gave to Thomas's great-grandfather. I'm told it comes with three wishes, and they're all unwished. No one's ever used them. I know it's not much, but it's all I have.'

Not much? As it happens, it was going to prove how much it was worth. Almost as much as the gift of a daughter. Hazel's gift. Emma's daughter.

'A daughter,' Emma said, almost in disbelief, as she looked into the child's eyes.

A *dohtor*.

She would become known as Doht.

XV

Thomas and his cousin-sister Doht were offered a feast of stories.

The fables of Tom Thumb and Old Mother Haggard. The tales of Bas the Bold and his Viking girl, Ynga. The exploits of Alfie the Wise and the scars he bore on his back as a sign of his love for his Emma. Harry's bumbling courtship of Hazel with her marred and beautiful lip. Or Harry sweeping Hazel manfully off her feet. (It depended on who told that particular story.) There were some tales with only shallow roots in family history, and some that sprang entirely from the depths of imagination, lodged in the seat of the soul.

Stories aplenty. They loved them all, though Thomas – small in body, but harbouring a giant's heart – dreamed most of all that he might grow to be like his grandfather, Bas. As tall as a tree and able to sling his foes halfway across the Bristol Channel to the island of Steepholm.

'So. If we're ever in trouble,' Hazel whispered, 'we'll seek your late grandfather's help.'

'Or the silver penny's.'

'Or the silver penny's,' she agreed.

Part Four

THE FIRST WISH

I

I'm playing softly on my whistle, ordering my thoughts, when Aart knocks on the door. Fresh from wooing young Edie the novice nun, no doubt. My poor, long-suffering scribe must be tired of my ramblings. Eager to get out there and follow his young man's desires. Aart's far too polite to inform me he wants me to get to the point and tell him – tell you – about the miracle-making penny King Edgar gave to Great-Grandfather Tom. The penny with the power to grant three wishes.

Well, let it be known, Pup. Your wishes will soon come true. My whistle can't be rushed, though. Not even this pale replacement for my favoured first whistle, wrenched from me when . . . No, I won't be coaxed into telling you that, either, just yet. A story can't be hurried for fear it'll be spoiled, that it'll disappoint, like half-brewed ale, supped before it's ready. My whistle knows this. It tells my stiff old fingers to take their time.

'Come in, Pup,' I say. 'You must be itching to etch my words on that vellum. But think on this. If the earth grew impatient and rushed its course around the sun, you might be denied the joys of the first flowers unfurling or the pale leaves bursting.'

'Yes,' he says. 'And might we not be spared the depths of winter?'

Fleet as a falcon, he is. I have no answer to this, but my whistle's unmoved by his wit. It taunts us, when I pick it up, with a bright trill that calls to mind the sunlight catching the tossed coin as it arced its way into Great-Grandfather Tom's grubby hands. As if to say: patience will be rewarded. Wishes will be granted. But wait awhile . . .

'Are we ready to proceed, Eam?' he offers, gently.

A shy nudge in the right direction.

'Forgive me, Pup,' I say. 'It's words we need. Not music. Besides – though whisper it, for fear the brothers who kindly gave me this whistle might hear us – this instrument's no match for my first one. Perhaps whistles are like maidens, Pup. Sometimes we love our first with a passion we struggle ever to conjure again.'

II

It was time for Emma and Hazel to bundle the men off to the borough again, though no one had allowed for the fact that the fish broth would have it in for Alfie – and Alfie alone among them – and be waging war with his guts all night. For the first time, Harry would need to go alone. Being a father and a lover might have fortified him, but he was still not one to blag his way through life. Harry would have his work cut out. Time for some advice. First things first. The simple matter of a shopping list.

'Say it after me,' Hazel instructed Harry. 'Five good egg-laying hens and one young cockerel, the randier the better, cockerels being a bit like men: only good for one thing.' She smiled that marred but winsome half-smile as she said it.

'. . . a sack of wheat, six yards of cloth and a new axe.'

Harry repeated the list.

'And if you can scrape a few extra pennies as part of the deal, they'll be welcome.'

He ran over the list again.

He set off for the borough market, a freshly slaughtered young hart and the hopes of his family draped limply over his square shoulders. A good pair of shoulders. As you'd expect the son of Ynga and Bas to have on him.

Tucked in his belt was a knife to carve up the beast. Safely stored in his head was his shopping list.

Harry still felt overwhelmed whenever he arrived at the borough. You heard the wall of sound before your eyes were assailed by the mass of people and your nostrils by the stench of so many men crowded into one walled town. He felt his chest tighten, but clung to the deer, to the knife, to the advice that Alfie had imparted.

'Hold your n-nerve,' Alfie had stuttered, while still doing

battle with the fish broth. 'They'll be going m-mad for your d-deer. You don't get m-many d-deer in the borough. P-plenty of chickens and axes, though. You'll have what they c-call *the upper hand* . . . Just keep t-telling yourself, Harry. They've got *the lower hand* and d-don't let them t-tell you otherwise.'

Alfie was right. Harry kept a straight face. Kept it in mind that he'd got the upper hand and instead of walking around with hope and a limp young deer on his shoulders, he was soon dragging around his axe, a sack of wheat and a generous length of cloth from the toothless crone who seemed so hungry that she definitely had the lower hand. (In truth, Harry felt quite guilty, the way he'd struck such a bargain, only agreeing to part with a leg, the liver and other offal for all that material . . . but the way she was salivating, she was probably happy enough.) Last of all he landed the sack of six chickens who, judging by all that wriggling and squawking going on, were probably already getting up to some meeting of flesh in there. The two pennies in his pocket were a source of satisfaction. Perhaps one of them could be used to slake his thirst. Hazel could have the other.

Ah, but one drink leads to another. And too much strong ale can play the foxiest of tricks on your mind. Such as telling it that the room you're standing in is rocking like a boat. Or muffling the words spoken to you so they don't quite make any sort of sense.

A man with a pinched face and thinning hair came up to Harry. He looked like an ageing rat. His warm smile was at odds with the mean look in his beady black eyes . . . but, as they say, you can't always judge an apple by its skin.

'You're a brave Viking boy to be showing your face in these parts,' Ageing Rat greeted Harry, eyeing that pale wheaten hair.

'You ever seen brock-baiting?' one of the measly bunch of drunkards asked.

'Never . . . though my father once did. The badger and

the dogs were fine, but I reckon my father scared the shit out of the men watching when he turned on them.'

Rat's eyes narrowed. He twitched but said nothing. Yes, the young man must surely be the right age and yes, you could see the likeness.

'You ever seen Viking-baiting?' the drunkard persisted.

There was laughter: menacing, not hearty.

Rat raised his right hand.

'Easy, boys. Give the lad a break. Let me buy our Viking friend another drink.'

Harry sensed it wasn't the moment to turn down Ageing Rat.

'Do I know you?' he slurred.

'Everyone knows *me*,' Rat responded. 'But if your story about the brocks is true, I reckon I knew your father well and your mother very, very well . . .'

There were smirks.

'I reckon the man you'd call your father is Bas the Bold. Am I right?'

There were gasps of awe.

The room was lurching uneasily. Harry didn't quite catch what Rat had said to his cronies.

This is the son of Ynga. The only boy with twelve fathers, it sounded like.

Harry smiled and shrugged his shoulders.

'Oh yes, Viking boy. I knew Bas very well . . . I still live in his old settlement. We bring provisions to the borough market each week for your father's old thane, Winfrith. You're not a giant yourself, I see. More of a pretty one. Like the fair Ynga . . .'

Just vulgar banter.

'You must give my best wishes to your charming sister,' Rat continued.

Rat seemed all right.

'How does Tilly fare?' Harry asked.

'Ah, Tilly. Your other mother. She fares well enough to

say she's wedded to *that*—' Rat pointed in the direction of a man slumped in the corner, snoring heavily. '—though I dare say she'll have earned herself another beating by the time the sun sets.'

Harry vaguely recognised the man who'd fumbled under Emma's skirts. He stood up.

'I reckon someone should . . .'

A few blows to the head would show the thug a thing or two. But his feet collapsed beneath him and he lay crumpled on the floor. The room was now not only spinning, it was laughing at him. He spewed heavily at Rat's feet.

'Come on now, Viking boy,' Rat said. 'We need to get you home. Here. Let me help you up.'

'The chickens,' Harry muttered. In his prone position, he could see them wandering around the floor, between the feet of the drinkers. Pecking away. Happy to be free of the boisterous cockerel, who – having done his duty five times over in the dark, confined space of the sack – had less of a strut about him now.

'Don't worry about your chickens,' Rat reassured Harry. 'My friends'll help me keep an eye on them for you. You put that other sack of yours over your broad shoulders and don't forget the cloth. The lads and the chickens'll have no need for your six and a half yards of cloth.'

Harry slung the sack of wheat on to his back, picked up the length of material and – embracing Rat – lurched from the tavern. By Frig, a sack of wheat dug into your shoulders after a while.

III

'You've been drinking,' Emma scolded Harry.

'It was Rat, from Winfrith's place. I've stories to tell, Emmem. Rat sends greetings.'

'The stories can wait.'

'I got six chickens. Rat and his mates are taking care of them.'

'*Taking care of them?* You mean they stole them?'

'Not really. They sort of . . . I've a story to tell about that, but I imagine it can wait.'

'The cloth.'

'Six and half yards. I swear it hadn't been pissed on when I bartered for it, though.'

Emma shook her head. Alfie didn't dare to look up. It was too painful to behold.

'The axe?'

'Shit. I forgot the axe. It was a good sharp one.'

'That's all right then,' Emma mocked. 'He's lost his axe, but at least he's lost a good one. And the sack?'

'The finest wheat. Look.'

Harry put his hand in and fished out a sample of the contents.

'Soil and stones?' he groaned.

'Well done, Harry. A sack of the finest dirt and stones. Shall we plant these stones or shall we eat them?'

Harry fumbled in his hem for the remaining penny. It was gone. He put his head in his hands.

'Frig help us,' Emma sighed. 'Next time, you're not going without Alfie.'

Harry said nothing. There was nothing he could say.

'And by the way. That Rat character who seems to be your best friend . . . I thought you might like to know he was one of the scum who raped your mother.'

Alfie put an arm around Harry's shoulder. 'I'll c-come w-with you, next time. Besides, I reckon I m-might be able to c-come up with some use for those st-stones.'

Though perhaps that challenge could wait until Alfie's guts had won their war with the fish broth that had laid him low.

IV

The next trip was more successful. Two heads are better than one and four arms better than two.

'For you,' Harry said, handing the hart's liver and several yards of tripe to the old cloth lady. Still feeling guilty for having pushed her too hard last time, what with her having had the lower hand.

'Thank you, kind sir,' the crone gasped. 'No one's ever given me offal for free before.'

'Every w-woman's d-dream,' Alfie joked.

They did well. Some healthy-looking fowl. More docile than the last lot. An axe, a sackful of wheat and a couple of pennies.

'Just wait here, Alfie. I'll only be a moment.'

Harry strode into the tavern, waiting briefly at the doorway while his eyes adjusted to the lack of sunlight.

'Well, if it isn't Bas the Bold's boy come to buy his old friend Rat a drink.'

'I can do better than a drink, Rat. I've a gift for you, from my mother.'

'Ah, the fair—'

Rat fell to the floor, clutching his face. Words stopped flowing from his mouth. Blood poured from his mangled nose.

Harry strode out, smiling. No one tried to waylay him. No one was taking any chances now where Bas the Bold's son was concerned. Not while he was sober. There was a rumour doing the rounds that some thane or other had started flogging Bas's son and the lad had just stood there smiling until the thane keeled over and died with exhaustion. No one was going to go playing the hero.

'You ready?' Alfie asked.

'Oh yes,' Harry replied. 'I reckon Hazel and Emmem are

going to be pleased with our efforts this time round.'

'Penny whistles,' shouted the man sitting at the borough gate. 'Half price. Everything must go.'

Why not? Harry thought.

He tried one out, then snapped a penny in two and handed half to the whistle-seller.

'May your whistle bring you much joy and happiness.'

Ah, Thomas the Piper's first whistle.

'A plaything for my little *sunnan*,' Harry says, handing the whistle to Thomas, who's run to greet him at the edge of the clearing. Harry's called Thomas his *sunnan* ever since that moment he held the child in his arms and pointed up at the night sky.

'*Steorra*.' Harry had said the word slowly. Star.

Thomas had then pointed up in wonderment and said:

'*Tom-sunne*.' Little sun. Because he'd worked out in his young wordsmith's head that anything called Tom must be small.

A ha'penny whistle for Harry's *tom-sunnan*.

V

A ha'penny whistle that would bring music and dancing into their lives, but, in the short term, torment to the ears of his family as young Thomas toiled to master the instrument, learning which notes fell most easily on the ears like a thrush's song and which were as harsh as an owl-screech.

Thomas was teasing out a melody when the whistle conjured a magic of sorts. His mother Hazel joined him and all the chattering suddenly ceased because Hazel – bashful Hazel – had never before sung with the rest of them around the fire. Alfie stopped in mid-stutter. All eyes turned to Hazel, singing so tunefully it could have wrung tears from the very pit of your being.

For years, she'd been hiding her voice as modestly as a maiden hides her body beneath her skirts. She'd feared that if she were to sing, folk would look at her mouth and see her marred lip: the harelip that Harry seemed to love but that she – and all those mindless boys who'd danced giddily around the maypole back at her old settlement – thought of as a curse. Now the ha'penny whistle had drawn her voice out of its hiding place and everyone else sat silently, rapt.

Hazel became aware she was being watched and started to falter. So Alfie joined her, lending his support because he didn't want her to stop. And Alfie's voice was notable not just because it was rich and a wonderful accompaniment to Hazel's, but because when he sang, he did so without ever once having to hesitate while he fetched a word. Emma had always said that life would be a lot easier if Alfie sang all the while, instead of trying to speak. Alfie had laid down the law about that.

Emma joined them and then Harry. Harry's voice was like the bear's growl that had afflicted his brother who'd died as a baby. Not a note was in tune. Meanwhile, Doht was jigging happily and unsteadily.

In time it would dawn on Thomas the Piper that a story wrapped in music can hold folk more spellbound than mere words.

For now they played or sang or danced, less quietly than they might have done back in the days they'd feared being found. While they did so, evil – unbeknown to them – was stirring under their noses.

Thomas was three now. His memories of what happened are imperfect. Not that this stops a story-weaver's flow . . . The peace was fractured, not by any marauding warriors or a thane's brainy-and-brawny search party, but by fire. Fire and revenge.

During Cnut's strong and often ruthless reign, calm had descended on the kingdom. But, just as he couldn't tame the sea, Cnut couldn't douse fires. Nor could he crush the niggling little disputes that poisoned some of his subjects. The reach of the law may be great. The king's *candelboran* – his circle of administrators, the so-called candle-bearers – might shine their light on the dark corners of the kingdom. The reeves – corrupt or otherwise – might impose their justice on the shires. But sin and hatred and retribution will always fester somewhere unseen.

Evil blew into the forest hideaway on a westerly wind, bringing fire with it. Thomas will always believe it was Rat, wreaking his revenge. As he sits summoning his story, he'll think he saw a wizened man twitching in the shadows, a man with a mangled protrusion that looked as if it might once have been a nose. He might hold up his hand and tell you he can't be sure, that some memories can't be coaxed beyond the shadows, not even by the strains of his whistle. But nothing will shake him from the view it was Rat who'd started the fire and the westerly wind had then ushered in the flames. Without the blessing of rain for more than three months, the forest had become parched and thirsty. The flames soon began to destroy everything in their wake. Everything. Their homes and all the possessions they'd cobbled together over the years.

There was no choice but to flee their home. Alfie picked up Doht. Harry grabbed hold of Thomas. Thomas hung on to his ha'penny whistle.

VI

Rat had judged things well. The fleeing family faced a stark choice. Heading off, perhaps across to the Mendip Hills, to start afresh. Or falling back on the fettered life of serfdom. It tastes bitter, does swallowed pride. More acrid even than inhaled smoke. And the ashes of a burnt past are a forlorn and soul-destroying sight.

'We need rest and food. The children need beds,' Emma had said. So they'd trooped into the borough, smoke and despair clinging to them. Hoping to hitch themselves to a friendly bunch of men and women. Troop back to those serfs' thane. Throw themselves on his mercy in exchange for a roof over their heads and a supply – yes, probably a meagre one – of food.

'It won't be for ever,' Harry had promised his *tom-sunnan*. Perhaps he sensed already that Thomas the Piper was fated to have itchy feet and an unslakable thirst for the new. Just as Great-Grandfather Tom had done. Tom Thumb: a dwarf foolhardy and foot-itchy enough to walk twelve wearisome years in search of love.

And who was there, waiting in the borough and greeting Harry like a long-lost friend? Ageing Rat, of course, his mangled nose twitching uneasily.

'Viking boy,' he said, opening his arms. 'Not come to give me another sharp lesson, I trust? We push our luck, we rats. It's the way we are. But we know when we're beaten.'

Harry agreed that hostilities should cease. Too-trusting-for-his-own-good Harry, who always gave everyone the benefit of the doubt.

'Perhaps you'd like to buy an old rat a drink to seal our friendship? As I always say: supping ale together is the best way to swallow your pride.'

'Nothing to pay for it with,' Harry muttered.

'My good man,' Rat gasped theatrically. 'No goods or chattels? Then we must find you work. My thane, Winfrith – not long for this world, bless him – is looking for good men and women. He's the best sort of thane, is Winfrith: decrepit, cowardly and no sons or daughters, so he treats us all as his own . . . Now, if I'm not mistaken, this must be the fair Emma. A comely wench, like your mother.'

Emma's pale-blue eyes narrowed. Something stank. Ranker than the stench of Rat's filthy tunic.

'I know all about you and I know all about Winfrith,' she said quietly, 'though I'm grateful for the tidings that he needs some good men and women.'

'Good. Good.' Rat slicked his hair nervously with his right paw. 'Then perhaps you'll allow me to use my influence with my thane to secure you all some comfortable quarters. Winfrith's settlement's less than half a day's walk from here, to the east.'

'I imagine Winfrith will remember the children of Bas the Bold without any prompting from one of his serfs,' Emma replied curtly.

The Viking wench needed to be taught a lesson. But a rat knows to bide his time. Choose his moment well.

Alfie had been watching his wife admiringly, not daring to open his mouth lest he should stammer. Doht slept against his shoulder. Hazel stood staring at the ground, grateful that no one had noticed her marred lip. Thomas peered at Rat's nose, convinced this was the man who'd set their homes ablaze.

'Well, as you wish, fair Emma. I see you're a single-minded woman, set on addressing the thane directly. Follow that road over there and it'll lead you to Winfrith's hall. I wish you well. Forgive me. I've work to do, my friends'

VII

They were greeted by a rotund man, who sweated heavily, despite the fact that the worst of the heat had relented.

'How can I help you?' he wheezed.

'Are you the lord Winfrith?' Harry asked.

'I'm Gross,' the man replied. 'My lord Winfrith's master cook. As corpulent as my thane but steadier on my feet than his lordship is these days. Who shall I tell him wishes to disturb him?'

'The children of Bas the Bold,' Harry replied.

Gross raised his eyebrows. His manner changed. Suddenly more helpful. Less cocky.

'Indeed?'

There'd be plenty of stories about Gross to add to the mixing bowl of the family's history. He'd been sent to brighten dull lives with food that sang as wonderful a tune as could be summoned from the finest ha'penny whistle.

For the serfs, he could render the most unlikely fare edible. And for the thane and his wife, he served up heavenly meals. One of the perks of being master cook is the limitless scope to spoon into your own mouth the wonders you've brought into the world. You must keep testing it until it's perfect. You're almost obliged to wolf down in a day what most peasants get their hands on in a week.

But not all was well for the man who lumbered off to speak to his thane. Gross was a troubled soul, tortured by his appetite for fresh young kitchen hands. His wife had openly mocked him. She'd railed at him in the coarsest of tones for his inability to undertake his manly duties. He served up tasty enough fare, but he starved her of the meeting of flesh. What sort of a husband did that? Humiliated by her ridicule, he'd slink back to his kitchen to find comfort in the food that he sampled so freely. And in the delight his meals wrought.

Gross's downfall had come in the form of a young lad whom he'd pinned to his kitchen table and raped vigorously in a moment of overwhelming need. The following morning, the boy had been found dead in the kitchen, as lifeless, now, as the salted meat hanging beside him. He'd hanged himself.

Lust is an all-consuming monster. Beware, lest it should ever devour you.

All fingers had pointed at Gross. Breaking down in tears, he'd begged his wife to forgive him. She'd told him to save his tears for the dead child.

By rights, Gross should have gone to hell. His wife thought so, anyway.

The reeve had been called to pass judgement.

A victim might hope for a sense of fair play and incorruptibility in a judge. But to this reeve clung the stench of corruption, masked only by the pungent odour of garlic. He was so overweight he had to be carried everywhere by his two helpers, known mockingly as High and Mighty.

High was a short man, a head and shoulders below most of his fellow men. Mighty lacked not height but strength; he was a weed of the gangliest, spindliest sort. High and Mighty carried their master on a specially crafted chair. It listed towards High, the smaller of the two men. This was a blessing, because it meant that Mighty had to suffer very little of the weight. Both men bore not just the weight (in differing degrees) of the reeve, but a florid glow, too. They would be gasping as they lowered him down.

'I come borne by the High and the Mighty and by the twin virtues of Law and Order,' the reeve would announce in his lordliest voice, unaware of the indignity of it all.

People stood well back from the reeve in apparent awe, although this might have been down to the overpowering smell of garlic he gave off. He ate it raw to protect him from the curses thrown his way by the wretched victims he'd sentenced. He smeared it on to the sores that erupted on his bloated flesh. And between each of the toes of his feet, tortured by infection, he wedged a clove.

Tradition has it that the condemned man's treated to a hearty meal to send him on his way into the next world. In this case, such was Gross's reputation that he'd been called on to provide a meal for the man about to sentence him.

Gross, still racked by guilt, had cooked out of his skin. Perhaps it was his last chance to glean a morsel of respect from his fellow men before he made his exit. The pigeon, jugged hare, partridge, pheasant and heron had all danced across the palate of the reeve. High and Mighty, unable to join their master at table, had drooled longingly.

'Bring the man here,' he'd ordered them.

High and Mighty had slunk out of the room to track down their quarry.

'A fine feast, my good man. You may have erred from the path of rightness, but I've a mind not to judge too harshly one who can offer fare so pleasing to the palate. Tell me: are you guilty?'

'Yes, my lord.'

'And do you feel remorse for your sins, your *gyltas*?'

'Indeed, my lord. There is not a day that passes—'

'Yes, yes. Enough. Tell me. The mother and father of the child whom you . . . whatever. What have they said to you?'

'The child had no living parents. I should have treated him as a son but I despoiled—'

'Yes, yes. No mother or father. This makes everything more straightforward. I've a mind to spare you, cook. Now fetch me more wine and we'll see how I feel on the morrow. Meanwhile, I shall let these two mangy curs taste your fare.'

He'd motioned to High and Mighty that they were now allowed to pick over the remnants of his meal. Then he'd belched with evident satisfaction.

Gross had been spared. The reeve had reckoned there

was too little evidence to convict him and that the so-called victim was clearly not of sound mind.

'Shame on you,' someone in the crowd had murmured. It had sounded suspiciously like Gross's wife.

His food had saved him from the gallows, but not purged him of his guilt. Unable to live with the whispers and ridicule, Gross had slunk off and happened upon Winfrith, a thane determined to enjoy the last few years of his life and not ask too many questions. Had he stayed, Gross would have had to put up with a lifetime being despised, with his wife leading the chorus. Hidden away in Winfrith's settlement, he'd been spared his wife's taunts, though he'd struggled to suppress his attraction to young kitchen hands.

'Bear with me while I inform the lord-and-master,' Gross said to Harry. 'Enchanting,' he added, nodding towards to the elfin child piping a tentative, uncertain tune on his ha'penny whistle.

The master cook waddled off.

VIII

The tidings were good, Gross informed the newcomers. Winfrith welcomed the return of the children of Bas and their kin, though he was too frail to greet them. Gross would show everyone to their quarters . . . though if their presence caused the unrest the Viking woman Ynga and that irksome crone Old Mother Haggard had caused, then they'd be out as quick as shit from a cow's arse . . .

'My lord's words, not mine, ladies.'

'Is Tilly still here?' Emma asked Gross.

'Just,' Gross replied. He pointed to her hovel. 'A diet of nightly beatings seems to have knocked most of the sense from her.'

Indeed, Tilly recognised neither Harry nor Emma.

'This place is dying,' she informed the strangers. 'I'm dying, the thane's dying, the soil's dying . . . This place is cursed . . .'

Stumbling wide-eyed into a settlement for the first time, Thomas the Piper is as moved by dread and excitement as Bas once was. The gentle notes of a well-wrought tune can usher in calm, though. His nimble fingers skip over the whistle and have the newly met children and their parents spellbound. Doht is dancing as if the fire and the long trek have never happened. Yet the tunes can't steady Alfie's stammer and they can't persuade Hazel to look up from the ground. Emma has led them around the place; she's found she remembers a number of the landmarks and buildings. They've not changed much, but they're smaller than she recalls. They'll be all right here. Harry, meantime, is a man intent on sorting some unfinished business. He tells the others he'll not be gone long, waits for Tilly's oaf to return and pins him against the wall.

'If you lay another finger on your woman, I'll break your nose the way I broke your friend Rat's, you understand?'

The man slumps to the ground. Laughing. Oblivious. Harry would have to wait until the brute was sober and try again.

IX

Alfie was a canny sort. Here he was, reverting to the role of simpleton, as easily as pissing into a puddle. Making out the heat of the fire had evaporated his wits again. He was a bright man, was Alfie. Knew that the best way to get on was to keep your head down and play the fool.

Conscious again of her marred lip, Hazel put her lovely voice back in its box.

Harry and Emma are fêted by some: the babes of the wood, the prodigals returned, the children of Bas, about whom no one has a bad word to say. Though not everyone wishes them well. There are hackles rising in some quarters. Hackles risen and poison brewing.

And what of Thomas? Hindsight is never clouded, never dusky, always sunlit and clear. Thomas the Piper is as blessed with faultless hindsight as the next man and he reckons he knew from the first that Tilly had been right. Claims, as he sits here now – cajoling his memories and shepherding his stories – that he looked into the future and saw Death. He took out his ha'penny whistle and tried to drown the silent spirits who wanted to tell him the place was dying.

Music masks silence. It heals wounds. Makes the heart sing.

It was a battle of wills. He practised day in and day out: songs to lift everyone's flagging spirits as they worked the unforgiving soil; tunes to bring peace when conflict threatened to brew into violence. Thomas brought smiles to faces. Hope to the downhearted. Light where there was darkness. Calm to troubled souls – and not only the folks. The oxen forsook their stubborn ways and followed him meekly as he led them through the fields while Harry guided the plough with those strong, square shoulders Bas and Ynga had gifted him. Gross the master cook, moved by the child's whistling, slipped him extra portions. But some people are beyond the spell of music. Scheming, untrustworthy Rat and his woman Catte – to name but two – remained full of venom and spite.

Perhaps the ha'penny whistle restored order where Winfrith lacked the will to impose a thane's control. Perhaps. Perhaps not. His powers weren't unlimited. Try as he might, the young piper still couldn't draw Hazel's voice from its hiding place, couldn't persuade his mother to sing. Maybe she could taste Death on her marred lips.

So Thomas the Piper played the whistle. His cousin-sister Doht danced beside him and Emma told stories. All to dispel the murk.

Emma was a wonderful story-crafter. She'd glean her ideas from the humblest of sources and shape them into something fresh and compelling. She told tales of how two young fools named Harry and Alfie went to the borough market and mislaid their wits. Inspired by the beans in their broth, she reshaped Tom Thumb's stories of a giant at the end of an ivy twine into ones about a magical beanstalk that grew all the way up to Bas the Giant's castle in the sky.

Thomas listened and learned. But still refused to grow.

Gross called the piper his *elfin trickster* and invited him into the kitchen.

'Play a song for me with that whistle of yours,' he instructed Thomas. Gross longed for his self-loathing to be banished to oblivion. To *ofergeate*. He wanted to rid himself of all the memories of his wife's mocking taunts.

'We artists,' he sighed. 'They should be thankful for our art and not judge us as men. Art springs from suffering as the stately oak rises from the unclean soil.'

Thomas didn't think his own art stemmed from any suffering, but wasn't inclined to argue. Reckoned he'd been put on this earth to calm frayed nerves, not to stir up discord. He sat in front of the fire, fanning the bellows and imagining spirits cavorting in the flames.

As fat fell into the flames and they spat and hissed, he sensed trouble lurking in the kitchen. A melting pot of evil sprites. And stirring it up was the master cook.

Thomas watched – playing his whistle – as Gross hovered over the turnspit, guiding another new boy's hands, every now and again brushing against his buttocks. Thomas saw the boy tensing. Gross wasn't going to get far with this one. Forewarned, he'd be ready to decline the master cook's attempts at seduction. Poor Gross. He'd be further diminished. Without respect or love we become undernourished. Food's no substitute.

X

Your worst enemy isn't a tortured soul such as Gross, preying on others. Not even a corrupt official such as a reeve who has the power over your life and your death. Not even someone like a vengeful Rat or a spiteful Catte, biding their time, waiting for their moment. Your worst enemy's an unseeable force at work. It breathes on you, bringing you low with the plague and pestilence. It stalks you and leaves you sleepless with worry, wondering when it might strike. It invades you in an unguarded moment and then wrenches your life and soul from you, from within. And never has the grace even to tell you how you've wronged it to merit its anger.

Tilly was the first to go.

'It's come,' she rasped to Alfie the Stammer.

'What are you s-saying? If you've been beaten . . .'

Tilly wafted her hand, airily. Not a beating. She could soak up a beating any night of the week. She'd had enough practice. Though, when she came to think of it, the thrashings had dried up of late.

'The end,' she whispered.

'Yours? M-mine?'

'The end,' Tilly repeated, shedding no light.

Alfie shrugged his shoulders.

But Tilly was right. Tilly, who'd stepped in, raised and then freed Bas the Bold's babes in the wood. She'd seen what her grandson-of-sorts Thomas the Piper had also seen. Perhaps when you're young like Thomas and without cares or you're old like Tilly and beyond caring, perhaps these are the times when you hear what the spirits are telling you. Like warnings that Death stalks a place. Because however loudly and tunefully Thomas piped his music, he could still hear Death in the silences.

Tilly was the plague's first victim. It laid her low and

consumed her. Her oaf was next. Then others.

'Eat. Eat,' Gross urged his most-favoured kitchen hand, Thomas. 'We must all eat. In my experience, it's the fatties who can fight the invisible menace. The plague prefers the taste of lean flesh. You're too small. You must eat, eat, eat or you'll die,' and he shovelled more food into his own mouth. 'Mark my words. Winfrith and I, with these bellies of ours, will be the last two standing, though Winfrith's so old, he might not be long for this world anyway . . . Eat, eat. If I'm to survive this pestilence, I'll want the company of my cheerful little piper.'

Alfie was as slim as a birch tree. Tall, with his head in the clouds, and thin. No stores of fat to fight the curse of the plague. Its rank stench started emanating from him. Although Emma bathed his black, rotting flesh, she knew hers was a lost cause. Alfie became more and more delirious; he was slipping away from her. She knew, too, that to kneel beside him and to touch his flesh was to risk incurring the further wrath of the unseen plague. But such was the force of her love that she clung on to his dear life until the very last.

'I c-c-c . . . I c-c-can't hold . . . hold on, Em-Em-Em-Em,' he whispered. The stammer that she loved but had sometimes driven her to distraction: back to haunt him again. Sparked by his blind terror of the loss of Emma.

She kissed him on his putrid lips, and didn't shudder.

If he'd held me once more in his arms
then would he have left me less longing?
Would I regret his death, his departing a
heart-warming bear-hug bit less than I do?
And if I had told him ten thousand
more times that I loved him, then
might I have managed to stem just a jot
of my battered-and-broken heart's grief-flow?

Elric and Rat oversaw the burials. Elric: friend to Bas the

Bold while he'd lived and tortured by guilt after he'd died. Rat: twitching the mangled remnants of his nose and waiting for his moment. Still stung by the way Bas's half-Viking son had made a mockery of him, undermining him in front of an alehouseful of men. If the brother didn't have the come-uppance he deserved, then maybe punishment would have to be meted out to the sister. That would taste sweet enough.

'Eat, eat,' Gross was telling everyone. 'More food for those of us who've not *had the call*, now the others *are gone to a better place*.'

Why could none of them address Death by its proper name?

'Take, take to our lord-and-master,' he said. He pointed to the meal prepared for Winfrith, who could barely ever rouse himself to leave his hall these days. 'Wasted on an old and dying man, I know,' Gross said, looking at the handsome helping of pork and vegetable broth, 'but if the master keels over, heaven only knows what sort of thane we'll have foisted on us.'

Thomas waited at the doorway because he heard low mutterings and could smell untruths and spite in the air.

Catte was talking to her thane.

'I tell you, my lord, it's the Vikings . . . and the witch with the marred lip. She's brought her sorcery with her. And the child who plays to the evil spirits on his whistle. And the daughter who dances like a dervish, summoning all manner of ill upon us. The simpleton's gone. I suspect they'd cursed him, too. They've cursed us all. And unless you remove them, we're all finished.'

Winfrith shook his head.

'Bas's children . . .'

'I understand, my lord, but the Haggard's Bastard Boy is long dead . . . We're flesh and blood.'

Then the spiteful little Catte (who'd do anything to get her way) had her hand fumbling inside Winfrith's undergarments.

Nothing stirred. The old thane's flesh was unable to respond to her caresses.

'I understand, my lord,' she whispered. 'Perhaps it will please my master to feast his eyes on what he once feasted his lips and his manhood on.'

She has her back to Thomas but he can see she's raised her skirts. She takes Winfrith's hand and places it on her tuffet. Starts sighing, pretending he's bringing her pleasure. Maybe he is. Thomas has seen enough. So he takes some steps back and re-enters the adjoining room with the heaviest tread his small-but-perfectly-formed feet can muster.

Catte heard him this time and gently lifted Winfrith's hand away, allowed her skirts to fall back into place.

'Perhaps my lord recalls why he takes special care of his little orphans,' she noted. 'Perhaps when the reeve comes, he might have the facts put before him . . . and if your Catte is called as a witness, she'll remember not to tell the reeve of her thane's errant ways.'

She was off through the other door before Thomas entered.

'Food,' Winfrith sighed, 'the greatest pleasure in life. Greater even than . . .' His voice tailed off. He paused a while, perhaps wallowing in memories of lusty exploits in the dim-and-distance. 'Now play me a tune, my big-hearted little dwarf,' he said, recovering himself.

Thomas pulled his ha'penny whistle from his belt and summoned music to calm the old thane's troubled soul. He crafted a melody to drown the silence of impending Death.

Winfrith looked happy enough, though that may have been down to Gross's loin of pork. So tender he could tear at it with his gums, no longer populated by any teeth. And the vegetable broth was like nectar.

'Good lad,' he dismissed Thomas, waving him away when he'd had enough. 'You eat up the scraps. You need to do some growing if you're to catch up with your grandfather.

You're master of that whistle, though, the way Bas was master of the sword he held in his hand. Now there was a warrior and a half . . .'

But within moments, he was dozing in his chair. One of the blessings of being decrepit. Thomas tucked his whistle back in his belt and wolfed down the rest of the loin of pork.

XI

'Garlic, Thomas. How much garlic do we have?'

'Ample,' the tiny piper told Gross, who lurched into a state of panic whenever he knew the reeve was on his way.

'And what do I add to my lord thane's stew? Onions to stir his blood so he's bright-eyed . . . and beans instead of meat so he's not sluggish. Just for a day. Then he can sink back into his usual torpor.'

Gross started cooking as if his life depended on in. Maybe it did.

'Some explaining for us all to do,' he muttered to himself. 'The reeve will be displeased. He'll see that Death comes at us from all sides. The fields are weed-ridden and trouble and unrest are brewing.'

Who cared about what the reeve thought? Tilly and Alfie were already gone; Harry was now lying on his bed, burning up as he fought the unseen evil stalking their settlement.

Time for the child Thomas and his whistle to become masters of events. Not slaves to them.

XII

There was a stir, as someone spotted them on the horizon. The lord reeve sat astride his horse. At his side walked High and Mighty, carrying an empty chair. Winfrith's band of serfs got their heads down. It's wise to look busy when the reeve visits.

'Come,' Thomas told his cousin-sister Doht. And they were off to greet the three honoured guests. You could smell the garlic on the reeve from twenty paces. No wonder his horse was snorting.

Thomas played a merry tune of welcome and Doht danced happily beside him. The Reeve scowled, but Thomas reckoned his lordship's scowl had been softened by their efforts.

He watched as the man was helped down from his horse. He'd a lot going for him, had the reeve. Girth. Power. Wealth. But not much dignity. The horse was led to the stable by Elric, still untroubled by the plague, though tortured by conscience. By *ingethanc*.

The reeve was lowered into his chair; a breathsome heave from High and Mighty and they were off, the whole carriage with its alarming-but-comical list. They were panting, were High and Mighty, because the hall was perched atop a steep incline.

Catte had placed herself beside the road and mustered a coy, provocative, vixenly pout, which seemed to please the reeve and his cohorts.

'I come borne by the High and the Mighty and by the twin virtues of Law and Order,' the reeve barked loudly.

Yes, yes. We've heard that one before . . .

Thomas led them to the hall and summoned something close to a fanfare blast on his ha'penny whistle, intended to stir Winfrith from his torpor. He might have been old and useless, but better the demon you know.

It did the trick because, although not exactly sprightly, Winfrith had managed to get to his feet.

'Welcome, my lord reeve,' he said, bowing as low as his stiff, aching back would allow.

'Garlic, Winfrith,' the reeve responded.

The thane looked a trifle confused.

'Your serfs need more garlic. The best defence against the Devil and his unseen plague,' the reeve explained.

'My master cook, Gross, has been saving the best of the garlic for your lordship. Perhaps I should—'

'No, no. The cook Gross is right. I can forgive you the loss of the odd serf, but to despoil your reeve's supper would be an unimaginable evil. What tidings, Winfrith?'

The thane began a bumbling, ill-informed account of life in the settlement but the reeve soon grew bored and restless. He summoned High and Mighty, who groaned as they lifted his chair.

'Perhaps I shall see for myself.'

XIII

'Witchcraft?' the reeve challenged the wench who'd thrown herself at his feet.

How dare she approach him unbidden? Though that tunic hung becomingly on her, allowing more than a glimpse of her flesh.

'Garlic,' he panted. 'The best defence against witchcraft and the best way to bring life to a man's fleshly weapon.'

Something of a miracle, this garlic.

Catte looked up at him and smiled that vixenly smile again.

Perhaps he'd have her tonight, he mused. If he couldn't lay his hands on a younger wench, this one would have to do. Then, when he'd finished with her, he might cast her to High and Mighty. Allow them to taste the leftovers. A mangy couple of curs. The best way to tame curs is to keep them in their place but throw them the odd scrap. What did she want?

'Witchcraft, my lord reeve,' Catte repeated.

A vile accusation . . . but a chance for some sport.

'Then we shall have to ask your thane Winfrith to sort out this unholy mess.'

A thorny problem. The woman accuses four newcomers of bringing witchcraft and the plague to this place. One of the newcomers is dead, the other one is clearly at death's door, incapable of stirring from his bed. That leaves the word of the accuser – a woman – against the word of the two accused – two women. The law is clear. Hazel and Emma will deny the charges and their testimony will outweigh Catte's . . . unless she can find others who'll testify.

'Indeed I can, my lord.'

She tells him more. Interesting. The word of a comely

slut and a rat-like man with a mangled nose against the two wenches: the one with the marred lip and the Viking. Let judgement begin.

XIV

Winfrith had been hauled from his bed without ceremony.

'Your chance to impress me with your ruthless leadership and sound mind,' the reeve informed him, mockingly. 'A mouth-watering case. Either way we have two culprits. Two wenches guilty of witchcraft or a wench and a serf-with-no-nose guilty of bearing false witness.'

Perhaps garlic is also good for easing the flow of creativity – *thought-smithing* – because the reeve has now given the instruction that four ropes are to be fetched. Four nooses. If Winfrith dithers and can't come to judgement then all four will be despatched to the afterlife.

In which case, the reeve muses, *the sad truth is that Winfrith will have to be replaced.*

Fearing the worst, Hazel had already cut the three-wish penny from the hem of her innermost skirt. She'd handed it to Thomas.

'Guard it well. Something to remember . . .'

Her voice had tailed off. She might not believe all that stuff and nonsense about its miracle-making powers, but it's something to remember her by. Something for Thomas to remember his forebears by. And a symbol of hope: something to cling to if Doht and he are left to fend for themselves.

Winfrith cut a sad figure. He bore a forlorn, hangdog look as he listened to the evidence. Catte and Rat kept glancing anxiously at the four nooses hanging from the boughs of four venerable oak trees, wondering if it was wise to have stirred up this trouble.

Rats have a nose for the main chance. Maybe that was Rat's problem. Since Harry the Viking had removed his nose, Rat had lost the ability to smell when the time was right. Or maybe the fault lay with Catte, who should have kept her mouth shut, kept all that spite inside her instead of letting it spill out.

Hazel and Emma looked hammer-struck and bereft of hope, fearing not just their own fate, but also that of Harry, lying on the floor of their hovel, dying of the plague with no one there to bathe his sores. And who'd look after Thomas and Doht? For all Thomas the Piper's elfin pluck, he was still no more than a boy.

Thomas resisted the urge to draw the ha'penny whistle from his belt and tune some lament about treachery and false witness, sensing the reeve might have been displeased.

The facts were laid out. Catte did most of the talking. Rat stood beside her, twitching nervously. Only Winfrith and the reeve were seated.

'In my experience, it's best to keep them all standing,' he'd said. 'That way they stick to the point. Allow them to wallow in comfort and they'll drag it out for days.'

Catte was at her spiteful, fluent best. She crafted a riveting story of Vikings, witches, the bad blood of Ynga the Danish slut (Rat's eyes darted uneasily; Elric swallowed hard), a child dwarf and his pipe, the boy schooled in the craft of summoning the plague from the very stones that litter the unyielding soil they're all cursed to till . . . and there was more.

'I need proof,' Winfrith informed Catte.

'Her lip's proof enough,' Catte said, pointing at Hazel, whose face was, as ever, cast downwards. The harelip that Harry loved so much and on which he'd planted his first longingful, lingering kiss. Harry, who was lying on his bed, drifting closer to the afterlife.

'In the moonlit hours, she becomes a hare. See how her own husband has been laid low while she slips off to cavort with evil spirits. That half-starved cat who arches his back and hisses at all of us. We've all seen how the witch is the only one it'll come to.'

'You ask me to condemn her for her kindness to an ill-tempered cat?' Winfrith asked.

'She'd want you to see it as soft-heartedness and, if this were a cat, then perhaps that could be true. But this is no cat. It's a demon dressed to fool us all.'

'And the other accused?'

'The Viking's a wedlock-wrecker like her mother before her. She cursed her husband with a stammer and then she despatched him to the afterlife to free her to cavort with any husband of her choosing.'

'And who are these happy menfolk?' Winfrith asked.

Catte held him in a steady gaze.

'In my experience, a man knows to keep his lips sealed when a woman's granted him favours. He stands by the woman – even to the point of taking her side in a court of law – lest she should tell all and sundry of his misdemeanours and risk incurring more than the wrath of the wife he's let down . . .'

Emma put her case. By turns she looked directly into Winfrith's and the reeve's eyes. None of the coy fluttering of the eyelashes that Catte had resorted to. Emma's was a defiant gaze, a look with which she unwittingly conjured longing. *Maybe she is a witch*, thought the reeve, falling under her pale-blue spell. Such a waste, though, to see a comely wench hanging from a bough. Still, he could do worse than settle for that Catte joining him in his bed.

'Enough,' said Winfrith. 'Does any other person wish to have their say?'

Elric shuffles uneasily. Does he speak up for the daughter of Bas and Ynga and put a stop to this madness? Does he make his peace with the departed souls of those two and, in so doing, does he condemn his sister Catte and his friend Rat to death? What of Bas's grandchildren? Does he spare them the fate of becoming orphans? Or does he find redemption by taking them in as his own while Emma and Hazel swing from their oak trees?

Elric shapes to speak but his nerve fails him.

'Line them up. All four of them. Put their heads through the nooses while I deliberate.'

A delicious piece of theatre, thinks the Reeve. *Perhaps there's life in old Winfrith yet.*

Catte cast Winfrith another warning glare. He smiled an almost fatherly smile as if to acknowledge he'd chosen aright. So Catte bit her tongue. Rat didn't look so sure. Hazel's eyes were cast downwards, though she looked up briefly at Doht and Thomas. Smiled that lovely, marred half-smile.

'Remember to bathe your father's sores,' she said quietly. 'Give him comfort and tell him I'll be waiting for him. Tell him my lips will be perfect in heaven.'

Emma stared in pale-blue Nordic defiance on them all, inspiring maybe awe as well as longing.

The four were in place. Each standing on their stool, their hands all bound, their heads through the nooses.

The reeve looked on, strangely aroused by the sight he beheld, though perhaps this was down to an excess of garlic coursing through his veins.

There was silence as Winfrith raised himself from his chair and waddled forwards. There were gasps as he drew his sword from its sheath. The sword was still stained by the blood of the victims of the avenging giant Bas the Bold, in whose hands it had fallen as heavily as an anvil from the sky.

'It is finished,' he announced, quoting the Galilean on his cross. Perhaps he was referring to the bad blood that had besmirched his village for too long. Or maybe to his own life. Or else – less fancifully – just announcing that he was about to bring proceedings to an end . . . He lifted his sword and sent one stool flying and then another and the two bodies plunged sickeningly and then lurched side to side, side by side.

XV

Two bodies hung. Two lives snuffed out because spite had stalked the place, lain festering inside Rat and Catte and then erupted like a sore that despoils the skin. Some people turned their heads, unable to stare into the face of summary justice, for it could so easily have been them. Others were unable to look away. Catte gagged and swallowed her spite. Rat stopped twitching.

Thomas opened his eyes.

'What's happening?' Doht asked.

'Winfrith's finally brought justice to this place,' someone responded. 'Hopefully peace as well.'

Elric helped first Emma and then Hazel out of their nooses and off their stools. Just in time, because Hazel's legs were in danger of buckling beneath her.

'Leave the other two. Perhaps once the hidden spirits have a taste for them they'll leave the living alone,' Winfrith wheezed.

Perhaps not, because it would be a while yet before the plague subsided and not before it had taken Harry, whose last hours were the more comfortable for having Hazel bathe him.

Thomas offered Hazel back her three-wish penny.

'Keep it, my love,' she said. 'I've no use for it.'

Hazel was holding Harry's cold right hand.

I shrank, unseen, into my silent and unpeopled space,
sought solace in my spirit-dwelling world,
away from all the wild and wanton revelry, the
maypoling, the mayday-dancing merriment.
Crushed and comfortless, unloved and all alone,
I traced the taut and twisted lines of my cursed lip.
What spell was it you summoned when you set

down, on the rough earth, the ring you'd wrought?
I placed it on my palm, then felt it on my finger,
your joy-giving and load-lifting gift.
You brought song into my sorrowed soul,
 melody and music to my cursed, marred mouth,
laughter and love to my baned, unlovely lips.
I was bruised and broken, you were my balm;
crushed and cursed but you brought comfort.
You were my all, my love, my life because
you looked on me and loved me as I am.

'I'll miss him,' Hazel said, tearfully. 'More than anyone will ever know. But of course I love you just as much. Why don't you pipe another of your tunes on that ha'penny whistle? Let Alfie and the others know Harry's on his way.'

XVI

The community was shrinking fast. But justice and peace had fallen on it. Thomas and Doht were brother and sister again, sharing not a mother and father, but two mothers.

'Eat, eat,' Gross was still urging them, throwing yet more garlic into his meals to keep the demons at bay. 'I must make you all fatties to fight this thing.'

Everyone was doing their best. Pretty soon a mere handful clung to their lives as an eerie silence fell on the place. Thomas kept turning the spit as Gross served up what was left in his larder.

'Turn, turn, my little elf boy,' Gross urged his charge. But all that spit-turning was taking the breath from the young piper's lungs. And the tell-tale signs of plague began to inscribe their handwriting on the flesh of mothers, daughter and son. The black, rotten pustules swelled on their bodies and the rank smell of death was on their breath. Hazel seemed resigned to it.

'At least we can all stay together in the afterlife. Harry won't have got far by now.'

Emma had more fight in her. Reckoned on taking her chances and waiting a few years before she caught up with Alfie. Knew Alfie wouldn't go wandering off without her.

At such moments, you turn to whatever help you can. Thomas picked up his ha'penny whistle to muster as happy a tune as he could. You don't want dirges adding to your gloom. You want gleeful spirits to fill the room . . . Except a jolly jig of a melody wouldn't come and nor would a song form on Hazel's lips. Doht was too weak for dancing.

'The penny,' Hazel rasped. 'Your great-grandfather's penny.'

For all her reservations about its powers, she knew it offered their only hope.

Thomas fumbled in the hem of his tunic and found the silver penny graced with King Edgar's noble face. With the four of them huddled together, Thomas the Piper – great-grandson of the far-famed dwarf Tom Thumb – made the first of his three wishes.

He wished for the *Gift of Health*.

And, just to be on the safe side, he managed to pipe a final, feeble, doleful prayer to the soul of his great-grandfather, seeking the old man's intercession with the spirits. The spirits whom they must have wronged for them to have visited the plague so mercilessly on them.

If Thomas the Piper was expecting something dramatic to happen, then he was to be disappointed. One by one, the four of them sank first into dizzy, thirsty apathy and then into a state of unlife-and-undeath. Emma went last of all, because she was the fighter. Before he passed out, Thomas was dimly aware of Gross placing him on a bed of fresh straw. The cook had been working tirelessly to ease the lot of the dying: his penance for the death of the young kitchen hand he'd raped. Without a flicker of revulsion, he'd also picked up the bodies of the dead and buried them, allowing them the sort of dignity in death he coveted in life.

He clung to the belief that his ample flesh was what saved him.

'Too big a man for the invisible spirits to bring me low,' he reckoned. All those years of gluttony had served him well.

XVII

It could have been days or weeks before Thomas was freed from Death's hold, overcome not by relief but by a raging thirst. He crawled to the nearby trough and sank his head into the water, drinking as greedily as any wild animal. Only after a while did it occur to him he'd made his first faltering steps free of the plague's clutches.

The dwarf-piper Thomas's first wish – for the Gift of Health – had been granted.

Still weak and exhausted, he found a vessel. Filled it with water and took it to Hazel, already back from her long sleep, but unable to stir from her bed. She gasped as the cold water gripped her throat.

'Back from the dead,' Gross observed. 'A grandson worthy of Bas the Bold.'

The sound of the master cook's voice startled Thomas.

It was a mercy, a relief that Gross was alive and well enough to continue his penance.

'Our lord Winfrith's left this earth to go and explain himself to his Creator,' the master cook informed Thomas. 'Along with most of the others. Everyone else has fled to throw themselves at the feet of some other thane and bind themselves into serfdom . . . I suggest we build up your strength – yours and the rest of your family's, if they decide to come back from their unlife. We must scoff what's left to glean and then scarper.'

Gross found what foodstuffs he could and turned them into dishes so tasty that it was hard for Hazel and Thomas not to believe they'd drifted to heaven. The plague left Doht alone a day or two after Hazel had been spared. Then Emma stirred. What do you feel after your three-wish penny's wrenched you from the grip of Death? Exhaustion and thankfulness above all else, though the two mothers were still suffering pangs, hungering for Alfie and Harry. They forsook conversation for a while: grief had knotted their tongues. Speech seemed unimportant, though the stories, the music and dancing would slowly flow into their lives again. As they do, given time.

Once they'd emptied the storage rooms of food, they moved on, and following them – a few paces behind – walked their uninvited guest, Gross. Still keen to serve out his penance.

'At least he cooks like an angel,' Hazel muttered. 'I suppose we ought to put up with him for that alone. But if he expects to become part of the family, he's another think coming.'

The rules were made clear. If Gross wanted to stay with them, then so be it. But his job was to keep the animals they'd rounded up from straying, to cook and to keep himself to himself. Helpful he might have been and, yes, they were all full of gratitude. But the man was tainted by the sin of sodomy; the shadow of his past still stalked the place. You didn't want such men to come too close.

Gross stepped meekly into line.

XVIII

It had been agreed. Binding themselves in serfdom would be ill advised. Not many thanes were as lax as old Winfrith had been.

Those itchy feet were ready to walk again and lead them back into the forest.

'Not as bad as working yourself to the bone and spending your life half starved, but it'll be tough. More so without Alfie and Harry,' Emma reckoned. 'Mislaid their brains more times than I care to recall, but they knew how to grapple with a wild beast and slaughter it.'

'I can't see Gross giving chase to a hart,' Hazel whispered.

'The hart might die laughing,' Emma suggested.

If Thomas had two mothers and no father, then he was brother-and-father to Doht. In the day he played as a brother might. Piping his beloved ha'penny whistle, he coaxed his sister's feet to jig again as her strength returned. In the evenings he cut his teeth as a story-weaver. To a youthful Thomas the Piper fell the role of keeper of his family's story hoard.

'Tell me the story of *The Babes in the Wood*,' Doht demanded.

And for the umpteenth time, Thomas recounted the tale, which had started its life as a truthful enough account of Harry's and Emma's beginnings, but – like all good stories – had become embellished in the telling and ended up as the tale in which Uncle Alfie the Stammer is now recast as the conscience-stricken Rawbones, who, sent to track down the two babes and rob them of their worldly goods, finds redemption when he becomes their protector.

So what if there was barely more than a grain of the original story? The whole point of fairy tales is the truth that

242

the falsehoods are trying to convey.

Thomas and Doht took to their roles of storyteller and listener as if they were old hands. Some children prefer tales that are bursting with sweetness. Not Doht. She had a taste for the grim and gruesome or for gently mocking tales of the glutton Gross, who – listening in – took it all in good heart.

'I wonder if it mightn't be kind to invite Gross to share our home with us?' Thomas asked his two mothers when the time seemed right.

He laid out the facts. The cook had helped them to build their home. Done the bulk of the work, in truth, though it wasn't the best of efforts, needing constant repair. Also in Gross's favour were the meals that had sustained them. Their animals already shared the home on the coldest nights: three pigs and a group of hens, lorded over by an insufferable cockerel. Even the bad-tempered cat (accused in the past of witchcraft and unarguably something of a demon when it came to hunting vermin) treated Gross with contempt rather than animosity. Poor old Gross. Still made to sleep beneath the stars, exposed to the snow and the rain, while the cat curled up without a care.

'I wonder if he's served his penance?'

'You're too soft for your own good, Thomas, like your father was,' Emma answered him. 'Though perhaps we could let him sleep in the corner with the three pigs. But you might warn him that if we catch him molesting them – or if he tries any funny business with any of us for that matter – then he's out on his ear. And he won't get around me with one of his bowls of broth, no matter what he puts in it.'

'Molest? The pigs? I hardly think . . .' Hazel said.

'You can never be sure with his sort.'

Thus it was that Gross squeezed in beside the three pigs at night – behaving himself impeccably, as far as anyone was able to judge.

XIX

They survived. That's what you do in the forest. You survive. Once in a while you might meet a passing stranger. Nobody bothers the woodland-dwellers these days. No need to take cover when you hear voices in the distance. Not like the days when a hard-pressed thane could send out his thugs to round up any fugitives and have them bound in serfdom.

One traveller – lured, perhaps, by the smell wafting from Gross's bubbling cauldron of chicken stew – brings tidings that Cnut is dead. He tells them that the Dane's sons are fighting over the throne. It must have been in the year One Thousand and Thirty-Five.

Emma shrugs her shoulders. What does she care of kings and queens. She doubts that the late king or the grieving queen – her namesake, Emma – would have cared much about her, had they come across her. Nor did she care one apple pip about them.

'We've had enough of kings and queens in our family,' she says. 'What with all the woe and heartache Edgar and Elfrith rained down on us.'

True enough. Emma doesn't know, of course, that kings will again, in time, weave their way into our lives and into this wordsmith's tale. Three kings to complement three wishes. Edgar, Harold Godwinson and . . . I can barely spit his name . . . William the Bastard.

My scribe speaks up. He knows how the Bastard wronged me, but I suspect he thinks I should let bygones be bygones. A simmering grudge makes for a troubled soul.

'You and Tolland are always talking of the good times before the Bastard came, but I hear your stories and I wonder if it was really so great, Eam. Apart from King Alfred, you make the Anglo-Saxon rulers sound a motley bunch. Maybe it isn't such a bad thing to have the Bastard rule us with a rod of iron.'

'I forgive you such obscenities, Pup, because you're young. Rulers are no different to us. There are bright ones and dimwits. Who would you rather have ploughing a furrow beside you? A bright one who spends his time ordering you about and telling you how you should be furrowing your plot, rather than lifting his own plough? Or a silent dimwit who leaves you in peace?'

'The dimwit, I suppose.'

'Quite. So be grateful that most of the men who've ruled this island have been dimwits. Let's hope William of Normandy – a meddling, intelligent, vicious bastard – proves the last of his kind. Long may we be ruled by dimwits.'

'Tell me, Eam. What happens if you're lorded over by a dimwit who won't stop talking and meddling?'

Banter of the friendliest sort. The best kinship is with those who feel at ease with you enough to mock you. The best sort of penman pricks his wordsmith's pomposity every now and then.

'I must be cursed to have a scribe with a sharp pen *and* a sharp tongue. A two-bladed sword indeed,' I scold Aart. But I'm smiling as I say it.

The years passed. In the summers, enjoying their unfettered life. In the winters, sometimes frozen from the very tips of their teeth to the ends of their toenails, gleaning whatever food they could. And rarely offering up scraps for this wordsmith to glean stories from. Sometimes, history is elsewhere, stories spawned by our family are as thin on the ground as whortleberries are on the floor of the Quantock woods in the darkest months. Yes, I admit it. Our family hasn't always taken history by the scruff of its neck. The Saxon world beyond the forest continued its slow lurch towards oblivion. To *ofergeate*. The pulse of English history continued to beat its irregular rhythm, but from a heart that was by now as much Danish as Saxon. Kings had come and gone. Edmund,

Cnut, Harold, Harthacnut. And now a new king, Edward the Confessor, an ineffectual, godly man – more interested in prayers to his and Tolland's Galilean Redeemer than he was in royal decrees – who'd manage to cling to his throne longer than most. Thomas was sixteen years old (though still no bigger than a child) when the Confessor began his reign. Storms, fire, famine, severe frosts and pestilence might all come and go, but Thomas the Piper and his kin will survive it all. Free, for a while, from the reach of history.

XX

Gross's attempts to hunt down animals were becoming increasingly despairing. Trying to outrun them hadn't worked. After giving up the chase, he'd collapse to the forest floor, panting. Stealth had also proved hopeless. When you had a belly the size of the master cook's, you'd little idea where you were placing your feet as you stole up on your prey. Nor was it easy to lose yourself behind a birch sapling.

'Perhaps if I flush them out and chase them towards Thomas?' Gross had suggested.

'Then what? Does my little pixie wrestle the beasts to the ground?'

'Wolves manage to hunt and they have neither arms nor spears.'

'No,' Hazel scoffed, 'but they have brains.'

Gross bore her insults without complaint.

'Hedgehogs,' Hazel suggested. 'Even you should be able to outrun one of those.'

Indeed, this had led to some success. He'd baked his hedgehogs in clay; cracked them open to expose that lovely soft meat. Wonderfully tasty, they'd been.

Word must have spread among the hedgehog community. The supply had soon fallen away. Two whole days it had taken Gross to track down the last of the hedgehogs.

Thereafter, their diet had gone downhill. In quality as well as quantity. Their own animals – the bad-tempered cat included – had long since been eaten. The cat had left a more lasting legacy than filling their stomachs, Gross having laid claim to its pelt.

'. . . Assuming no one else wants it,' he'd said, meekly.

'You take it, Gross. It's crawling with fleas, anyway,' Emma agreed.

'And I wonder if I could ask another favour?'

This was called *pushing your luck*. But, before she knew it, Emma was sewing Gross a headpiece to protect his bald pate from the summer sun and the winter cold.

It didn't sit easily on his head, although, as Hazel pointed out, it was a blessing the cat had been a modest tabby and not a flamboyant stripy ginger.

To be fair to Gross, he'd made a good fist of the grass snake, serving what could have passed for a chicken soup. The moorhen had turned out less well. They'd been hampered, for a while, by the absence of a fire, on account of weeks of unrelenting rain, which had dampened their kindling as thoroughly as it had dampened their spirits. Raw, the bird had tasted vile: the texture of drying sludge and the taste of rotting vegetation.

They were driven to try luring a more hefty beast by the sound of Thomas's melodious piping. Unsurprisingly, this had failed.

Thomas had had his doubts and sought some clarification. 'Which animal is it we're trying to lure?'

'A big one,' Gross replied.

For the first time since he'd dipped his ladle into his master's broth to test it – setting a pattern of over-feasting – Gross had started to lose weight and taste the bitter gall of aching hunger. He'd felt the life-tinder draining from his very bones.

Perhaps our best ideas come when our need is greatest. Yes, neediness is the begetter of thought-smithing.

'We could try a trap, possibly?' Gross muttered, unsure if this was a good idea or a bad one. All that weight he'd shed wasn't the only thing that had left him. Much of his self-belief had cantered off over the horizon, too.

'That's not a bad thought,' Emma remarked.

Gross glowed in the heat of her praise.

They scratched at the ground with stones, working between them to dig a pit about six feet square and six feet deep. Then they laid intertwined branches and twigs over the whole and smothered it with dried leaves and loamy soil.

They retreated a fair distance and watched. Not much happened until the evening. Gross's heart began to pound as he saw a boar emerge into the clearing. He nodded to the others.

'Just keep talking,' he whispered. 'It'll have smelled us already, anyhow. Act naturally.'

As it happened, Emma was in full flow with a pretty story about Silvanlocks, the spirit of the forest, from whose mouth leafy shoots grow. She was telling the tale of how the ivy, the holly and the mistletoe had arrogantly refused to shed their green leaves for the winter and how once the north wind began to bite, and they felt the full weight of the winter snow, they began to regret their foolhardiness and pleaded to Silvanlocks for forgiveness. Silvanlocks had granted their leaves a coat of wax to keep them warm. In return, he'd punished the mistletoe by taking its roots away.

'You'll have to rely on kind strangers to be your host,' he'd said. 'And, in return, you'll bear white berries to remind all and sundry during the darkest mid-winter that the stars will always shine white and brilliant in the sky.'

Silvanlocks isn't a vengeful spirit, so he'd softened by the time he spoke to the ivy. He'd punished it by taking its trunk away.

'You'll have to rely on others to give you support,' he'd said. 'And, in return, you'll bear black berries to remind everyone that though the moon wanes to darkness, it returns to its full beaming glory without fail.'

By the time he'd got to the holly, Silvanlocks had mellowed even more.

'I'll grant you roots and a trunk,' he'd said, 'though your leaves will forever be sharp to prick your conscience. And, in return, you'll bear bright red berries to remind folks during the darkest mid-winter that the sun will always hang in the sky, bringing daylight and the promise of summer warmth.'

The boar snorted loudly as it bumbled around the clearing.

'Keep talking,' Gross whispered.

'Someone else's turn,' Emma breathed.

The boar advanced a few paces, sniffed at the trap, seemed to shrug its enormous shoulders and then turned away, as if to make clear its utter contempt for the human race and its feeble attempts at entrapment.

'Oh well,' Hazel muttered. 'Let's hope there are some daft animals out there. I don't mind eating daft animals, so long as they taste good. Play us another tune, Pixie, a melody to take my mind off food. I'm so hungry I could eat one of you lot.'

Gross shuffled uneasily on his buttocks. He was still – by some way – the most succulent specimen in the group, for all the weight he'd lost.

Thomas drew his pipe from his belt and summoned a tune to numb their hunger pangs and calm Gross's worst fears. And perhaps to lull some unwitting dimwit of a beast into their animal trap.

XXI

There was a kerfuffle during the small hours. A crash. Then silence while whatever beast had fallen into the trap recovered its senses. Then some faint whimpering.

'Leave it 'til morning,' Emma whispered. 'It's probably a mouse, anyway, knowing our luck.'

'Can I have the best bits?' Doht said, hopefully.

'I don't think there are any best bits on a mouse, my little love,' Hazel commented. 'I reckon they're all paltry.'

'Better than a slap in the face,' Emma said.

'So long as it's not another moorhen. Definitely no best bits on a raw moorhen.'

'If it's a moorhen, I'll take the slap in the face, instead. Back to sleep everyone.'

Good news. The beast was still whimpering in the morning light. Thomas crept forward.

'Careful, Pixie,' Hazel called. 'Don't going being a hero like your grandfather Bas.'

The beast was cowering in the corner, curled into a ball and shuddering with the cold. Thomas laid down the roughly hewn spear he'd been carrying and pulled his ha'penny whistle from his belt.

The pitiful sobbing stopped as the beast in the corner looked up. A boy of about fifteen. Not much younger than Thomas.

'What's your name?' Thomas asked him, putting his whistle back in place.

The entrapped boy peered up at him.

'I'm called all sorts. *Earfothe* mostly . . .'

Trouble.

'. . . though I'd like it best if you called me by my birth name, which is Wulfie. Reckon I've twisted my ankle.'

'Hang on, Wulfie. I'll get someone to help get you out
of there.'

Wulfie was hauled out of the hole he'd got himself in. It was
soon clear that the reason he was *earfothe* was that he was
as ill sighted as a mole.

He looked a sad and comical sight as he peered at them.

'How many of you are there?' he asked.

'Five of us, Wulfie,' Thomas said. 'Six, counting you.'

'Heaven help us,' Hazel muttered. 'Gross sets his mind to
capture a beast and he ensnares another mouth to feed.'

'I've something in my sack,' Wulfie said, pointing towards
the pit.

'What is it?' Thomas asked.

'A swan or a goose,' Wulfie said. 'I couldn't tell which.
I reckon it's got a broken wing. I chased after it and it just
kept flapping along the ground. By the time I'd got it, I was
lost. I've been wandering around ages. Then I fell into that
thing.'

'Well done, Wulfie,' Emma said. 'You don't mind if we
share your swan-goose before you go home, do you?'

'Don't mind if you do, though I've not got a home since
I lost my mother and father, so I'd rather stay.'

'Lost them as in *passed away* or lost them as in *wandered
from earshot and eyeshot*?' Emma asked.

'Both, as it happens. Though they did the passing away
first and I've not seen them since they were buried.'

'Well, you're welcome to stay then . . . Gross and
Thomas'll fetch the swan-goose.'

It proved to be swan.

'What about these earwigs and beetles that have fallen
into the trap?' Gross asked.

'Swan will do me for the time being,' Emma replied.

A rare treat. By Frig, it tasted good.

And everything was just fine for a while. Wulfie reminded

Emma very much of her Alfie. Tall, slim as a sapling and with Alfie's muddle-headed bright mind. The same infuriating head-in-the-clouds, eyes-on-the-distant-horizon absentmindedness. Though, considering he was surrounded by the thick fog that had dogged him since birth, it was forgivable for Wulfie to be looking to the dim-and-distance.

The rest of them were story-gleaners, but Wulfie plucked thoughts from the far yonder.

'What are you thinking, Wulfie?'

'I see a time when all men and women might wear reading stones if they're afflicted by mist.'

Wulfie also reckoned he could foresee a time when all men would be free from the yoke of serfdom. He'd heard of some idea the Ancient Greeks had come up with: everyone had a say in deciding who their oppressors were. That way, if they started oppressing you too much, you could boot them out and get a new oppressor.

'Sounds good to me, Wulfie,' Thomas commented. 'Though what about leaders who don't oppress?'

'Like King Alfred you mean?'

'Yeah, like King Alfred.'

'Leaders like him are one in a million. You can't go building up your hopes that another one like him will ever come along . . . He reckoned everyone should learn to read and write, too. Not that I could read or write with these mole's eyes the Creator gave me.'

'You'd be all right with some of your reading stones, Wulfie.'

'Fair point . . . Anyway, I've heard tell that if we could all read and write we might be free. You have these thoughts and you take your *fethere* – your quill-feather – and dip it into ink and then entrap the thoughts on vellum . . . and only then can you give them the wings to fly. You share your ideas with your fellow men and in knowledge lies freedom. If I had a son and he could see better than I can, I'd find him a teacher who can help him to read and write, even if it cost me my life.'

'You're too earnest and misty-eyed for your own good, Wulfie,' Hazel told him. 'Though I'll give you a prediction of my own. You're a lovely, well-meaning lad and some girl out there will fall for your charms.'

She nudged Doht, who scowled at her. The exchange passed Wulfie by.

'I reckon I'm more likely to end up in a monastery or some such. Getting in everyone's way and crashing into things,' Wulfie muttered modestly.

XXII

Winter passed. Spring came and with it, food. First the eggs, taken from birds' nests or sometimes the young, unfledged birds. Gross in particular relished the crunch of those soft young bones. Broth of fresh, unfledged bird – rendered even more tasty by the roots of wild garlic – made the heart sing, got Doht dancing again and put extra life into Thomas's piping, There was nothing better, though, than a plump, amply fleshed adult beast, with wild boars the most prized of all. That needed stealth but, after their initial botched attempts, they were getting better at landing their quarry. They decided it might be best to leave Wulfie behind, rather than have him bumping into everything, startling most of their potential prey into flight.

'You prod the fire for us, Wulfie. We need someone to keep it aflame to cook the meat. Be careful what you put on it, though . . . You sit down over here and do some of your thinking about what the future might hold and tell us all about it when we get back.'

It was the first time Wulfie had been left alone and he realised, as he thought about them, how happy it made him, having his new family. The happiest he'd ever felt in his life. This family he couldn't quite make out. He was fond of the fuzzy outline of the two mothers, the boy and girl and the fat man who – as far as Wulfie could see – had tabby hair on his head. Wulfie couldn't figure what this man's relationship to everyone else was; he wasn't the husband or father, given the way they spoke to him. He seemed at the bottom of the pecking order. Though perhaps Wulfie himself had now taken on that role. He missed his first family, of course. But things had never been the same after first his mother, and then his father had passed away. He and his siblings had had to fend for themselves. As the youngest – and, yes, the most useless because of his eyes – he was a source of annoyance to them or, when the mood was lighter, the butt of their jokes. It was cruel what siblings could do to you when the Creator had cursed you with a mole's eyes. Briars on your stool, stones or foul-tasting haw berries in your stew. This family might tease him, but he was warmed by their love.

Wulfie looked into the flames and, before he knew it, his thoughts were off beyond the here-and-now. He was picturing that time when he was old enough to be a father. Of course he'd have to get a girl to wed him first. One who loved him enough to put up with the fact he couldn't see an awful lot.

The sound of many footsteps and of Gross's rasping breath, as he struggled under the weight of a carcass, cut short Wulfie's daydream. Wulfie must have spent a fair while looking into his future, because the fire had burned itself out.

'Well done, Wulfie,' Emma quipped.

Wulfie was crestfallen.

'Don't take it to heart, Wulfie,' Hazel said. 'You're in good company, what with King Alfred and his griddle cakes . . . What were you thinking about, anyway? We're all dying to hear your words of wisdom.'

Wulfie blushed.

XXIII

'What's Doht like?' Wulfie whispered to Thomas.

They were sitting side by side at the privy. You could share some of your best secrets by the privy, because no one else hung around there for long.

'What sort of a question's that?'

'Does she look like she sounds?'

'How does she sound?'

'Her voice is as sweet as honey . . .'

Wulfie's face reddened. There. He'd managed to tell Thomas about how he felt.

'Can't say I'd noticed,' Thomas grunted. 'Don't think brothers look at their sisters much.'

'Try to think.'

'She sort of looks like Emma. Wheaten hair, pale eyes. Pretty, I suppose. Yeah, she's all right.'

'Her lips, her nose?'

'Frig only knows. Why would you want to know what her nose is like? Or her lips, for that matter? Tell you what: I've an idea. I'll ask her to let you touch them and you can work it out for yourself.'

'I couldn't do that. Emma and Hazel would laugh at me.'

'If it's that important, I'll say you want to feel what everyone looks like and you can work your way through all of us and finish off with Doht, 'cause that way you'll be quite good at it by the time you get to her.'

'You sure, Thomas?'

'Trust me, Wulfie. But for Frig's sake remember to scrub your hands on some dock leaves and wash them in the river before you go pawing everyone.'

'Not a word to Doht about how I feel.'

'Don't worry about it, Wulfie.'

XXIV

Thomas outlined the problem.

Gross offered himself up first. Wulfie tried not to shudder as he felt the cook's sweaty, sagging face. The man's breath smelled like a dog's fart. And that hair on his head was more like cat fur. But he concentrated hard as he built up a mental picture of Gross and each of the others. As he traced the lines of Emma's face, he realised he couldn't remember having ever touched his own mother in this way.

Then Hazel. Surprised by the scarred lip, Wulfie dwelt on it a moment too long. He blushed.

'It's all right, Wulfie,' Hazel said.

'Sorry.'

Thomas was next. Small but perfectly formed.

And then Doht.

Wulfie feared his knees were about to fail him as he dwelt on Doht's face.

He mustn't take too long, so that Thomas is the only one who knows his secret . . . but his hands have begun to tremble. He strokes her hair. It is long and plaited. He holds a hand against each cheek and traces her face. He feels her eyelids, then her nose, and then moves his hand across her lips. He tries to feign indifference, but he fears his voice is wavering.

'Thank you, everyone,' he says.

Now Doht's blushing, though Wulfie's the only one who doesn't see this.

XXV

Gross had helped himself to his share of young kitchen hands over the years. But never, in all that time, had a young lad touched his skin like that, awakening feelings the cook thought he'd long since managed to quell. Emma and Hazel were enjoying their preferred sport of banter as everyone sat down to eat. Soon, they'd be in their stride with stories to tell. Thomas would lie back and play his pipe. Doht was strangely subdued, in no mood for dancing. Wulfie had a contented smile on his face.

Gross hoped no one would sense what he was thinking. He'd bide his time, however long it took. Days or weeks if need be. Get Wulfie on his own and make his move. These feelings welling up inside him: they needed release.

Not tonight, because Gross has had his fill of roast boar. He's feeling sluggish, beginning to doze off.

Then, when the rest of them are asleep, Thomas tells Wulfie a short story. One born from the mouth of his great-grandfather. He says it quietly, so as not to wake the others. He recounts it as the old man himself first told it. Thomas isn't even sure it all makes sense.

'The rose,' he begins. 'Lovely to behold but a brute to pick with your bare hands. You try tearing one of those thorny beasts from a bush . . .'

Picture the first man who ever plucked a rose for his lover. Came back to his cave tired after a day crafting his latest work of art: two round discs joined by a pole. He'd begun to wonder why on earth no one had thought of this before. But isn't that true of all the best ideas? Their very straightforwardness is why they're overlooked.

He opted to call this new wonder a *hweol* – a wheel – because the word brought to mind the sound it made when it was spun.

Lost in his work, he suddenly became aware the sun was setting. He'd be in trouble again. On the other hand, his girl knew how forgetful he was. She forgave him his lack of manliness, she forgave him his absentmindedness. So she must surely love him.

Why?

Why is a rose worthy of more love than a humble sow-thistle?

A rose. He'd hand her a rose. Because wrenching a rose from its bush would let her see the pain he was prepared to suffer to bring her such loveliness.

'Where have you been all day?'

'Thinking,' he explained, handing her the first rose a man ever picked for a woman.

She wasn't sure why, but her mood lightened and her gaze softened.

'Thinking about what?' she asked him, warily.

'Something I've decided to call *romance*,' he replied, very satisfied with himself.

Lovecraft, he might have said, but the meaning was the same.

'One of my great-grandfather's tales,' Thomas concluded. 'Probably another of his tall stories. He was fond of tall stories, to say he was a short man . . . but I reckon you should hand Doht some flowers and see how it goes.'

'Worked for me, when Harry left me a bowl of flowers during our courtship,' Hazel whispered.

The boys fairly leaped out of their skins.

'You weren't supposed to be listening, Mother,' Thomas chided Hazel.

'Just checking you're not leading young Wulfie off the straight-and-narrow. We want to make sure he doesn't let Doht slip through his fingers.'

Wulfie blushed. It was becoming a habit.

It takes inner strength to woo your beloved. The courage to spill the words that are coursing through your mind. Boldness enough to risk the fear of being ridiculed. It's bad enough when the Creator's gifted you two proper eyes, eyes not just to drink in your beloved, but to draw you to the brightest or daintiest flowers to melt her heart.

Wulfie breathed in deeply. He summoned some strength of purpose and made his fumbling first footsteps from the clearing, peering down in the dappled shade for the finest flowers his mole's eyes could spot. Garnering a heart's worth of heart-melting flowers took him most of the morning.

What did Doht make of the flowers? Not much, it seemed. Doht wasn't sure about flowers. Not sure about boys, either.

'Don't give up at the first setback, Wulfie,' Hazel whispered. 'A girl likes to be sure a boy's not just playing games.'

Summer came and Doht seemed to have become slightly more responsive to Wulfie's bumbling attempts at lovecraft. Progress was slow, though. So slow that when the following winter beset them, Wulfie still hadn't moved on any further than the odd bit of bashful hand-holding. The cold began to bite. Hunger started gnawing at them all again. The berries had all been stripped. There were no beasts left to slay. Survival was the only thing that mattered. They lay pressed against each other for warmth. All bar Gross, who knew to keep his distance.

But even in the depths of late winter, Wulfie hadn't given up all hope of winning his girl. The moment came to try his luck again when Doht announced she planned to go off foraging for food.

'Your chance to be alone with her,' Thomas whispered.

'Don't feel at my best,' Wulfie said. 'Got a streaming cold. Besides, what do I say?'

'How about you tell her she's the sun who brings cheer to your murky gloom, the girl who brings hope to your visions of the future, who brings joy into your life when she dances—'

'Thanks, Thomas. That'll do for now.'

Wulfie bumbled off in pursuit of his quarry. Tripping over a fallen trunk as he left the clearing.

XXVI

Wulfie wouldn't remember how long it was before alarm gave way to the certainty he was lost among the trees. To lose one family is an unhappy mistake, but to lose a second one . . . Feeling utterly dejected, Wulfie was torn between sinking to his knees and sobbing or crying out to Doht for help. Either way it wouldn't look good. Not very manly. Maybe he wasn't cut out for this lovecraft. Maybe he should stick to what he did best: sitting down and mulling over what the Wyrd might have in store for him and his fellow men.

Then he heard the snap of a twig and someone's tread. What if it was a stranger? No, it must be Doht. They'd not seen a stranger for more than a year now.

'Wulfie.'

Thank the saints: a familiar voice. Though he would have preferred it to have been Doht's.

Gross's breath was heavy as he approached. He held Wulfie firmly and turned him. Wulfie shaped to offer his thanks, but then sensed something was wrong. Gross was pressing him against a tree and now the cook was fumbling with Wulfie's tunic.

Wulfie struggled, but the cook was too strong for him. His cries were stifled as Gross clapped his greasy right hand over the boy's mouth.

Now Wulfie was whimpering.

Then the weapon plunged hard into him. The rusty old *seax* that had once belonged to Tom Thumb, now held in the hand of his tiny great-grandson, Thomas the Piper.

Gross slumped to the ground. He looked up pathetically at Thomas.

'Forgive me,' he bleated.

Thomas ignored him.

'You stay here, Wulfie. I'll run and get the others.'

'No. I'd die of shame,' Wulfie whined.

'It's all right, Wulfie. They need never know what happened.'

In their weakened state, they all had to work together to drag a groaning Gross back to the camp.

'Why?' Hazel asked.

'He tried to grab some acorns and we got into a fight.'

'So, where are these acorns?'

'He scoffed them,' Wulfie said. 'That's why Thomas stabbed him.'

Quick thinking, that.

'He deserved it,' Hazel observed. 'Though you should try to be less hot-headed next time you're in a fight. And you'd better hope he recovers, because none of us has the strength to bury him.'

XXVII

Gross was lying beside the fire. The others were up and about.

'Should I make my peace with him?' Thomas asked Emma.

'Probably a good idea, my love.'

Thomas walked over to Gross. Coughed loudly.

'I was too quick to anger. I regret the spilling of blood.'

Gross was still turned away from him. He seemed in high dudgeon.

'I'm sorry, Gross.'

Thomas looked up at Emma.

'He's asleep. Seems a shame to wake him.'

'Nonsense,' Emma said, giving the cook a sharp kick on his ample buttocks.

She bent down, peering at him.

'Shit. I think he's dead.'

She rolled him over; Gross was staring blankly up at the sky now. The cat pelt had slipped to the side of his head, robbing him of any shred of dignity. No doubt about it. Dead.

'Oh, Frig. I'm too weary to dig a hole big enough for his fat body.'

True hunger can drive a man to madness. Have him howling at the moon for the aching, soul-destroying longing to go away. Hunger such as I hope my scribe, Aart, who looks at me warily now, will never know. It was Hazel who came up with the idea. It was a thought that had occurred to her before.

'Eat him?' Emma asked, in disbelief.

'Why not?' Hazel said. 'I've heard human flesh is a bit like eating a pig. He might be quite succulent . . . though there are certain parts I'd not want to touch. His head, for a start. I reckon we should bury that. Maybe cast his entrails aside or use them to lure some other beast for when we're hungry again.'

'I can't imagine any of us would ever feel hungry again if we ate Gross,' Emma said.

'Nonsense. Once you've eaten an uncooked moorhen, you've the stomach for any food you can get your hands on, though I'll pass on his cock and balls, if it's all the same to you. Let the crows have them.'

'So who's going to carve him up?'

'I'll do it,' Wulfie piped up. 'The way I see it, with my eyes it could just as well be a wild boar as Gross.'

'In that case, I'll help Wulfie,' Thomas added. 'Make sure he doesn't slice off his own fingers or anything.'

'Well done, boys,' Emma said. 'We'll get the fire ready for a good roast. Toss over his clothes when you're ready. I don't suppose any of us wants his old clothes, do they?'

'I'd rather freeze to death than wear his things,' Doht said. 'And I've got my doubts about eating him, too.'

Wulfie did the best he could. There was as much cursing and gagging as there was severing of body parts.

The head – gleaming and bald without the tabby cat's pelt – was hardest to dislodge. Wulfie lined up the axe on Gross's neck and then raised it slowly before bringing it crashing down. The axe bounced up and Wulfie staggered back a couple of paces.

'How did I do?' he asked Thomas.

'Not bad, Wulfie. Another blow should do it.'

Wulfie was working up a bit of a sweat now.

'What are we going to do with the head?' he asked.

'Don't like the way he's looking at us, all accusing,' Thomas said.

He carried the master cook's head to the hole he'd prepared. Not quite the same as a boar's head borne to the mead table on a platter, but he did it with at least some sense of occasion. Placed the head carefully into the ground. Then, to allow the cook some dignity in death, he put the cat pelt on the dead man's head.

'Sorry, Gross,' he said to the head. 'Hope everything works out for you in the afterlife.'

Then he shovelled some earth over the cook, lest he should be invaded by some woodland sprite and start up a conversation.

The carcass now looked something like a pig's.

'I reckon it won't be too bad sucking the meat off those ribs,' Emma noted, now warming to the notion. 'We'll maybe bury his hands and his feet near to the head. He may need those in the afterlife. Not a bad job there, Wulfie.'

XXVIII

'Here we are then,' Emma said, ladling out the food. 'Your first taste of Redemption Stew.'

Doht gagged. Hazel – beset by doubts now – looked at the stew uncertainly. Emma was right, though, wasn't she? Redemption at last for Gross. The master cook who, in life, had made food sing on the palate. Now, in death, staying the hand of their hunger. And such terrible hunger. Emma knew you needed laughter to strengthen your resolve in the face of hardship or uncertainty.

'Shame old Gross isn't here to enjoy it. I reckon he'd have been full of praise,' she joked. 'Should tide us over 'til the worst of the foodless weeks are past. I was thinking that maybe once the famine's over we should try our luck in the borough: find out if there's any work going. Maybe Thomas and Wulfie could offer their services. See if we can earn a few seedling crops to plant in the clearing.'

She was already tucking into the stew, talking between mouthfuls. Hazel and the others followed her lead. Not Doht, though. Even aching hunger was preferable to the taste of a fellow human, any human, but particularly one such as Gross.

XXIX

It was a mistake to let Wulfie loose in the borough. Misty-eyed and too gullible by half. Thomas was skipping around happily. So many people. So much excitement.

'This place is alive,' he said.

'What are we going to do then?' Wulfie asked.

'You could offer your services butchering carcasses.'

'My, you're on good form, today . . . Slow down, Thomas. Don't go running off.'

Thomas was still jigging merrily, piping a playful tune on his ha'penny whistle.

'You should be a beggar, with talent like that,' a smiling stranger noted. 'You a dwarf or just a child?'

'A dwarf of far-famed lineage,' Thomas chirped, cockily. 'I'm Thomas the Piper, wordsmith and tunesmith to boot, my forebear being the renowned Tom Thumb.'

'Well I never. What they call a perfectly formed *homunculus*. You set yourself up against that wall there, play your pipe, dance your dance and maybe conjure a story or two and you'll soon be a rich man.'

'Wulfie tells folks about his visions of the future.'

'Less call for that sort of thing, I'm afraid, Wulfie. And why are you peering at me?'

'Wulfie can't see too well. He's got the mists.'

'Poor boy. A curse indeed. Anyway, you two settle down there and watch the pennies come . . . Perhaps I should introduce myself. Isaias the Broker.'

'What do you broke, then?' Thomas asked.

'I broker deals,' Isaias informed Thomas. 'For a reasonable cut, I thrust talent into the public gaze and nurture it. Yes, I am a broker of deals, though I'm not averse to broken bones when crossed by thieves and villains.'

'If it's all the same to you, Isaias, Wulfie and I'll look

after ourselves.'

'Very well, but if you ever need a wise old head, you come running to Isaias, young Thomas the Piper.'

'I didn't like the sound of him,' Wulfie muttered.

'Didn't look too pretty, either. Now you sit there looking poor and miserable, Wulfie, and bag up the coins. I'll do the talking and piping.'

Isaias was right. There was money in this begging lark. Thomas was really getting into his stride, throwing himself into the storytelling the way Tom Thumb had done . . . He was cobbling together a tale – inspired by the master cook Gross's demise, but given a new gloss – about how Bas the Bold had grappled with a twenty-foot-tall giant and how the giant had roared with his dying breath to say he'd been slain by Bas. How the reeve had heard the roar from many miles away and instructed his two helpers, High and Mighty, to carry him to the place, so that justice could be dispensed and Law and Order enforced . . . Meanwhile Bas had been wolfing down the bones of the giant, leaving only the winkle and balls, which was all that was left when the reeve, borne by High and Mighty, hove into view.

'I come borne by the High and the Mighty and by the twin virtues of Law and Order,' the reeve panted. 'What say you to the charge of murder?'

'I say I'm Bas the Bold whom no man dares to cross.'

'What are you holding in your hands, if not proof of your guilt?'

'I hold in my hand a prick borne on a couple of bollocks, which bears the look of something else I behold.'

He flung them at the reeve.

'Now be on your way before I eat the three of you.'

'A bit near the knuckle,' Wulfie remarked as the crowds cheered and the odd quartered penny landed in his lap.

'The best ones often are,' Thomas said.

Wulfie tucked the winnings safely into his pouch.

'I reckon we'll be all right for crops, Thomas . . . Thomas? Where are you?'

A group of thugs had collared Thomas and though he was flailing at them, he was overwhelmed.

'Old Isaias wasn't lying, then,' one of them said. 'Could be worth his weight in gold, this one.'

'Thomas? You there?' Wulfie repeated, forlornly, peering into the mist.

Thomas took one last, desperate look at Wulfie, wriggled briefly free of the hand clapped over his mouth, managed to shout over to him:

'Look after Doht for me, Wulfie.'

And he was gone and Wulfie wondered how he could possibly ever find his way back to their clearing on his own.

It would be some while before Thomas would receive tidings as to whether or not he ever did.

Part Five

THE SECOND WISH

SECOND YEAR

I

I start tracing Wulfie's forlorn wanderings on my ha'penny whistle. The notes run in no particular direction. There comes a rap on my wall. Clearly Tolland has quickly tired of this song without structure or melody. The whistle issues Tolland a piercing, short and sharp rebuke.

We'll be friends again soon enough. Tolland bears no grudges. He might be starved of sleep with all that incessant praying of his, but he's the most forgiving of men. Once he's up and about he'll see clearly that my whistle must search in every corner, take my memories – every one of them – by the scruff of the neck and draw the truth from them.

If the notes the whistle demands of my old fingers are not to his liking or mine, then we must suffer them.

Just for once, I impose myself on my wilful ha'penny whistle. I play a hymn of devotion, the one Tolland loves best. I hear him settle his head down again to snatch some sleep. He'll be smiling already. The best friendships are as timeless and enduring as the best music . . .

He's snoring by the time Aart slips into my room, greets me politely and settles at his desk.

Thomas the Piper would be troubled by the faint echo of Wulfie's sad whimpering for many years. Stories without endings can haunt you.

Isaias's words of praise still ring in his ears. A wordsmith should be wary of flattery. A flattered fool is worse than a derided one.

'You, my dear *homunculus*, are verily worth your weight in gold,' he says and Thomas fairly swells with pride.

'. . . But we must hone those story-weaving skills before we set you before kings,' Isaias continues. 'And, skilful and heart-rending though it is, we must take the shrill edge from your piping.'

'Where's Wulfie?'

'Probably bumbling through the streets of the borough, unaware that night's fallen,' Isaias laughs. 'But we'll find him in the morn. Lead him back to his kith and kin. Though if they're all half as talented as you, dear boy, we'll perhaps encourage them to join us.'

'Wouldn't if I were you,' Thomas warns. 'They'd eat you for breakfast, they would.'

'Bravado as well as a story-weaver's tongue. I've heard tell the great Tom Thumb was much the same.'

II

A man with a whistle, a bag of stories, a deal of talent and the right sort of backing can go far. Even claw himself all the way to the presence of Harold Godwinson, the future King of England. But there's a price to be paid. The young man with itchy feet and an aversion to serfdom found himself fettered by Isaias and his thugs. Sweet and honeyed his words of praise might have been, but here was a man who'd cut off his young charge's tongue rather than let him slip into anyone else's hands.

'You're a rare jewel, Thomas, and I understand that a boy might pine for the lost family he held so dear. But consider me your father now. And be warned: I have eyes everywhere. No one crosses Isaias the Broker. And if he does live to tell the tale then he does so *sans* his tongue. A wordsmith with no tongue is as fruitful as a bull with no balls.'

Thomas the Piper decides to take the law into his own hands and late one night, when he's been feigning sleep for some hours and Isaias's thugs have supped too much ale, he slips from his bed in the corner of their quarters. He hears the beat of his own heart as he slides out as silently as a shadow. He knows in those moments how Great-Grandmother Fleda felt as she slipped from the grasp of Queen Elfrith. But it's worth it for the blessed taste of freedom, albeit freedom still soured by fear, because soon the thugs will find he's gone.

He asks questions: does anyone know the way to the borough? And finally a man says: yes, he does know, but Thomas must beware. Isaias must not find him. The man has a closet where Thomas can hide until it's safe for him to be spirited away.

So Thomas climbs into the dark closet. He has misgivings at first: a closet is no place for a young man with itchy, wanderer's feet. But he has no other choices worthy of the name. He thanks the kindly man. Yes, his is a face he would choose to trust. The muffled sounds of his host's movement cease after a while. Silence falls, save the sound of his own heartbeat until it calms. Peace descends at last in the darkness. Finally, eternities later, he hears the man's voice telling him it's night now. It's safe. He unlocks the door. Beside the man stands Isaias. The man clutches his paltry reward in his right hand.

Thomas cowers as he's struck across the head.

'Foolish dwarf,' Isaias rages. 'Did I not offer you the hand of friendship?'

Isaias orders his thugs to take the story-weaver away and shackle him in chains.

'This time, story-weaver, your tongue will be spared. If you try my patience once more, I'll show you no mercy.'

So Thomas the Piper continues to ply his trade under the cold, watchful gaze of his master. He plucks a number of stories from the canon, moulds them afresh and paints tuneful pictures with his beloved whistle.

Each night he returns to his chains. Isaias needn't have bothered with those irons, because Thomas is fettered enough by fear not to chance another break for freedom and the family he misses so sorely.

But it will be a long while before those shackles come off. Isaias isn't a great one for second chances. What forces the change of mind is not soft-heartedness, but a broker's concern over his takings. Thomas the Piper's stories are losing some of their sparkle. The crowds don't take to misery. Something has to give. The storyteller is allowed at last to sleep in his locked room without those cursed irons around his wrists.

For the best part of ten years, Thomas has been enslaved by his keeper. In that time, not a penny has passed into the wordsmith's hands.

'You must understand, Thomas,' Isaias tells him. 'Yours is what we brokers call an *apprenticeship*.' Not serfdom or slavery or daylight robbery, then.

'We need to find you a woman, Thomas,' Isaias says, one day, in a sudden turn-for-the-better of mood. 'Perhaps that might take your mind off your troubles. For far too many years you've moped about that family of yours. Your stories are becoming dulled by the shadow of sadness. Look at me, Thomas. I have no family but my charges. Do you see me moping?'

She arrives within a week.

'This should put the sun back into your tales, Thomas. Perhaps a pinch of spice and bawdiness, too, as you learn to put your dwarf's weapon to good use. She's yours to do with as you please. You have the room to yourselves for one hour only. And' – a cold edge sharpens his voice again – 'you know what will happen if either of you tries to escape.'

She's sobbing quietly. She's as fresh and pretty as the first primrose of spring. She's no taller than Thomas. He asks her her name.

'Ottillie,' she sobs.

'Don't fret,' Thomas says.

'I've never lain with a man,' she says.

'Nor I with a maiden. It's your friendship I wish for. The meeting of minds.'

She looks up. The sobs give way to fully fledged tears. Thomas takes these to be relief. For an hour they talk. Thomas holds her so that they're both comforted. She's been taken from her family, too. Her pain is fresh where Thomas's has been dulled by the years.

When their time's up, Isaias returns.

'You have a flush to you, Thomas. Your fellow dwarf's served you well. Let's hope she can draw your best story-weaving skills from you. Come now, wench.'

Ottillie is put to work serving at a local hostelry. It could be worse, she tells Thomas. Some of the girls are asked to do unspeakable deeds with strangers. Their eyes are dead, she says, and their thoughts away in the distance. This is the only way to bear the pain, they've told her.

Thomas tells her how much he misses his sister, Doht, and the rest.

'Let me be your sister,' Ottillie says. He kisses her, as a brother might. He feels he could love her as a lover, but the moment would have to be right. The risk of spoiling their friendship is too great.

They talk for an hour. Isaias takes her away.

With every passing hour together, their friendship deepens. Thomas the Piper, who thought he knew some of the ways of the world, finds out something new. That it's easier to declare your love – the love that leads to a meeting of flesh – to a stranger than it is to your best friend. At least his stories are now blessed with a bright spirit of chirpiness and an undercurrent of longing.

'You craft stories the way a nightingale sings,' Isaias notes. 'The gift of that wench has heralded the rebirth of your talent. Good thing, too. I need you to be at your riveting best. Word has it that tales of your story-weaving have reached the ears of one of Harold Godwinson's inner circle.'

Harold Godwinson. King-in-waiting. And a restless man, according to Isaias. Impatient for Edward the Confessor to die and vacate his throne. Impatient to get to the end of any story. A man who liked action, whether in the field of battle or in the stories he listened to.

'Forget about the Confessor, Thomas,' Isaias added. 'The man has neither the robust appetite for an earthy story nor the will to govern with any resolve. Godwinson's our man, though we must start at what we call *the bottom of the pile*. Impress the housecarls and their wenches and word will reach the top man before you know it.'

Isaias was right. Word soon reached the top.

Once upon an eternity ago, Tom Thumb had been placed

on King Edgar's mead table, trembling with fear as they waited for him to speak. There had been nowhere to hide as he'd stood there, tongue-tied and terrified. Then the king's comely, reluctant whore had gazed on him with her ocean-green eyes. Words had come babbling from his mouth and the king had drooled in delight as the dwarf brought nuns and wolves to life.

What was it about kings like Edgar or kings-in-waiting like Harold Godwinson that had storytellers groping for words? Perhaps it was the thought that if you displeased them, your reputation was in tatters and, worse still, you might be about to part company with your head. A beheaded storyteller is neither use nor ornament.

When Harold Godwinson walked into a room, he filled it with his presence. If he glowered at you, he filled you with terror. When he smiled at you, you felt you'd walk to the ends of the earth for him . . .

Oh, yes. Thomas walked for Harold, all right. If not to the ends of the earth then all the way up to Stamford Bridge and then back down south again. Kept on walking until William the Bastard came and helped himself to a new country, stripped it bare of everything. Left barely a morsel of hope for a cowed and beaten people to cling to.

But we're racing ahead of ourselves. To a time when Thomas the Piper – an old man, now – will muse:

'Verily the land of the hopeless. A land bereft of joy. This is *Un-glee-land*.'

Tolland will be sitting beside his old and dwarfish friend. His soulmate. As Tolland had known he would be when he'd saved Thomas's skin the first time and, again, when he'd stridden forward, picked Thomas off the floor and carried him away from . . . from . . . he couldn't summon the words to describe their brutality.

'*Brutalité*,' Tolland will say. 'Yes, the Norman oppressors have wrought *forspillednesse* – desolation – on the land they wrenched from us. But they'll not get their hands on our mother tongue, our *Englisc*. Let them foist new words on us . . . Brutality, servitude, subjugation, surrender, legislation . . . and any other fancy words they wish to slip from their forked tongues. But they shan't take that which matters to us. The stuff of life. Our rawest, most heartfelt urges . . . Our love, lust, hate, fear . . . Our sun or our moon. Our wind and rain. Our day and night. The days of the week . . . *Sunnandæg, Monandæg, Tiwesdæg, Wodnesdæg, Thursdæg, Frigedæg, Sæternesdæg* . . . Nor our daily bread.'

III

Back in One Thousand and Sixty-Five, when everyone was waiting for the Confessor to vacate the throne and every Englishman was praying for strong leadership (with a fervency that every Englishman would come to regret), Thomas stood in front of Harold and groped for words. Simple stories about wolves dressing up as grannies or three bears grumbling about Silvanlocks eating their porridge wouldn't do . . .

Thomas picked up his whistle and began to pipe a tune about a weak but astute king who bought peace by offering his throne to Hardrada the Dane, who'd threatened to arrive from the North in his longships. Then he'd offered the same to his brother-in-law, Harold, son of the Earl Godwin and possessor of more lands and wealth than the king himself. And then – and this is the gravest error of all – he'd offered it to the bastard spawn of the Devil. William, first-begotten bastard son of Robert le Diable, Duke of Normandy, and his Harlotta. Why in Frig's name does he offer his throne to the Bastard? To stop him invading from the south, perhaps. Well, let him come now.

Thomas the Piper has placed his whistle back in his belt and, to loud cheers, is spinning a yarn about shipwrecked Norman boats, about Harold's loyal troops lining the Sussex shore and picking off the Norman scum one by one as they struggle on to the beach. And there is William the Bastard, hanged drawn and quartered and just a doodle in the margins of the history chronicles while Harold and his Saxon heroes live in peace and plenty.

A story that met with loud, ringing cheers. But no more than a fairy tale.

'If only,' Tolland will sigh. 'If only . . . In the years since then, these have become the two saddest words in our mother tongue.'

Even Tolland, the most hopeful of men, can't foresee a time when the English people will feel whole again. No longer like turd-weevils, grateful to be feasting on the crap left for them to glean, but fearing all the while the heavy tread of their lords-and-masters. A time when sane men and women will no longer be driven to walking, straight as the flight of an arrow, into a mere and – unable to take any more of this life – throw themselves at the mercy of the Almighty. Risking hell and damnation-without-end rather than bearing another day of life.

'You're blessed,' Tolland will add. 'You can't see the *forspillednesse* wrought on our land or etched on our faces.'

'I may have been robbed of my sight, brother, but I'm not blind.'

Yes. There you have it. Thomas the Piper will end his days as blind as a log. Blind. But able to see things far more clearly.

IV

Thomas the Piper had won over Harold and his housecarls. And for the first time since Fleda and Tom Thumb had fled from Queen Elfrith a member of that far-famed family of fable-mongers had his hand back on the pulse of English history. A pulse that was going to quicken in the fateful year of One Thousand and Sixty-Six.

Wulfie, on the other hand, was not one to go feeling the heartbeat of English history.

Still fresh in his memory was the time he'd bumbled forlornly around in the forest and fallen into an animal trap, though that had ended well enough when, as the new day dawned, he'd discovered he'd found himself a new family. Wulfie had felt the same sense of loss when he'd become aware that Thomas was gone. Alone in a borough full of people – too many people – none of whom he could see clearly. He'd cried out to the mist, shouted out Thomas's name, but Thomas had been spirited away.

He'd sat down on the ground and sobbed. His feeling of panic had given way to something worse. Utter hopelessness. There is no greater blow than the absence of hope.

But then a gentle voice had swum towards him through the mist. A woman's voice. Whether it was an angel or flesh-and-bone Wulfie couldn't say as he peered at the form. When she laid a hand on his arm and asked what ailed him, Wulfie tried – unsuccessfully at first – to stop his sobbing.

He was lost, he told the angel-woman. He'd mislaid his friend, his family and his hope. Couldn't see his way out of the mess he was in because he was afflicted with mist.

Well, according to the angel-woman, you might not be able to stop people from robbing you of your hope, especially if you couldn't see what was going on, but nobody can rob you of your trust, however many times your trust is abused.

It's down to you whether you trust someone or not. It's not down to anyone else.

'So you tell me where you think your friends and your family might be and I'll take you there.'

The angel-woman teased it out of Wulfie, bit by bit. The rough lie of the land. The sort of trees. How wide their trunks were. The way the flow of the water sounded. The smells and the birdsong. The dip of the valley.

They got there in the end.

She led Wulfie home and, sobbing again, Wulfie confessed that he'd lost Thomas. Emma shook her head in disbelief. Hazel wrapped her arms around him and told him it wasn't his fault.

She turned to the angel-woman and thanked her for her act of kindness in rewarding Wulfie's trust and restoring his hope. Ah, if only . . . if only such unconditional goodness weren't rarer than gold. If only those who ran the world were full of such charity.

If only the kingdom hadn't been about to be claimed with brutal efficiency by William the Bastard, Duke of Normandy.

If only. The two saddest words in the mother tongue.

Though things were far from perfect, of course, before the Bastard laid waste a once-verdant land.

Indeed, my sharp-witted scribe has been known to remind me of this fact.

V

Unrest was in the air. The troops were itching for action. In the absence of a foreign invasion, some local sport would have to do. Thomas the Piper was being dragged in through a church door and towards the altar. He pulled and squirmed but what chance does a dwarf have when he's in the clutches of a group of drunken goons? Harold Godwinson's thugs ruled the roost when they'd a mind to. Where was Isaias when finally he was needed to save his charge's skin? Beating a hasty retreat is the answer. Clutching his ill-gotten gains to his bosom as he deserted Thomas. The boldest of bullies make for the worst of cowards.

Ottillie was already there, no longer resisting them: like a trapped animal who's been forced into meek submission.

The priest, kneeling by the altar, praying for deliverance, was hauled roughly to his feet. He managed a weak sign of the cross, as if that might absolve him of the sin he knew he'd be forced to commit.

His hands were shaking as a huge vellum book, which the illiterate warriors took to be a copy of the Bible, was slammed down in front of him.

The poor old priest had never stumbled so haltingly over his lines before.

'Our Father who abides in heaven . . . hallowed be your name . . . your kingdom come . . . your will be done . . . and forgive us our *gyltas* . . .'

Ottillie and the priest kept their eyes cast downward. Thomas glowered at the rabble: the sort of withering gaze that Emma could muster when the mood took her.

'My master will have your guts for garters,' he shouted.

'The little man has a big heart,' one of the warriors laughed.

Thomas turned to Ottillie, who was shaking with terror.

'Let them have their sport. At least walk away with your dignity intact. Unlike theirs. In the eyes of God, you'll still be an unwed maiden. A priest can unmake wedlock as readily as he makes it.'

Though this priest had been reduced to a gibbering wreck.

'Get on with it, fool,' the ringleader shouted.

Someone lifted him from where he stood and placed him between the tiny couple, in front of the altar.

Father, forgive them, for they know not what they do . . .

'Do you take this man to be your lawful wedded husband, your *ceorl*?'

Ottillie looked up at Thomas. She worshipped the ground he walked on. She loved the lilt of his story-weaver's voice. She adored his tall stories. Knew that she'd have given anything to be his wife. The sisterly love she'd always felt for him was no longer enough. She gazed at him the way she had done so often from the dark corners, as he'd stood there, wordsmithing on the stage. She looked into his eyes and said:

'I cannot.'

If wedlock of the priestly sort was to be denied the drunken crowd, then so be it. Wedlock of the commoner sort was a better idea, anyway.

One of the men lifted the girl and sat her on the altar.

Thomas was thrust forward and instructed to deflower her, make her his common-law wife, with witnesses aplenty.

A kneeling stool was needed for him to stand on.

'This is sacrilege,' the priest said, trembling.

Then – right on cue – a loud, insistent ringing of the church bell cut the air and suddenly the mob became aware of itself.

Thomas and his nearly-wife. Saved by the bell. And who was it who'd rung the bell? The bell that had sounded to save them, that rang to mark the beginning of a lasting friendship?

It was a godly man named Tolland, who'd been plucked from a life of quiet devotion in Exeter Cathedral by Harold Godwinson. Charged with curbing the baser instincts of the troops and, more importantly, interceding on Harold's behalf with the Almighty. Because Harold, although steadfast in his faith, was far too busy to say his own prayers when he could pay a holy man such as Tolland to do his praying for him. It was Tolland who'd had enough of his wits about him to save the young piper from a sorry mess. Not for the last time.

VI

'Ottillie,' Tolland will sigh, as he relives the tale with Thomas. 'She was the sweetest girl. I imagine she could have made you happy-ever-after, the way she loved you.'

And Thomas will take up the thread of the story:

'Ottillie was sobbing as I helped her down from the altar. "Dry your tears, my friend," I said. "I would rather have died with a knife in my back than force the meeting of flesh on an unwilling maiden . . . Remember, I know what it is to be a worthless wretch. I may strut on the stage and hold an audience in my thrall, but I never stop being a dwarf inside."'

And no doubt Ottillie had marvelled at how dumb a man could be. How could Thomas not see that he'd already found love? Those eyes could see a story hidden in the most unlikely, hidden-away places but they couldn't see love when it stood, blushing, in front of them.

'Love,' Tolland will say. 'It's like poetry. It's everywhere. Poetry's in the soft tremble of a newly burst leaf, a cloud gilded by sunlight, the soundless flight of a barn owl or a child's contented gurgle. Yes, Love is like poetry. Everywhere, but you must understand it to see it.'

> *Love is as tough as a twisted tree-bough*
> *that bends but refuses to break beneath*
> *the blast and buffet of the strongest storm.*
> *Love is as long as a life that takes its time*
> *to spark across the slow, eternal starlit sky.*
> *Love is as far-up-high as a falcon might fly*
> *were it not for its wound-weakened wing.*
> *Love is dug deep as a sheer drop cut steep in*
> *a waveless and water-starved, dried ocean bed.*

'And Friendship? Is Friendship the same as Love, Tolland?' Thomas will ask.

'Friendship and Love are like a cloak and a tunic. One and the same, but different.'

They often speak in riddles, these educated types.

Ottillie watched from the shadows with unrequited love in her eyes. Thomas was striding confidently on to the stage as though he were a giant. Ottillie marvelled at the way he could raise his spirits, forget about being so small. She couldn't do that. Suddenly she felt tiny, unneeded, unloved, invisible.

Thomas had been tasked with weaving another story. Harold Godwinson gnawed on a chicken's thigh. Spat out a splinter of bone on to the floor.

'What tale have you for us tonight, dwarf?'

'A story of a comely maiden, set upon by thugs, who little knew that she was a sprite who'd return to poison their dreams—'

No one detected Ottillie's blush in the shadows.

'Get on with it then.'

A man in a hurry. Not one for reflection. Indeed, when the wait is over and the Confessor has finally slipped off to the afterlife, Harold will demand a hasty coronation. Unmoved by the splendour of the newly wrought Westminster Abbey, Harold will grab the crown from a startled Archbishop of Canterbury and bring proceedings to a sudden conclusion.

Harold wanted a story and he wanted it fast.

In the front row, the warrior who had lifted Ottillie on to the stone altar hours earlier shifted uneasily on his stool. Thomas the Piper cleared his throat. Gazed, unblinkingly, at him. A painted woman, the worse for drink, was draped on the man's lap.

A hostile audience, this was. One of Thomas's toughest.

'This is the tale of a warrior who thought he was the top dog. He turned to the woman seated on his knee and told her what a hero he was. He told her how, that very day, he'd lifted his foe in the air to subdue them, how they'd pleaded for mercy, but, having the heart of a warrior and knowing that he had the better of a stronger, wiser foe, he'd been deaf to their pleas. The woman seated on his knee asked him how he'd managed to disarm the foe. Ah, there's the rub: his foe was without any weapon . . . Nevertheless, it must have been a mighty heave to lift a foe in the air, what with the weight of all that armour.'

Thomas the Piper has kept his unblinking gaze on the soldier.

'In truth, they had no armour . . . Nevertheless, he must have been a well-muscled foe. No. This one used guile rather than brawn . . . Still, he must have put up a good fight with his fists. Well, yes, though – to be completely truthful – it was a woman, barely more than a girl, a dwarf . . . But still, it must have been a ghastly battlefield. Well, it was a church, if he was being honest. He'd lifted a dwarf-girl on to an altar in a church.'

The rest of the warriors are laughing at their ringleader. It's as if they're absolved of the blame.

'But the girl sitting on the warrior's lap knows that lapping up flattery is the greatest of the man's many weaknesses, so she coos to him that he's still her hero and he can lift her on to an altar and have his way any day of the week. The warrior shapes to lift the woman, but he can't because he's spent all his life-tinder lifting the dwarf-girl earlier in the day.

'"Still," he says, "perhaps I can have my way seated on this stool, with you astride me."

'She lifts her skirts, but the warrior's weapon won't stir, because he spent his weapon-wielding powers when he subdued the little dwarf-girl. The woman sitting on the warrior looks up, bored, and sees a sprite, watching in the shadows. It's the dwarf-girl the warrior had bullied earlier.

'"You're wasting your time with that one," the sprite tells the woman. "There's more life in a corpse than there is in that one's weapon. I've cursed him for eternity. You should take your money and run."

'"Money?" the woman gasps. "I'm no common whore."

'"Then you're as big a fool as your warrior," the sprite says. "You could make a pretty packet selling your body. You tell me you don't take a penny from all these warriors you've lain down with. That makes you worse than a whore. It makes you a fool."

'The woman thinks about it for a while, demands her dues from her fool of a warrior and then climbs off him. She leaves; so there's now only one fool in the room. An impotent, impoverished, cowardly fool.'

There's thunder in the ringleader's eyes. His woman has stormed off in high dudgeon, the jeers ringing in her ears. In the shadows, Ottillie smiles. Her face is radiant when she forgets herself. Regrettably, Harold looks bored senseless.

VII

Did Thomas the Piper's mocking tales curb the indiscipline of Harold Godwinson's men? Not enough to ready them for the battles that lay ahead, it seems.

And what of Ottillie?

She watched Thomas the way Great-Grandfather Tom Thumb had watched his Fleda. Ottillie was unwavering in her love, but never dared to speak of it. And nor did Thomas, because best-friendship had stood in the way of love of the meeting-of-flesh sort. And now the moment was gone. Thomas and the king's men were readying themselves to leave. Word had reached them that the Confessor had finally breathed his last. Harold had taken history by the scruff of the neck and claimed the throne for his own.

Thomas kissed Ottillie on her cheek as he parted.

'Take care,' he said. 'Make sure you find that family of yours again.'

She was unable to reply lest she should shame herself by choking on her words.

'You'll live happily ever after,' he added. 'The prettiest sprites usually do.'

He shaped to tell her he loved her, that he always had from the moment they'd met, that he always would. But the words lodged in his throat. Then he was off. To witness Harold Godwinson's coronation, which would spark an orgy of story-spawning, history-making events.

VIII

A good listener and able to dance the merriest jig, Doht was no mean story-crafter, either. It ran in the blood of brother and sister alike. She also knew her own mind when it came to choosing her life-partner.

There are two sorts of men and you can tell the right sort by watching the way he looks – not at you but at other women. Some men are always hankering for more. These are the ones who'll look you tenderly in the eye and then turn away and wonder what other women might be out there. Oh, they can love you rightly enough, but they have discontent lurking in the pit of their being. The other sort of man is the one who looks at you and counts his blessings. Thankful for what he's got.

Doht knew she'd found her man. Perhaps it had been a dose of luck. Perhaps it was down to fate and the guiding hand of the Wyrd. Some might think that Wulfie looked no further than Doht because of the mists that afflicted him. But Doht saw the turmoil in his eyes as he summoned the courage to stake his claim. That appealed to her. She wasn't one to be impressed by the bold types who come strutting up to you like roosters. Let him take his time. She was in no hurry.

'Easy as falling into an animal trap, ensnaring our Wulfie,' Doht would come to tease him.

And yes, he'd need a nudge in the right direction. Just as he'd needed to be led by the hand when that stranger had found him . . .

Doht remembered the time he'd finally arrived back from the borough, two days after he'd left, covered in dust, his tunic and leather shoes all torn and scuffed. His guardian angel at his side asking him, patiently:

'Does this look like the right place, Wulfie?'

The look of relief on his face when he'd heard their voices. How she was secretly leaping for joy that he'd returned until she heard what he was saying. Those crushing words that snuffed her joy as soon as it had been lit.

'I think I've lost Thomas.'

As if he'd lost a purse of money or a ring. Harry loses six chickens, an axe and a sack of wheat. Wulfie loses Thomas.

'What do you mean, you've *lost* him?' Doht had asked.

'One moment he was there. The next they'd taken him.'

'Who's *they*?'

'I couldn't see,' Wulfie had whimpered.

Time passed. The pain subsided. But the wound of Thomas's absence would never heal. Neither for Wulfie nor for Doht. But she'd long since decided to forgive her Wulfie. It was hardly his fault that he was afflicted by mist.

Doht was watching as Wulfie held his hand in front of his face and moved it towards himself.

'What you up to, Wulfie?' she asked him.

'The only time I can see clearly is when my hand's pressed right up against me. What sort of a curse is that? The only things you can see are the ones pressed up against your face?'

'Would you like to see my face, Wulfie?'

'If it's not too much to ask.'

'You stand still, while I move my face towards you and you can tell me when you can see me.'

Wulfie stood rooted to the spot.

'Can you see me yet?'

'Not clearly.' Though even the fuzzy outline of Doht's features was enough to get his heart pounding.

'What about this?'

'I can nearly make everything out. Not quite, though.'

Doht stopped talking and shuffled a few inches forward so that Wulfie could make out her eyes. Her pale eyes in which he could now see every detail, every fleck. She was so close that she was pressed up against him. She said nothing because her lips were touching his. She felt Wulfie's heart, hammering away. Or was that her heart?

Doht was in no rush to pull away. Not that she could have done so without a struggle. Because Wulfie, who'd spent what seemed eternities summoning the courage to make his move, had now secured his beloved in a bear hug.

'Like a great grizzly bruin,' Doht would confide in Emma. 'Barely able to see and a bit slow coming out of hibernation but a fair old grip with those arms when he has a mind to it.'

IX

Wulfie's heartbeat was slowing back down to a mere canter and Doht was walking around with a smile on her lovely face. The face that he only ever got to see each time his lips were pressed against hers.

Now he had to work up the courage to ask Doht to be his wife, with all the delights that might bring. How many years would that take? Dear Wulfie. Timorous as a dormouse – soft as a *sisemus*, as Doht put it – but a stubborn streak to him. Wulfie, who wouldn't have harmed an earthworm, even if his life depended on it. Others might laugh at him, but Doht knew better. She liked inner strength in a man – the courage to acknowledge his own timidity – much more than any displays of brute force. Wulfie was a man who was never likely to try to mould you into a wife you didn't want to be. Such a man was worth his weight in silver.

Doht would tell the story (no doubt a tall one) about how Wulfie had been looking up into the night sky trying to make out the stars. Doht reckoned she'd found him after he'd just walked into a tree. Claimed she'd heard him apologising to the tree as he knelt on the ground, rubbing his head. Doht had helped him up and brushed him down.

'The way I see it—' Wulfie had begun.

'*The way you see it*?' Doht had scoffed. 'You don't ever see much. Apart from all that guff about what's lurking beyond the here-and-now.'

Wulfie stuck to his task. Perhaps the blow to his head had caused him to mislay his inhibitions.

'That's not what I'm saying. The way I see it, we should become man and wife.'

'About time too,' Hazel had spoken up.

Doht had been too taken aback to reply to Wulfie.

'. . . and while you're at it, you'll need to know about

how you make babies,' Hazel had continued. 'Let me explain a thing or two to you, Doht. Emma can give her version of how these things work to Wulfie and then we'll both make ourselves scarce for an hour or two. Maybe glean some food or perhaps even a few stories. Emma gathers stories the way a squirrel gathers nuts.'

Wulfie had peered plaintively at Doht's fuzzy outline.

'I'm not sure if you said y*es*.'

'Yes, Wulfie,' she replied. 'Now come a little closer so you can see me more clearly.'

Emma's and Hazel's words of wisdom about the making of babies were a success only in so far as they were the spark that lit many nights of unbridled joy. But just as Alfie – all pith and no pips – had seemed unable to plant his seed in Emma, so it was with Wulfie and Doht.

Whatever the reasons – perhaps it was the fact that Doht was always too half-starved to conceive – it would be some fifteen or so years before the blessing of Doht's first pregnancy came about, heralded, as were many other momentous events, by a comet that blazed brightly across the April sky for seven nights in One Thousand and Sixty-Six. Perhaps even Wulfie was able to make the comet out.

X

Wulfie and the rest of them were happy with the slow, gentle heartbeat of the seasons that marked their lives. Thomas the Piper danced to a different rhythm: the throbbing pulse of English history, which seemed to have quickened. Thomas pulled his whistle from his belt to draw music from it. The music of momentous events to come. A song for the comet that had flashed across the night sky, filling heads with foreboding. And then – to comfort and lull the king's men – soft notes, to make-believe all would be well. Thomas the Piper put into music the most make-or-break, all-or-nothing, no-turning-back of years. One Thousand and Sixty-Six. A year when the pulse of English history was racing fast enough to give itself a seizure.

A comet lighting the night sky for seven nights. It was a warning for anyone who cared to note it.

A messenger came and whispered in Harold Godwinson's ear. The newly (and hastily) anointed king pushed back his chair.

'I swear it wasn't a look of thunder but a lightning-strike of exhilaration on his face, Tolland,' Thomas will recount the story to the man who saved him by his bell-ringing. '"The time for music and story-weaving is over, my friends," Harold announced. "Destiny has summoned us." And before long we were off. Not to guard the southern chalk cliffs as we'd all expected. Not to bar the way to the Bastard, but to York . . .'

And when trouble brews, you find out who your real friends are. Isaias, grown fat on the dwarf Thomas's storytelling talents, is gone. Like any broker worth his salt, he fled at the first sign of trouble. But Tolland's friendship is of the all-weather sort. He's going to stay by Thomas's side.

The invaders were led by Hardrada, together with Harold's brother, Tostig.

The enemy were still sleeping when the onslaught began. Caught – quite literally – with their pants down. It gives you a bit of a boost when your foe's still in bed as you start laying into him. A mite inglorious, but who cares? The winners live to tell the tale and they can put a starry afterglow on events.

It was a bloodbath. The victors plundered vast quantities of gold and silver, which would prove something of a curse. Because hot on their heels came a messenger to say they all needed to head south. William of Normandy was about to set sail for the Sussex coast.

The Saxon army could have done without dragging several hundredweight of metals with them, but such is the nature of greed . . .

'Should we not return it all to the monasteries whence the Vikings have just plundered it?' Tolland asked.

'God has thought fit to grant us this bounty,' a housecarl informed him.

So they carried on with their journey. Exhausted, half-starved and about to face a bunch of bloodthirsty butchers, but – on the positive side – rich beyond their wildest dreams.

Tolland was still troubled by the theft. He turned to Thomas.

'So God has generously yielded up his wealth to the cause . . . Strange that our king should claim God is with us. I imagine the Norman duke will claim the same, which has me pondering: is God hedging his bets or does He have no interest in our trifling affairs and cares not a jot who wins? Which must mean that all our leaders are misguided at best and have an inflated sense of their own import? Perhaps my little friend might work this little riddle into one of his stories.'

'Perhaps your little friend values the continued presence of his head too much, Tolland.'

XI

The Battle of Hastings.

William, Duke of Normandy, was a determined man. William the Bastard. A man with an unslakable thirst for power and a man in search of a new name.

William's single-minded ruthlessness was matched by Harold's *ofermodignes*. His arrogance.

The two armies were encamped by the thirteenth of October. William sent more than one message to his counterpart, but Harold made it clear he was in no mood to yield his crown or his kingdom.

'Perhaps Tolland will lead us in prayer before we feast ourselves and then Thomas can bind us in his storytelling spell while the Bastard and his curs hear our happy revelry and salivate with hunger. A final fast for those Norman and French scum before we put them to the sword.'

Tolland prayed that God would see fit to take the side of the English. That He'd grant wisdom and patience to their king. That He'd speed the arrival of the supporting troops coming from the west. That he'd allow peace to fall like refreshing, fine rain on a happy people.

Tolland's prayers fell on deaf ears.

A night of drunkenness and storytelling. The Saxons awoke the following morning, sleep-starved, shattered and with sore heads. Had common sense prevailed, Harold would have waited for reinforcements to arrive. Perhaps held back, even then, and waited until – dejected, terrified and weak with hunger – the invaders gave up and slunk back home. A few thousand men would have been powerless against the Anglo-Saxon hordes. But perhaps Harold was thinking he needed to show his men he was a fearsome leader. Perhaps he was thinking that if he didn't crush the Bastard now, he'd be back again and again, like some niggling infection. Perhaps Harold just wasn't thinking straight because he had a gutful of ale and a headful of pain. At least he had the sense to choose the best site: the top of a wooded slope fronted by marsh.

Meanwhile, Tolland was despatched to a nearby church and ordered to spend the best part of the day on his knees in prayer.

'God speed you,' Harold said to the man of God. He patted the rear of the mule Tolland was seated on. The beast snorted at the king and ambled off a short distance before giving in to temptation and stopping to help itself to a piece of English sward. Then either the mule or Tolland farted and they were off.

'Let's not pin all our hopes on Tolland and the Almighty,' Harold exhorted his housecarls. 'I suspect they'll not get to their church before we're done.'

Tolland, the Almighty and the mule notwithstanding, the Bastard would be insane to press ahead now. But the Bastard *was* insane. At that moment, the Normans became beset by doubt, believing they were doomed. It took the intervention of the French to restore order. The Frenchmen were led by Eustace, Count of Boulogne, who'd subsequently be double-crossed by the Bastard and who'd do his own bit of double-crossing with a botched attempt to rid the English of their Tyrant-King William a couple of years hence.

Eustace's *jongleur*, Taillefer, ventured out from amongst his fellow countrymen and, sitting on horseback, started juggling his sword in the air to rally the troops.

There was a bemused silence from the English as he finished:

'Dear God, our Father, let not France be shamed.'

It occurred to those Normans who'd caught his drift that they were fighting for the Danish enclave of Normandy, not France, but they cheered along all the same. They could get back to their usual hostilities with the French once they'd stuffed the English. Never a good idea to fall out with all your neighbours at the same time. Try to keep at least one of them sweet.

Harold was affronted that the enemy had the gall to insult them so. That they should claim his God, the God of the English, for their own. Without allowing his own wordsmith any time for preparation, he called forward the storyteller on whom he'd leaned many times before to rally his exhausted warriors.

'Follow that one, Thomas,' he instructed his man.

What was he expecting? Did he want Thomas to outperform Taillefer with his sword-juggling showmanship? Or – more likely – declaim a stirring Anglo-Saxon epic to keep everyone in the story-weaver's thrall for a few hours while their headaches subsided and further troops dribbled in from the west? Either way, Harold didn't, of course, hang around long enough for Thomas to ask his lord-and-master.

Defying convention, Thomas found a way to upstage the French *jongleur*. He strode forward, stopped, turned and, facing his fellow Saxons, his back to the Normans, inspired by the example of Tolland's incontinent mule, he dropped his pants. Holding his pipe carefully in position to give some melody to his efforts, he delivered a good, old-fashioned fart. Much more eloquent than all that French gibberish. Yes: Thomas the Piper broke wind with great gusto in the direction of the enemy. To enormous home cheers.

First blood to the English.

But a pyrrhic victory, as it happened. Not wishing to decry the efforts of those who were to spend the next few years leading failed uprisings, culminating in Hereward's last stand at Ely, this was to prove the last defiant gesture by a race that was about to be crushed.

Taillefer was livid at having been so insulted by a fellow *raconteur*. He led a suicidal charge into the massed ranks of the Saxons. Battle had at last been joined.

The history books tell you what happened.

Once upon a time, a ruthless bastard came in search of a new name . . .

The invaders slaughtered the English, who'd been holding their ground until William's troops feigned a ragged retreat. Our boys dived in and suddenly found that the Normans had conned them and were picking them off like fleas.

The Almighty was still dithering about whose side He was on. Three times, William lost a horse beneath him, weakened by all the arrows lodged in them. He mounted the fourth one as Tolland's stubborn nag managed to amble as far as the churchyard and was helping itself to some of the lush grass there. Tolland left the beast to get on with it as he entered the church to begin his entreaties.

Perhaps if he'd . . . No. There's no point in torturing yourself, wondering how things might have turned out. You can rewrite the past but you can't change it.

You can reweave history the way those patriots who stitched up their embroidery did. Their slave-labour of love for Odo, Bishop of Bayeux. How were Odo and his brother, William the Bastard, to know that, by threading that arrow into Harold's eye, the seamstresses were having their little joke at the invaders' expense? That arrow was a nod towards Zedekiah, leader of Judah. Forced under fear of death to swear allegiance to the pagan Babylonian tyrant Nebuchadnezzar. Blinded by that ruthless thug of a king when he dared to stand up to him. The Normans might have won the war, but, when it came to anarchic humour, the Anglo-Saxons won by a clear head.

Once the Normans and their allies had broken through, there was carnage. Thomas the Piper became aware that the chain-mailed, sword-wielding victors were bearing down on the remaining Saxons, from north, south, east, west and every point between. Never in his life had he felt such overwhelming, bowel-emptying, leg-crumpling fear. As others turned to flee, Thomas lay prone. Rasping for mercy.

Perhaps it was the prayers of Tolland, now on his knees, calling on God and all the saints and all the pagan idols to come to the aid of his friends. Perhaps it was the distraction of the fleeing Saxons, who seemed to be more interesting quarry. But, if you believe in hope and wishes and fairy tales, then it was the silver penny that saved him.

Thomas felt the hem of his tunic, clutched the penny bearing the head of Edgar: a black-and-white Saxon king, but one who'd have sent William scurrying back to Normandy in next to no time . . . Thomas the Piper made the second of his three wishes.

He wished for the *Gift of Life*.

The Gift of Health he already had, but at that moment mere survival was more pressing. What benefit in being a perfect, unblemished specimen, if you were a corpse?

The clash of iron sword on iron sword had ceased. The groans of the wounded abounded, only to subside as the invaders ran them through with their weapons, eliciting sickening final, curdled screams of terror as the Saxons met their ends. Then the sound of chainmail being pulled from bodies. The clanking as it was thrown into piles, along with the knives and swords.

Then came the softer percussion of bodies being overturned, dropped to the ground.

Keep saying your prayers, Tolland. Pray for the life of your little friend. His second wish may have been granted, but let's not take any chances. We've seen the outcome of ofermodignes *already today.*

Someone picked Thomas up.

The end, surely. But no. Thomas slumped. Fell limply to the ground as the Norman discarded him. He closed his eyes. Dreamed of days when he and Doht had piped and danced. Where was Doht now? Hazel? Emma? And Wulfie? Had Wulfie peered into the future and seen this carnage coming?

And Tolland . . . Tolland had walked towards the rising

sun to seek the help of the Almighty but the Almighty had not been prepared to listen.

When Thomas dared to raise his head, an uneasy peace had descended. Crows picked at the eyes of dead warriors. The birds scattered as the odd person, scavenging for clothing or other bounty, moved among the corpses. Thomas rose to his feet. His beloved pipe had been snapped in two. Perhaps by some Norman or Frenchman, still smarting at the insult the little Saxon entertainer had blown their way. He picked up the two pieces, but then thought better of trying to summon any music. He discarded it and turned to leave. A free man. No longer beholden to King Harold, or bound by the people-peddler Isaias. But – like every other Englishman – enchained by a conqueror.

Thomas walked towards the rising sun. Determined to track down Tolland and his trusty farting mule. And while the beast stood there, munching grass and breaking wind, Thomas would chastise the man of God for his feeble attempts at intercession. Then he would explain how he came to be in possession of the Gift of Life, perhaps the greatest gift that can be granted.

XXII

'Praise the Lord,' Tolland rejoiced, stretching his arms out to greet his friend Thomas. 'He's spared you. The most fervent of all my prayers has been answered.'

How many Englishmen lined up against the invaders on Saturday the fourteenth of October, One Thousand and Sixty-Six? Hard to say for certain, but Thomas the Piper, as Tolland's Almighty is his witness, says he reckons on some seven thousand or more.

Many died. Many fled. Only one stayed on the field of battle, clutching a three-wish penny. Remained there, but survived until the Sunday morning.

They'd all had faith in Harold. Start believing too strongly in a man like Harold Godwinson and you may even be prepared to die for him. Pin your hopes on the wrong man, though, and your belief comes back to bite you. Saxon faith had taken a battering from which it would be hard to recover.

'From now on, Tolland, I shall have faith in nothing or no one. Not in the leaders who inspire. Not in this Almighty of yours who's never at the right place at the right time. From now on I believe only in *me, mec, ic*; in me, myself, I.'

'And in love, friendship and hope, Thomas.'

'True enough, brother. I believe in love and friendship. Though I'm less sure about hope, having seen what our new leader's capable of.'

'He's mortal, like the rest of us. He'll not be around for ever. In the meantime, might I suggest we go and spread some love and hope and friendship and perhaps the odd story? Though I see you've mislaid that whistle of yours, so I trust you'll still be able to enthral the crowds. Now if we can get this blasted beast to shift, we can be on our way.'

The mule let rip a resounding fart that engulfed the three of them.

XIII

Yes, William of Normandy was as mortal as any other tyrant. But it would be another twenty-one years before he proved it.

When William the Bastard landed at Pevensey Bay, he came in search not of immortality but of two other things: a kingdom he believed it was his God-given right to rule; and a new name. Well, he found the latter. And though Providence might eventually rob him of his dignity in death, nothing could ever take William the Conqueror's new name away from him.

'A worthy cognomen for an unworthy thug,' Tolland will mutter.

Part Six

THE LAST WISH

I

One of the Bastard's henchmen snapped my ha'penny whistle in two. The way they broke a nation's spirits. The way they'd break its resistance. Break its heart.

Tolland would thoughtfully hand me a new whistle in time, but, though it can blast a merry enough melody when the mood takes it, things have never been the same. Perhaps it's the four walls of my room that fetter me. Perhaps the brothers hold me back, what with their quiet words of admonishment when I play with loud abandon. Perhaps my leathery old lips can't conjure the unbridled joy they once could.

Whatever the reasons, I miss my first ha'penny whistle the way I miss the people I love. My new whistle knows this. It comforts me. Draws its soft tunes gently from my old lungs. Uses my breath sparingly. Not long, it encourages me.

They broke your first whistle in two. They broke your heart. But you lived to tell the tale. They haven't broken you . . .

Not long. My scribe no doubt draws comfort from these words, too. I know he'd rather be dancing his lovers' dance with Edie the novice nun. He'll not say so, though. He's such a polite, modest young man. My scribe, Aart. My sister's son. He didn't even catch his breath when I told him the Creator sent a comet to herald his coming. Maybe that's because he believes only half of my tales. Or maybe he's heard them so many times that they no longer have him on the edge of his bench. Or perhaps he's so tired of his scribings he just wants it all to be done.

'The end is nigh,' I encourage him.

'So say some of the brothers,' he replies, 'though I hear and see nothing in heaven or earth to support their claims.'

'I've brothers-in-Christ in the glorious citadel of Exeter,' Tolland announced, thwacking the mule with a birch twig to get it moving. 'Far enough from the Bastard for you to relax, my tiny, stout-hearted friend. Close enough to civilisation for us to taste life. We'll shelter in the house of God. Perhaps I'll continue my conversations with the Almighty. Seek clarification over why he's visited the Bastard on our land.'

'Conversations with the Almighty tend to be a little one-sided, brother. I've never heard tell of the Almighty getting a word in edgeways.'

'I should have thought such one-sided conversations would be to a storyteller's liking. Aren't they the stock and trade of a storymonger?'

'One puts up with the sound of one's own voice for what follows: the laughter, applause, the cheering. Your Almighty tends to prefer plagues and pestilence to applause.'

'You forget about the joys He grants you, Thomas. The bounty from the earth. The warmth of the sun. The gift of life you cherish so. Ah, my friend, we have many years of banter and friendship ahead of us.'

Thomas the Piper. Tolland. A tongue-tied, tight-lipped Almighty. And a foul-smelling mule.

The mule had stopped again to tear at some tufts of grass. Tolland struck it smartly across its rump.

'Exeter's a long walk, Tolland. Are you sure we want this beast slowing us down? Should we not part company with it?'

'Patience, my friend. I'm sure the Almighty granted me this beast for a reason.'

'Just as he's granted us the Bastard.'

'Besides, it may repay us handsomely if we need to trade it for food.'

'Perhaps it might be easier to eat the mule. I've had worse in my time.'

'All right, I'll admit it . . . I've only known the brute for a day or two but I've already grown fond of it. Not least because it bore me away before the carnage of Hastings.'

'Your choice of friends must be very poor indeed, Tolland.'

They came with their hounds. The Normans – aided and abetted by turncoat Saxons – searching for signs of life in the forest. Let it be known, they proclaimed. These were now the cherished hunting grounds of William of Normandy. Anyone sullying them or plundering them would be dealt with mercilessly. They must now bow before their new overlord and his henchmen.

The usurpers spoke in a strange tongue, though the meaning was often clear enough.

'*Vite! Vite!*' a man in chainmail barks, pointing his sword in the direction of the borough.

'I think he means: Fleet! Fleet! Go to the borough,' Hazel ventures.

Stay within eyeshot and work for the new master as he thinks fit. There will be work aplenty in the borough. The new king has plans – many plans – to build towering structures to the glory of God, in thanks for his victory. And, of course, a place for the victors to lie safely in their beds.

Wulfie had the right idea. Doht, too. Don't look beyond the end of your nose. Hear no evil. See no evil. Only curse your Norman oppressors when you're well out of their way.

Emma, though, was unable to keep her lips buttoned. Telling folks her spellbinding, near-the-knuckle stories. Fixing the mangy, misfit Norman thugs who were now supposedly her masters with that withering gaze of hers. It was surely only a matter of time before one of them would lose their temper and she'd be finished. Just one casual but well-aimed swipe of their swords was all it took.

'You can see the fear in their eyes. Look how they scour the land hunting in their packs,' she said to Hazel.

True enough. You could most definitely see fear in

their eyes. You'd feel fear if you were in a strange country, outnumbered by about a thousand to one, even though you're mounted on your steed, you're dripping with chain mail and helmeted, you have your sword in your hand and you have the right to grant life or death to your subjects on a whim.

But consider this. Why does a grown man step on a harmless spider the size of his hand? Not to snuff out the spider's life but to snuff out his own fear.

'Be careful, Emma.'

Wise words from Hazel's marred lips. Don't insult your new master; try something much more satisfying instead. Pluck any one of a number of Norman words to describe it, because there are plentiful supplies of Norman words to describe all manner of evil. Call it *subterfuge*; call it the most delicious subterfuge of all: *irony* (although admittedly these are Roman words that slipped into the mother tongue in Norman clothing).

When you're without weaponry (because every Saxon has been denied the right to carry his knife – his *seax*, which gave him his Saxon identity) you use your language. Your language and theirs. You develop the knack of speaking to your oppressor in mock-servitude and in the most glowing, praiseful terms. You walk away, with your head suitably bowed. Then you and your fellow men snigger in triumph as your Norman overlord rides off with his chest puffed out and his head held high. Yes: oppression is the root of all irony. When you're starved of food and hope, irony is a deliciously tasty brew.

Hazel understood the healing power of irony. Emma was too stubborn to listen.

Hazel's telling them about the latest piece of subterfuge. One of the men who serve at the mead table in the newly wrought castle has told her all about it. His Norman master demands the finest wine; no English mead or wine or ale is worthy enough to touch his lips. His wine has a lovely golden hue. Unbeknown to the overlord, the wine has been fortified with a quantity of the best English urine. As he carries the jug to the table, the waiter is not carrying the finest wine but taking the *micgan*.

'We need action, not buffoonery,' Emma says, bitterly. 'The Normans should be burned from the land like a blight.'

Maybe she's right. Merely taking the piss is a futile little gesture. Then again, the uprisings that are going to take place in the forthcoming years, led by Harold's sons, by Swein and the lords of Mercia, by Eustace of Boulogne, by Edgar the Ætheling (true heir to the throne), by Hereward, by anyone who's anyone . . . maybe those uprisings will prove just as hopeless. Maybe they'll be worse, because they'll stiffen William the Bastard's resolve to the point he starts laying waste the land he's conquered. Hell-bent on crushing all hope from his brutalised subjects.

Wulfie speaks up.

'By my reckoning, one ruler's just like any other. They're all Bastards and Conquerors, when it comes to it.'

If you looked no further than the end of your nose, tried not to peer into the middle distance, life was tolerable enough, he reckoned. As long as you spent it with the people you loved.

'Well said, Wulfie,' Doht agreed.

Wulfie was so happy these days, it was as if the invasion had never happened. What did he care about such things when he could hold his hand against his beloved's swollen belly and feel the child kicking inside her?

He still recalls the day he found he was to be a father. Doht had been on her knees, her left hand pressed against her stomach, her right hand held out against the trunk of an elm tree for support. She'd groaned as she'd retched.

'Can I help?' Wulfie had asked.

'Yes. You can help by going off and garnering some pennies for your family,' Hazel had replied. 'She's suffering nothing more than a dose of *morgenspiwing*.' Morning sickness.

Wulfie had peered at her. Blankly.

'She's carrying your baby,' Hazel had explained. 'Babies are a source of much happiness and copious amounts of sick. First their mother's, as you can see. Then a lot of their own.'

'Well, when she's through with puking, please tell Doht I'm the proudest of men,' Wulfie had informed Hazel, grabbing his over-cloak.

III

They made their way to the borough, as instructed by the chain-mailed thug with the sword. Wulfie felt the usual wave of remorse at the loss of Thomas as the town hove into view. This time it was heightened by the fact that he was unable to share the good tidings of his impending fatherhood with his friend and brother-of-sorts.

The first task was to find somewhere to live. If they'd hoped for something to match even their mean and lowly forest homes, then they'd have had a rude awakening. They haggled over and finally secured the crudest of lodgings. What was good for the Virgin Mother and the unborn Redeemer was good enough for them. Though you imagine it must have been a deal warmer in Bethlehem.

Wulfie then found some ill-paid, dispiriting work clearing scrub to make way for the new master's fortification.

Wulfie and a scythe . . . It was a sight to strike fear. Distracted by thoughts of what the future might now hold, Wulfie was wielding the scythe with wild abandon. The other workers left him a wide berth.

The Creator had granted Wulfie a useless pair of eyes. But Wulfie reckoned on telling his child – whom he prayed would be blessed with Doht's perfect vision – to put those eyes to good use. Clumsily, he'd grope for his hands and then hold them. Explain to the child that he must put these hands, nimble as their mother's, to good use, too.

Only by grafting until you've mastered the gifts of reading and writing will you become free. Because when you can read, you can glean all manner of knowledge. And when you can write, you can spread knowledge. And in knowledge lies the power to shape the dreams of others.

Wulfie's dreams of distant horizons were brought to an abrupt end when the blade came down on him. Someone came over when they heard Wulfie howl. They tore a strip from his over-cloak and tied it tightly around his foot. Wulfie was determined to carry on with his work. He needed the meagre pay. But, as blood continued to seep from the wound, he felt himself weakening. Someone offered a shoulder to put his weight on. They held Wulfie's bloodied scythe for him as they led him home.

Emma rolled her eyes.

'What are we going to do with you, Wulfie?'

'Comfrey,' Doht suggested. 'We must gather lots of it, to bathe the wound.'

'You stay put,' Emma told Doht. 'Hazel and I'll go gathering the comfrey. You need to keep your strength up enough to look after two children: one curled up inside you and this helpless great lummox lying groaning on the floor.'

IV

Progress was slow and not just because of the recalcitrant – the *fæstan* – mule. Thomas and Tolland stopped at each settlement and often found themselves party to stories of the atrocities wrought by the usurpers. Some bragged boldly of how they'd send the scum scurrying back to their homelands. Some spoke with forlorn acceptance of defeat. One fortunate old man, his memory having dimmed like a spent candle and his mind already somewhere in the afterlife, was surprised to hear that the Confessor was no longer their king.

'Perhaps there's bliss to be had in living in happy ignorance, in darkness,' Tolland mused.

Wasn't this the firm foundation on which the Church had been built? Thomas bit his lip. He wasn't ready for another discussion on the nature of belief or the whims of the Almighty.

Wherever they stopped, the threesome was rewarded with food – scarce though it was – and shelter. Tolland's ragged habit and Thomas's silken story-weaving skills were also enough to release them from the odd setback as vagabonds approached them, looking to fleece them of their worldly goods. It was clear to anyone that they were carrying nothing of any value (the three-wish penny having been secreted again in Thomas's hem). The mule seemed to elicit at best sympathy or at worst scorn, and (more often than not) revulsion on account of the stench it gave off. On just one occasion, a vagabond, having established that there was no money or other goods to be filched from the two travellers, made the unwise decision to mount the mule and make his getaway. Thomas and Tolland, travelling at the slow pace of two men who'd already covered too many miles for comfort, soon caught up with the beast, who was snorting noisily and farting loudly as the vagabond thrashed it repeatedly. Tolland smiled at the man.

'Heed the message of the Almighty,' he implored the man. 'Hear the words of He who rode into Jerusalem on a humble donkey. Repent of your sins, and He shall set you free.'

Miraculously, the man seemed to be swayed by Tolland's powers of persuasion and joined him in a prayer for his blemished soul before he departed, seemingly on the best of terms with the man whose mule he'd just tried to rob. Though the vagabond cast a distinctly unchristian look at the mule.

'A sinner saved,' Tolland sighed happily. 'Go forth and sin no more,' he shouted after the man.

'You think he'll avoid temptation then, brother?' Thomas murmured as they set off again.

'For at least a week,' Tolland observed. 'Though I doubt he'll try his hand at the sin of mule-theft again.'

He ruffled the beast's coarse, dusty coat. They looked at each other with something that could have passed for tenderness.

'Help yourself to a little grass, my friend,' Tolland whispered. 'We're on the final stretch now. Exeter must be no more than two days away. Then we can all rest our weary bodies.'

V

'I thought your time had long past, but it's not a bad idea, getting in the family way,' Emma informed Doht. 'I know exactly what men are like. These Norman usurpers are mad with the taste of power. They make slaves of the men and whores of the women.'

'Not whores,' Hazel corrected her. 'A maiden taken by force is still a maiden, to my thinking.'

'Though not to the thinking of any but the most love-struck of suitors,' Emma said, prodding at the fire the way Fleda had done. She'd inherited so many of her grandmother's mannerisms, including that outspokenness.

'Well, if anyone defiled Doht, I'd love her no less.'

'You're a good man, Wulfie,' Emma conceded. 'Though I'm not sure I'd want to be protected by a man who slices open his own foot with his scythe. Anyway, as I was saying: not a bad idea to be in the family way to keep the Normans at bay. Dress as modestly as you can and never look your Norman masters in the eye.'

A fine piece of advice from a woman who was never quite able to avert her withering gaze from the lords who were unlikely ever to master her. She was right, though. Those Norman had no qualms about deflowering the more pleasing-on-the-eye of the Saxon girls whenever they chose to, indifferent to the heartache and pain they left in their wake or the years of suffering they sowed.

Wulfie lay in the corner, his leg throbbing. He felt miserable and powerless.

'Dearest Wulfie,' Doht sighed. 'Let me dress your wound again.'

Emma watched. Recalled how, eternities ago, she'd bathed the whip cuts Alfie the Stammer had borne to save her from a beating. Wulfie and Alfie would have rubbed along well: a couple of the wisest of fools.

VI

'Civilisation, at last.' Tolland beamed as he saw the city walls. 'What do you reckon, Thomas? How about the far-famed tale-weaver, the Piper of Hastings entering the east gate astride a mule? Not unlike our Lord on his donkey . . . What do you think, Mule?'

'Mule reckons the dwarf would be better walking and the dwarf agrees. The Galilean might have been foolhardy enough to enter Jerusalem on a donkey, but he'd have had more sense than to sit on this beast.'

'I fear we must be a gruesome sight, my friend. Many months marching around this country of ours will have taken its toll. Nonetheless, we should all feel at home in this city. I've heard it said there are upwards of two and a half thousand souls crammed within those ancient Roman walls. Enough humanity to mask the stench of our mule . . . and enough listeners to line your pockets when you regale them with stories of your heroism.'

'I think I need water and rest before I can summon any stories, Tolland.'

'Then rest you shall have aplenty, my friend. While you restore that little body of yours, I'll minister to my flagging soul. First we must seek sanctuary for the two of us in the great Bishop Leofric's care, and before that, I've my tonsure to attend to. His Grace insists we brothers should all shave our heads to represent our Lord's crown of thorns. He's a stickler for a well-groomed tonsure.'

'Why?'

'Must you ask why? Do you ask why the moon is white or leaves are green or why our mule should fart without ceasing?'

'Once a story-crafter stops asking *why* his craft will be

diminished.'

'A fine wordsmith you may be, Thomas. But to my mind you lack faith, my friend. A faithful servant of the Redeemer asks not *why*, but *how* he may serve the Almighty.'

'Oh, I have faith enough, Tolland. I have faith that when I fall asleep I'll wake again and faith that the sun will rise each day. I even have faith in you. Faith, as well, that words will come pouring from my storyteller's mouth when needed. I just lack faith in this Almighty, who seems to have taken the side of the usurpers who've wasted no time in spreading their poison over our land.'

'Well, either way, I suggest we clean ourselves up and I beg some barber to trim my tonsure before we throw ourselves on the mercy of Bishop Leofric. I also suggest you curb that adder's tongue of yours if he's not to throw us out on our ears.'

'You have my word, brother.'

'And another thing, Thomas – I'll whisper it, so we're not overheard – we'll need to sell Mule, here, to provide ourselves with pennies for my haircut and some food to fill our bellies before we announce ourselves. Bishop Leofric's not a great one for feasting and revelry. More of a bookish type. Finds nourishment in the written word.'

Ridding themselves of the stinking mule. This was something they might perhaps agree on.

VII

Wulfie had braved the scrubland again, hobbling along awkwardly and painfully. Comfrey or no comfrey, that wound was refusing to heal. Perhaps something stole into him when he gashed his leg so horribly with his scythe. How would Wulfie know what it was? He wouldn't have seen it anyway. According to the others, all blessed with clear-sightedness, the spirits that bore plague and pestilence were never seen by the eyes of men. Just supposing, Wulfie thought. Just supposing that, as a tiny seed falls on the land and grows into something larger and more powerful, there are living things flying in the air, so small that not even Doht or Emma or Hazel could see them. What if they were sown like seeds in your wound and grew into something more powerful . . .

Wulfie cast his thought aside. If it were that simple, he told himself, some clever person would have told of such things already.

It had been a long day. They'd moved on from clearing scrub to piling earth to digging what seemed to be awesomely large foundations and Wulfie was ready for home. He ached with hunger. Prayed that there would be something to eat that night. Surely Hazel and Emma would have gleaned something? Starvation was biting, though.

The Norman master and his fellow thugs watched with indifference as the peasants began to give up the ghost. A peasant was only as worthful as he was skilled. They weren't good for much, these Saxons. Fair enough, they knew how to work silver and how to stitch fine embroidery or bring a manuscript alive in the fairest hand. But what use were such skills in this day and age? True, these Saxons were hard working enough when it came to heaping up earthworks for their masters to build their castles on. Though that sort of labour was easily replaced. There was an endless supply. Those who could work timber were perhaps of some worth. But a wooden castle was a mere fleeting structure: offering shelter before you raised up stone strongholds and stone cathedrals to make these serfs gasp in awe. And if you wanted men who could work stone, you looked not to the Anglo-Saxons but to the French. A moody bunch, but they understood stone all right.

The long and the short of it was this: the likes of Wulfie and his kin were as useful as a horse with two legs. If men such as Wulfie wilted and fell by the wayside, then let them die.

Wulfie groaned each time he thrust his spade into the ground. He was racked with pain. Growing weaker by the day. They all were. As thin as willow fronds, the four of them. Afflicted by sniffles and sores. What manner of life was this? No life for their child: that much was sure.

There comes a time when a man must take control. Wulfie knew what he had to do. The others would try to talk him out of it, but they were wrong. They might be able to see the birds alighting from the trees. They might be able to see the pain etched on each other's faces. They might even be able to summon the fearlessness to look their Norman overlord in the eye and see his hatred and contempt written bold. But none of them could see beyond their own hinterland the way that Wulfie could. None of them could see the trouble that brewed. This was just the start. It was as far removed from the suffering that would follow as the first spots of rain are from the full-frontal, thunderous, lightning-striking storm.

VIII

As it happened, neither the barber nor the baker would take as much as a farthing from Tolland or Thomas the Piper: a man of God and a story-weaver who'd survived Hastings. Furthermore one who'd aimed a well-judged *pettum* – a wholehearted Anglo-Saxon fart – at the Bastard. These were not two men you could charge for a tonsure-trim or a loaf of bread. Not without fear of damnation.

'I only ask that you take that malodorous mule away from my stall,' the baker gasped. 'Such a presence is not good for trade.'

Thus Mule was spared the indignity of being sold for the price of a neat tonsure.

'Peace be with you, my friend. May God bless you for your kindness.'

Mule snorted as Tolland smacked him on his left haunch to get him moving.

'I suspect Leofric will be assailed by similar misgivings, Thomas,' Tolland continued.

'Perhaps Leofric has gleaned a morsel or two of wisdom from reading all those books, then.'

Exeter was a glorious, foul, awesome, filthy, beautiful city. It had only been a bishopric for less than twenty years, having wrested its status from the less impressive town of Crediton, whose claims lay in antiquity as the birthplace of St Boniface. Edward the Confessor, fearing for the safety of the saint's dusty old bones, had agreed they'd be safer entombed in a house of God behind the sturdy Roman walls that ringed Exeter.

'Inside this cathedral sits one of the finest libraries in the land,' Tolland assured Thomas and the mule.

'What use is a library against our Norman oppressors?

Do we throw the books at them?'

'The thrust of the quill cuts deeper than the sharpest sword, Thomas.'

'I fear we live in different worlds, Tolland. I'd rather be stabbed by a feather any day of the week. Even Mule's looking at you as if you're talking bollocks.'

'Ah, my friend. The glory of written words is that they can fly from one place to another. From one age to another. I can dip my *fethere*, my quill, in vitriol and can wound an enemy I haven't even seen. I can stir up unrest. And I can dip the same pen into my gleaming, glory-be-to-God liquid gold and craft images so bright and beautiful they'd have you gasping.'

'Talking of gasping, I reckon Mule's dropped another one. Maybe we can use his hide for one of your beloved books. Make him more useful in the afterlife than he is in this one. What do you think to that, Mule?'

Mule didn't deign to reply.

'Anyway,' Tolland droned on. 'All this talk of swords and feathers is so much hot air. The Bastard will have been sent packing back to Normandy within the year. You mark my words, Thomas. If I'm wrong, I'll eat Mule in one sitting as my penance.'

Mule looked up a mite anxiously. Bared his teeth in a grimace and shuddered. The flies that had taken to his coarse coat all scattered, momentarily.

'On second thoughts, I might suggest some other less demanding penance . . . Anyway, we're approaching the gates of the cathedral. Your best behaviour, Thomas. Keep your godless thoughts and doubts to yourself. And none of your bawdier stories until we're settled in. Just think about the bed and the food. And, Mule: try to desist from farting while we greet our new-found friends.'

'Ah, brother,' Tolland greeted the man at the cathedral door. 'We have travelled far, fleeing the wrath of the Bastard. Our faith has been sorely tested by our trials and tribulations, but, like Job before us, we have remained as steadfast as this mule we bring as our humble gift. We come in peace and love and fall at your feet in the fervent hope that you'll grant us beds in your sleeping quarters and a place in your hearts—'

'Enough, my brother. Come on in.'

IX

'I'll brook no argument,' Wulfie growled masterfully. 'My mind's made up. I've seen into the yonder and before us stretches *orwennes ond forspilledness* . . .'

Orwennes. Hopelessness. When you say the word, you expel the air from your lungs, then draw breath again. *Forspilledness*. You spit the word as you would a curse. If you say them in the Norman way that's wheedled itself into the mother tongue – if you utter the twin evils of *despair* and *desolation* – they have a sly, deceitful charm. They fall from your lips: soft, sensual, as seductive as sin.

Wulfie had never been more determined.

Then someone tapped him on the shoulder.

Wulfie leaped where he stood. The bane of misty eyes was that life was always full of such surprises. Unexpected taps on your shoulder when your mind was elsewhere. Fallen trees that tripped you as you walked. All manner of other bothersome burdens.

'Talking to yourself, again, Wulfie? You ready to leave?' his fellow worker asked.

'Just trying out a little speech I need to make.'

Wulfie gathered up his things. Of course his resolve would wilt, the way a frail seedling might wilt on a summery day. What was the point of being able to see beyond the distant horizon if you lacked the will to take life by the scruff of the neck?

'Isn't that Hazel coming towards us?'

'You tell me,' Wulfie replied. 'I can't see anyone.'

'I think she's looking for you.'

'Wulfie,' Hazel panted. 'It's a boy. Sooner than we thought. Kept us waiting all these years and now he's arrived early . . . Come quickly. Doht's calling for you.'

Hazel led the way, stopping at intervals to draw breath.

Wulfie hobbled along behind, his foot still throbbing from that scythe wound which refused to heal.

'Well done, Wulfie,' Emma greeted him.

She handed him the bundle of fleece containing his son. Wulfie held the child in his arms. Drew him towards his face so that he could make out his features. Their noses were more or less touching. The child struggled to make out the detail of the face in front of him, as newborn babies, as yet unable to see their wondrous new world, are wont to do.

And Wulfie wept for joy. At such moments it was possible to forget all about hopelessness or desolation. It was possible to have faith and belief.

'Thank you,' he said to Doht.

Emma smiled. Yes, he was just like her dear, departed Alfie. Kind and loving. A wise, bumbling buffoon.

As for Wulfie's masterful idea: that could wait.

X

Trouble was afoot. As far as Bishop Leofric and the good citizens of Exeter were concerned, they owed no allegiance to the Bastard. Those lily-livered Londoners might have crumbled, but the men of the West were made of sterner stuff.

Mule was actually earning his keep, helping to shift boulders and stones as the task of strengthening the old city walls was undertaken.

'Never seen you looking fitter,' Tolland said, patting the beast in encouragement.

As stenchful as ever, though.

Mule looked at Tolland accusingly.

'Sorry, old son. Not my decision. Frankly, I'd have just opted for the easy life. If that means letting the Bastard run this country, so be it. Even the spawn of the Devil can't be everywhere at once. Lie low, live a life of quiet study and devotion. Steer well clear of trouble. That's my credo.'

Mule didn't look convinced.

Tolland might have wanted the easy life, but it isn't always an option. In this case, Exeter's two most far-famed residents each had a different axe to grind. Gytha, mother of the late King Harold, wasn't going to become a vassal of William of Normandy. Bishop Leofric was damned if he was going to accept a hike in the *geld* he was expected to pay to the new king. Edward the Confessor had made a similar – and not unreasonable – demand. Exeter was no longer a crumbling backwater but a bishopric and a city of note. One of the most populous cities in the land. A tax increase was only fair and right. The locals disagreed. Edward the Confessor had caved in. William the Bastard was not as easily fobbed off.

So, his Christmas feasting cut short, he braved the grim English winter and set off to lay siege to the place and teach the yokels a lesson in who was lord-and-master.

Things began well enough. For the locals, that is. The Norman casualties were high and Mule's efforts at strengthening the city walls were proving fruitful. Thomas the Piper, urged on by those who'd heard of his exploits at Hastings, gave a repeat performance of his *pettum*-popping party piece from the safety of the ramparts.

'Is this wise?' Tolland had asked.

'It's safe up here, brother.'

'I meant: is it wise for a man lodging in a house of God to risk the loss of his dignity?'

'I'm a story-weaving dwarf, my friend. I'm an object of curiosity and amusement. I *have* no dignity.'

'On your arse be it, then.'

An arrow whistled past Thomas the Piper's bared buttocks. Too close for comfort. He gathered his pants up hastily, clinging to any vestiges of that dignity, as a cheer went up and the mule brayed loudly.

This act of defiance was his first big mistake . . .

It's often those with most to lose by their defiance who are the first to weaken: the property owners in particular, who'd no wish to see their houses rased to the ground by a wrathful king.

'At least send out a spokesman to reason with the Bastard. Let him hear our objections,' one of the burghers suggested.

'How about Thomas the Piper? He's been blessed with the gift of the gab.'

'And he was steadfast at Hastings. The Bastard will respect the words of a fellow warrior.'

Thomas's second big mistake was to agree to this proposal. Perhaps his head had been turned by all that praise. Had Isaias not similarly lured him with flattery?

'If Thomas goes, I go, too,' Tolland announced. Then he

turned to Thomas. 'Perhaps we should take Mule as well. I'll lead him while you sit astride him.'

'Thank the Redeemer for small mercies,' someone said as the two of them led the fetid beast out through the city gates.

'We come in peace to hear your terms,' Thomas announced.

The king's interpreter relayed the words. William turned away, dismissively.

'Take the hostages away from my sight.'

Hostages, emissaries. All one and the same, as far as the Bastard was concerned.

'But, sire, the laws of the land—'

'— are mine and mine only to craft. Place the hostages in full view of the citizens of this godforsaken city. My patience is nearly exhausted.'

'Yes, my liege.'

The interpreter broke the news to Thomas and Tolland.

Mule aimed a vicious kick at William's steed as he sidled past.

That was the third big mistake.

William brought his sword down hard on Mule's neck. The beast lurched and fell.

'Feed that thing to my hungry men,' he barked at one of his soldiers. 'Now bring me a brazier . . . And shout word to the burghers of Exeter that King William will only talk when they have laid themselves at his feet in complete surrender. Tell them their overlord demands that they open the gates *immédiatement*.'

It took rare skill to imbue one simple word with so much menace. The interpreter did as he was bidden.

But the gates remained firmly bolted.

The brazier was roaring. A sword was placed into it. William nodded at the soldier.

'The dwarf,' was all he said. William bore the monk no

malice. But, unless he was very much mistaken, the dwarf had twice insulted him. There was a price for such insolence.

'Forgive us our *gyltas*,' the interpreter whispered. 'My friend here has a steady hand.'

Two Norman soldiers held Tolland, a third held Thomas, who shaped to cry out for mercy, to beg the Bastard's forgiveness, but was struck dumb with terror.

Such was the man's grip that Thomas was unable to turn his head as a fourth soldier lifted his sword and, deftly, touched one eye and then the other. Thomas sank to his knees, clutching his face, as the light we're gifted for a lifetime was snatched away. The light that guides and comforts us and the air we breathe. No man has the right to take either of these from us.

Darkness and pain bore into him.

It was Tolland, not Thomas, who wailed so loudly he might have shaken the very walls of the city. The soldiers had released their grip and he ran forward, placing a comforting arm around Thomas, who raised his head as if to look at his friend. Tolland turned to one side and vomited.

'My dear, dear brother. Hold my arm.'

Carefully, he led Thomas away. Grabbed him to stop him from falling whenever he stumbled.

'Cold water, Thomas. We must find cold water to ease your torment,' Tolland said, quietly. 'The soldier has shown great skill and mercy; he must be practised in such arts. But what they've done is barbaric, my friend. We're put on this earth to be God's eyes, to see his creation over and again in many and various ways. They've denied you this, brother. They've sinned against God.'

William nodded to the four soldiers. A job well done. Let them be. Let the hostages enter the city and the place wouldn't hold out for much longer.

A few of the ringleaders slipped away, Harold's mother, Gytha, among them. The rest of them were soon falling over themselves to swear unwavering loyalty to their king.

For eighteen days in the month of March in the year One Thousand and Sixty-Eight, they'd held out. Why did William not trample on the Saxons lying prostrate at his feet? Perhaps it was Leofric's intercessions that led the Conqueror to stay his hand as he breached the walls of Exeter. Maybe the king was not yet sure of the crown and had no wish to stir up more festering hatred of him and his men in this godforsaken part of his new land. Whatever his reasons, William showed mercy to the vanquished. Spared them. Warned them – his eyes narrowing – that, henceforth, nothing and no one would withstand the might of William the Conqueror.

XI

Wulfie knew they'd reached a point of such utter despair that there were no other roads open to them. The shadow of a motte loomed over them: the slave-made mound on which the *seigneur* planned to build his stronghold. Wulfie and the rest had been forced into building the structure. Doht, Emma and Hazel had had to play their part, lugging rocks, while they took turns at carrying their boy, whom they'd named Aart.

'We might as well be digging our own graves,' Emma cursed.

Half the community had already been struck down by disease, hopelessness or starvation.

'No more,' Wulfie muttered. 'We must leave.'

'If we're caught, we face certain death,' Doht counselled Wulfie.

'If we stay, we face certain death. We'll not see out another year. Look at us.'

'Where will we go?'

'A house of God.'

Any house of God would do. Throw themselves on the mercy of some abbot or bishop.

'Your best idea yet, Wulfie,' Emma agreed. 'Hazel and I will stay. The journey would finish us. We can cover for you. Throw those Norman curs off the scent.'

'I couldn't leave you.'

'Wulfie, I command you. Take Doht and Aart. Our life stories are complete. Death will be a release. You have a son with a lifetime ahead of him. Don't deny him that gift. Take to the road as soon as dark falls.'

Perhaps Emma was right. The Creator grants us our life. The beginning and the end are mere moments in time. Beyond them is the kingdom of the unknown. It's how we weave our story in between that matters. If not a story, then think of it as an embroidery on which we stitch our lives, our loves, our laughter and our sorrow, our friends and our kin. Let Posterity judge us all by the embroidery we stitch or the story we weave.

So Doht, Wulfie and Aart – still a babe in arms – set off. Fate would bear them, though they didn't yet know it, to Exeter.

XII

'Look on the bright side, Thomas—' Tolland checked himself. Not the best advice to give a blinded man. 'Count your blessings, my friend.'

'Which are?'

'First, your fate could have matched that of our dear, departed friend, Mule. Second, the soldier who blinded you stayed his hand. Your wounds are painful, but slight. The flesh will recover. Third, they didn't remove your tongue. You can still regale us with your life stories. Fourth, you have me. I shall never leave you nor forsake you. I shall be your eyes as long as we live.'

'When put like that I am indeed blessed . . . Perhaps if you pray for me hard enough, your Almighty will restore my sight.'

'Some things are beyond even Him, my friend. Beyond God or indeed that three-wish penny of yours that's served you so wondrously.'

'Well, brother, I'll have enough time for wordsmithing now. Enough time, too, to mull over the third of my wishes . . . though to wish the Bastard dead might be the greatest gift I could grant to my fellow men.'

'Wishes tainted by hatred or revenge are unworthy of you, you must see that—' Tolland grimaced. 'Not *see*. I beg your pardon, Thomas. There are things I must remember not to say to a man robbed of his eyes.'

'Don't stay that wagging tongue of yours on my account, brother. Hearing you speak is one of the few pleasures left to me.'

XIII

Wulfie tripped and fell. There was a dull splashing as he stumbled into a waterlogged ditch.

Doht smiled.

'Heaven help me,' she sighed.

She held Aart against her with her left hand. Pulled Wulfie up with her right hand.

He looked as thin as a blade of wheat. His face was racked with pain from months of suffering. He now smelled of rank, rotten slime. Doht gagged. Aart began squalling, so she rocked him, guided his thumb into his mouth to stay his hunger pangs.

'Hush, my little one,' she whispered. 'Let me tell you a story about a tall gangly man who can't see beyond the end of his nose and trips over stones and falls into ditches and drives his wife to distraction, but she loves him as much as any woman could ever love a man and wouldn't change him for the world. She'd walk through deserts and sail through storm-tossed seas to stay by his side . . . Why? Why would a silly woman do this? Because he gave her two gifts more than the rarest jewels. He gave her the gift of his love and he gave her the gift of a son.'

Wulfie snuffled, overcome by feelings of gratitude and unworthiness. Aart began to cry. A thumb in your mouth and a softly spoken story were not enough when you craved your mother's milk but her breasts were dry.

Love only goes so far.

Which is greater: love or charity? Perhaps charity, because it's undeserved and unrequited. A gangly, well-meaning husband, limping along and wincing each time he puts his weight on his wounded leg, can only elicit so much in the way of charity. But a starving, crying child melts the steeliest of hearts.

They were given food, shelter and something else. Tales of a story-weaver dwarf who'd defied the odds and survived Hastings, who'd rasped his very particular insult at William the Bastard but lived – by the will of the Almighty – to tell the tale. Who'd then stood firm against the usurper, marched out to confront him outside the old Roman walls of Exeter . . . But the Bastard, unable to bear the dwarf's defiant, unyielding gaze, had ordered that his sight be plucked from him with a firebrand, and now he languished in darkness under the care of Bishop Leofric.

'It can only be Thomas,' Doht gasped. 'My brother's alive. What do you think, Wulfie?'

Wulfie wasn't listening. He was biting on a stick to stave off the pain. The hunger, too. The foot had become putrid. It had begun to swell.

'Don't give up on me, Wulfie. We must get to Exeter. Thomas will take care of us.'

Wulfie didn't hear her, couldn't hear anything as he tried to shut out his suffering, though he didn't resist as she led him forwards.

XIV

Word was spreading about the usurper's ruthlessness. Any hopes that the Bastard would soon be scurrying back to Normandy, sent packing by some Saxon – any Saxon would do – fired by the spirit of King Alfred or maybe Bas the Bold, were beginning to evaporate. William had been showing restraint when he'd dealt with the Exeter uprising. Playing a waiting game. If your enemy is bigger than you, stronger than you, you crush him as a serpent would, slowly squeezing the life from his lungs. You don't try to savage him as a lion might. So it is with a people who outnumber you by so many. The word that best encapsulates this is *attrition*. *Asmorung* – suffocation – will have to do in the English tongue. Perhaps the fact that the Saxons don't understand attrition – the art of slow conquest – explains why Harold dived in and led his men to defeat at Hastings. And William is able to pick off the rebellions one by one. Crushing each one with steadily increasingly hard-headedness, leading to the North of England being laid waste . . . though, as Tolland guides Thomas to the table to eat, the rebellion by the burghers of Exeter has just been quashed, rather than crushed. They should have been grateful that they were among the first to flex their muscles and not among the last.

'Will we ever recover, Tolland?'

'Your wounds are healing fast, Thomas.'

'I was thinking more of my fellow men. The whole English race.'

'It's the women who'll save us, Thomas. Mark my words. The *peace-weavers*.'

'And how will our women save us when the Norman thugs believe they can rape them at will and cast them aside, and plunder the most courtly of them for their wives?'

'Perhaps you've answered your own question, my blind

but sightful friend. With no women of their own, they'll turn to English maidens.'

'Some of the Normans may be tamed by the womanly spell cast on them. I reckon most of them will remain the barbarians we know them to be.'

'Ah, yes. But who'll raise their sons and daughters while the Normans are out soldiering, hunting, raping, horse-whipping their Saxon slaves into building their new castles and suffocating the hope from this bleeding, wounded land? The English wives. Their English kith and kin. Their English teachers. That's who . . . And though the sons and daughters will speak with forked Norman and *Englisc* tongues, it's the lessons and the stories learned at their mothers' and their wet nurses' knees that will forge them. They'll speak their Norman French in their fathers' hearing and they'll strut around as Normans. But somewhere deep within their hearts, they'll be English. Because the tongue with which you speak in unguarded moments is the tongue that shapes your thoughts.'

'I admire you're hopefulness, Tolland. Your glass of mead is ever half full, never half empty. I pray – to whatever saint, whatever pagan god is likely to hear me – that you're right. A few more years of this barbarity and the only Englishmen will be those as fortunate as us, holed up in abbeys and minsters. Those of us whom the Almighty has chosen to have more than our fair share of the fat of the land.'

'I sense your disapproval, Thomas, but how would our giving up the opportunity for meat or mead help others?'

'The others aren't some bunch of heathens. They're flesh and blood: Hazels, Emmas, Dohts, Wulfies, Ottillies . . .'

Thomas's voice trailed off.

'I'm sorry, my friend. Do you miss them?'

'I miss them more than I miss the gift of sight, brother. My mother and my sister, and my dear … friend, I suppose we must call Ottillie. I'll admit it, Tolland. Much as I'm grateful for your friendship and I never take your strong, guiding arm for granted, I'd not complain if it were Ottillie bathing my fevered brow. I fear I passed up the chance for love. I should have seized my moment and asked her to be my lawful wife. Sometimes you can think too much, instead of letting your heart speak. Sometimes your head's so far up your own arse that you can't see what's staring you in the face.'

'A very unwholesome picture you paint . . . and one likely to result in a hernia, to add to your other woes, Thomas.'

XV

Wulfie sank to the ground. So this was how it felt when Death came stalking you. Don't expect a light touch on your shoulder to summon you to the afterlife. Expect the mist to darken and the pain to enshroud you. Expect Death to press so hard that you fall to your knees.

'Not far to Exeter now, Wulfie,' Doht whispered hoarsely. But Wulfie wasn't listening to her. He only had ears for Death.

Every last morsel of his strength was gone. He lay crumpled in a heap, his face racked with hopelessness and agony.

He was finished. Doht knew it.

'I haven't the strength left to bury you, Wulfie. You'll be carrion for the crows, though there'll not be much meat for them to glean on those bones of yours.'

She muttered a last, heartfelt prayer of pleading. To the Almighty. To Edmund, the one true patron saint of the English. To the Wyrd. And most of all to the souls of the late, long-departed Tom Thumb and Fleda. But though the wind rustled in the leaves of the distant, now-girthly oak in whose shade their bones lay, neither Tom Thumb nor Fleda heard her. And Wulfie heard nothing either as his breathing ground to a halt and his heart lost the will to beat.

When Thomas and Gross had laid their trap it wasn't some wild beast but Love that had come tumbling into it. All misty-eyed, gangly and lost.

Sometimes love lands lightly
with a soft and tingling touch,
sometimes at first sight like the
flash of a falcon-swoop,
or overwhelms you like a

washing-all-before-it, wind-whipped wave.
Sometimes loves seeps slowly like
warm water welling from a spring,
steals softly as the footsteps of
a sly and stealthy fox.
Sometimes love comes soaringly,
summer-skyfully, high-flyingly,
heart-hoppingly, doubt-defyingly,
walls-come-tumbling-downfully strong.

Doht barely shrugged her shoulders as she rose up and dragged her weary body towards Exeter. Two more days it took her to walk the last few miles.

She fell against the great cathedral doors and slipped down, still clutching the baby. Aart at least had enough life-tinder stored in him to summon a pitiful wail. Thank the saints for that, because one of the brothers opened the door and, seeing the two bodies as much dead as alive, called for help. Had them carried in and laid on to beds.

'Thomas the Piper,' Doht rasped, as the man of God raised some water to her lips.

The water was like the loveliest balm.

The man could make no sense of the words Doht was trying to form.

'Your son will be safe,' he said.

She tried again.

'Thomas . . . The dwarf . . . Now blind.'

'You wish to see Thomas the Piper?'

Doht nodded slowly.

'Ask Tolland to bring Thomas,' the man whispered, urgently.

They found the men in the library.

'Quick,' the man hurried them along.

'Who is it?' Thomas asked.

'A woman.'

'Her name?'

'She's beyond telling me her name, brother. To call her voice anything as loud as a whisper would be a falsehood.'

They entered the room. The woman was lying on a bed, still as a stone. One of the sisters was cradling a child.

Tolland led Thomas over to the prone figure.

'I fear she's beyond speaking, my friend.'

'Put my hand to her face, Tolland.'

Tolland held Thomas's wrist and placed the dwarf's right hand beside Doht's cheek. Then with both hands, Thomas felt her features. She stirred and looked at him. Some distant memory was awakened. The memory of how her Wulfie had once felt the lines of her face. She recalled how she'd felt both excited and ashamed to be longed for by a boy.

Thomas was unable to recognise the gaunt features that he was touching, but then she mouthed his name and he knew it was Doht.

The baby was crying again.

'Your child?'

'Aart,' she breathed.

'Wulfie?'

'Gone.'

'Enough,' the sister said. 'Let her sleep . . . And more milk for the baby, please.'

Thomas the Piper wept.

'I am a brother again and I have a nephew, a *sweostorsunue*,' he said.

'Though prepare yourself, Thomas,' Tolland whispered. 'I fear Death is knocking at her door.'

XVI

But Tolland, more schooled in the whims of the heavenly Father than the ways of earthly mothers, hadn't reckoned on a woman's unbending iron will to do right by her child. Doht thought Wulfie could wait for her a while. He'd taken his time in courting her. She'd take her time now. She'd fight for every breath.

It was three days before she was able to speak again. Another week or so before she raised her voice to a whisper. And she'd cling on to life for a while yet. Bedridden, her body broken, she cradled Aart, and then watched as he gained his strength and learned to walk.

Joy of joys. He could walk without bumbling into her bed or tripping over the stool. Eyes that worked as well as hers. Thank the Creator for that. Already the image of Wulfie in other ways. He even had that slight apologetic stoop. Comical in a child, but winning.

And then the stories, of course. So much to tell Thomas and so much to hear from her cousin-brother about where those itchy wordsmith's feet had taken him. To Hastings, no less. Now there was a tale and a half. She wondered whether most of it was true or not. Thomas the Piper was as guilty as his great-grandfather when it came to the matter of facts.

Facts, Tom Thumb had said, *are there to serve the story.*

The story is lord-and-master: the facts must do its bidding.

I'm guided over the treacherous flagstones by one of the nuns who comes to collect me each time Doht has the strength to see me. We're privileged indeed: Doht and I. Tolland, too. The hero of Hastings and his venerable friends have each been allotted cells of their own.

'It's been more than a year now,' Doht whispers one day.

'A blind man normally learns to find his way over familiar paths.'

'Stay your wagging tongue, woman,' I tease her. 'That nun has a voice as soft as a snowflake. Resting on that arm of hers I can forget my cares. I'll let her guide me at least until Aart's old enough to take over and shatter all my daydreams.'

'Have you had many loves?' she asks me.

'I didn't come here to be questioned so,' I laugh. 'But yes, I did love a maiden once, though I never took the chance to tell her.'

'She'll have known you loved her, Thomas.'

'Her name was Ottillie. And, yes, I'll admit it. When they said a woman was at the door, rasping for the Piper, I thought it was her.'

'I must have been a disappointment.'

'A lie, as you well know, my dear sister. I'd thought you were dead, but you rose again, like Tolland's Redeemer.'

'Ah, but he only took two days and nights.'

'. . . I hope Ottillie found the family she'd been taken from,' I sigh.

'She will have.'

'How can you know that, Doht?'

'I've been gifted neither Merlin's foresightedness, nor your unerring hindsight—'

'You mock me, sister.'

'—but I have a woman's inner-sightedness. She'll be well, Thomas. All the better for not having to endure the worst of your tales.'

For nearly two years, Thomas the Piper is blessed with the presence of his risen-from-the-dead sister. Her body's frail, her dancing days are done and dusted, but her mind's as spritely as an elf's.

'He'll be safe with you and Tolland,' Doht whispers, when she knows – with her woman's inner-sightfulness – that her time is up. 'I'm ready to see Wulfie again. He's probably crashing around up there, now. Greeting every woman he bumps into, thinking it's me.'

'I imagine the Almighty will have restored his eyesight by now,' Thomas says. 'I certainly hope I don't have to spend eternity afflicted by this cursed blindness.'

XVII

'You and I will be the best of friends,' Thomas says to Aart as he breaks the news to his sister's son.

Aart doesn't fully understand his loss. Not yet three years old, he's not bruised by the blow of his mother's death. Nor, in truth, is Thomas. He just gives thanks that they met again. That Doht was able to whisper her tales. That he can stitch them into the embroidery of his life stories.

Aart spends his days with his Uncle Thomas. He stares in wonderment at the miracles of creation. He describes to Thomas what the butterfly alighting on a flower looks like. And what the flower looks like. Thomas demands more sharp-sightedness. Young Aart takes a closer look and sees that there are four wings, not two, and that the butterfly's wings are made of thousands of tiny scales. And then he sees that there are as many colours as there are scales and that his eye has been tricking him all along, trying to make sense of this world by simplifying it. In this way, Aart learns about the many-hued, more-complicated-than-it-seems world.

Sometimes Aart goes wandering off, studying some nondescript weevil and discovering that it is in fact something delicate and beautiful, when he hears his uncle calling, pleading with him to come back.

'You're my eyes,' Thomas reprimands his sister's son. 'You bring my world to life. You make it as vivid as a butterfly's wing.'

What Aart doesn't yet know (but he'll soon find out, because as the years pass, he's growing into a bright lad) is that Thomas the Piper is offering something more important than the gift of his well-travelled wordsmith's wisdom. Aart is offered protection from the brutality and extinction of hope besetting the English. Holed up in this place, protected by the Church and, if Tolland's protestations are to be believed, by the loving arms of the Almighty, they're safe from the wrath of the Conqueror and his chain-mailed henchmen.

Aart's taller than his uncle, now. Isn't everyone? He even bends his neck when he talks to Tolland. He still has that willowy look of his father, Wulfie, too. And the same fleet mind.

'Your father gave you the gift of your mind, young Pup, and your mother left you the gift of the gab when she went. Now I have a little something to show you.'

'Another story, no doubt, Eam.'

Eam. Mother's brother.

'Not another story, though I've plenty more before we're done, you cheeky rascal.'

Thomas shows Aart the three-wish penny, with its final wish still intact.

Fairy-tale wishes come in threes. There's shape and reason in this. Most of us fail to choose our wishes well. Unhappy with our lot, we make our first wish. Later, disgruntled with our new world, we wish for something else . . . Only then does it dawn on us that the grass doesn't always grow lusher on the other side of the wattle fence. We have a final chance – the third wish – to go back to how things were when we started.

'Have I told you about this penny, Pup?'

'Many, many times,' Aart replies, feigning weariness. Clearly itching to be off somewhere.

'Maidens,' Thomas scoffs. 'I see more than you know with these hollow shells that used to be eyes. I hear the turn of your head as the squeals of the young novice nuns caress the air. I hear your mind wandering as you pick up the sound of one of them skipping along the cloisters. Don't be ashamed, Pup. All this time reading and writing, learning in the company of old men, is useful enough, but you were granted this life to take a maiden in those arms of yours . . . Let me tell you a story, though, before you go rushing off into the big wide world.'

Aart sighs.

Once upon a time a wise old man sat beside a road. A storm had passed and now a rainbow arched across the sky. Two lovers came by and the young lad greeted the old man, asking him:

'Tell me, wise old man, is there gold at the end of the rainbow?'

'You answer me first. Do you love this maiden?'

'Oh, yes. With all my heart.'

'And you, young maiden, do you love this boy?'

'Oh yes, with all my soul.'

'You've answered well. Go to the end of the rainbow and you'll find your gold.'

They searched but found no sign of the treasure they sought. Disappointed, they returned to where the old man had been sitting patiently all the while.

'What did you see?' he asked the young lad.

'Nothing,' came the reply.

'And you?' he asked the maiden.

'Nothing,' she agreed.

'Think again,' the old man said. 'You must have seen something.'

After racking his brains for a while, the young lad admitted defeat.

'No,' he sighed. 'The only thing I saw was my lover.'

'Me too,' the girl added.

'Then you're truly blessed,' the old man told them, 'for you both found gold at the end of your rainbow.'

(Did Thomas the Piper hear his sister's son stifle a groan, there, as he endured that little homily? Poor boy. He's too well brought up to make his true feelings known and leave the room as, say, Wolf-Dog or – latterly – dear old Mule might have done.)

Thomas holds the penny on his upturned palm.

'Take it,' he says.

'I don't know what to say, Eam.'

Aart's looking intently at the coin.

'Then say nothing. You're free to go, Pup. Run along now. And don't go rushing into any foolhardy wishes you'll live to regret. Between you and me, I've more faith in the powers of that silver penny than I do in the Almighty those poor brothers spend their lives on their knees praying to.'

'Thank you, Eam. Thank you for everything.'

XVIII

Tolland had been full of praise for his young charge from the outset.

'A good listener. Perhaps he has a story-weaver's ear. Took to his reading and writing like a fledgling eagle to flight. I reckon Aart's ready to move on from copying out bibles and bestiaries. I've in mind a splendidly bound scribing of your life stories, Thomas. Perhaps the effort will stop the boy's mind wandering, though I have to say that pert little sister I've seen the lad dancing around and flirting with is easy on the eye.'

'You may be right, brother, though I imagine crafting such a tome would serve only to delay the inevitable. As sure as bees are drawn to the sweet-smelling honeysuckle, lads will be drawn to maidens.'

'So are we agreed that it might be a good thought to entrap your stories on vellum while there's still breath in your old storymonger's body?'

'Agreed, too, I hope, on the even better thought that you'll be the one to break the news to the lad, Tolland.'

When Tolland tells his young charge the good news, Aart greets it with a shrug of his shoulders. He's spent nearly twenty years in a house of God where discipline is the order of the day. He's not been schooled in the art of defiance.

He's a good lad, is my sister's son, Thomas thinks. Then, when they're alone, he confides in the boy.

'We'll take it slowly, a snatch at a time, Pup. There'll be plenty of time for you to go plying your lovecraft with that delightful little novice with the voice as soft as fine rain.'

When does history really begin?

Perhaps it doesn't have a starting point. Water wells from the ground, fills a spring and flows by trickle, brook, stream, river, mud and marsh to the sea. But then it rises skyward and falls by way of droplet, cloud, then rain and storm to start its journey again. No beginning and no end.

'Mark these words, Pup,' I instruct my scribe.

I take a deep breath.

'Some call me Thomas the Piper. Great-grandson of the far-famed Tom Thumb. At night, I pick up a whistle and place it to my lips. I play softly, so as not to awaken Tolland and the others. My piping coaxes memories – one hundred years of memories – from their hiding places. I line them up and dust them down, ready to call my young scribe into the room at first light, so that he can pin them, wriggling, to the vellum. Stories of how we danced, my forebears and I, to the tune of history, felt its pulse, played our part, wove tales of our own, and how each of our wishes, even in the face of hopelessness, was fulfilled.'

Ah, yes. That was some sort of beginning. My whistle takes me to the year Nine Hundred and Eighty-Seven. To Great-Grandmother Fleda and her wolf-dog. To the far-famed Tom Thumb and his twelve-year search for love. The words would flow, now.

Thomas the Piper speaks in short bursts. Listens as Aart's *fether* bites into the vellum. It's as Wulfie foresaw it. The stories hidden somewhere in Thomas the Piper's head come tumbling into the room and Aart etches them on to the vellum leaf. And they'll be bound one day in the finest pigskin, closed from the light of day. They'll not be imprisoned but freed for others to read.

'I think you've earned your freedom for another day, Pup,' Thomas says after many hours. 'Though slip away quietly so Tolland doesn't know I've let you off so lightly.'

Aart springs from the room. Then Thomas hears the boy stop in his tracks, turn and place his head sheepishly through the door.

'Thank you, Eam.'

A good boy.

XIX

There's a tremble in Aart's voice the day Thomas wheedles from him a declaration of the boy's love for the novice nun, Edyth.

He longs for her, he says.

Thomas, because wordsmiths are sometimes better versed in the ways of lovecraft than their own paltry deeds might suggest, tells Aart how to woo his beloved. With patience, with flowers. Perhaps with the odd story or two.

It's during one such storytelling sitting – leavened by Aart's ardent protestations of his undying love for Edie – that Tolland lumbers into the room. The book of Thomas the Piper's life stories is maybe three-quarters penned.

'Wondrous tidings, Thomas . . . The Bastard's dead.'

Not any common-or-garden bastard, but the patron saint of evil bastards everywhere. The ruthless leader of a bunch of heartless thugs who'd managed, in little more than twenty years, to rob a once-proud nation of its self-belief and more or less snuff out the one thing that can shed light on even the darkest of places. Hope.

'I feel I should dance for joy, Tolland, but I've lost the will for such gestures.'

Here's a tale. A tall tale dressed as history.

Just before she gave birth to the Bastard, Le Diable's Harlotta had a nightmare in which her bowels were dilated and extended all over Normandy and Britain. William took this to be a premonition about the bounds of his kingdom. His faith was rewarded in full measure. Fate had the last laugh, when, in One Thousand and Eighty-Seven, his corpse would swell up as it rotted, while his followers argued over where to bury him. When finally they tried to squeeze him into his sarcophagus, his body erupted. And whilst his bowels didn't quite shower over the full extent of Normandy and Britain, they made one unholy mess of everything and everyone in their immediate vicinity. Providence had kicked him rudely in the guts.

XX

'I've some tidings to spill,' Aart tells Edie.

'Tell me. Tell me,' she says excitedly.

'Not unless you promise to pay me for them.'

'I've nothing to give, as well you know.'

'Then you may pay me with kisses.'

'How many?'

'These are wondrous tidings, worth a fortune.'

'In that case, if you tell me, I'll judge how many kisses they're worth.'

'Very well, then. William the Bastard's dead—'

Edie shrugs her shoulders.

'—and there's more. Nobody could agree where to bury him, so his body started to swell in the heat until it burst.'

'Yuck.'

This isn't going well.

'So. How many kisses?'

'None.'

And Edie's off, running away from Aart.

He chases after her, soon catches up with her, presses her gently against a wall and launches into their first giddy kiss.

Taste her moist and tempting mouth:
the lightning flash, the lovely flush.
Breathe her breath: a blissful blast,
as bright as light, as free as flight.
Feel her skin, as soft as touch,
while time stops, life stands still.
No gravity to ground us, grind us down.
Hear her music, soft as silence, slight as love.
Drink her. Drown in her. Devour her.

'Sister Edyth. Come to my room at once,' a voice echoes

through the cloisters. 'And you, young man, be off to your quarters.'

They pulled themselves quickly, guiltily apart.

XXI

Poor Aart comes into my room: forlorn, when he should be joyful. His beloved's been snatched from him by that fearsome abbess. Edyth is to be spared the contagious influence of the hot-blooded young beast who's frolicked with her, may the heavenly Father forgive him his *gyltas*.

'I have a plan, Pup,' I reassure him. 'Trust this one to me . . . But first you must promise me we'll both knuckle down and finish this tome.'

'Very well, Eam,' Aart sighs.

And his quill's scratching its way lightly across the pages of history. Racing towards an ending of sorts, though history really has no beginnings and no endings. Even the Battle of Hastings is in the twilit past, now. Tamed by time, dulled into something that once all those who took part and witnessed that turning point are gone will be just so much ink penned to vellum or silk stitched on to the famed embroidery that the Bastard's loathsome brother, Odo, had the sisters of Canterbury toil over.

'I've never heard you work so earnestly before, Pup.'

'Perhaps I'm lost in your tales, Eam.'

'Perhaps you're schooled in the un-Saxon art of flattery, Pup. Edie should beware. Your flattery's wasted on me. But it'll go to the head of that girl like a cup of mead. As sweet as a newly plucked flower.'

'What's as sweet, Eam? Edie or the flattery or the mead?'

'Possibly all three.'

'I thank you for your advice, Eam, though I'd rather we didn't talk of Edie. It pains me to think of her shut away from me.'

'The abbess will have a change of heart, lad. You mark my words. She may be a crusty old haggard but she'll have been besotted with some young brother in her time. Don't be in a rush. A break will serve to stoke Edie's fire. I might not have landed a catch of my own, but I've watched others strutting their stuff – though with your mother and father there was much more bumbling and stumbling than strutting. So, on with the story, Pup. We'll have this done before you know it and you'll be off again, skipping your lovers' dance.'

XXII

One Thousand and Eighty-Seven. A fiendish sort of a year. Foul weather, famine and fever. While the Norman thugs feasted and fornicated, the English were brought to their knees. Bribery and corruption were rife. In every shadow, weasels worked to ingratiate themselves with their overlords, bearing tidings of any man who dared to curse and spit at the usurpers. Only the young, who knew no different, accepted that this was how it was to live in such a godforsaken land. The Bastard seemed intent on squeezing every last drop of hope and every last farthing from his long-suffering subjects (though there was one little piece of silver, bearing the features of King Edgar and carrying the promise of one final wish, that William of Normandy would never get his hands on).

One Thousand and Eighty-Seven was a real pig of a year. But it wasn't all bad because – on an unwaveringly positive note – it was the year in which William the Bastard was finally kicked in the guts by Providence and died unloved, facing an afterlife bereft of all the lands and possessions he'd coveted and then brutally clung on to while he lived.

And One Thousand and Eighty-Seven – one hundred sometimes gruelling, sometimes joyful years since Great-Grandmother Fleda had sat there, with her life-tinder nearly spent – was the year in which, hot on the heels of that other tome – the Domesday Book – Thomas the Piper pushed back his chair, stretched and said to his sister's son:

'It's finished, Aart. Your toils are over. Perhaps we shall see whether or not that pretty young novice nun has slipped from the abbess's grasp.'

Aart looked out of the window. No sign of Edie. Not since she'd been hauled from his eager embrace.

'Don't give up just yet. I've had a thought: we've finished

my book, so now it's your turn to begin a new chapter. Perhaps you might make that final wish.'

The Gift of Health and the Gift of Life had been granted, though Thomas's life was nearing the end of its course.

'May I suggest you wish for the *Gift of Love*, Pup? I reckon that would have been my third wish, if I'd had my wits about me.'

Aart fished the coin out of his sleeve. A tarnished old silver penny that didn't look as if it was quite up to the task of granting three wishes.

'You sure, Eam?'

'Trust me, Pup. It's never failed me yet. Now run along and fetch Tolland for me. I'd like a word with him.'

Aart left the room, looked at the penny again.

Though he'd doubts aplenty about the true reach of its miracle-making powers, it was worth a try.

'Grant Edie and me a love so strong that it melts the iron will of that fearsome abbess,' he prayed.

XXIII

'Ah, my dear brother, my faithful friend . . .'

'A prelude to some request for an unlikely favour, Thomas?'

'You catch the stench of flattery the way a hound picks up the scent of a fox, Tolland. Aart has finished his scribing. Perhaps I can entrust my ramblings to your safekeeping.'

'I'd not have it any other way, Thomas. Though we should perhaps keep some of your stories well away from our more godly brothers. Heavily spiced fare is not fitting for those accustomed to blander food.'

'And there's another favour I ask. I wonder if you might speak with the abbess. Perhaps persuade her that a life of devotion is no life for young Aart and that delicate flower he so adores. Tell her the boy's intentions are good. That the *sweostersunu* of the story-weaving hero of Hastings deserves the chance for love. That he bears in his heart the gift of love and in his loins the gift of children and with them hope for our future.'

'Perhaps the abbess doesn't need to hear about the lad's loins, Thomas. But I'll see what can be done.'

When I speak to Aart – my sister's son, my scribe and my treasured Pup – I'll speak to him not about Tolland's efforts to soften the temper of the abbess, a woman as *fæste* as Mule ever was. Instead, I'll talk to him about choices, because he must make them, now. Tolland and I have protected him from the savagery of the Norman usurpers the way his mother would have wished. But now, if he follows his heart and opts for love, and he wants to step from this place with those itchy feet of his, then he must do the choosing. Right or wrong. Me? I've a hunch he should seize love, live with joy as often as he faces hardship. Yes, this place is as safe as any. But, I admit it. After twenty years here, life has become dull. A dull life is bad enough for an ageing wordsmith. For Aart, if his feet are half as itchy as mine, it will be soul-destroying.

Yes, I'll tell him about choices, though he must do the choosing. I may be wrong – it's perfect hindsight I've been blessed with, not foresightedness – but I reckon he'll let that aching heart of his rule his scribe's head.

XXIV

Thomas the Piper rouses himself from an afternoon slumber.

'Sorry, Eam. We'd not intended to wake you.'

'Come in. Come in, Pup.'

'I've brought you this,' Aart says.

He hands Thomas the book, bound in the finest pigskin leather.

Thomas strokes it. Smells it. Opens the clasps and feels where the words have bitten into the vellum. The witnessed truths of Thomas the Piper, though what's true and what's not is all a matter of opinion.

'Thank you, Pup. Thank you, with all my heart.'

A heavy tome, but a tiny sliver of Saxon history. Preserved for posterity.

'And you have someone with you . . . Bring them forward.'

A young woman takes a step towards Thomas, who reaches out and touches her face.

'One of the blessings of blindness, my dear. Such moments bring a little light into my dark world: I can caress a maiden's soft face without fear of having my own slapped. And yes, I can feel her hot blush as I say how fair she is. You've chosen well, Pup. I'm happy for you both. You and your children will be my future now. I only hope I last long enough to hear the cries of your firstborn, if only to satisfy myself they have a storyteller's lungs in them.'

Somewhere out there, in an unknown place, deep in the Quantock Hills, the spirits of Tom Thumb and Fleda chatter in the chill wind that sweeps through the oak, the family's tree, tugging at any autumnal leaves that cling on. Somewhere Wolf-Dog howls, but only in the faintest plaintive whine that you'll struggle to hear. Bas the Bold growling a giant's low, rumbling growl, wishes he could wring the necks of those Norman swine who've laid waste his land. Ynga weeps for a past where we can all be cleansed, made whole again. Harry and Alfie are bumbling their way around paradise like a couple of clowns. A kindred spirit named Wulfie, groping through the clouds but free of all pain now, comes crashing into them. Hazel and Emma are in a better place than those who've lived to tell the tale. Somewhere, Ottillie – not yet ready for the afterlife – sits down and rests her weary old bones. Sighs as she thinks of the little storymonger who could hold a group of listeners in his thrall. Wonders what might have been if he'd made her his wife. Doht has eyes only for the boy who, left in her brother's safekeeping, has grown into a handsome, lovestruck scribe.

Edie, too, can't take her eyes off young Aart. Bewitched and powerless against the forces beyond all of our control, she gazes at her lover's face. Her look betrays great tenderness towards the willowy, wheaten-haired young man who mightn't be suited to the cloistered life of a monk but would be a fine father to her children.

Thomas turns his wizened face up and smiles into the darkness.

'Remember this, Pup. My life stories are safe in your and Edie's hands now. Refresh them. Add to them with tales of your own. Embroider them. We're all part of the endless fabric of history. It's up to each of us to leave our mark.'

**Beautiful
Books**